BREAK OF DAWN

VAMPIRE BABYLON
BOOK THREE

Chris Marie Green

ACE BOOKS, NEW YORK

THE BERKLEY PUBLISHING GROUP
Published by the Penguin Group
Penguin Group (USA) Inc.
375 Hudson Street, New York, New York 10014, USA
Penguin Group (Canada), 90 Eglinton Avenue East, Suite 700, Toronto, Ontario M4P 2Y3, Canada
(a division of Pearson Penguin Canada Inc.)
Penguin Books Ltd., 80 Strand, London WC2R 0RL, England
Penguin Group Ireland, 25 St. Stephen's Green, Dublin 2, Ireland (a division of Penguin Books Ltd.)
Penguin Group (Australia), 250 Camberwell Road, Camberwell, Victoria 3124, Australia
(a division of Pearson Australia Group Pty. Ltd.)
Penguin Books India Pvt. Ltd., 11 Community Centre, Panchsheel Park, New Delhi—110 017, India
Penguin Group (NZ), 67 Apollo Drive, Rosedale, North Shore 0632, New Zealand
(a division of Pearson New Zealand Ltd.)
Penguin Books (South Africa) (Pty.) Ltd., 24 Sturdee Avenue, Rosebank, Johannesburg 2196,
South Africa

Penguin Books Ltd., Registered Offices: 80 Strand, London WC2R 0RL, England

This is an original publication of The Berkley Publishing Group.

This is a work of fiction. Names, characters, places, and incidents either are the product of the author's imagination or are used fictitiously, and any resemblance to actual persons, living or dead, business establishments, events, or locales is entirely coincidental. The publisher does not have any control over and does not assume any responsibility for author or third-party websites or their content.

First edition: September 2008

Library of Congress Cataloging-in-Publication Data

Green, Crystal.
    Break of Dawn / Chris Marie Green.—1st ed.
        p. cm.—(Vampire Babylon ; bk. 3)
    ISBN 978-0-441-01629-7
    1. Madison, Dawn (Fictitious character)—Fiction. 2. Women stunt performers—Fiction.
3. Missing persons—Fiction. 4. Hollywood (Los Angeles, Calif.)—Fiction. I. Title.

PS3607.R4326B74 2008
813'.6—dc22

                                                                                    2008021613

PRINTED IN THE UNITED STATES OF AMERICA

10 9 8 7 6 5 4 3 2 1

To Sheree Whitefeather and Judy Duarte—
stars who watch over Babylon

Thank you to Ginjer Buchanan, Cameron Dufty, and the Ace staff, for all their hard work; to Wally Lind and the *crimescenewriter* web loop, for their guidance (by the way, any and all errors in this book are my own); and to the Knight Agency, for their support.

BREAK OF DAWN

VAMPIRE BABYLON

BOOK THREE

ONE

Lights . . . Camera . . .

CHARITY Flynn had sold her soul to experience another moment like this.

The doors of Grauman's Chinese Theatre burst open to the night, showering the actress with camera flashes, pinpoints that flared like exploding stars. She posed, summoning her brightest, sexiest smile, knowing which angles would make her shine. She pouted her lips ever so slightly, tilted her head, then allowed her Allure . . . just a touch . . . to reach out to every man, every woman out there.

Another flash went supernova, worship in motion.

For a hushed instant, the late-summer air went still, the crowd silent in the presence of such magic. It was as if Charity—their Charity—had reached into their chests and stolen their breath away.

Their adoration filled her, fed her.

But this superstar wasn't reckless. She hid her Allure, trained to know when enough was enough during decades of practice. Time spent Underground, time spent waiting for this second comeback to glory.

Such a long, long wait away from the screen. . . .

The cameras came back alive. A paparazzo shouted to her over the blinding lights as she stepped out of the theater's lobby, where the special late-night premiere after-party was in full swing. Her diamond-studded pumps met the red carpet.

"Charity," the photog yelled, raising his monstrous camera above the heads of the others. "How do you think it'll feel to be queen of the box office?"

She swayed to a stop, allowing more flashes to devour her. "It already feels like a million bucks." Her smile grew, and the crowd smiled right back. "Several million, as a matter of fact."

They all laughed at her sly nod to the salary Charity Flynn would be commanding after such a big response to her first inevitable blockbuster.

Before she could move on, another voice piped up. "You really *look* like a million tonight, Charity!"

"Vintage Chanel." She spread her arms, showcasing the long creamy white silk sheath that flowed over her curves, a sparkling brooch clasping the material together at her cleavage. "It used to belong to"—another smile, this time a very knowing one that toyed with their expectations—*"her."*

Her.

The press had been calling Charity "the new Amanda Grace" ever since she had arrived on the Hollywood scene a few months ago. They had also referenced a second name, "Delia Wright," to describe whatever Charity had that the camera loved. But Charity didn't hear this other name as often since "Delia" wasn't the original. The template.

Platinum-blond Charity—and Delia—with her cherry lips and just-had-sex smiles, evoked the legendary, carnally inclined, tragically dead Amanda Grace from the late fifties. She reflected her in manner, in style, in . . .

In *everything.*

And it wasn't just a coincidence.

Charity winked at the cameras and continued to her limo, where she climbed inside to be enveloped by dark grandeur: plush velvet seats and mahogany detailing. Her veins fizzed as if shot through with champagne and, now that she was sequestered, her mouth began to sting with thirst.

Just a taste, she thought. *Something to keep me high until the end of the month when the Master infuses me with his own blood again.*

Charity shuddered, leaning back against the seat while the vehicle took off, away from the pulsing camera lights. But a voice from across the large sitting area jarred her.

"Amanda."

Her heightened sight cut through the darkness, settling on a shadow. In return, he leaned forward, catching some light from the passing streetlamps. Based on his delightful scent, she determined he was human. A Servant, as a matter of fact—one who did much of the Underground's footwork here Above. His face, punctuated by a cleft in his chin and piercing, pale eyes, was something out of a thug's casting call. But upon second look, the casual way he moved in his long leather coat, his jeans and boots, made him more approachable.

"Mr. Lonigan," she said, "I'm 'Charity' now. Charity Flynn. Remember?"

The private investigator made a conciliatory gesture. "Sorry. Charity . . . Delia . . . I like your first name more than the other two you've used."

She didn't know him well, so her curiosity almost overwhelmed her surprise at seeing him in her limo. Almost.

"Probably wondering why I hitched a ride?" he asked.

"It crossed my mind." She used her smile on him. "Is it too much to hope you're here for a little . . . fun?"

Charity rubbed a hand over her neck, her nails scratching her jugular.

Matt Lonigan calmly stared out the window, a subtle rejection, even if she'd seen interest in his eyes before he'd turned away. But she could sense a deeper purpose to his visit, even without having to reach into his mind. Not that going into someone's head was ever a good idea—especially while Above. Here, it could lead to detection from the "others" the Master had always warned them about.

She followed the Servant's gaze out the window. They weren't traveling to the Regent Beverly Wilshire, where the after-after-party would be held. No, she knew where they were headed: near one of the abandoned quarry entrances of the Underground, where the rare hiker wandered and where no production units had ever set foot.

Unease stole over her, because she had an idea about what was going on, about why the Master's Servant was here with her. She'd all but tuned out the disturbing rumors from Below lately because her attention had been anchored Above, on the resurrected career she deserved.

"What's going on?" she asked.

"The Master is gathering every one of you. I was assigned to see you came back instead of partying your big night away. The Master wanted you to understand the seriousness of this call home."

A gathering. It iced her spine. She'd given *everything* for this third chance at superstardom.

Well. Amanda Grace wasn't going to tolerate any threats to what she'd worked her ass off for, to what she'd invested so much in.

Suddenly she couldn't bring herself to care about the after-after-party she'd be missing.

Soon, the limo disappeared down into the black of a massive cave. Once stopped, surrounded by rock, they alighted. Charity walked ahead of Matt, never looking back at the Servant, even as they passed the wailing echoes of the removed Guard chambers.

She pretended to be unaffected, even as she pictured the lower-level vampires and their red eyes, their barbed tails, their freakish way of moving, like stuttering heartbeats in transit. Guards were their first line of defense, monsters manufactured to protect the Underground.

The damned, she thought, hurrying her steps, hearing the *click* of her heels against the cold walls.

She slowed only at the entrance to the emporium. There, Matt opened the door, allowing her to anticipate the usual splendid cacophony, the exotic incense, the vivid laughter, the tang of blood.

But . . . there was merely a hint of that normally free-flowing blood tonight as she entered, and no more.

This *had* to be serious.

Pulse tapping in growing concern, Charity greeted a contingent of Groupies, silver-eyed vampires who had entertained her for so many hours Underground while she'd waited for her comebacks. Now, as they sat cross-legged on the marble floor, holding hands, they weren't the lively, erotic creatures she'd always treasured; they weren't sidling up to her, playfully biting her skin, or stroking her to pleasure.

Tonight they merely watched her return to them, their eyes wide as Charity made her way past the waterfalls, the pools, the blanked grand television screens, and to the amphitheater.

Levels of stone seating held her brothers and sisters—other high-ranked Elites who had been just as worshipped Above as Amanda Grace. When they heard her, they turned their heads as one, every face a beautiful mask of waiting terror, every pair of eyes swirling in preternatural worry.

A hollowness seized Charity, and she placed a hand over her breastbone. She felt empty there. But when she thought of the crowds tonight, the cameras, the utter joy of being loved, she knew her sacrifice had been worth it.

She would do anything to preserve it.

She sat next to Jesse Shane, one of the world's biggest action stars who'd "died" in blood-soaked mystery eleven years ago. Next to him was the Underground's newest Elite, Tamsin Greene, who had "expired" just as tragically as Amanda Grace, once upon a time.

Charity sat straight, attempting to seem unruffled. She was one of the oldest Elites, and the young ones were looking to her for serene guidance.

"Is everyone here?" she asked Jesse.

He spoke in that carefree cowboy voice that'd made him millions. "Every single one. You know what happened?"

At Charity's raised eyebrow, he continued.

"We've officially been exposed Above."

Horrified, the actress held a hand to her stunning face.

To the eternally youthful visage she'd paid for with the currency of her soul.

TWO

ABOVE

Hours Later

EVEN while priming a lethal weapon, Dawn Madison struggled to keep her eyes open.

Made sense, because she hadn't gotten any sleep after what'd happened last night. And when the sun had risen and things around the Limpet house had calmed down, burning daylight by grabbing a snooze had seemed a colossal waste of time because there was so much to take care of.

Besides, there was the little matter of her being filled with rage, terror, impatience—all of which pretty much put the kibosh on lying back against a soft pillow to let her mind and body chill. Hell, wasn't there even an old saying that went, "There's no rest for the wicked"?

Problem was, Dawn couldn't help wondering who "wicked" applied to, now that she didn't know who . . . or what . . . to trust.

And that included herself.

Currently, she was putting all her strength into winding a crank.

In turn, it coiled a wire that was attached to a bladed disk in a modified crossbow. Nearby, the hum of a massive fridge competed with the clang of an old-fashioned clock on a nightstand in a sublevel lab. The timepiece was striking the twilight hour, every beat a countdown to what waited for Dawn and the rest of her team outside these walls.

Vampires. The past resurrected, when it should've just stayed buried.

Her muscles—honed from a life of athletic habit, stunt work, and hunting—strained as she stabilized the crank. Then, attempting to be as smooth as death's whisper, she hefted the saw-bow upward, propping it against her shoulder, aiming. Pulling the trigger.

In a shower of sparks, the weapon spit out the circled blade. *Swick!* across the room, where it bit into one of the wooden poles Dawn had propped against the far lab wall.

Lowering the bow, she inspected her target. Damn, too low of a hit to count as a decapitation. How'd Breisi been so good at using this thing on the vamps?

Dawn stalked toward the poles, intent on retrieving the blade and getting it right, even though every inch of her was screaming with discomfort. Last night's battle royale with their enemies was twanging every muscle and joint.

But the scent of jasmine interrupted Dawn, enveloping her. A voice sounded in her ear—or maybe it was in her head. Either way she hadn't gotten used to it yet.

"Just picture your target, and you'll be fine."

It was Breisi in her new spirit form, coaching Dawn about her old saw-bow—a favorite weapon back when she'd been alive and hunting by Dawn's side.

"I'm trying, Breez."

Overcome by the jasmine, by everything that went with the scent of the new Breisi, Dawn leaned the bladed crossbow against the nearby stone wall, slumping her own frame against its coolness, too. Absently, she locked eyes on her friend's worktable in the middle of the room, a table that mostly held Breisi's lab equipment and projects. Then she scanned left, past the collection of computers, taking in her coworker's bed and the nightstand with a shattered-glass picture of young Breisi and her grandma.

Dawn's suddenly blurry gaze returned to the table, where the remnants of a different bladed crossbow lay deserted, half-finished, a metal carcass. Before dying last night, Breisi had been building this second weapon for Dawn but, with the turn of events, Breisi had ended up giving her protégée her old saw-bow instead only a few hours ago. She couldn't manipulate it in the spirit world.

"*Dawn . . . ?*" the Friend whispered, her tone troubled now.

Dawn felt Breisi—her good friend *Breisi*—hush over her skin, then rest on her shoulder like a comforting hand. Mental agony lanced her at the touch. Last night Dawn had seen Breisi choking on her own blood. *Murdered*. Yet—

A sense of joy twisted into the strands of her pain. Dawn swallowed, trying to contain it.

Yet here Breisi was again, one of the guardian Friend spirits who helped the Limpet and Associates team in their quest to find the vampire Underground that haunted Los Angeles.

"I'll get back to practicing with the bow soon," Dawn said, reclining her head against the wall and regulating her breathing. It was the only way she could control her emotions right now. But at least she was able to force a grin, mainly for Breisi's sake. "You watch— I'll be better than you ever were with that snaggle-toothed contraption. Vamps are gonna shiver in their boots when they know I'm coming."

Her bravado sounded empty in the face of reality, because soon, there really would be a fight. Jonah Limpet, the boss of this operation, had promised that much, and based on last night, the dogs of war had been unleashed. It was only a matter of who would be attacking whom, and when.

In simpatico, Breisi's essence sank against the wall next to Dawn. She had no words of wisdom this time.

Why? Hadn't Dawn's book-smart Friend learned the ropes of the spirit world yet? Or did it take a lot longer to acquire all the answers Breisi's new state of being required?

The question beat against Dawn's temples. New state of being. Dead. *Murdered.* Breisi . . .

As tight emotion welled in Dawn's chest, traveling upward until it choked her, Breisi's voice soothed.

"Lo siento. . . . *I'm so sorry this had to happen, Dawn.*"

"What, it's not your fault you went and died." She'd tried so hard to be more open to what she was feeling, but it was too hard. Hurt too much. "If Cassie Tomlinson were still alive, I'd kill her myself."

Last night's horrors had been waiting for this kind of invocation. They attacked Dawn again with slashing memories of the Vampire Killer. Limpet and Associates had sought the culprit because Jonah had believed that the serial killer might lead to the Underground. So the team had investigated, never knowing that one of their interviewees, the sister of an already-jailed suspect, was their quarry. When they'd discovered the murderer's identity, it was too late, because Cassie Tomlinson had already captured Breisi, taking her to a remote camper in the woods, intending to publicly broadcast the murder and make herself a celebrity in the process. To make matters worse, Cassie had been in cahoots with the Underground, working with their red-eyed Guards.

Before Dawn and her father, Frank, had stormed the killer's hideaway to get Breisi back, someone had tipped them off about the unholy alliance. The same informant had also detailed how the murders fit into the Master's plans, goddamn him.

And that someone had been Eva Claremont, Dawn's vampire mother.

But all the helpful information in the world wasn't enough to endear Eva to her daughter now. Not by a long shot. Even if it was possible that the Underground vamps had witnessed Eva going turncoat when she'd helped her daughter and husband rescue Breisi, even if Eva had chosen family over the interests of her Underground, there was no room for forgiveness.

Because not only had Eva most likely turned Dawn's father into a vampire himself.

She'd also allowed Breisi to die.

That was right—Cassie Tomlinson wasn't the only one responsible for the death. When Eva had refused to stop Cassie from killing Breisi, she'd made herself a murderer, too. She'd sacrificed Breisi—the woman Frank Madison had fallen for during the years Eva was Underground—for a second chance to win her husband back. Then she'd captured Frank and stolen him away from Dawn again.

Anger seethed through Dawn. Still, in spite of herself, she wondered if her hell-spawn of a mother had already been punished by her own kind—the Master.

The big vampire responsible for everything.

She calmed down, because the reminder of the Underground leader pointed to even bigger issues: what would the Underground do now? What was their next move?

Actually, what was *Dawn's* next step?

She wasn't sure how to hunt down her mother and father, how to bring this Master to justice. She had no idea who her real allies were and weren't. She wasn't even sure she could turn to Jonah, her own boss, for aid, because he'd done his own share of hurting Dawn in the past.

Maybe there was no next step.

A clang and a clutter sounded at the top of the stairs.

At first, Dawn's body electrified, anticipating Jonah. Before last night, she'd called him The Voice, because that was just about the only thing she'd known of him. He'd always given instructions via speakers, staying out of sight. He was a shut-in, never facing his team . . . until Dawn had called him out for all his hidden agendas and manipulations.

Even now, hours after he'd finally revealed himself to her, she still couldn't measure her response. She hated how her body reacted around him—blood vibrating through every limb in sharp awareness. They'd known each other in a carnal sense many times, with his essence entering her, fulfilling her, but it wasn't until last night that she'd looked into his tortured gaze, seen the angry wounds slashing over his face. . . .

As footsteps descended the staircase, Dawn held her breath, in spite of all the distrust she still felt for her boss.

But when Kiko Daniels, little-person vamp hunter extraordinaire, popped into sight, she sank back against the wall. In relief? Or . . . ? God help her if it was disappointment at not seeing Jonah. She was one pant away from being the guy's sex slave.

"Hey, Kik." She went to him, intending to help with the massive picture frame he was struggling to carry.

He nodded back to her, watching his step as he hit the floor. Since going upstairs earlier, he'd put on his back brace under a dark T-shirt. He had to wear the gear every so often, seeing as a vampire had once thrown Kik against a wall. But his injuries were healing on schedule, and everything was improving except for the pills the Limpet team's psychic had been downing. He'd claimed he was going off of the medication, but Dawn had her reservations.

As she reached for the frame, he maneuvered it away, frowning. Oh, yeah. The chip on his shoulder. Offering to help him nowadays was like brandishing a castration knife, so Dawn backed off.

But he recovered pretty quickly, offering a tired smile that told her how much he was hoping she wouldn't comment about his 'tude. And, damn it, it just about broke her heart. He was good at making people forget he was in his late twenties while working the little-boy-charm angle; the trick caught their interviewees off guard, persuading them to believe Kiko was harmless. Even Dawn was susceptible every once in a while.

Breisi's exotic scent grew stronger as she whisked past Dawn to her other coworker. His smile widened in greeting, then he moved toward the bed, expending a lot of effort to cock the picture away from Dawn's gaze.

"All the rest of the Friends are napping," he said. "Breisi probably needs more rest than they do, even if they're working overtime out there."

It was true that Friends had been exhausting themselves while helping the team; they were trying to cover for their missing numbers. Friends had been disappearing at an alarming rate, and Dawn had discovered why: Elite vampires were captivating the spirits.

"So," Kiko continued, "it's bedtime. Right, Breez?"

A soft sound of acknowledgment brushed the air.

Dawn couldn't stop herself. "And the boss? Where's he?"

"He's still holed up, planning strategy, trying to 'logic out' the vamps' location."

A tremor edged Kiko's small voice, probably because he knew this was it—the calm before the storm, the fading of the lights before the projector flickered on and the action began. The Voice had always told them that once a vamp lair was discovered, the team needed to leave it alone because it was his domain from there on out. *He* would be the one to crush the Underground, not the team. Too dangerous, he always said. Too unnecessary.

It was just another sign of Jonah's maddening secrecy. But Dawn just wanted to know how the hell he was going to attack an entire community of bloodsuckers all on his own.

Or did he have something other than vanquishing in mind?

Her betrayed instincts soured once again, making it easy to conjure up scenarios of The Voice using his team to usurp this Underground. She hoped she was wrong.

Kiko added, "The info you got from Eva is what he seemed to need before starting to figure the rest out."

"My mom's a savior all right."

Obviously Kiko didn't say anything because he knew Dawn would just jump down his throat.

Her beautiful actress mama had supposedly died when Dawn was just a month old: Eva had been murdered, martyred, held up in the Tinseltown heavens as a legend. But over a month ago, when Dawn had been called back to town to find her missing father, Frank, Eva had insinuated herself into Dawn's life as sweet, innocent "Jacqueline Ashley," an emerging starlet. When Jac had revealed herself to be Eva, a product of the vampire Underground, Dawn also discovered that the bitch had abducted Frank in a warped effort to get the family back together.

Touching.

But Dawn hadn't so much gone for it. And now, after Eva's refusal to save Breisi's mortal life . . . no way.

Kiko had reached Breisi's bed and was staring at the picture, face arranged in silent devastation.

She knew, even before he propped the frame on the mattress to lean it against the wall, what his painting would show.

The background featured this very lab, with its stoic walls and sky blue ceiling. But there was nothing else in the frame. Not yet.

"I'll hang it later," Kiko said. "It's not like I won't have enough time during this lockdown."

"How did it get painted so quick? Don't these take . . . well, longer than we've had?"

Kiko scratched at the soul patch he was growing; he'd shaved it off for a recent assignment and wanted it back. "The boss did it. Don't ask how."

"He probably, like, mind printed it onto the canvas or something." It was kind of a joke, but the fact that it rang true just went to show how bizzaro things were.

"However he did it, it's perfect." Kiko blinked. "He said he wanted to welcome her home as quickly as possible."

Dawn heard a laugh. A jasmine breeze flowed around the room, as if Breisi were running around in excitement at the thought of finally being able to rest. Then the scent burst toward the frame, and the portrait began filling with a familiar shape.

Moment by moment, Dawn's throat ached more.

Ghostly brush strokes painted a petite Mexican woman in her early thirties. Her dark eyes were wide, her lips caught in a gasp, her black, bobbed hair carefully styled. She looked surprised at how the world looked from this vantage point.

As Dawn noticed the Nemo clownfish on her shirt, she almost lost all composure at the Breisi fashion signature.

She'd seen other Friends in their portraits. She'd even seen one bloom into color and form like Breisi just had. But now, witnessing her coworker doing it was too much.

Kiko was clearly undergoing the same anguish. He clenched his jaw and marched to a butcher paper chart attached to another wall, hiding his face.

"Sounds like everyone in this haunted house is asleep or at rest but us." Her voice croaked as she tried to give Kik some comfort by diverting him.

He had his back to her, inspecting the chart instead. They'd created it hours ago, back when Dawn had revealed to the entire household, including the eavesdropping Jonah, what she'd found out from Eva. When her mother had kidnapped her, she'd attempted to win Dawn over by melding minds and arrogantly sharing how much of the Underground worked: it'd seemed to be more of an orientation than a breach of secrecy, since Eva explained that the Master was bent on getting Dawn Below, too. Even at that unsettling news, Dawn had retained all of Eva's mind meld: the levels of vampires, what killed them, how they functioned. Many, many details that would come in damned handy.

However, Dawn realized now that Eva hadn't colored much in when it came to the Underground's actual location or even its Master. Was that last part because the head vampire wanted to tell her everything about himself when he welcomed her?

He and Eva seemed so confident that Dawn would give in to

them. But the Master had been the one who'd planned to kill Breisi by using Cassie Tomlinson as their assassin.

I'd love to meet the prick, right along with Eva, Dawn thought. *Bring him on.*

She took a step toward Kiko and the chart. "Have you gotten enough rest to function? The boss is probably going to use us as advisers before he goes off on his lone crusade."

"You're not my nurse." He'd picked up a marker from an art supply box on the ground, opening and poising the implement as if to write something. "Besides, I don't see you making yourself at home in some bed here."

The Voice had commanded them to move into the Limpet house for security purposes, and Dawn couldn't argue the wisdom of it, even if she would've loved to face off with him again.

Maybe it just had something to do with his refusal to ever tell her what was going on. Even last night, when he'd been on such a roll in revealing information, his answers had been vague. In fact, she had more questions than ever, especially now that she knew Limpet and Associates existed only to find this particular Underground. He'd led other teams to hunt down various Undergrounds in the past, but the only reason he'd given for doing it was that he couldn't stop himself.

Cryptic. And typical. Damn it, Dawn had taken just about enough of—

The clock on the nightstand began to shudder. Next to it, Breisi's broken grandma picture tinkled in shattered-glass discord.

Dawn closed her eyes, and it all stopped.

When she opened them, she found Breisi's painting staring at her, but then her Friend's eyes closed. Freaked out, Dawn faced Kiko, and she suspected he knew what'd just happened. Another unexpected mind push—a so-called talent she hadn't been able to master yet.

Keeping an eye on his coworker while turning back toward the butcher paper, Kiko said, "When *you* sleep, *I'll* sleep."

"I'm not the one under doctor's orders."

"Come on. What good is rest gonna do me if these vamps end up beating us? Sleep ain't gonna matter."

"We can't fight them without sleep." Listen to her. Kettle, did you know you're black?

"Okay, okay," Kiko said. "How about we both get some shut-eye after tying up a few loose ends. Then I'm sure the boss is gonna wake us up when he's ready."

Sounded reasonable. "So what's keeping *you* awake?"

He pointed to the flow chart, where the title *Elites* reigned near the top, above *Groupies*, *Guards*, and *Servants*. Under every heading, there were lists of their many differences. So damned many. Different ways they could die, different ways they could survive.

Unfortunately, right above *Elites* was a nearly empty space topped by *Master*. All it said was "Dr. Eternity, plastic surgeon and resurrector."

No written advice about how to kill the bastard or what else to expect. Hell, Jonah had even told the team that *all* masters had different talents, based on individuality.

"That blank spot is really bugging me," Kiko said.

"I guess we should be grateful for what Eva did tell me."

At the name "Eva," Kiko dropped the marker. He didn't bother to pick it up.

"I know," Dawn said. "I thought she was pretty decent, too. When Eva was pretending to be Jac, I mean."

"I can't believe we go to watch movies with them as stars. How many Elites have I accidentally idolized over the years?" Kiko looked like he wanted to puke. "I tell you, if Foxy Brown is a vamp, I'm going to fall on a sword."

"I know. I don't think I can ever watch a film the same way again."

"I said it before—don't trust what your eyes tell you."

"What do we trust then?"

Dawn caught a glimpse of remorse from him. Since one of his premonitions had been the reason she was lured to L.A. and recruited on this team—supposedly she was "key" to them beating these vampires—he felt guilty about his part in keeping information from her.

"I got a nightmare when I tried to sleep this morning." Kiko said it so softly, she wasn't sure he'd talked at all. Then he spoke louder. "All this stress brought back what happened with Robby Pennybaker back at the Bava nightclub. I keep seeing him before he threw me against that wall. Jeez, Dawn, I know you saw Eva all vampy and tempting, so maybe you're getting used to it, but I'm not. I mean, what if the *boss* can't even beat them?"

She hadn't gotten used to anything. Elites were far worse than their lower counterparts. When they were in human form, all you knew was that you wanted to be them so badly. You wanted to be touched by them, accepted, and nothing else mattered.

She cut herself off, realizing this was true about her own relationship with Eva at the core.

Kiko faced the chart again, as if it was some oracle. "Their Allure is what scares me, when they let it loose, like Robby did. He went from being a boy with funny eyes to something so beautiful it went beyond imagining. He was like . . ." Kiko searched for words. "An angel in a mist. And in that mist, they can show you everything you want; they can lure you with it." He didn't tell her what he'd seen.

But Dawn remembered how Robby Pennybaker had tempted *her* with her heart's desire. He'd shown her Frank and Eva reunited, the happy family she'd always craved. Then he'd attacked.

"But they don't always stay in that beautiful vamp mist." Her voice was garbled.

Kiko rubbed his hands over his arms. "No, next comes Danger Form."

Neatly printed words on the chart blurred in front of Dawn's tired eyes:

- Elites can walk in the sun
- fire, decapitation, and stake or silver through the heart can kill them . . . silver in bloodstream weakens them, but they can drink blood to cleanse themselves
- can be seen on film and resist religious objects, even though they get confused by them at first
- can resist garlic
- can "mind screw"
- killing an Elite makes their immediate children mortal

Something popped into Dawn's head at that, clarifying her gaze. A terrible idea took root.

Killing an Elite would free anyone they'd turned into a vamp. And Eva had turned Frank. . . .

But one more look at the chart showed her exactly what she was up against. And this was what she would face for Jonah, a man who had proven that he wasn't beyond using her. Damn, she wished she knew what was in his head, who or what the hell she'd already helped.

Kiko had lost himself in staring at the chart, so Dawn let him be, knowing it was useless to bother him until he was done. She glanced back at the sleeping portrait of Breisi, then around the lab.

Quiet, everything was dead quiet with the countdown so close to zero hour.

Her gaze strayed to the darkness that hovered in an alcove near Breisi's bed. That was where The Voice had emerged as Jonah. That was where he'd disappeared, too, never coming out again, not even to hear her sharing what Eva had imparted, even though she knew he'd been listening in.

With one last glance at Kiko, Dawn ambled toward the black.

Cool blankness enfolded her, and her heart began to beat in her ears. She blindly felt around the pitch space, coming up empty. She searched for a wall, a door, *something*. . . .

She crashed into a wall, sucking in a breath at the contact.

Frustrated, she pushed at it, wishing she could just get to Jonah and continue where they'd left off when they'd been alone last night.

But she knew when she found him that it wouldn't do any good, even if all she wanted was a little control, a little honesty.

At her wits' end, she wandered back to the lab, into the light.

Not that it ever did any good.

THREE

THE HIDEAWAY

As she entered Breisi's lab again, she heard The Voice whisper to her from the darkness.

"Are you searching for me?" His old-world-accented words sounded weary; he was as drained as she was.

Heart in her throat, she gauged Kiko, who was still staring at the chart on the other side of the room. He hadn't even noticed she'd returned.

Without hesitation, she headed back into the nothingness.

"What other kind of loon would be hanging out in these shadows?" she said. "Hey, where are you anyway?"

As usual, he didn't immediately respond. His reticence was one of the things that drove Dawn ballistic.

"Jonah." Her tone was final.

Another beat passed, then his resigned voice sliced through the void. "Follow me."

He echoed all around her, his tone a tear in the fabric of blackness—a rip that separated her, too, reducing her body to a needful shiver. She was used to his power over her, and sometimes she wondered why she didn't fight it more, didn't use the control she knew she had over *him.*

His voice continued to waver through the air, pulling at her, guiding her through what must have been a tunnel. *Secret rooms in an old house,* she thought in her haze. Now the scent of something minty and unidentifiable beckoned her, too.

She parted the atmosphere, as if swimming through ink. It was only when she felt a shift in temperature—a chilled huff—that she blinked to alertness. Ahead, a vertical slit of light waited, and she reached for it.

A door. When Dawn opened it, dull illumination washed over her. Awakened, she scanned the area to see where she was.

Stark, monastically white walls where candle flames slanted shadows and angles. A plain bed, bearing only a pillow. A time-scarred wooden chest at the base of the mattress, locked tight. A low table boasting a single, lit candle and a standing silver crucifix—much like the iron one hanging over the front door of this Hollywood Hills house.

And near the crucifix, a man on his knees with his back to her, his midnight-hued hair curling near his shoulders.

Dawn couldn't move. Besides the usual frenzy of cells crashing against her skin, she was afraid she would disturb his peaceful plotting. Oddest of all, he reminded her of . . .

Of a knight dedicating himself to the art of war.

He was wearing a long, black coat that covered his wide shoulders, hiding the rest of his body. But Dawn knew he was tall, whipcord lean. Just the thought sent a new rush of blood blading through her veins, serrating her with a longing, a hunger so intense that she battled to overcome it.

This was his private domain, and she'd finally been invited in. No wonder Breisi had protected her lab door like such a bulldog—she hadn't wanted Dawn to stumble across his sanctuary.

It made Dawn wonder what else Breisi hadn't told her.

Jonah didn't turn around. He kept his eyes on the crucifix, maybe because he was too ashamed to look at her after everything that'd happened. Or maybe because he'd tried so hard to hide what all his crusades had done to his face. . . .

"You wanted a word?" he asked.

She reveled in a shiver, then fought it off by glancing around the room again. Actually, it was more of a cell. "Don't you ever go crazy with boredom in here?"

A mirthless laugh. "Answering a question with a question. Breisi and Kiko taught you how to interrogate too well."

"I've learned a lot of things in a real short time. And not all of them have been compliment worthy."

Images attacked: hacking off Robby Pennybaker's head; almost piercing an innocent bystander with one of her throwing stars and hearing the woman cry out in terror as she laid eyes upon Dawn . . .

She shifted, noticing how Jonah's crucifix captured the darkness of her jeans and the white of her sleeveless tank top, then warped them in its silver. She looked away.

"So . . . this is where you live, huh?"

"Live. That's a subjective word."

"Listen, I didn't come here to engage in philosophical riddles with you, Jonah."

"Then what's your mission, Dawn?"

Her name, saturated with his tone, did it to her every time. She sank to his bed, crossing one biker boot over the other to fight the ache between her legs. "You know what my mission is."

That got a response out of him. He turned his head to the side, offering a vague profile, a candle-burnished hint of high cheekbone, soft lips, the violence done to the rest of his face.

"Don't act surprised," she said. "You know I'm not going to let Eva get away with what she did to Breisi and Frank."

"When you finish with Eva, then what comes?" Jonah's jaw tightened. "Are you planning to take on the entire Underground for seducing your mother and beginning the chain of events that has caused you such grief?"

"I'd love to."

He turned toward the crucifix again. "You know that is out of the question."

"Right. If you've told us once, you've told us a thousand times—*you'll* do the dirty work after the team uncovers the vampire lair. Somehow, after you pinpoint where they are, you're going to go into a community of vamps all alone and vanquish them. Sounds realistic."

"Don't doubt me."

The words all but gleamed in the low light. They had an edge to them. A double edge, as a matter of fact, because Jonah wasn't just talking about his strategies.

She blew out a frustrated breath. She couldn't help doubting him and he knew it. Hadn't he been the one who'd hired her dad in the hopes that he'd lure her back to L.A. to join the team? Hadn't he believed in Kiko's "Dawn is key" premonition to the point of forgoing any ethics while using *her* to draw out Eva? Where did his plans for Dawn end?

She realized that finding this out was almost as important as tracking down Eva and exacting vengeance. In the slowly approaching showdown between Jonah and the Underground, Dawn didn't know which side she should be on: with the man who'd dangled her very life as bait? Or . . .

No. Siding with her mom, even if Eva said that all she wanted was to have her family back, wasn't an option. Not after her mother had betrayed her so thoroughly, and not after this Master had plotted to take Breisi's life.

Still, the reminder of what Eva had done to be with her daughter and husband kept shredding Dawn into pieces. And what Eva had told her about Jonah . . . That made it even harder to sort this out.

You work for a monster. Jonah Limpet wants to take over our Underground, and he's using you to accomplish that.

Dawn's worst fears embraced the memory.

She had to get down to the bottom of all this. *That* was her only option.

"Jonah?" she asked, testing.

"Yes."

The candle wavered, making eerie objects come alive against the walls.

"If I nicely asked you to help me hunt down Eva, to get Frank back from her, would you do it?"

Pause. "Oh, Dawn . . ."

Tortured. She was putting him in an impossible spot, because they needed to be concentrating on just the Underground now. That was all that mattered—not her petty personal issues. He'd told the team time and again that he would only emerge from his sheltering house when they were sure an Underground existed, not before; secrecy and suspense were his best weapons.

Accordingly, he'd hired a team who would place blind trust in his plans. Both Kiko and Breisi were loyal to a fault, driven by notions of justice on a save-the-world scale, and that was what Jonah promised them.

So why would he sacrifice the high ground to right Dawn's little wrongs?

"Doesn't it bother you that you brought me back to this god-awful town to track Frank down and you aren't willing to carry through with what you offered?" she asked. "Eva took him again, just when I found him. Do you seriously think I'm going to give up *my* mission for yours?"

"Getting back at this master does not sway you? Also—"

"I know, I know." She didn't even have to say it out loud: *the good of the many outweighs the good of the few.* She was sick of the justification.

What Jonah didn't know was that he wasn't the only one she might be able to turn to for help. So maybe there was another option, after all.

Matt Lonigan, a fellow vampire hunter and PI.

Last night, hurting and impulsive, she'd gone to him, trying to enlist his aid. He'd hesitated, but only because she had a misguided sense of her own loyalty to the team and hadn't wanted to tell him everything that'd happened.

Ironic, huh? She'd done to Matt what Jonah had been doing to her for over the past month: keeping her in the dark.

Should she go back to her PI, even though he'd done his share of making her distrust him, too?

Jonah slowly rose, looming before the low table and blocking out the candlelight. Dawn hitched in oxygen, her pulse snagging on the mere sight of him coming to his full height. Every movement, every word . . . He owned her.

Disgusted with her lack of control, Dawn used her mind to push at him, to keep him out of her head and body. It was like punching at a rock wall.

"Don't worry," he said. "I'm not asking to enter you."

At his rejection, she snapped, giving one last mental shove.

Something crashed in front of Jonah, and he defensively stepped to the side. The candle's flame jerked.

She saw that she'd knocked over the crucifix.

Troubled, Dawn rose from the bed, moving toward the object with her hands outstretched.

"No." Harsh, protective.

Dawn halted, palms raised helplessly. But she wasn't religious, so why did she care about what'd just happened?

Yet she did. In fact, something like despair made her back away as Jonah cradled the crucifix in his hands, then set it upright once again. With one last caress, he let it go, turning all the way around.

His eyes, a topaz gleam, caught hers in his quiet fury. She barely had the presence of mind to see the rest of his ravaged face: the scars mapped in terrible welts, making him so much older and more pained than a man in his tender thirties normally was.

"I'm sorry," she said. "I didn't mean to do that. It's just another thing I . . ."

She faltered, finishing the rest of the sentence silently. *Just another thing I can't control.*

"I'm not . . . angry." He'd started to tremble.

"If you're not pissed at me, then why do you look like you want to maim me?"

He bowed his head. "Leave, Dawn. Please . . . leave now."

Suddenly, she knew. He wanted her, *needed* her, as he'd admitted before. But he didn't like it.

"Do you need to enter me?" She was shocked by how gentle she sounded. It'd occurred to her that whenever Jonah came into her body with his essence, he seemed to be feeding. Made sense, since she was an expert at sexual feasting, too. That was how she used to endure her days on movie sets—by filling herself up at night with men and their satisfied responses. She used to compete with Eva with every thrust, every climax, because at that point, Eva had been dead and she wasn't around to please men like Dawn could.

Jonah was shaking his head, in denial.

"Is that how you survive?" she asked bluntly, wanting to hear him say it. "Is that another reason you've kept me around, because sex is what fuels you?"

"Dawn—"

Instinctively, she blocked against any entry. "I thought you weren't one of them!"

He raised his head, his eyes flaring golden heat and hunger. "Go!"

At the horror of his low, mangled voice, she stepped backward, caught off guard. And when he began to quake in earnest, sinking to his knees, she reached out a hand again, just as she'd done with the crucifix.

I need you, he'd told her, but now she saw just how much.

"Jonah, you can come—"

What happened next occurred before she could suck in a breath: his body flattened against the floor. Immediately, something invisible slammed against *her*. She felt the weight of it, the hard lines and demanding length. An unseen mouth went to her neck, pressing against her skin.

Dawn shifted, spreading her legs to accommodate him. He hadn't come to her this way since the night they'd fought about Jonah using Frank as bait to get her here. . . .

Without warning, the essence pulled away.

"Jonah?" Dawn reached for him, grasping air.

He returned to her with a crash, soaking into every pore with orgasmic heat. His essence, inside of her now. The force of him laid her out on the ground, panting, open.

In spite of all the ill will between them, she welcomed him, clinging to the addiction of him, knowing she couldn't get enough . . . would *never* get enough.

He felt hot, like bubbling oil. He simmered everywhere: against her skin, under it. On the tips of her breasts, in the pit of her belly, in between her legs. Physical and not physical.

She groaned, pushing a hand against the center of herself as if to bottle him in.

Burning, burning from the inside out, feeding on her until she was raw, gnawing at her like an unseen wild thing.

Too soon—too late—with a blast of ripping heat, he exploded within her, catapulting her, forcing her to rise off the floor and land on her hands and knees with one tight scream.

She clutched the sheet off his bed and grasped for air as she pressed her face into the linen. Minty smell . . .

Her body pounded, still wet and swollen. It'd never been this primitive between them; he'd never used her so quickly. . . .

She leaned forward, cheek against the mattress, depending on the bed for balance as she sought him with her gaze.

What she saw froze her.

From his prone spot, Jonah—the body itself—was smiling, obviously having watched his separated essence as it fucked Dawn. Obviously having enjoyed it.

Yes, he was smiling, and his eyes were . . .

. . . blue.

Before Dawn could blink, he heaved in a breath, arched his back, closed his gaze, and wrenched to a sitting position. When he opened his eyes again, they were topaz.

He rapidly turned away from her, body canting toward the crucifix. "*Now* go," he roared.

Feeling somehow dirty, even if she'd lived her life banging one man after the other for the sheer gratification of it, Dawn rushed out of his room, chopping the door shut behind her. She sought the walls, hoping they would guide her back to Breisi's lab, where she could hear Kiko talking to someone.

What'd just happened? Sensual, savage, even tender . . . He'd been all those things before, but never like this. Never.

She stumbled into the lab, where Kiko was standing on a chair at the raised steel worktable. On the surface, a vial was being pushed toward him by an unseen force.

Breisi's voice came through strongly for Dawn. *"Thorns from a wild rose make the concoction even more potent—"*

As Kiko spotted Dawn, Breisi stopped talking. Pulse throbbing, body damp, she could feel other awakened Friends in the room checking her out, too. She had no idea how many had gathered, or how long she'd been with The Voice.

Smoothing down her sleeveless tank top, she walked toward them, acting as if everything were A-OK. But then she caught sight of herself in a corner vanity mirror.

Her dark brown hair was streaking out of her low ponytail, making her look like a mad housewife who'd just opened the knife drawer and was going to slice up the curtains. Her color was high, bringing out the bewilderment in her light brown eyes and emphasizing the scars over her eyebrow and on her cheek. She looked tough, but also more vulnerable than ever.

Ignoring her state of dishevelment—maybe no one would comment on it if she pretended things were cool—Dawn nodded to everyone.

"Short nap, Breisi?" she asked, poking around for information.

"Couldn't sleep . . ." came the ethereal reply.

None of them could rest. Then why not go back to work?

Real work.

Dawn gestured to Kiko. "When you're done here would you mind chatting with me for a few? In private?"

"Sure." Kiko raised an eyebrow at her while motioning at the table. "Breisi's divulging the secrets of her healing goo so all of us can make it. Don't you want to—?"

"Maybe later."

She managed a casual smile—*acting!*—then went to the stairs, climbing them even as her body protested. Muscles, hurting.

Soul . . . hurting.

She avoided thinking too hard about it, instead entering the foyer, where a black-clawed iron chandelier reigned over the heavy curtain–blocked windows. An archaic suit of armor guarded a stone mantel and, above that, another portrait rested.

Right now, there was only a background column of red flame, but it usually held more. The Fire Woman, Dawn called her. She scared her with her taunting gaze.

But maybe Fire was on some job for the team since the portrait didn't show her body. Good. Dawn could deal with most of the other Friends, but this one . . .

The scent of jasmine swept by and almost knocked Dawn over.

Okay, maybe Fire Woman was home.

FOUR
THE KIKO VIEW

WHAT'S your deal, you crank?" Dawn said as she recovered her balance.

Around her, the air was still, the scent of jasmine gone.

Normally, she would've just rolled her eyes at something so weird and dramatic happening around the Limpet place, but now she knew better. Besides, this wasn't her first run-in with a Friend. Not long ago, a female spirit named "Kalin" had given Dawn trouble during one of her stranger encounters with Jonah. He had ordered Kalin to subdue Dawn while initiating a discomfiting sex game that included a blindfold, and the spirit had seemed all too happy to make Dawn squirm.

Wait. Now that she thought about it, Jonah had seemed off *that* day, too. He hadn't acted like the man . . . or whatever he was . . . she'd come to know.

But back to more immediate matters—was Kalin the one messing with her right now? Dawn had no clue what the spirit's vendetta against her might be, but if that was how it was, then she wasn't above throwing down with the ghostie.

She got into a readied stance, expecting another attack while scanning the foyer.

Kiko's voice sounded from behind her. "I'm not gonna ask."

Dawn relaxed, facing him as he shut and locked the door to the lab stairway. His forehead was furrowed as he tucked his hands into the pockets of his cargo pants and approached.

"Just thought I'd get some practice in." Dawn's to-do list didn't include complaining about a crotchety spirit. "So, you have a few minutes? I need to bounce a few things off you."

Clearly wary, he raised an eyebrow. "Until the boss calls us together again, I've got lots of time."

Here it went—an investigation that would decide everything from here on out. She was ready to play hardball if it got her what she needed.

Information about Jonah's intentions.

"I'm leaving the team," she said, going full-throttle bullshit. Or maybe not.

For a second, Kiko just stared at her. But little by little, his blue eyes grew wider. "You can't do that."

"Kik, I know you've got these vibes about me being the 'key' to beating the Underground"—he'd envisioned her covered in the blood of a vampire, victorious, no big interpretation there—"but I don't get how that could ever happen."

"What do you mean?" And . . . cue Slightly Panicked Kiko.

"First of all, how am I going to be covered in vamp blood if Jonah keeps us locked down in this house and away from the big fight? Doesn't that make you go 'hmmm'?"

Panicked Kiko gave way to Relieved Kiko. "Listen, I only saw the end result, Dawn, not how it all comes about. Is that all you're worried about, the lack of brawling? Yeesh."

Answer a question with a question; that was how to conduct an interrogation. "What I'm really wondering is why should I stick by a boss I don't trust? Because you tell me to?"

Kiko opened his mouth, but Dawn cut him off.

"Weren't you the one who just told me not to trust what I see? Excuse me if I'm confused."

He raked a hand through his hair. A sheen of sweat formed on his upper lip. "You *can't* leave, Dawn."

"Watch me."

In an Oscar-worthy moment, she even took a step toward the door. He grabbed her arm before she could make any progress, leaving her to wonder if she would've really walked out. If she would've deserted the closest place she had to a home.

"Wait, would you?" Calmer Kiko took her hand in both of his, cupping it, begging as much as he would probably allow himself to. "I don't know what's been going on between you and the boss—I mean, yeah, I kinda know, and I don't wanna go there—but I'm sure he'd do anything to get you to stay. We need you."

"Where have I heard that before?" Time to soften her tone. "Kik, I'm not like you. I didn't come loaded with that noble loyalty you and Breisi have. I should be out there looking for my own dragon to slay. Eva could be halfway across the country by now, far away from the Underground she turned her back on last night."

"Look at this another way. . . . Wouldn't supporting the boss in bringing down the Master—the thing that planned Breisi's death—go a long way in satisfying you for now? *Then* you can get Eva."

A flicker of interest lit through her, but she doused it. "I'm not stupid enough to think Jonah can go into that vamp lair and come out the winner. Have you thought about what happens if he loses? Will the Underground hunt *us* down for being a part of Jonah's posse? Are we going to be sitting ducks?"

"The boss can handle any and all vamps."

"And you know that because . . . ?"

He shuffled his oversized feet. "He's done it before."

Dawn took her hand away from Kiko's. "And that's where I have to start trusting in this whole process again. Not going to happen. I'm not staying around to be Jonah's pawn anymore."

Wow, she sounded pretty confident about all this—almost enough to convince even herself.

"We're not *pawns*," Kiko said, not looking at her.

"Oh? Then tell me all about what Jonah wants with these vamps. Tell me exactly why he's going after this Underground. Something more than a pawn would know."

Her voice seemed to bounce off the walls. She didn't care if Jonah could hear all this. She hoped he could.

Shaking his head, the psychic looked at a loss again.

"You don't know why," Dawn said.

"I just *feel* I'm doing the right thing." His eyes seemed so honest, clear. "It's like the first time I caught a bad guy by using my talents—I knew I couldn't stand by while he raped his way around L.A. when I had the power to stop him. With these vamps, how can I just sit around knowing they're out there? How can I *not* help?"

"You really think the boss's intentions are for the best, that he isn't a megalomaniac who's using us to take over this Underground?"

"Yes." Kiko swallowed. "Yes, I believe in him."

In spite of his odd reaction, she still wondered how anyone could go through life with so much faith. If there was one thing she knew about herself, it was that she was incapable of being so pure. Eva's supposed death had warped her from the beginning, and it wasn't so easy to change.

Kiko had eased his hand over Dawn's again in a tacit plea for her to stop doubting, to stay.

It was time for her to strike. Now or never—before she lost courage.

"If I just knew everything *you* did about Jonah, maybe I'd . . ." She allowed the thought to wisp away.

Jackpot. Kiko grimaced, as if debating with himself.

"You know more than what Jonah revealed to me last night,"

Dawn said quietly, bending down to his height. "Shit, you *have* been withholding while I've been bumbling around in ignorance."

"What I know might not be what it seems on the surface." Like his upper lip, his hand was moist. "There was never a need for you to know what I . . . Dawn, the boss has good reasons to keep us in the dark. He's learned the hard way with his past teams."

Jonah had already mentioned something about this difficulty with his previous hunters. It made her wonder exactly what had occurred during his searches for other Undergrounds, what had become of the vampire communities in the end.

Hell, she wouldn't be surprised if Jonah was ruling all the Undergrounds he'd conquered. What if he was actually using this house as headquarters and the Friends as regents? What if he *was* a bad guy, just like Eva had said?

Dawn got back on track. "Okay, Kik, so basically, when the boss keeps information from us, he's protecting us. I'm not so down with that kind of leadership."

"Think about this: what if one of us gets captured by the Underground? Those vamps can mind screw. If we knew everything about the boss, they'd take that information and use it to destroy him."

Okay, that made sense, but it didn't make her happy.

"Besides," Kiko added, "I know that, one time, there was a team member who really bungled an operation because she knew too much and decided to act on her own great wisdom instead of listening to Jonah. He doesn't want a repeat."

"And how many team members has he lost because they wanted to know why they were fighting?"

"Don't know."

"Big surprise there." She patted his hand. "Good luck with all that, okay? I'll be pulling for you guys—"

"Stop." Now his face was truly scrunched, as if he were downing a bitter pill.

He didn't say anything for a full minute, but Dawn waited him out, knowing he was close to doing what she wanted. He believed so much in his premonition about her being "key" that he would move mountains to make her stay. More powerfully, she suspected that he wanted to make up for all the psychic damage done by the painkillers he'd been taking; he wanted to prove that he was still a meaningful part of the team—a person who mattered.

She was depending on that.

When she made a show of getting up to leave, that did it. He yanked her toward the massive, curved staircase that led to the hushed second floor. When they reached the top, he guided her past the portraits of sleeping Friends: women so beautiful they made Dawn cringe in self-aware inferiority.

Finally, they came to Jonah's office at the end of the gloomy hall, the scent of that minted something waiting as Kiko pushed open the door.

Inside, bookshelves towered, offering the scent of must. Burgundy drapes blocked the windows in fallen glory. A huge plasma television screen loomed like an eye that was closed in its own temporary slumber. Below that, a wide desk stood resplendent, the leather seat behind it empty.

Throughout the rest of the room, more portraits hovered, filled with sultry women at rest. But one painting didn't feature a person: right now, it showed only a field of fire. Once, Dawn had seen a shape in it—but only once. The subject had been hiding its face while a red cape shrouded its body. Long, dark hair had been the one discernable feature. Even though the painting brought to mind the Fire Woman over the downstairs mantel, there'd been something slightly off. . . .

Kiko took Dawn to a door in the room's corner. It blended seamlessly with the wall, making the entrance all but invisible.

Without any fanfare, he cracked it open, then paused. "The only reason I'm doing this is because things are coming to an end. Besides, if I know what I do, then why can't you know the same thing, too?"

"Now you're talkin', Dr. Seuss."

Serious Kiko forged on. "I think the boss has always known that I found this out, but he never did anything about it."

Dawn caught a glimmer of—what was it?—fear? in her co-worker's eyes. It shut her up good and well.

In fact, for the first time, she wondered if there was more to Kiko and Jonah's relationship than merely trust. Was it possible that the psychic's obedience had been earned through some terror, too? Was it the same with Breisi?

Suddenly, she wasn't so sure she wanted to be doing this.

Kiko looked away from her and into the dark room. "This isn't off-limits, so don't be afraid about coming in."

"I'm not afraid."

A soft laugh was his first response. Then a dragging pause. Then, "I'm not sure what all of this means anyway, but . . . Ah, what the hell, here we go."

He pushed the door open all the way and pulled her into the room with him. Her breath caught on the same time-stalled scent you would find in a museum.

Kiko hit the lights and, at the blaze of soft gold, Dawn took a step back, especially when her brain registered what she was seeing. An armory? When her eyes adjusted, she saw it was a small collection.

At the far end of the slim room, a suit of heavy leather armor stood bodiless while on display. It seemed to guard all the weapons posted on the walls and stands: bows and arrows, maces, swords, pikes, lances, spears, crossbows, staffs, muskets, and rifles—all sorts of firearms. Handheld goodies.

"Interesting," Dawn said noncommittally. "But . . . ?"

"Here."

Kiko led her over to the wall, where a dagger was posted. It was simply designed except for a symbol etched into the wooden hilt. A deep, rough C. An identifying mark?

He didn't touch it. "When the boss first hired me, I was poking around the house, just like you've done a million times."

Dawn nodded, finding no shame in admitting to her nosiness.

"And I came across this hovel." Kiko gestured around. "As you can imagine, I got kinda excited."

"You started touching everything." Dawn knew that Kik had a definite hard-on for warfare; this was a guy who splooged like a porn star when she used her whip chain, for God's sake.

But then she understood what he was getting at. "When you grabbed stuff, you sensed images or feelings through touch." Besides having telepathic and precognitive talents, he had psychometric powers, too.

"Yeah, I got a reading. *Someone* was holding on to this dagger throughout the memory. The rest of the objects in here come up empty. I can't get a damned thing from them."

"'Someone' was holding it?" He'd made the word sound spooky.

Sweat had really started to bead over Kiko's upper lip again. He fidgeted, and Dawn wondered if he was nervous or was feeling the effects of his cold-turkey pill withdrawal.

"I'm not sure who's in this vision," he finally said, coming to stare at the dagger. "I'm not really sure I want to know."

Gaaaaah.

But she couldn't help wondering if Jonah had been so lenient about Kiko's touchy curiosity in this room because any residual readings the psychic was bound to come up with didn't concern the boss much. Shouldn't that make her feel better?

Then why keep these weapons?

"So," she said, forcing herself to move on, "if this memory has nothing to do with the boss, why are you sharing it with me? How's that going to make me stay?"

"I'm showing you what I *do* know, and that I'm not covering anything up. And . . ." A drop of sweat trickled past his mouth. "I'm not even sure it's *not* the boss in the vision I got from this dagger."

Okay. Freaking out now.

"Once," Kiko added, "I dragged Breisi up here and actually

took her into the memory with me. She didn't last through hardly any of it."

It took Dawn a second to comprehend that. Breisi, who had the calmest guts out of any team member, save for Jonah.

Kiko kept on going. "She told me never to bring her with me into a vision again. That's why I don't allow you guys to ride my skin, to touch me while I get readings. It's too much for most people to handle."

Now Dawn wondered if he was just scaring her off. Good try. "Are we going to do this or not?"

"If I have to."

She wanted this, the answers—*any* answers. If she experienced what Kiko had, maybe she could decide for herself whether this vision belonged to Jonah. After all, he'd been inside her. Wouldn't that give her judgment an advantage over Kiko's?

She moved to the dagger, holding out her hand, pulse banging.

"I'm ready," she said, oxygen tangled in her lungs.

Without preamble, Kiko took her hand and put it over his own, almost belligerently, as if he hoped he would teach her a lesson.

As he touched the dagger, ice thrust into her chest, her head, and she jerked back.

But she was unable to disconnect from what she was seeing. . . .

Sitting at a long dining table in a room composed of stone, torches flaming to provide light that wavered over the tapestry-ridden walls—sanguine hunting scenes.

There were many men at the table, all facing front, all silent as they watched whatever was playing out before them. Rough men, bearded and leathered, hunched over their dinner plates. Meat and grease clung to their facial hair.

Looking down, she saw that her hands weren't her own: they were big, strong, callused, one of them gripping the edge of a wooden table as a plate of half-devoured lamb and bread waited for her to finish them off. Her . . . *his* other hand was clenching a dagger, and it was coated with strands from the meat.

Then a blast of something coppery, something foul—feces and urine—hit her full force.

Slowly, she raised her gaze from the table, and she saw the reason for the stink. A nude man, drenched with blood, his mouth stretched open in sheer terror. His wrists and ankles were tied to two posts, blood and waste dripping from his body to the ground. One eyeball hung out of a socket, and upon closer look, the skin had been flayed from his legs.

Next to the victim, a commanding man stood. It wasn't that he was tall; no, in fact, he was built like a cannon, strong and stocky. But his face—his *face*. The thin shape of it boasted a long nose with flaring nostrils and large green eyes that left no doubt as to who was in charge. He held a bloody dagger as he assessed his prey.

Eat, eat, Dawn heard herself—him, the seer—think. The words were steeped in a foreign language, but somehow she understood everything. *If you do not continue feasting, you will displease him.*

Dawn didn't even taste the meat as she shoved it into her mouth. The seer wanted to retch on it.

But looking away would prove a weakness that could result in the seer's own terrible death.

So he ate. As did the other warriors at the table.

In the meantime, the commanding man addressed his guests. He had invited his most faithful followers to attend tonight, a group proven trustworthy through battle.

His long, black hair curled past his shoulders, his mustache cruel over his calm smile. "Witness the wages of ineptitude," he said, gesturing to his victim, a captain who had the misfortune of disagreeing with his sovereign's own plans.

Their leader was noted far and wide for both his ferocious deeds and crusading spirit. Though he reigned through fear, he had done much to keep his throne and his people protected. However, at this moment, this *night*, a deeper streak of brutality was emerging as the man traced his dagger blade over his victim's stomach.

"It is said," their superior began, "that the enemies of the cross of Christ intend to challenge us, if not on this night, then the next. Or the next. It is said that, soon, I might even find my head delivered to a most grateful sultan."

The men at the table made low noises of appeasing disagreement. As their sovereign turned back to his victim, the seer glanced at the warrior seated next to him. Dawn knew instinctively that he was a good friend who often served as a conscience, tempering the seer's own discreet indulgences. It was known far and wide that their superior expected piety in those around him, though he had been no saint himself. Still, it was prudent to appear a loyal man of virtue.

In the next chair, the seer's companion was quiet and still. His mouth remained in a line, his meal unfinished. He believed in their sovereign's strict code of ethics and held their leader to high standards.

Nevertheless, under the table, the seer nudged his friend, reminding him to obey. His companion paused, then ate a hunk of bread.

Their leader had paused in taunting his victim, who had been reduced to quaking. He no doubt knew that if he lost consciousness, the sovereign would revive him, merely to visit as much agony on his prey as possible.

Tossing his blade to the ground, their superior held up his hands to his warriors and continued his speech. "I think I should not ever make an appearance with my head on a platter!"

Soldiers slapped their hands against the table in agreement. And although the seer still clutched his dagger, he and his friend responded in kind, as well. After all was said and done, they did not wish to see their leader—their land—vanquished by the enemy. They had often risked their own lives to make certain this never came to pass.

Their leader held up his palms, and silence tightened the air.

"I will not perish at the hand of an adversary. *We* will not." He tilted his head. "I have made it so."

Without warning, he reached out to the bleeding victim,

snatching the man from his bindings in a motion so swift that the eye barely caught it. A sickening *rip* sucked through the room.

Gradually, the seer's eyes focused on the abomination in front of him.

On a human beast gripping two halves of his prey's body in each hand.

A collective gasp from the warriors led to utter quiet.

"I," their leader said, a giddy tremor in his voice, "shall never be destroyed." He dropped the two halves like so much discarded meat, then approached the long table. "And you shall be as I am." His tone had turned low, strangely persuasive. "I ask you to join me in eternal dominance where, together, we shall always rule. We shall have the strength to conquer not only the infidels, but all."

A pause stifled the room, and their superior lowered his gaze at his men. The seer's gaze blended in confusion, as did his mind.

Enthralled, Dawn heard him think. *Swayed* . . .

Moments later, thunderous noise grew in force as the soldiers rose in forceful compliance. In spite of himself, the seer stood, too, under a compelling, unquestioning sway. His loyal friend also obeyed, his voice raised in the same primal glee.

"Immortality," their leader yelled as he ran his blazing gaze over his followers, connecting with them one by one. "It is ours!"

The very idea thrilled the seer. No fear in battle. A life of glory and joy. It could all be his. . . .

He loosed a gut-level yell of agreement, too.

Their leader's gaze traveled the table, the roaring men. Then he came to the seer, his eyes resting on him.

He reached out a hand.

The seer did not notice anything in his path; he did not even take the time to drop the dagger he was still fisting. Vision going red, he barged over the table, upsetting plates of food in his rush to obey.

He came to bow at his leader's feet. His sovereign helped him up, laughing as he flicked a glance to the seer's dagger.

"My first," the god said, his eyes glowing with such promise that the seer could not resist. "Do you vow your soul to me in exchange for the world? Do you promise always to fight in this glorious war we will wage for our land and our people?"

"Yes." Fevered, needing, hungering. "Yes, I do."

With care, the sovereign brushed the seer's hair back from his neck, cocked his head back. Then struck.

The seer's sight bled to gray, though he could still hear his own shocked cry of anguish.

Empty, piercing pain, his veins like hollows in his very body—

The world turned black, drained. His soul, the very essence of him, dying.

Yet, then, like a flower as it blooms, darkness was replaced by glorious images: riches, women, all that the seer's heart had ever desired.

He fell to the ground, heaving in air. Something within him grew, building, consuming his body. Rage, arrogance . . .

Craving.

The seer turned his head to his fellow warriors, locking eyes with his constant friend, who was watching him with blank wonder. Saliva flooded the seer's mouth as his companion smiled, just as their superior had.

Then the seer caught scent of it: blood. He sniffed, guided by a twisted desire to the torn body. Crying out in ecstasy, he pounced on it, burying his face in the meat, lapping up thick liquid. In his excitement, he dropped the dagger—

With a push of horror, Dawn jolted to reality, slamming against the ground. She gasped for breath, jarred by her fall, by what she'd seen. A film of defiled nastiness coated her skin, her bones.

Above her, Kiko stood, his shirt soaked with sweat as he shivered. "Didn't I tell you? I knew I shouldn't have—"

"What the hell was that?" she grated out. "Who were those . . . things?"

"I don't know. . . . I don't know. . . ." His eyes were reddened, haunted and pained.

"Where were they?" she asked. "And when . . . ? What happened after . . . ?" Then comprehension descended as she started putting two and two together. "Vampires. Oh, God, who was that guy with the crazy eyes—the one who tore that man in two, Kiko?"

Now the psychic looked scared, as if she'd asked a question he'd been wondering about, too. As if he'd been afraid to know the answer.

"You've studied vampire lore, Dawn."

This was a joke. One big cosmic hah-hah. The only cruel big guy she remembered from vampire literature came with names like Vlad. But maybe there were others like him . . . maybe?

Or, yeah, maybe Jonah had gotten ahold of some artifact from the Impaler's era? There were so many rumors about the prince, so many so-called facts that'd been bent and turned into fantasy throughout the years. . . .

The next thing she knew, Kiko slumped to his knees, his arms wrapped around his torso while his shaking got worse.

This vision had gotten to him, and he'd summoned it for her. Or was he reacting to his medication withdrawal?

She wasn't amping out half as much as Kiko, so it had to be about the pills.

"Kik?" Dawn darted over to his side, everything else but worry for him disappearing.

"Don't give me any . . . pills. . . ."

Dawn took him in her arms. "Right, you don't need them." That was probably why he'd been able to get such a clear vision, she realized. He'd gone cold turkey, and his powers were coming back full force.

"I can make it without . . ." he said, sweat drenching his face as he cast a pitiful glance up at her.

"I know, Kik. You've got your mojo back. It's all there again."

He squeezed his eyes shut. "Hurts . . ."

Unsure of what to do, she hefted him up in her arms. He was little, but still heavy. Struggling, she made her way out of the weapons room and into Jonah's office. There, she eased Kiko onto a velvet couch.

"Someone get in here!" she shouted. "Breisi? Kik needs help!"

She didn't want to leave him alone, so she glared around to see if one of the Friends had awakened and could lend aid. Then she saw the portrait with the fire landscape, and she stopped cold.

Because it had just filled up with a shape boasting long, dark hair and a red cape that hid all identity.

FIVE

Below, Take One

As night gathered strength, so did the vampires under the streets of L.A.

The Master adjusted a silk pillow on a sunken bed, the round mattress surrounded by netting held back by ribbons. He mounted the stairs to look down upon his work, then smiled.

At the moment, he was in his original human body, feeling more complete than what his usual nebulous form allowed. In this solid shape, he was unfettered by the sorrow that had imprisoned him for years; instead, he felt liberated by the events of the past few months.

Benedikte was someone again, and when Dawn Madison finally joined him here in the Underground, he would never have reason to go back to being nearly invisible.

The door to Dawn's future room slid open, and without even glancing, the Master knew his second-in-command, Sorin, had entered. He heard his son's thoughts via their Awareness, a direct link between maker and high-vampire child, or also between . . .

The head vampire's sight darkened. Or also between the other masters in Benedikte's brotherhood.

As Sorin surveyed the decadent room, his words were silent. *I would have guessed Dawn Madison to have simpler tastes.*

At her name, Benedikte's vision cleared. He took in the chambers he'd designed just for her: a bed fit for adventure and peaceful dreaming, walls adorned with peacock feathers, an urnlike fountain dribbling water. But he'd also addressed her more aggressive side, including gymnastics equipment artistically built into the walls so she could amuse herself.

Benedikte didn't bother using his Awareness, preferring to speak out loud. His recent activities Above—pretending to be "human" in order to perform spy work—had given him a taste for life as it used to be. "Dawn doesn't really know what she wants yet, Sorin. She might not dress in silk now, but once she joins us down here, she'll admit to desiring prettier things."

"You know her well enough to be certain." His son sounded doubtful.

Benedikte finally looked at Sorin: shoulder-length brown hair, a haughty bearing revealing a handsome contempt usually reserved for his siblings, the Elites, who weren't as pure-blooded as he was. Since the other high-level vampires received a once-a-month dose of the Master's blood to maintain themselves, Sorin believed he was superior since he'd been born from merely one bite over three hundred years ago. He didn't like knowing that Dawn would be receiving the same treatment when she finally arrived.

"I suppose I would know what Dawn wants," Benedikte said.

In a playful mood, he decided to taunt his favorite son by shifting shape. He melded into the body of a Servant, Matt Lonigan, a visage he'd recently been using to seduce the unknowing Dawn to their side, to extract information from her—unsuccessfully, until last night.

Sorin glanced away to register his protest for this dangerous charade. For security's sake, he believed Benedikte should stay shielded Underground, safe until absolutely needed to fight Jonah Limpet when they finally lured him to their territory, where they would destroy him through greater numbers, power, and strength.

"I do not understand the reason you insist upon wearing that body, Master. A mere PI is not worthy of you."

"But *she* likes it." Benedikte peered into a mirror slanted to reflect the bed. There, he saw the pale blue eyes of a tough face he would've never considered attractive, himself.

Sorin remained still. The Master didn't need Awareness to know that his son believed Benedikte was taking an obsession too far. That he was transferring the love he once had for Eva Claremont and lavishing it on her daughter now. Vengeful love. But the old vampire knew it was more than just that. No, he'd finally found acceptance in Matt Lonigan's body. He was finally the object of a deep, romantic passion, just like in the movies he'd studied for decades.

"Ironic," Sorin said, wandering down to the bed and carelessly reaching out to test its filmy netting between his fingers. "It is so very strange, as well as insulting, that you would choose to masquerade in the body of a human who has never even expressed the willingness to become one of us."

"I know Matt Lonigan, and I understand why he wants to keep being a human. He has heavy commitment problems, Sorin. We know from TV and all the stories we hear that children of divorce usually feel that way."

"I do not trust anyone who refuses to pay the ultimate price of admission."

"You don't trust much." Benedikte went to Sorin and patted his head. "That's why you're my second, *my* most trusted."

As Sorin glowed with contentment, a perverse need seized the Master. He glanced up at a different mirror, this one poised over the bed, and caught sight of his "human" Matt Lonigan body next to the vampire Sorin. The difference in image was almost enough to make Benedikte believe *he* was human again.

He sighed, then began guiding his son toward the exit. There was a lot to do tonight: he needed to go Above to see Dawn and follow up on last night's progress with her. After the death of her friend Breisi, Dawn was in need of "Matt" 's help. It was time to reel her in.

After that, the Master would have to keep tabs on the preparation for Limpet's expected attack. The plan was to draw the suspected rival master and his team to this lair since it was unthinkable to launch a battle Above, where humans would discover their use of vampire magic if it wasn't properly disguised or buried.

That was just one of the reasons Benedikte had assumed the identity of a real human Servant: to cover up his intentions. To dig for information from the Limpet hunters without them knowing. Up close and personal, he'd been able to monitor the moment Dawn was ripe for recruitment.

When Limpet attacked, he'd be surprised to see that Dawn wasn't on his side.

This subtle plan had been so much more acceptable than outright destruction of the team. The Master made certain his vampires never, ever attacked humans who would be missed by families or other loved ones. And that was why he'd persuaded another human, Cassie Tomlinson, the so-called Vampire Killer, to do away with one of Dawn's team members *for* them. Too bad chances like that didn't come around more often.

Once out of Dawn's room, the Master and Sorin traversed a hidden tunnel connected to the emporium. Reluctantly, Benedikte shifted from Matt's form to an almost invisible mist as they entered the opulent amusement area from behind a velvet curtain.

In his new shape, he hovered over Sorin's head like smoke from burning incense. Being "Matt" was normally his preference: it made him feel closer to Dawn. However, since most of the populace, except for the Elites, knew Sorin—not Benedikte—as their Master because of the body doubling instituted as a safety precaution, near invisibility was prudent for the Master now.

As they strolled through the spacious area, vampires flew around them, training for the moment Jonah Limpet would enter their domain. It would be a mercilessly short battle, just like the time they had lost their first Underground to another master who'd wanted to usurp what Benedikte had built. Except this time Benedikte would come out the winner.

Something like rage made the Master's misty form expand and pulse. He still couldn't comprehend how boredom and greed had urged his brothers, the men who'd also taken the blood vow, to turn on one another while the ultimate master lay sleeping, gathering power, over the centuries.

But Benedikte held himself together because, when his own maker rose again, more powerful than before, more capable of conquering nations and winning back more than just his throne, *this* master would have remained faithful.

Go forth and create societies, the ultimate master had told them just before going to rest in a location only one unknown master knew. *Populate so I might have an army when I awaken.*

And Benedikte had done just that, obeying like the soldier he'd been in life.

His reverie was interrupted when a ghostly misted Elite swooped through Benedikte's own cloudy form, parting him. He contracted in pleased shock, watching as the comedian named Danny Dukes continued on his way and darted up to the emporium dome. There, the Elite vampire crouched upside down, tendrils from his white, angelic body wavering against the golden leafing. Then he zoomed downward, his body a rocket aimed at whatever was unfortunate enough to stand below him.

But instead of hitting the ground, he pulled up and landed gently next to another Elite, his tentacles waving. He was laughing, as if at death itself.

The other high-level vampire, Amanda Grace, toyed with a pearl-studded fan in her "human" form. Ever since her return last night, her siblings had been attempting to win her over, as if she were their queen. And why not? Above, she was royalty. In fact, the press had been in a dither about the story her Servant PR manager had whipped up to cover her absence from a big promotional tour for her new movie. As far as her fans knew, she'd checked in to an ultrasecretive clinic for exhaustion and wouldn't be back in circulation for a while.

It was a shame, really, the Master thought. Due to the Underground emergency, Amanda had been forced to halt the momentum of her third career just as it was gaining speed. Her second career had ended when the public started commenting on "Delia Wright" 's chronic youthfulness, so she'd come back Underground for another chance.

And she was going to have it, the Master thought as he and Sorin headed for the grand hallway leading to the Elites' private chambers. She would have it.

Near the hallway entrance, Sorin stopped to accept the salutes of the lower-level Groupies, who had halted in their flashing hand-to-hand combat exercises to acknowledge the vampire they believed to be their master.

The Groupies were looking good: ready and nimble. Benedikte made a mental note to ask about the Guards—soldier vampires—and how ready *they* were to face Jonah Limpet and his team. The lowly creatures had just finished training and Sorin, their keeper, would have them resting now.

As the Master and his son moved on, Benedikte caught a glimpse of the Servant station, where volunteer, vow-bound humans had come Below to offer blood as meals so the Groupies wouldn't have to travel Above.

Everything was in place—now they just needed Mr. Limpet to show himself. And the Master needed Dawn, too.

The moment the door to the Elites' palace was closed, Benedikte shifted back into his original form. Benedikte's body. He wanted to be himself when he saw Eva Claremont. He wanted her to see what she'd rejected when he'd so often tried to win her over in the other, less attractive, featureless form he'd worn during his years of not caring about anything *but* Eva. Was it any wonder she'd turned him down, though? He'd resembled nothing more than a shadow with a colored outline, anonymous and almost lifeless.

Since meeting Dawn, that had changed. He was back.

They arrived at Ms. Claremont's colossal door.

Eva, the Master thought, using his Awareness instead of a more common knock.

A few seconds passed before she answered. *Yes, Benedikte?*

He wouldn't ask permission to enter this time. Instead, he pushed her door open. It revealed quarters that smacked of old Hollywood charm: jazz-age pictures on the first-floor walls, a Greta Garbo–type bed located upstairs. When Eva had been released Above for her comeback as a starlet named "Jacqueline Ashley," she'd decided to decorate her retro-Tinseltown home just like her Underground chambers.

They moved to the stairs, climbed them. The soft perfume of Eva beckoned as they approached the guest room where he knew she was located. As always, Benedikte was overtaken with a craving for her. He was transported back to the moment he'd first seen her on the screen: larger than life, daisy beautiful.

After falling for her, he'd set a Servant, a manager in her employ, the task of winning her over. The man had skillfully introduced the idea of long-lasting beauty and unending fame to Eva and, soon, she'd faced the fear of losing her youth, her career, her paycheck, which sustained an overspending husband and their little baby girl. Eva had panicked. Not knowing how else to preserve what she had, she'd gone along with staging her own legendary murder, making her an instant superstar, eternally loved. But she hadn't died. No, Dr. Eternity—the Master's "professional name"— had ushered her Underground at the cost of her soul. In exchange, he gave her a monthly infusion of his blood, which kept all Elites young and coveted.

But that was not where Eva's treatment ended. For years, she'd stayed Underground, waiting for her legend to grow. Then, when the world was ready for her comeback, Dr. Eternity performed his final feat of transformation, using surgery to alter Eva's appearance enough to make the public think she was someone different, all while remaining the same star underneath. It was this star who drew the adoring masses, both on the red carpet and on the silver screen. While they believed she was the "new Eva Claremont," she was nothing more than the old, made better by a touch of vampire Allure and ambition.

An unending career that could last eons with enough returns to the Underground . . .

Sorin's Awareness shook Benedikte. *Master?*

His son stood at the guest room door, waiting to open it, a concerned expression on his face. He'd always thought Eva would be his father's downfall, but that wasn't true. Dawn had taken Eva's place in Benedikte's affections, so Eva didn't have the power to hurt him anymore.

At least, that was what he kept telling himself.

Resolutely, Benedikte opened the door, then walked inside. Eva appeared from behind a silk dressing screen. A light blue robe flowed around her, the hem kissing the floor. It brought out the glimmer of her long, blond hair, the swirl of colors in her Elite eyes, the high flush on her cheeks that her last infusion had caused. He'd overfed her—an impulsive mistake—and he wondered if she'd become stronger because of it.

She came to stand by the four-poster bed where some*thing* was chained to the posts with enough silver in the bindings to restrain a lower vampire.

Benedikte fought to avoid what was on the mattress, his vision washing *it* out.

But, in the end, it was no use, no denying that Frank Madison, Eva's husband in life—the man she'd captured Above when he'd tried to save Breisi the hunter—was her guest.

An unwilling one.

Benedikte knew that Sorin had his doubts regarding Eva's story about how she'd gotten ahold of Frank and wrangled him Underground as her captive. Yet the Master hadn't approached her about the wild claims. Not yet. He would later, but reaching into her mind would anger her and . . .

The Master didn't want to think about why he wasn't forcing answers from his favorite Elite. Maybe it was because, after Jonah Limpet was destroyed, he would have to live with Eva for centuries, and her ire wasn't an appealing notion.

But . . . Benedikte cleared his throat, clasped his hands behind his back. He would get to Eva soon.

Sorin spoke out loud, since he had no Awareness with Eva. She wasn't his maker, after all. "I see Frank has been misbehaving again."

The burly man chained to the bed didn't stir at the noise.

"He'll come around." Eva stood protectively at her husband's side.

"Why is he slumbering right now?" Sorin asked.

The actress played with her belled sleeve. "We had a disagreement about Dawn entering the Underground. You know he doesn't want her here."

"Ever the vampire hunter." Benedikte tilted his head while inspecting this member of Limpet's team. He had been missing from action lately, supposedly because he had been on a sort of walkabout, staying true to his restless nature, deserting his job only to return to it at a most inopportune time.

Sorin laughed sarcastically. "Are we to assume, Eva, that you were forced to give your husband a . . . How do they say it? A love tap?"

Eva stiffened, prompting Sorin to really laugh.

Call him off, she said to Benedikte through Awareness. *You don't want a miniwar on your hands between siblings, do you?*

The Master sent his son a look of such reproach that Sorin immediately quieted, then raised his chin defiantly, aiming his superiority at Eva. It was odd, because Sorin had always shown tolerance for this one Elite since she really did miss her family—even more than her once-stellar career. His son admired that. But after last night's questionable events with Eva, Sorin's attitude had changed.

"When do you expect Frank to wake up?" the Master asked. "I'd like to chat with him since I haven't had the honor yet." Time had been at a premium since Frank had arrived. There'd been meetings, attempts to sort out what was happening, then rest during daylight, even though the Master was a strong enough creature to walk in the sun.

Eva tentatively stroked the dark hair back from her husband's forehead, obviously free to do so as he slept. It twisted the Master's heart—or whatever it was—in his chest. A stab of unbearable hunger accompanied the twinge.

"I'll tell you when he's up and about," Eva said softly.

Will you? Sorin asked silently through Awareness to Benedikte, even though he knew Eva wouldn't be able to hear him. His show was for the Master.

She will, Benedikte said.

His son remained quiet, even though he lifted his chin even higher.

Still wearing his Benedikte body, the Master bowed respectfully to Eva, his hair, which had been long and black when he'd taken his blood vow, spilling over his shoulder. "Then I'll see you later tonight, Eva. You *and* Frank."

She bit her lower lip, nodding at him. So beautiful. Her every move made him ravenous.

Wasting no time, Benedikte left her chambers. Someone else was waiting Above for him. Dawn. But there were ways of getting Eva out of his system before then. . . .

Sorin followed in his tracks as they wound through the tunnels to the Master's secret room.

Master? Sorin asked.

His son sensed his madness. And when Benedikte didn't answer in his haste, Sorin turned on a deeper level of Awareness they'd been practicing lately.

The Master felt Sorin in his head, looking out of his own eyes as he nearly stumbled in an attempt to reach for his door lock. Ignoring Sorin's invasion, Benedikte allowed his son to linger, to see what he saw.

To feel what he felt.

He scratched at the buried lock and, at the muted *click*, pushed the door open and headed for the shelves that held all his collected vials. He went straight for his favorite.

Unbeknownst to himself, he'd shifted from his Benedikte body to his nebulous, pulsating form—his nobody shape. He fumbled in an attempt to reach for Eva's vial.

The soul she'd given him in exchange for long-lasting youth and fame.

Behind him, Sorin made a strangled sound. The Master barely had the presence of mind to glance at him, to find his son's eyes glowing, swirling, in attached hunger.

For no good reason, Benedikte cut off Sorin's Awareness, but that didn't change the fever in his son's gaze.

"What is it?" the Master asked, voice rough. "Do you want to drink one, too? Maybe your own?"

"Master—"

"Then have *you* finally reached the strength of hunger I've experienced for centuries?" Would his progeny finally develop the power to assume other shapes, too—like father, like son? The mere thought of it lingered like a threat that Benedikte didn't want to acknowledge.

"Have you crossed a line, Sorin?" he added.

"No." The second-in-command sounded horrified. "No, I don't want it. I don't . . ."

As his son sank to the floor and barred his arms over his head, Benedikte couldn't stand any more. He ripped the cork out of Eva's vial.

A slight scream hit his ears before he drank her in.

Her soul pounded through him, ghostly fists against his ribs and skin, prey begging to get out. But the Master fed off that anguish, fed off her innocence.

Fed off the love for a family she wanted so desperately to return to until he was convinced that he felt it, too.

That he was, once again, wonderfully human.

The Night Caller

In a guest room punctuated by iron bird statues and a mural depicting a dark forest cove, Kiko was snoozing while Dawn sat in an overstuffed velvet chair by his bed. She was killing time by channel surfing the TV.

After the dagger adventure in the weapons room, Breisi and a couple of other anonymous Friends had rushed upstairs, urged on by Dawn's summons. Even though she had managed an explanation for his weakened state—Kiko was getting sick because of his pill withdrawal, right?—she'd left out the vision itself. She would tell Breisi all about it later.

Or maybe advertising that she was launching a full-scale investigation into Jonah wasn't to her advantage right now.

At any rate, as Kiko had sweated and shaken on the office couch, he'd muttered, "No painkillers. I won't be . . . a mental gimp. . . ."

He'd also refused to go to the doctor, insisting that the team needed to stay locked down. Breisi had agreed, so she and the other spirits had seen to Kiko in their own way. It was amazing to hear them putting him at ease: the Friends' voices had melded together, churning into something like a soft song that faded toward their patient. Actually, the whispers seemed to be funneling into his *ear*. Something low and soothing, something Dawn couldn't translate.

He'd sighed and closed his eyes.

"What did you all do?" Dawn asked.

Breisi skimmed by on her way out, leaving the usual trail of jasmine. *"No time for details. I'll come back later. . . ."*

Obviously, Dawn had interrupted some kind of important Friends meeting. Well, lah-dee-dah. Shut out of the club.

As the rest of the spirits followed Breisi, Dawn again felt isolated from her coworker, as if there were a crevice separating her and the woman she'd just started warming up to recently.

No time for details . . .

Now, sitting here in Kiko's room, where Dawn had transferred him, she felt like maybe there was too much time while all of them waited for Jonah to finish strategizing.

Or maybe there was too little.

She mindlessly zapped the remote at the TV, using more force than necessary.

The dagger vision wouldn't leave her alone. God, if she had believed she was in over her head before, what was she now? Whoever was in that nightmare was a vampire or . . . *something*.

And in spite of her attempt to get Kiko to enlighten her about the reason Jonah was hunting the Underground, the vision had come up short on that, too. Or should the images have given Dawn a clue—a big, fat, huge, hairy clue that she was failing to grasp? Man, she sucked as a detective.

But as she sat there shooting at the TV, theories began to creep up her spine, settling in her head with the cold prickle of footsteps trailing a person in the dark.

Jonah had kept that dagger for a good reason. From what she knew of him, he wasn't the type to collect needless things, whether it was team members or artifacts.

Was the seer in the vision Jonah himself? Was that the reason he'd kept the antique?

She jumped in her chair from the creeps, and her feet itched to run right out of the house. But then she told herself to get to the bottom of everything before she made a rash, irreversible decision. If anything, Dawn liked to think she'd learned *something* from Limpet, whether it was a touch of patience, a smattering of logic, or even . . .

The memory of brutally killing Robby Pennybaker consumed her.

Maybe she'd learned too much.

She calmed herself. *Think rationally, Dawn. Don't be the girl who once flew off the handle and hucked that throwing star at a human homeless woman because of an urge—a thirst—for violence.* Think, *ya dumb cluck.*

Okay, okay. What if Jonah wasn't the man in Kiko's vision? Maybe he was just acquainted with the seer in some way?

Or maybe the seer was the master of a different Underground. Or maybe he was even the Underground master they were looking for right now.

Even though the conclusion made her feel slightly better, the first scenario bugged her the most. Jonah, a vampire.

But how could he be one of them? The Voice had never sucked Dawn's blood, had never sucked anyone's blood as far as she knew, and that was what had given birth to the seer in the vision—blood. Wouldn't he still crave *that* instead of the sustenance he'd been taking from Dawn?

Just as she was getting scared again, she aimed the remote at a newscast, then pulled back as she registered what the reporter was saying.

"—murdered in jail this morning by a guard."

Volume, up. Way, way up.

"The victim, Lee Tomlinson, who was awaiting trial for the murder of struggling actress Klara Monaghan—"

Dawn shot to her feet.

"—has been in the spotlight since his arrest. Speculation about Tomlinson's innocence has been rampant ever since a second Vampire Killer began terrorizing L.A. while Tomlinson was incarcerated."

Neither the public nor the media realized that Cassie, Lee's sister, had been the second Vampire Killer. For some reason, Jonah had instructed them to remain quiet about that doozie for now. Shocker, but he was no doubt temporarily keeping things under wraps in order to bar normal society from interfering with vamp business: the team wouldn't be able to work as well if, say, reporters were always around. Besides, the killer was off the streets and wouldn't be doing any more harm. As far as the regular world knew, the culprit was a copycat psycho, which was pretty much the truth anyway.

Dawn clutched the remote. Justice for Klara Monaghan wasn't top priority. The team's focus couldn't be anywhere but on the Underground, and it left Dawn feeling crappy.

She recalled Klara and her surgery-enhanced face, her clearly desperate ambitions of making it in Hollywood. Sad. Awful. *Shit*.

Dawn's attention fixed on the screen as it switched to a taped interview with a ubiquitous legal talking head who made his living on Crime TV shows. His high forehead gleamed in the spotlight.

"Would Lee Tomlinson have been set free eventually?" he said in a smoker's rasp. "We won't know now, thanks to a prison guard who seems to have cultivated an even bigger fame-whore complex than Lee Tomlinson himself. Rumor has it that the murderer, Dexter Tyson Hallicott, was obsessed with Tomlinson, and I guess we have an idea of why now."

Lee Tomlinson's mug shot blipped over the TV, showcasing his Brandon Lee looks, his matinee beauty. His empty stare.

The newscaster spoke over the image. "Tomlinson was an aspiring actor who moved to Los Angeles before he was arrested for allegedly murdering Miss Monaghan. At one time the celebrated Hollywood lawyer Milton Crockett represented Tomlinson, until handing over the reins to Enrico Harris. The investigation is ongoing, so stay tuned while we bring you more as it's revealed."

And . . . on to the next headline.

Dawn shut off the TV. Should she bug Jonah with this?

Images of the seer burying his face in flesh and blood nauseated her, weakening her knees to the point that she had to sit down again.

No. There were way bigger issues than the Vampire Killer murders they'd already left behind. Besides, her boss probably knew about the newsflash since he was always one step ahead of the team. Still . . .

She glanced at Kiko, who was sleeping away. When he woke up, would he have any more answers about Jonah or the dagger?

Damn it, she couldn't just sit here waiting to find out.

Moving to the bed, she bent down, brushing a hand over his cooled forehead, then headed for the exit.

In the shaded hallway, she encountered the scent of jasmine lingering near a picture that usually contained a woman soldier dressed in silver armor, her curly red hair flying away from her body in a paint-textured wind. Now, it was empty, except for a desolate background filled with craggy mountains.

A Friend who had just awakened out of her portrait. Good.

Quickly, Dawn told the spirit everything about Lee Tomlinson's murder, hoping she would do whatever it was Friends usually did with the info. Then the perfumed cloud drifted away, leaving Dawn alone.

She walked to the computer room to do another time-killing search about Jonah Limpet, but her encrypted cell phone rang. When she checked her screen, she knew she had to answer.

Her last option was on the line.

But what could she say to Matt Lonigan here in the Limpet house, where she would probably be monitored?

Ah, screw it. What did she have to hide from Jonah? He knew how much she wanted to get Eva, and if he wasn't up to joining Dawn in a search, he had to expect she would turn to other resources.

She answered, telling herself to keep it cool because she still wasn't sure where she stood with Matt after last night, when she'd actually drawn blood from him at one point, striking out in frustration when he'd tried to comfort her. The only thing she'd wanted to hear was that he would team up with her to find Eva, and he hadn't come through.

"You heard about Lee Tomlinson?" she said in greeting.

"It's all over the news."

"Yeah, say . . ." She ran a hand over the top of a computer. "Sorry I didn't get back to you sooner."

"You've probably had a lot on your plate." Calm, rational, so levelheaded she didn't know what to make of him. "How about we meet to talk about this?"

The last thing she should do was go out of the house. True, Eva/Jac and her fellow Elites could walk around under the sun, but nightfall was different. It seemed to be the time when vamps didn't give much of a doink about hiding anymore.

Yeah, PM strolling wasn't such a great idea, even if Dawn could wear Breisi's locators, which would track her if she went missing. It was something they should've done *before* Breisi had been kidnapped. Stupid lack of foresight.

"You'll have to excuse me for not being all that excited about dancing with the devil in the pale moonlight," she said, knowing he would appreciate the *Batman* allusion. He was . . . a big fan. "I'm on Severe Alert Level when it comes to vamps, Matt. You should be, too."

Then again, hadn't Eva hinted that the Underground vampires wouldn't hurt Dawn or Frank?

Better to err on the side of caution and . . . Good Lord. *Caution*. If anyone heard her spouting stuff like that, they wouldn't know who she was.

Matt laughed, cocky. "There's nothing to worry about out here. I can prove it. Why don't you go on over to a window that faces the street?"

Frowning, she nevertheless did exactly that. The Limpet house was a fortress that kept Jonah secure, so she was safe inside, too, especially since the team had found that their type of vamps needed to be invited into private dwellings. But this wasn't even a guarantee with these freaks since they had different vampire levels and, hence, different strengths and powers.

She found a good viewing spot past the stairway, near a front window that opened onto a small balcony. Pulling aside the heavy velvet curtain, she looked past the gothic iron window bars, knowing she probably resembled a ghost peering out of a *wooo-eee-ooo* mansion, what with the facade's crumbling stucco face and sleepy-eyed splendor.

It didn't take her long to find Matt across the street where the only backdrop was a canyon. Under the brandy-hued streetlamp, he looked lethal: his long coat gunslinger mysterious, his posture wary and coiled.

Her breath came faster at the sight of him, the danger of him. In spite of how nice he'd seemed at first, he'd shown her a real different side a few nights ago when they'd been hot and heavy with each other. Just when she thought they were finally getting somewhere in the hubba-hubba department, he'd brought out the sort of dress Eva would've worn, then hinted that he wanted Dawn to put it on. The act had created such a doubt-ridden distance between her and Matt that she hadn't wanted to see him ever again.

But that had changed after Breisi's murder and Eva's part in it.

"What the hell are you doing out there?" she asked.

He held out his free arm in supplication, using his other hand to keep the phone to his ear. "I'm waiting for you."

"Not going to happen."

"What if I told you I brought flowers? And they're not daisies, either."

She cringed at the reference to Eva. Her mom had worn daisies in her hair during her most famous movie scene, and Matt had played upon that in his failed seduction of her.

"Come on, Dawn." His tone sounded injured. "I'm trying to make it up to you. I'll even go so far as to say I deserved those scratch marks you gave me."

She leaned closer to the windowpanes, not caring how much of this conversation Jonah or the Friends could be hearing. "Stop trying to be sweet. It doesn't really work on me."

"A man can only give his best."

A smile fought its way over her mouth. Damn it, both Matt and Jonah really messed her up when it came to men. Couldn't she just go back to easy sex? It'd required a lot less fuss.

But . . . a bland taste lined her mouth. Her old way of coping didn't really appeal anymore. Other addictions, other wants and needs, had taken its place.

With too much force, she closed the curtains, shutting him out. Dust swirled and she batted the motes away.

"Dawn?"

"I'm still sorting out what I need to do."

"And I'm here to help. Actually, I can't stop thinking I'm the only one who can help you. Trust me. Let me take on some of your problems."

So tempting. She'd been weighing his offers since last night, when she'd all but stumbled into his house to see if his hunting services were for hire. He'd offered solace, commenting on how he'd seen the Vampire Killer broadcast and how he just might know what to do if she'd only give him more information about what was going on. . . .

Dawn raised a hand to her head, trying to think. Something about what he'd said was niggling at her, and she couldn't put her finger on what it was, even though she knew it had to be obvious. But there was too much debris floating around in her noggin to sort it out. Damn, was she going mental or what?

"You still there?" Matt asked.

Without answering, she peeked out the curtains again, just to satisfy the sadist in her that he was still hanging around.

He was ambling past a parked Camaro. Almost absently, he slowed his pace, canting toward the window and pausing.

Was he checking himself out?

She closed the curtains, not wanting to watch. Some of the actors she'd worked with, narcissists, never passed up the chance to admire themselves in a mirror or anything that reflected their glory back at them.

But she was overreacting. Years of hating the entitled golden boys and girls of Hollyweird had given her way too much attitude and it colored every second of her days. People were allowed to look at themselves every once in a while, right?

"I'm still here," she finally said. "But not for long."

"Why? Is your boss spying on you?" He said it with an edge to his tone.

"What's it to you?" Just for good measure, in case Jonah *was* listening, she added, "I'm not on his leash. I'm not on anyone's."

Matt went silent, and it made her bristle.

"I'll be in contact," she added. "Count on it."

Just as soon as she got over her Hamlet act and decided how best to go about her business without getting her or Frank killed.

A long pause arched her nerves until she quivered, fear stringing her together as she turned from the window to face the darkened hall and its empty portraits. Back to work.

Back to Jonah.

"I'll be waiting for you then," Matt said.

Dawn thanked him, then hung up. But his last words dug into her.

She couldn't help wondering if, based on the obsession Matt had once confessed to having for her, maybe he'd already been waiting long enough.

SEVEN

THE BREISI VIEW

No one in the Limpet house ended up remarking on her phone call with Matt. No one probably cared because, even hours later, Jonah was still sequestered, Kiko was still zonked out, and the Friends were still going about their weird, private business.

In the meantime, the walls seemed to squeeze in on Dawn as she waited for something to happen.

The grandfather clock in the hallway ticked, tocked. The house moaned under the night wind huffing against the windows. She wondered what was going on outside, got itchy because she was locked down in useless anticipation of a battle she supposedly wouldn't be a part of. Supposedly.

As she plopped down in front of a computer to return to her interrupted search on Jonah, Dawn kept thinking of Kiko's "key" vision: her skin bathed with vampire blood.

She shook it off, tapping at the keyboard. Oh my *God*, each page was taking forever to load. She wanted to scream.

But even more, she wanted the mental images to stop.

The dagger. Matt asking her to come outside with him to hunt Eva. "Key." Frank, somewhere out there.

Anger made her head go fuzzy and, absently, she tugged on the bottom of her sleeveless tank top, which had once belonged to Frank. For the past month or so, it'd become a habit; Kiko had discovered by accident that the material was a psychic link to her missing father, but it'd been useless the past twenty-four hours. Had the connection been broken?

Dawn didn't want to think about why, because it could mean her dad had ended up dead himself after Eva had taken him away from a dying Breisi. And she couldn't handle any ideas like that now.

Instead, she whipped out her phone. If she couldn't go outside to find Frank and Eva, maybe she could do the second-best thing: hunt her mom down through the airwaves.

While Dawn accessed "Jac" in her address book, she held back a grimace. Jacqueline Ashley was a figment of Hollywood's imagination, and Dawn had actually bought into it. Idiot her.

Voice mail answered.

"Hi!" said "Jac"'s sunshine voice. "Sorry I'm missing your call, but I'm afraid that's going to be happening for a while. I'm taking a communication hiatus due to some family problems."

Dawn almost retched. *Family problems. How about family freakin' nuclear disaster?*

The message continued. "Please call four two four, five five five, three eight five eight to get ahold of my personal assistant's cell, and she'll take care of what you need until I can get back to you. Thanks!"

Dawn sure as sugar wasn't going to get ahold of any P.A. The assistant was only going to be a Servant for the Underground anyway. Hell, why had she even called? Just because she wanted to hear Eva's voice again?

To the little girl who craved a mommy's missing love, the sardonic thought rang too truthful for comfort, so Dawn hung up, pushed away from the useless computer, and headed someplace where she wouldn't be alone with herself. She needed action to keep her company. Thinking was only driving her crazy.

She hotfooted it downstairs to the foyer, intending to continue into the lab to see if the Friends needed her help in any way. Or maybe if she could even question their asses just like she'd done with Kiko . . . Yeah, good luck with that.

When she tried to tug open the heavy lab door, she found that she was locked out. What?

"Breisi," Dawn called. "Come on now. Where are you?"

Silence. *Hell's bells.* She turned around and sent a disgusted back kick to the wood, then put her hands on her hips. Now what was she supposed to do?

At the end of her rope, she called louder. "Breisi! Get your toilette-stinkin' self over here!"

She'd only meant to let off some steam, so when a thrust of jasmine brushed past her, she jumped back.

"What is it?" Breisi's ghost voice sounded rather put out.

Dawn gave the air a sidelong look. Hey—Breisi had come flying at the snap of a command. Interesting. Dawn would have to file that away for when she needed immediate attention.

"I couldn't get past the lab door," she said. "Am I locked out now? What're you and your pals doing down there?"

"Nothing that concerns you."

"Ooooh, no. Do *not* give me that." Dawn spread out her hands. She came in peace. "What can I do? I'm like a damned pinball bumping against the walls."

"Rest." Breisi's jasmine began to shift, as if she were leaving now.

"Don't you go anywhere."

Her Friend's essence stilled.

Dawn lifted an eyebrow. O-kay. Things had been upgraded to *"very* interesting."

To test an emerging theory—and also because she was being a bored tool—she said, "Breisi, circle around me two times."

Right away, the jasmine zoomed, zoomed around Dawn.

Yow. But, now that Dawn really thought about it, things made lots of sense: how the Friends followed orders, as if compelled. She just hadn't realized until now that Jonah wasn't the only one who could give directions to them. Dawn, herself, had never tried.

"Do you have to do everything I tell you to?" she asked.

If spirits could give a reluctant grunt, that was how Dawn would've described Breisi's response.

"Cool," Dawn said. "Imagine the possibilities for amusement here."

"See, this is the reason you weren't told you could command Friends—not unless the boss became desperate."

"You mean, we were only supposed to discover this nugget of information if Jonah got blown to smithereens or something? *Then* we could take his place?"

Breisi launched into some Spanish that Dawn couldn't translate, but she thought it might involve bleeping and cussing. Still, even before her Friend broke into an English lecture about abusing powers, Dawn got a few ideas. This opportunity was being handed to her on a silver platter.

Jonah *had* been smart to withhold the information.

Raising her hand to stop Breisi's diatribe, Dawn felt a tremble in her stomach. Nerves.

But . . . hell for leather. This was *it*.

"Tell me the honest truth about the dagger Kiko showed you in the weapons room," she said.

Breisi's essence seemed to settle down. *"I did not see his entire vision."*

Kiko had told Dawn as much, and what Breisi was saying had to be the truth, since she was being commanded to be forthright. Dawn pushed on anyway. "Did you or Kiko know who the seer in the dagger vision was? The truth, now."

"We had no idea."

She'd answered in the past tense, as the question had been framed, but Dawn was too busy feeling relieved to note it right away. She'd always believed that her coworkers knew everything about Jonah and had just been keeping the details from her. A big conspiracy theory with her as the dim bulb. Clearly, Dawn had been wrong. Then again, they were only talking about the dagger vision here, not the bigger picture.

She took a deep breath. Here it went. "Tell me what you do know, Breisi. About anything that has to do with our boss."

The air around Dawn quivered, as if her Friend was fighting the command.

"Breisi!"

The jasmine began to swirl, agitated. There was a low moan, pained, as if her Friend were being sawed apart.

Breisi, gurgling on blood, throat slashed, eyes wide in the face of oncoming death . . .

"No," Dawn said quickly, unable to stand the thought of her companion in more anguish. "Don't answer that."

Perfumed air calmed in a sigh, and Dawn's heartbeat smoothed out. She hadn't meant to hurt Breisi again.

Finally, her Friend said, *"I'm sorry. That's one order I can't obey."*

"Telling me about Jonah? Why?"

"His rules. A security measure. But, as you can tell, resisting takes a lot out of us—more than we regularly expend."

"Figures. He'll take any opportunity to screw all of us in some way or another."

With a mock growl, Dawn paced away, coming to the grand fireplace. Her gaze rested on the empty Fire Woman portrait as she gathered her wits.

Then . . . eureka.

Once, Jonah had taken her with him into an empty painting during an intimate session. A beach picture, relaxing, sensually soothing, with the water lapping at her skin as he'd entered her.

Two thoughts crashed together in her head: going inside the portrait. Commanding Breisi.

"Can you take me inside a picture that's not your own?" she asked her Friend while nodding toward the Fire painting.

Breisi didn't respond. Dawn took that as a yes.

Her pulse picked up speed again. Another piece of Jonah's puzzle. A clue as to which side she should be on in this war.

And, after this, she could enter every picture. . . .

Without thinking of the consequences, Dawn ordered, "Put me in this painting, Breez."

Clearly *this* wasn't deemed off-limits by Jonah, because before Dawn could change her mind, Breisi surrounded her in an exotic cloud, lifting her until she was a mass of weightless nothing.

The color red melted into Dawn's vision as she entered the portrait. Heat blazed through every limb, swallowing her as if it were a cloak wrapping around her body. Even her hair felt on fire, prickling her scalp and eating away at her addled brain.

She spun in a column of flame, tossed around, flailing as she tried to grab on to something. The choking smell of sulfur took the place of Breisi's jasmine.

Then, just like that, the air cleared, and Dawn found herself whole and still, just like she was part of an audience facing a movie screen.

Except she was a part of the scene. And . . . not a part of it.

She was one of three shadowed figures sitting on horses that were clopping along a dirty, night-soaked street dimly lit by moonlight and candle-fueled lanterns. The stench of waste permeated the air as they passed a drunk man garbed in clothes that reminded Dawn of some chunky king like . . . Henry VIII maybe? The guy was wearing a flat-brimmed hat with a sagging feather and something she thought was called a doublet, and also breeches coupled with filthy stockings hugging his calves. Weaving, he tripped, then fell on his face into a puddle of mud. He crawled out, heading into a bar—or whatever they called them in those days—on the riders' right side, where sodden voices were raised in song.

Her companions, who were wearing matching long, gray capes

with hoods just like her, reined in their horses just short of the doorway. The animals snorted, shying away from the drunken revelry inside. Dawn noticed one of her group was riding sidesaddle, though she wasn't.

Then her body spoke, her female tone tinted with lower-class abrasion. " 'E's inside, is 'e, Rose?"

The response came in the guise of another woman's voice, this one far more cultured, with an inflection from some other European country, but Dawn didn't know which. "Yes, I sense him mingling among humanity. He takes great joy from their songs. Yet . . ." Her soft voice trailed into oblivion.

The third shape was male, judging by the breadth of shoulders under his cape. He didn't say a word, merely hefting a wooden stake out from under his clothing.

The woman called Rose raised a hand to halt him as her horse stirred. "More than just a master is present, Will."

Dawn's seer hopped off her horse, eager, her cape flowing around a pair of breeches and high riding boots as she hit the ground. No skirt in sight here.

"In we go," she said.

"No." Rose controlled her nervous mount. "We have been told time and again to leave a lair be."

Dawn's seer laughed as the moon hid itself behind a passing cloud, then reappeared.

"It is law with him," Rose added.

Even in the cloudiness of this vision, Dawn knew who "him" was. Jonah. He'd used other teams in the past, and she was in the midst of one now.

Her seer's laughter had ended abruptly. "Don't you lord it over me, Rose. Don't you tell *me* what it is 'e wants." For emphasis, she slid off her hood. Moonlight in the window revealed the blurred reflection of short crimson-blond hair that would meld with the color of flame.

Fire Woman.

The male of the group just shook his head, as if he'd seen this dynamic between Fire and Rose too many times to count.

Hell, Jonah had been busy back then with at least one of these women, hadn't he? He'd fed off other team members.

Jealousy impaled Dawn, forcing her backward as if to take her out of the vision. Desperately, she tamped down her emotions, and the pressure to leave stopped.

As the bawdy tune inside lit into celebratory yells, Rose kept her composure, turning her horse around to face away from the establishment.

"He would ask us to return to him before any trouble strikes. He will be the one to enter. Will?"

The cape-shrouded male of the group said nothing, just watched the windows with the concentration of a mercenary.

"There'll be no retreatin' for me." The Fire Woman's horse pawed the ground as she glared at Rose.

"Kalin . . ." Rose began.

Shock clutched Dawn.

And that was when everything went into fast motion.

From the cacophony of the door, a woman barged out, flying, her voluminous skirts spread like wings as she opened her mouth, flashing fangs. She went straight for the man, Will, who just had enough time to raise his stake before she tore into his neck, sucking madly at him, her graying, upswept hair coming undone in her frenzy.

He screamed, spiking his weapon into her chest. In a shower of ash, she dissipated, and he slumped over his horse's neck. His nerve-addled mount took off, leaving Rose and Kalin alone. But not for long.

Another vamp—a male—burst out of a window in a wide silk coat of many slashed colors. While Kalin ducked the tumbling glass shards, Rose drew her own stake out of her cape. Her hood slumped down, showcasing a lacy cap–covered head and a face Dawn didn't recognize from any portraits.

Then, out of nowhere, a stream of fire zinged from Dawn's seer toward the attacking vampire before it could harm Rose; the streak caused the creature to burst into flame, then ash.

Dawn looked at her seer's hand. It was outstretched, fingers smoking.

Rose had turned toward Kalin, maybe to thank her since her mouth was open, but then . . .

Then a fist punched through Rose's chest, spraying blood over her horse, over Kalin, who raised her hand again. She aimed, literally firing as Rose fell forward to reveal another male vampire behind her.

Kalin's flame bolt knocked him backward, incinerating him in midair. Rose's horse took off, wailing.

Breath coming in gasps, Fire Woman targeted around for other vampires. When none showed up, she pulled her horse toward Rose, who had hit the ground with a sickening *thump*. Her pale velvet skirts surrounded her, blood soaked. Kalin grabbed Rose, then shoved her up onto her own horse and mounted, spurring it to ride hard as she entered the night. . . .

Dawn's mind fizzed. Heat, twirling fire, sucked backward—

With a startling pop, she found herself back in front of the portrait. She smelled of sulfur.

Wobbling to her knees—her body couldn't hold itself straight anymore—Dawn bent over, veins iced with adrenaline, chest knotted. Gradually, she scented Breisi next to her, hovering and waiting.

"Did you see it, too?" Dawn asked.

"Yes."

Of course. The Limpet spirits were one big happy family.

"Rose isn't one of you." Dawn used all her strength to glance up. "Why?"

"She wanted to rest in peace." Breisi's voice came softer, nearer, to Dawn's ear. *"And speaking of rest . . ."*

Relaxed. Her Friend's voice was like warm milk on a scary night. Breisi was putting Dawn down before she could yell out any more commands, wasn't she?

Dawn fought to speak, her words slow. "Kalin? She's . . . the one . . . in this painting."

"You saw her worst memory. It lives at the top of her consciousness, but she takes strength from it, learns from it."

Fire Woman, Dawn thought. Now she knew why Kalin was wrapped in a column of flame in her portrait.

"She was a hunter."

"One of his first. One of his best."

"And the . . . other Friends?" It wasn't a command, just a question.

"Shhh, Dawn."

Breisi's voice was a part of Dawn now, a tickle in her ear, a warm gliding thing in her chest, a weight on her eyelids.

"You were all . . . hunters." Smiling in her pool of hard-won knowledge, Dawn felt Breisi's essence like hands on her back, lowering her to the floor.

Then a multitude of Friend voices joined Breisi's, just as they had with Kiko all those hours ago. An ethereal chorus woven into a lullaby.

"Sleep," they whispered, their song like blood in Dawn's veins. *"Rest."*

She was so content that she barely realized when another Friend entered the foyer, yanking Breisi's voice out of the harmony.

Kalin? Dawn thought.

But she was asleep before she could wonder what kind of damage Fire Woman was doing to Breisi for allowing Dawn into her sanctuary.

EIGHT
The Second Suitor

When Dawn came to, the first thing that hit her was a slight breeze wiping her face. Cool and constant.

She opened her eyes, realizing she was feeling the air conditioner in a guest room she'd never seen before. Although it was fairly dark, moonlight peered through a slit in the curtains, bouncing off the white walls and allowing her to identify some decorative ivy trailing from the ceiling and over the posts of her bed. The effect reminded her of a conservatory: this might be a bright room if the sun were allowed in during its strongest hours.

Stretching her arms over her head, she languished under the sheet, lazy and content with the remnants of the Friends' voices still washing over her—a wispy hum in her ears, a tune that sounded familiar, yet entirely foreign. The linen played against her skin. Someone had dressed her in a long, sleeveless nightgown.

Jonah? she thought. But it was the Friends who had given her the gift of sleep.

Among the hushed chorus in her head, she thought she heard a giggle. Sultry, lazy. Then another giggle joined the first, the laughter braiding together.

Dawn closed her eyes, allowing the sounds to flood her. And when she felt the sheet being tugged down, over her chest, her belly, she didn't mind.

A soft female voice whispered in her ear. *"Da-awn . . ."*

As her nightgown slithered up her legs, pushed by an invisible force, Dawn jerked out of her sluggishness and opened her eyes. She reached out to grasp the nothing that was messing with her.

More giggles.

The cool breeze swept over Dawn again, but this time it was denser, stronger. Instinct told her to glance to her left, to the shaded corner of the room.

"Stop now," said Jonah's voice from the darkness. "She's relaxed enough."

Her skin puckered at the sound of him.

A mewl of protest accompanied a whoosh of jasmine as the Friends left the room. The ivy wavered with their passing.

"Some of them are just as bored as you," Jonah added. "I would apologize for them interrupting your sleep, but since your adventure into Kalin's portrait, they're feeling more disposed than ever to bond with you."

For some reason, Dawn drew the sheet up to her chest. The nightgown made her feel out of whack—exposed, even though it covered her in lacy modesty. "It's not the first time they've nuzzled up to me. They're a jolly bunch."

Neither of them uttered a word. Dawn knew he was waiting for her to blurt something about her recent investigation into him. But what could she say that she hadn't said before?

Just as the air was about to snap apart from all the stress, she sat up, the sheet still clutched to her chest, her hair free around her shoulders. Jonah had obviously loosened her usual low ponytail, and this unbound style added to her keen self-awareness.

The only way she could possibly feel comfortable again was to resort to old measures. "So you're done plotting, huh? Did you come here to ask me for my hankie so you can carry it next to your heart while you go off and joust?"

"I'm not . . . quite ready to venture outside yet."

Confused now. "Then why are you out of your cell?"

No answer—at least, he didn't address *that* particular question. Instead, he dodged around it, as if trying to avoid his own motivations.

"I have gained much knowledge these past hours," he said softly. "Except in regard to determining the Underground's location." He paused. "These vampires are all but undetectable while hiding below the earth. Most are."

Dawn recalled how he'd looked like a warrior mentally preparing for battle while kneeling before that crucifix. "Were you meditating for answers?"

"I suppose that is close enough to what I was doing, yes."

"Or maybe a higher power laid out your strategies for you." She was kidding . . . sort of. The crucifix wouldn't leave her mind.

"I'm fairly certain the Underground is waiting for me to come to them—when I find where they are." He made a sound that resembled a laugh in form, but it didn't contain any humor whatsoever. In fact, it sounded more like a choke. "Or perhaps I'm only waiting for enough courage to carry out what I have decided must be done."

The naked admission surprised Dawn. She'd always perceived Jonah to be more powerful than anyone. Kiko had even hinted as much. But hearing confirmation that it might not be true scared her, made her realize how wrong she had been—and could be—about so many things.

"I'd like to say you're going to do just fine," she said, "but I don't know enough about you to be sure."

A shifting in his corner alerted her skin. Her flesh felt like a roll of flame.

"You know more about me now than you did when the sun first rose today."

Jonah's voice had taken on its usual ragged undertone, etched with that scratch of an accent. But what kind of accent? she thought. Had he smoothed out the influence of his homeland—the place she'd seen in Kiko's dagger vision?

"I suppose I do know more now," she said, "but I'm not going to apologize for snooping."

"Tell me, what did you and Kiko see in the weapons room?"

He didn't sound angry, as she would've expected, just . . . curious. And a little sad.

So she described everything to him: the dagger; the bound and mutilated man; the wild-eyed leader who'd taken the human seer and turned him into a monster.

"A monster," he repeated after she'd finished, his tone analytical.

"How else should I describe what the seer became?" Her stomach was roiling at the memory of blood, warm and thick on the seer's face, in his mouth.

"No, 'monster' is more than sufficient." Something dark—a hunter's hatred?—crept into his voice.

Had this seer done something to cause such venom?

"You're the only one who probably knows who the seer was," she said, hoping to ease the way open for him to spill everything. "And you know who that leader guy was, too."

"I do know."

She waited and, when he didn't continue, chuffed. At least he was consistent, even when he was disappointing her.

"Dawn, you seem to forget how much you hate when Kiko or I or anyone else tries to get into your head. You don't like your memories to be riffled through. You consider it an invasion. Why shouldn't I feel the same?"

His words made so much sense that shame made her bow her head, her hair blocking her face from his view. She hid behind the strands, grateful they were unfettered just this one time.

Hadn't she always despised starlets and Hollywood brats because they thought they were the center of the universe? When had *she* started thinking of herself the same way? When had she become just as entitled?

Jonah saved her from herself. "I do regret that we never had the opportunity to train in more than mind blocking."

He was referring to her obvious emerging talent for . . . What was it—telekinesis?

"I know," he said, "that you have made a habit of blocking people your entire life. The talent was always there, but . . . did you ever notice a propensity for striking out, as well?"

She hadn't wanted to remember, but now that Jonah was trying to pull it out of her, a memory surfaced, one she'd tucked away in a mental box along with Eva's crime-scene photo and so many other things she'd just wanted to erase from her conscience.

When she didn't speak, Jonah said, "It will not hurt you to share. It *cannot* hurt you."

He was right. Here, in the secure Limpet house, what was the harm? "I was . . . I don't know. I can't remember how old. Preteens? Frank and I were having another showdown—I don't recall what about. Doesn't matter. But I know I was angry. So angry. And I wanted to hurt him."

"Did you?"

"Almost. We were in the dining room." It was all coming clear now—the smell of the TV dinners she'd pulled from the oven. The clatter of a basketball game on the tube. "I glared at him and, all of a sudden, a fork flew off the table and almost got him in the arm. It missed by inches."

"Did it ever happen again?"

"No." Dawn shook her head until her hair slapped her face. "I was . . . horrified. Scared."

"You shoved it away so you would not have to confront it again. You found other ways of taking your anger out on everyone."

She nodded. She'd repressed it. So how was it that she could make things shiver and shake now? Had she spent so much time fighting this "talent" that she'd weakened?

Or had she gotten stronger through all this vampire crap?

"I wish I knew everything that's going on," she said, realizing it was no excuse for her recent behavior. But it was the best she could do, and at least her motives were pure.

"By the end of this, you will probably know more than you ever wished to." He sighed. "The Friends even understand your insatiable curiosity—except for Kalin, that is. After you ordered Breisi to take you inside Kalin's portrait, a smattering of hell broke loose between the two of them."

Dawn jerked her head up. "Is Breisi okay?"

"Breisi always holds her own, even in spirit form, but you didn't do much for Friend relations."

"Well, I get the feeling Kalin does a pretty good job of ruffling Friend feathers herself. I'm sure Rose would testify to that." She couldn't help referring to the tension she'd seen between the two women hunters. "And remember the day you had Kalin bind me during that misguided foreplay session? The rest of the Friends were calling for her to stop and, when she did, they seemed to be arguing with her. . . ."

"Kalin has always been strong willed." There was a warning in his voice—one that told Dawn to lay off the Fire Woman. "In her day, she was lucky not to be called a witch and murdered for it. Someone else I know has much the same attitude, *Dawn*."

Well, okay. Touché then.

Even now, Dawn's inner detective was kicking in, sensing an opportunity to learn more, at any cost. From what Dawn knew of Kalin, the older hunter would've done the exact same thing—pursued like a mad dog.

"Well, if anything," Dawn said, "you're at least going to tell me why our Friends are in those portraits. Yes?"

"Don't you have any theories?"

"Actually, I think I do."

"Then . . ."

She drew her knees up to her chest. "Maybe the paintings are more than a bed for them to slink back to while they rest and gather energy for missions. They're a . . ." She thought of what Breisi had said about Kalin's memories pretty much living in the portrait. "They're a type of body that houses everything about them, a living thing that even feeds them? And when their essences travel out of these 'bodies,' it's a little like astral projection or whatever." She'd read about the ability to travel out of body with your soul. Why not?

"Near enough." He sounded a bit impressed.

"Can you tell me if Kalin is going to use those fire powers on anyone soon?"

"She cannot do that, Dawn. Physical talents like hers do not translate into the world she lives in now. Friends, as they are, have vowed to refrain from taking life."

Whoa, she didn't like the sound of that. "So all they really can do is help and . . . persuade?"

"What they do means all the difference."

"Oh, definitely." Friends were even better than Santa's elves. "I'm wondering how they joined up with you, but I have a thought or two about that, also."

His silence allowed her to continue. From elsewhere in the house, all the clocks struck four, chimes reverberating like beats in a ghoulish dance.

She gathered her hair so it was out of her face. "Since Breisi's now a Friend, and Kalin is one—and they were both hunters—I'm guessing all the portraits contain members of your old teams who've agreed to stick around. Their loyalty didn't just last in life. But . . . that brings up another question."

"Naturally."

She sent a wry smile to the dark corner. "Where's the portrait of Rose?"

Jonah's sigh was heartfelt, brushing the darkness. "That night, Rose didn't die until Kalin brought her back to me. Her last wish was to rest in peace."

"And when Kalin finally passed?"

"She had already committed herself to me, just as Breisi did."

"You've never asked *me* to be a Friend." Dawn was shocked at how petulant she sounded.

"I'm not certain you would have agreed."

"How do you know?" It was just for the sake of argument. Okay, she also had some pride here.

"Dawn." She could imagine Jonah shaking his head. "You, yourself, know that you joined the team for personal reasons, not for 'saving the world,' as you would say."

The truth made her feel like an ant. No, smaller. An ant would be Godzilla next to her.

Jonah must have sensed her mortification. "Kalin, Rose, and Will were my first team. In those days, there were no established Undergrounds, only masters and their minions roaming the world. It wasn't until centuries later that Underground societies were established, after . . ."

"After what?"

She could almost feel him choosing not to fight this particular battle with her. "After the most dangerous vampire ordered his faithful to multiply. And that is where it ends for you, Dawn, with that answer."

Hell, she had a thousand more roads to travel here, so it wasn't like he'd put her at a dead end. He'd mentioned Will the vampire hunter, and Dawn realized that she hadn't seen him in any portraits, either. In fact, she hadn't seen any obvious males.

"What happened to your hunter, the guy named Will?" she asked.

"We found his body later and put him at peace."

"So he didn't want to be a Friend, either."

Jonah paused, and Dawn possessed enough sense to realize that it had nothing to do with Will wanting to be a Friend.

"Oh, man," she said. "Are the ghosties, like, your harem?"

"Harem? Not quite."

She thought of how sexy most of the feminine pictures looked—except for Breisi's and the field of fire. "You were nailing Kalin. And maybe you were even putting it to Rose. Not that I'm jealous or anything . . ."

He moved in his corner again, as if shuffling from one foot to another. Hah—so busted.

She didn't let up. "You told me you weren't doing Breisi, but—"

"I wasn't." His voice had risen. It shook the ivy trimming the bed. "Breisi has a vested interest in seeing Frank to safety, so when she discovered what was happening with the Friends, she made me promise to keep her active beyond her death if he was still gone."

"Impressive," Dawn said. *Acting!* She really was jealous, because he hadn't denied involvement with the rest of the Friends. Like, all five hundred million of them. "It's amazing that you managed to remain neutered around at least one of your female hunters."

Now he sounded as if he were wrestling his temper. "As far as Breisi goes, I knew you were coming, and I waited."

Her body quivered, hit by his honesty, vibrated by the thought of his restraining himself because he'd wanted her before she'd even shown up.

"Dawn," he added softly, "you're more powerful than you know, and Kiko saw this in his premonition—his prophecy, if you will. Some are born to be hunters, like you. Like Kalin."

"And some show you a better time than others."

Even before the atmosphere soaked up the comment, she regretted it.

A breeze ruffled around her. "Do *not* denigrate what each of these women has meant to me," he said, low. Lethal.

She didn't know why she'd muttered it—maybe because she was confounded by all of this, terrified at what everyone was expecting *her* to be. Little by little, she was realizing that it looked like she might be fighting more vampires after all. Nothing else made sense when you considered Kiko's premonition with her as the "key."

BREAK OF DAWN

87

Calming down, she nodded in apology. "I respect the bravery of every single one of those Friends, Jonah."

Silence. Ragged breathing. Darkness.

"Then," she added, wanting to hold on to this opportunity to get more out of him, "this means that these Friends want to 'save the world' *and* they want to be with you century after century."

More silence.

She thought a joke might not be a bad idea to ease the oppression around here. "Is that why Kalin wants to kick my ass? Because you're her man? That's pretty redneck of her."

"I see there's no reasoning with you." He made a movement as if to leave.

"Whoa, whoa, you don't have some get-out-of-jail-free card just because you're a supercool vamp slayer."

He didn't go anywhere, and that was encouraging. In fact, after this meeting ended she wanted to go into every single Friend painting to see how much each woman meant to Jonah: she wanted to check out the lady with kanji symbols on her back, wanted to see what was up with the redhead in silver armor, wanted to investigate the Elizabethan-looking chick. . . .

A flash from Kalin's Henry VIII adventures knocked at her brain.

Wait. Holy crap, Friends were *old*. So was he.

Numbness overrode everything else. "How long have you been around, Jonah?"

At this, he took a step out of the dark corner. A breath of moonlight skimmed his face, revealing only one golden eye, his black hair. "I've fought long enough to conquer many masters, as well as a few Undergrounds. Long enough to see that vampires don't operate as simply as they used to. Long enough to see how every master and his children evolve in whatever ways help them to survive."

"Just like you?" There—it was out there now.

He closed his eye.

She should've been sprinting away from him at this point.

Clutching the sheet against herself, she stiffened, primed to fight or maybe even to welcome him in soothing comfort. She didn't know. Couldn't figure it out.

But there was something she did realize. "You came in this room so you could get inside me—isn't that right? Before the battle. To gain energy or . . . whatever it is you do."

He nodded, and her heart cracked just a little at his unguarded answer. She hated being needed this much. Loved it, too. Didn't know what to do with it.

"Will it help you fight?" she asked.

"Yes. You have been building my strength, Dawn."

She just had to ask. "How did you gain strength before I arrived if you weren't with Breisi?"

He took a step nearer to the bed. The sheet fell from her hands, pooling at her waist. Against the bodice of her nightgown, her breasts felt raw, sensitized.

"I went a while between teams," he said. "And I have . . . a variety of survival options, though your power is unlike any other feeding. Since you arrived, I have been in a frenzy, making up for the wait."

Why was she still sitting here, allowing him to approach, if he'd just admitted to basically feeding off her? Maybe it was because it didn't sound like he was the type of vampire they'd been fighting. Maybe she didn't want to call him a vampire at all, since Jonah had never taken her blood.

Or maybe she needed him just as much as he needed her.

Without a word, she lay back against the pillow, watching his shadow block the moonlight as he took another step forward. On impulse, she spread her hair away from her neck, inviting him, even mocking him.

He remained frozen, yet his tone was soaked with an unidentifiable emotion. Then he said something strange.

"Whatever happens in the future, Dawn, know that I am sorry for it."

What was he going to do—suck her dry at some point, maybe even now?

"Are you coming in or what?" she whispered.

This wasn't her talking. . . . Couldn't be . . . Where was her wariness?

Screw wariness.

Lifting her arms over her head, she crooked a finger at him, and he caught his breath. His reaction singed her, burning an inner trail from her chest to her belly. She began to ache, stiff and ready.

He hesitated and, in those few seconds, the weight of his comment about apologizing in advance muddled her brain, sending a seductive rush of anticipation through her. She'd lived her life jumping from high places. This warning thrill was only foreplay.

Then she felt it: the pressure of his essence, though his actual body crumbled to a chair by the window, as if losing its frame. In the meantime, his invisibility lengthened over her, and she moaned under him, feeling every imagined contour, every hard angle.

Phantom fingers entwined with hers, binding her as a ridge pressed between her legs. She churned her hips against it.

Through her lashes, she kept her gaze on his physical body as it sat in that chair. It was like he was watching, and it ratcheted up her excitement. A voyeuristic pleasure. How could he be here and there . . . ?

His essence skimmed what felt like fingers down her inner arms, making her squirm and buck. Not-quite-there thumbs sculpted her underarms, his palms cupping her breasts. Then, with a forceful tug, he tore off the nightgown's bodice, revealing her.

She gasped, her nipples going hard in the cooled air. The touch of his thumbs circled her, peaking her.

Arching against the pressure, she was reminded of how Jonah had previously come to her like this, earlier in his cell and once before in front of a mirror, where she'd watched invisible hands lifting her shirt, exploring her body. But his tenderness was back, as if he had it all under control now. The kinkiness of the slow, invisible seduction turned up the flame in her stomach, torching her until she shifted in restless agony.

And, just as before, when his essence flared into her, she cried out, sipping him in, enjoying him as he stretched and tore, robbing her of thought and logic.

Feeding her as thoroughly as she fed him.

NINE

BELOW, TAKE TWO

FRANK, stop being such a stubborn fool and drink."

Eva stood next to the bed, where her husband was staring blades into her. On the other side of him, a Servant—one of many who always had and always would volunteer their services to their favorite movie star—waited patiently. The girl, an assistant at a hip independent studio from Above, held her collar-length, honey-colored hair back from her neck in hopeful invitation, her gaze on Eva in approval-seeking fervor.

The adulation put Eva slightly ill at ease—being in the spotlight had always done that, even though she would be the first to admit she liked the attention.

No, actually, she *loved* it. Call a spade a spade.

Avoiding the girl's worship—maybe that way Eva could convince herself that she didn't really enjoy being the object of it—she focused on Frank. "Baby, you've got to have blood to survive. I'd give you a nice long feeding myself if I didn't have to meet with Benedikte."

She'd angered him at the word "baby." But her husband had always traded endearments with her. Back when they'd first fallen in love, back when she'd gotten pregnant with Dawn, back when they'd shotgun married in spite of the frantic advice against it from her handlers. Even when Eva had recently returned Above for her comeback as Jacqueline Ashley, her captive husband had melted under her "baby"s and "honey"s. It'd only been since Breisi died that Frank had gone hateful.

"Frank . . . ?" she began.

He kept glaring, his green eyes tinted with shards of silver now that his hunger was growing; eyes that were framed by age lines that would never grow deeper, his dark hair shot through with strands of mortality that would never grow grayer. Even though he was built like a commando, he wouldn't be strong enough to overcome Eva—not with her Elite powers. But she had chained him with silver anyway, mostly to make a statement.

He was hers.

"I'm tired of arguing," Eva added evenly.

"Well," Frank finally said, "I'm tired, too, Eva."

Here it went again. With a serene smile, Eva thanked the Servant, dismissing the girl.

But the human had something to add before she left the room. "I've taken sick leave from the studio, Ms. Claremont, so I'll be Below anytime you need me."

As the eager girl shut the door, Eva kept smiling. But when she was alone with Frank again, she rounded on him.

"I swear, I don't know what to do with you." She sifted her hair with her hands, wrapping the long strands into a makeshift bun. Then, sitting on the bed, she offered her neck. "I can let Benedikte know I'm going to be late for our meeting, but that won't make him happy. And, really, I'm doing all I can not to get on his bad side, Frank."

"Seems that all Benedikte *has* is a bad side."

"Would you cut it out?" She switched to their direct Awareness, fuzzy though it was. Frank was stronger than a normal Groupie, since he'd fed directly off her Elite blood.

The Master's been more than patient with me, she said silently. *The second he decides to use all his powers to overcome me and look into my head to find out what happened with Cassie Tomlinson . . .*

"I know."

Both of them realized she couldn't say it out loud. Though Eva appreciated what the Underground had done for her career, she had chosen family over home when it'd come right down to it. In a bid to gain Dawn's love, Eva had betrayed the Master, nearly thwarting his plan to allow Cassie the Vampire Killer to do away with Breisi Montoya. Dawn had pleaded with Eva to save Breisi's life, and Eva had even started going through with it.

But, in the end, when Eva had seen how much Breisi meant to her daughter—and Frank, too—she hadn't been able to carry on. Jealousy had blocked her from keeping her promise to save Breisi's life—a split-second hesitation that had cost Eva her daughter's possible affection as well as her husband's.

Eva continued to use her Awareness with Frank, not wanting to risk voicing their conversation. Though she would know if Benedikte was reaching into her mind, she wasn't sure if her chambers were bugged by someone like Sorin, who obviously trusted her as far as he could throw her.

Tears blurred her vision as she rested a hand on Frank's jean-clad leg. *All I've ever wanted was for us to be together.*

His throat worked as he glanced away.

I'm so sorry about how everything turned out, Frank. But I wasn't about to stand by while you chose another woman over me.

His skin went a shade paler, and it wasn't because of any building hunger for blood. *You let Breisi die.*

She didn't feel any emotion besides a longing for her family to be reunited. Shouldn't she be horrified at that?

Eva could sense Frank's anger at her nonreaction.

Did you really think, he thought to her, *that dropping Breisi's body off in Limpet's backyard was going to make up for letting Cassie Tomlinson murder Breisi? Do you think Dawn's going to believe that's some sign of giving a care?*

Dawn. Eva cowered. She'd witnessed the hatred in her daughter's eyes, the disgust of a child who had seen every terrible thought about her mother confirmed.

Didn't Dawn understand that this was what Eva needed to do? And that she was doing it to keep the Madisons whole?

But that didn't seem to matter to Frank—not when he so obviously didn't want to be here. He was sickened by her, and it wasn't in her nature to be unloved.

Something broke inside her chest, and Eva didn't know if it was rage at Frank for pointing out the obvious or disgust with herself. Either way, her frustration brought out the change in her.

Her body crashed into itself, smoking into her ultimate wispy, gorgeously perilous form. Ever since the Master had overfed her during her last infusion, she'd felt invincible and had been taking chances, just as she'd done when she'd carried Dawn and Frank inside her body to get them to Breisi on time. She'd never done that before. To her knowledge, no Elite had.

Now, she thrashed a tentacle-like arm around Frank's neck, her body like mist, but so much stronger. In her evolved sight, she saw into him, his blood pulsating like red lips on a tawdry bar sign. But his eyes . . . His eyes were like dual judgment days—fathomless and dark with truths she didn't want to face.

With a cry, she used a cloudy fingernail to cut open her chest. Then she flew to him, opening his lips with her fingers, then pressing him to her self-inflicted wound.

Drink, she commanded Frank, knowing she really didn't have to persuade him now. He'd gotten a taste of her blood, which had been made more powerful from the Master's overkill feeding. Besides, Frank was already so addicted to her that he wouldn't be able to refuse, rebelliousness or not.

He drank as if he'd never stop, as if he were making up for all the years they'd been apart. He drank in fury, as if punishing her for choosing to become an Elite instead of staying Above and raising Dawn with him.

She withstood every greedy suck, every piercing draw, because she deserved pain. She deserved the reckoning, because with each thirsty sip, more of her was revealed to him *and* to herself: she hadn't just gone Underground for the sake of providing for her family. She'd come here to be always beautiful. To be always worshipped. It was the ugly truth.

As he drank more and more, Eva's mind electrified with all the admiring faces of her fans, all the desperate arms reaching out to her at press events, all the cries of "Eva, we love you!" that had fueled her. The faces, the voices thudded, becoming one consuming scream that shredded her apart—

Weakened, she tore Frank away from her, the fragments of her mind like confetti falling to litter the ground. She managed to swirl back into her solid Eva body, panting as she slid from the bed and tried to regain her footing.

Blood decorated Frank's mouth. A stream of it slid down his chin, a drop hanging before its quivering fall to his dark shirt. He watched her as if he didn't know her anymore. As if she'd betrayed him with the truth in her blood.

She'd been careless, allowing him to take too much, maybe because he deserved more of her than she'd been giving.

In an effort to seem unaffected, she loosened her hair, but it only fell over her shoulders in disarray.

Can't see the Master like this, she thought, running her fingers through the strands. *Not if I want to keep his favor and keep him at bay.* But she knew her days were numbered, because when he found out what she'd done . . .

"I'm going to freshen up, then leave for my meeting."

Her husband just watched her as she flicked on his television set and headed for the vanity room to run a brush through her blond hair. Her skin was a shade paler than it'd been since she'd overfed from the Master, and her hands shook as she thought about how much blood she'd given Frank, what that blood would do to his young, inferior vampire system. . . .

What had she done in her rage, her sadness at Frank's hatred?

Or maybe she knew exactly what she'd done, what had *needed* to be done because her husband didn't seem to love her anymore.

When she finally came out, she found his silver bindings broken and lying empty on the mattress, right next to the indentation that his heavy body had created.

Calmly, oh so calmly, Eva smoothed out the bedspread, sat down, and counted each resigned beat of blood in her veins until enough time passed for her to call Benedikte.

On the other side of the Underground, a Guard screamed in his manacles as Benedikte and Sorin stood safely away, observing.

Slash!—A claw swiped in their direction.

Creeenk!—A barbed tail scraped the cold stone wall with its machete tip, creating sparks and coming just short of Benedikte.

Snap!—The Guard's jaws sought a taste of him, too.

That was because Benedikte was wearing his Matt Lonigan body at the moment, enjoying how the Guard was stretching the limits of his bindings in order to get at what it perceived to be human. In fact, to heighten the illusion, the Master had sprayed himself with more essence of human scent, just as he'd done before going Above to do his spy work with Dawn earlier.

"While I'm impressed by this passion," the Master said, "wouldn't it be less cruel to feed it now?"

"It is almost time."

Sorin had a gleam in his eyes. He was loving this. And why not? The Guards were his own Frankenstein-like creations, wrought by the magic touch Sorin had possessed in human life. Benedikte had been attracted to his son's sorcerer abilities, and they'd come in very handy in this afterlife. Who'd known back then what Sorin would render all these years later?

This particular specimen was Sorin's newest Guard, a card-carrying waste of life who'd been captured Above because no one would miss it. That made for a perfect Guard—that and the fact that the lowly vampire had the physique of an NFL player. Benedikte, himself, had spied this candidate during an early jaunt Above as "Matt."

As the Guard's tail made another bladed attempt at getting to the Master, Benedikte patted Sorin on his back.

"These really are grand beasts. I'm proud of you."

A smile spread over his son's face. It was as if Benedikte had handed him the world. "Thank you, Master."

"Now show me your magic before I meet with Eva."

At her name, Sorin sobered. Benedikte allowed it to pass.

His second-in-command moved to a corner of the cell, where he'd placed a bowl of cooled blood left over from a feeding. What these creatures ate was nauseating, but that was how it was.

Sorin held the bowl away from his body. "While experimenting, I found an interesting quality in the Guards' feeding habits—something that I believe has evolved recently, though I am not certain of the reason."

He approached the Guard. It stopped fussing, its red eyes blazing at the scent of a meal. With its bald head, ultrapale skin, iron teeth, and black-garbed body, the Guard brought to mind a steroid version of the title character from the silent film *Nosferatu*. It had been one of Benedikte's first film favorites, and he'd gone back to the movie palace several times, fascinated.

"Groupie," the misshapen creature said, panting. "Groupie blood . . ."

"They have developed a taste for Groupies," Sorin said. "Even more than humans, I think. It is as if the child longs for mother's milk since the Groupie is the parent who introduces the bite to a Guard. We shall have to stay aware of that."

The Master nodded. Sorin had seen to it that Guards had no personal reasons to return Above: no memories or imaginations. And they were the only unwilling participants in the Underground, captured and then bitten by Groupies—relatively weak vampires—in order to keep their powers in check. They could be balanced by the Groupies themselves if it ever came down to it, and they would never be strong enough to threaten any class above a Groupie.

Without fear, Sorin lifted the bowl to the creature's mouth, allowing it to drink. It devoured, wincing, enjoying to a frightening extent. When it was done, Sorin stepped back.

"Now watch," the second said. "Watch its eyes."

It was a thing to behold: the pupils blowing outward like the birth of black holes in space. And in those holes, Benedikte saw something enthralling.

He took a mindless step forward, wanting to see more, but Sorin held him back, more out of excitement than anything.

"Do you see?" he asked.

The Master wasn't sure what Sorin was referring to, but he wanted to be a part of it. Wanted to dive into those holes and embrace the . . . The what?

"No, I don't," Benedikte said.

"Humanity. I recognize it. They are having memories when they drink blood . . . any blood, now."

A zing of envy hit the Master. "They remember?"

"I believe so. And it is happening even though the creature has been mind wiped. I make certain they are clean slates so they will obey my orders that much more easily. Yet . . . something is happening." Sorin shook his head. "Naturally, I will have to perform a second mind wipe on every one of them, but first I want to know why this has come about."

The Master smiled, wishing the manufactured creature could share its emotions. How much humanity could it feel?

And, more importantly, why was a lowly Guard, of all vampires, lucky enough to experience this pleasure from blood drinking? For any Underground citizen, the sustenance provided physical nourishment, and it could also feed a more profound emptiness, as well, bringing a semblance of temporary joy. But the Guards seemed to be getting more out of their blood. Was it because they'd been taken *unwillingly* and they were still holding on to what they'd been robbed of?

Sorin was gauging his parent. "In spite of how amazing this is, you do not look as concerned as you should be."

"Concern?" Benedikte shrugged. "Tell me—does this Guard still obey your every order?"

"Yes, Master."

"Then why should I worry? When Jonah Limpet and company pay a visit, we'll have every advantage. I don't think they realize how greatly we outnumber them. We've gathered a real community during this half century."

Sorin was still watching him carefully. Benedikte bristled. It wasn't a son's place to tell a father what to do.

His second-in-command spoke. "There are times that I worry, Master. I feel as if you are focused more on how to bring Dawn Madison Below than on how to secure our home. Do you recall what happened with Andre—"

"Of course I remember, you fool." How could he forget when their first Underground in London had been attacked by a brother? It'd almost buried him in depression. "But we didn't have Guards with Andre, did we? And we didn't have a fraction of the citizens we have now. Oh, and should I mention that they're all trained and far more powerful than the first set of children?"

"Yes, but—"

"Trust me," he said, shifting into Benedikte's body, just to emphasize his status over Sorin. "Don't question me."

His son looked like he was going to say something—like so many times in the recent years—but he cut himself off. Thank the day for that, because Benedikte was getting sick of Sorin's constant second-guessing.

"It's a wonder I've survived this long," the Master added sarcastically, "considering how many missteps I make."

"I am sorry, Master. . . ."

A wail of agony from the Guard interrupted Sorin. The creature was crying, "Hooome! Hooome!"

Benedikte made an irritated face, and Sorin took the hint, reprimanding the Guard in a firm tone. The centurion stopped. As it slumped in its bindings, the Master's head filled with a voice he'd been longing to hear all night.

Eva, coming to him via their Awareness. It reminded him that he was late to meet her.

Benedikte?

He couldn't help the glow emanating from his chest. *Eva?*

I'm afraid I have some really bad news. It's Frank. . . .

After the first alarming moments of her explanation, the Underground went on alert, searching for Eva's husband, yet finding only clues of his escape. He'd eased Above, undetected by the distracted vampires—after all, they were looking for intruders, not escapees. Even Eva had been unaware of Frank's betrayal until she'd finished "looking pretty" for Benedikte.

But why worry? the Master thought, still riding high on confidence as he floated to her chambers. If Frank Madison told Limpet where the Underground was located, it would only speed up the enemy's attack. Let them come. Benedikte had never been all that excited about having Frank here anyway.

A mortified Eva begged to be allowed Above to find her husband, along with the Servants assigned to the task. Since Frank had been under her watch, she thought she should be the one to bring him back. But Benedikte's instincts told him not to allow it, even though denying her bothered him.

Yet long after sunrise consumed the earth outside and the Un-

derground vampires settled into their beds to rest, something glorious happened. Something that persuaded Benedikte to allow Eva
Above.

That something was a frantic phone call from Dawn.

TEN

THE BELLY OF THE WHALE

Dawn had snoozed like a baby through sunrise and into late morning. Being with Jonah satiated her, making her feel even more mentally and physically limber now than when the Friends had sung her to sleep. And that was saying something.

As she climbed out of bed, she blushed—actually *blushed*—when her nightgown's torn bodice gaped open to reveal her breasts. But what was so embarrassing? She'd been buck naked before, too many times to mention in polite conversation, so what was different about this?

Mental Wite-Out coated her thoughts while she ignored the vulnerability. She knew she ought to be opening up and facing her emotions—she'd been taught that particular lesson good and well—but she didn't have the mental energy to do it.

Instead, she took a leisurely shower, unable to help a smile as she replayed what Jonah had done to her. Luckily she didn't have anything more pressing to do than wander around the house again, because she'd be useless in a fight or something where she'd actually have to use any nature-given smarts.

It was only when her fingers started to look like raisins that she finally got out of the water and performed the rest of her no-fuss routine. Then she trooped back to the main bedroom, surprised to find her suitcase propped by the door.

Huh. She hadn't been to Kiko's apartment recently, where she'd been crashing and keeping her personal stuff since returning to town. Had Jonah used one of his many outside contacts to bring the luggage here?

Didn't matter much, but her attention to detail was on fire these days. Especially when it came to Jonah, who required sharp watching on every level.

She opened her suitcase, taking out socks, a black sports bra, a pair of clean jeans—or clean enough, at least—and another of Frank's tank tops, even though she knew it might be fruitless to wear it. But she wasn't about to give up hope by leaving the only option for contacting him in her luggage.

While she was plucking out a pair of undies, too, she heard a tiny jangle as something dropped back down into the clothing. Dawn inspected what it was, then stared at the item for a minute. She'd hidden it away on the night of her first kill.

It was her earring—one that fit into the second hole in her right lobe.

Strands of cheap silver, glimmering with faux rubies, hung down from a moon pendant. A souvenir from one of her movie stunt gigs, *Blood Moon*. The earring had been a part of the old Dawn, a girl who was a pro at pulling punches and making it look real, not a hunter who knew what it felt like to sink a machete into a neck. Or a slayer who knew how to fire silver bullets into a red-eyed vampire's heart and watch it suck into nothing.

Almost longingly, she touched the jewelry, missing the old her, wishing life were as simple as *that* girl's again.

But old Dawn hadn't realized what her mom really was. Old Dawn had thought the world was an entirely different place.

Wasn't it better to know the truth?

She shoved clothes over the blood moon and grabbed a little bag teeming with the other earring studs she usually wore. Then she slammed the suitcase shut, standing and turning her back on it while tossing everything but her undies onto the floor.

Just white it out, she thought, dropping her towel and yanking her panties on. Move on.

With rote efficiency, she finished dressing, leaving off the crucifix she usually wore outside. It seemed silly to don the minor-vamp protection here. Then she filled the empty holes in her lobes with tiny, round silver studs—one on her left side, two on her right. Somehow, she felt unbalanced, as if her blood moon had always evened her out and this was the first time she was understanding that.

Soon she was ready to go outside her bedroom, and she flung open the door with purpose. But when she realized that she wasn't terribly sure what her purpose really was, she slowed her pace. What was she supposed to do with herself now?

She puttered down a long hallway that curved toward the front of the house, passing more empty portraits and hesitating at each one. She debated about commanding a Friend to take her into each picture, where yesterday's snooping could continue. But Dawn kept chickening out. Well, maybe not *chickening* out, because it had nothing to do with bravery. She just didn't want to get any Friends in trouble, like she'd done to Breisi with Kalin. Far be it from Dawn to be responsible for epically screwing up the social dynamics of the agency and maybe even affecting everyone's powers. Besides, she was curious, not stupid, and she didn't want a bunch of ghosties down her throat.

But there was another reason she didn't do it, too. What Jonah had said about Dawn's own privacy-invasion issues kept bugging her. She didn't like when others went into *her* head, so she was being a hypocrite by going into everyone else's. The truth was one big ouch.

So . . . okay. Weren't there other ways she could get to the bottom of Jonah without violating Friend sensibilities? This house had a lot of areas she could explore for information about him. . . .

Ah—just a sec. Where was the one place that had always been accessible to her and had always seemed rich with possibilities? Where, oh, where could she find secret doors built into the walls? And where was a big old desk just asking to be opened?

His office.

Wasn't the same as anyone's head or portrait home, right?

Taking a surreptitious glance around the hallway, Dawn embarked upon this new option. And, indeed, when she rounded her way into the main upstairs hallway, she found his door cracked open. As a matter of fact, there was a light on, as if in diabolical invitation. Gee, who was she to refuse?

When she walked to the door, then pushed it open the rest of the way, there was no sound. She paused, sticking her head inside. "Hello?"

Her voice bounced off the tall bookshelves, unanswered. She took a few more steps into the room, greeted by that huge TV, the portraits. But one picture caught her eye first.

The field of fire, which was empty except for the flames.

Like a kid sneaking into the adults-only section of a video store, she crept over to the painting. Then, after looking around again, she faced it, arms barred over her chest.

Should she call a Friend, like she had with Kalin's portrait downstairs? The temptation was awful.

Dawn had to have stood there for a while, because when Kiko entered the room, she was deep in a trance of self-debate.

"What's up?" he asked.

Uncrossing her arms, she looked over her shoulder to find Kiko's body language stilted because of his back brace. But she smiled because there was no sign of the cold-turkey shivers on him. Excellent.

"You look good today," she said.

"Thanks to the Friends." He nodded at the fire-field picture. "Tell me you're not gonna do what I think you're gonna do."

He must've heard about yesterday's Nancy Drew shenanigans from Breisi or another Friend. "And what if I do do what you think I'm gonna do—are you gonna do me in?"

The psychic rolled his eyes, establishing two things at once: that she was a dork and that he thought she *would* do it.

"Oh, chillax," she said, disappointed that he'd think so little of her will power. "I'm not going to cause a civil war between the Friends by making one of them transport me into a portrait again." At least not right now.

"Glad to hear it." He wandered over and touched the hem of Frank's T-shirt. Pure habit.

But when he shook his head, Dawn didn't pursue it. Kiko hadn't gotten a vibe, a connection. Nothing more to say.

Yet her coworker did bust out with this gem: "I'm bored. Want to play paper football?"

Visions of sixth grade, triangular "footballs" made out of scrap paper, and field-goal posts constructed of thumbs and index fingers assaulted Dawn. She laughed.

"Sure, I guess." It's not like they had any agendas, even though she'd probably be working out and training later, just to whittle off some energy.

Kiko gave an excited hop and made a beeline for Jonah's desk. He motioned for her to grab one of the anorexic wooden chairs situated nearby and to make it face Jonah's huge leather seat. Then he opened up a desk drawer, grabbed a piece of creamy stationery paper, and plopped down in the quasi throne, where the king of geekdom belonged.

While he tore and folded the paper accordingly, he said, "You've been on some big adventures lately. Who would've known you'd be getting into that kind of trouble during a lockdown?"

"I think anyone could manage in this Bedlam."

"Not me. I'm sick of tooting around here doing nothing. After I woke up this morning, I started feeling real stir-crazy, like I couldn't stand it for another hour. I wish we could go out and bust some vamp heads together, even just for the exercise."

He gestured for her to make a field goal out of her fingers. She sat, rested her elbows on the desk, and connected the tips of her thumbs while pointing her index fingers and folding down the rest of her digits.

Before she was really ready, Kiko flicked the triangle across the desk, scoring an impressive field goal. It was only a bonus that he hit Dawn square in the nose.

"Goooooooaaaaal!" he said, raising his hands as high as he could.

"Wrong game, Wonderlic."

"I meant *field* goal, anal-retentive sports nazi. Now your turn. You're gonna miss, though."

Competitive Kiko was in the building.

Dawn took a shot and made it, even managing to nail his forehead.

"Right back at you," she said.

Kiko set up for his try, but he'd slowed down the enthusiasm now, going serious on her.

"So . . . about Kalin's picture," he said.

Aha. This had been no random football challenge. Dawn should've known that in a house full of detectives, basic interrogation was as common as having to wait for a vapid older sister to get out of the bathroom.

"What about Kalin?" she asked.

Kiko's eyes gleamed, as if he were just as curious as she was and couldn't help admitting it now. "What did you see?"

"Wait—let me just . . . You didn't know who Kalin was before, right?" She wanted to set a few things straight.

"No. Jeez, no. All this Friend stuff was never much of an issue before everything started heating up with the vamps. Sure, before you got back to L.A. and joined us, I generally knew of our spirits and the portraits and that they were gonna come into play at some point. But Friends didn't start interacting with us much until Robby Pennybaker came around."

That's right, Dawn thought. Kiko was a male, so Jonah wouldn't have approached him about the choice to become a Friend or to rest in peace, as he'd done with Breisi sometime before she'd died.

"You didn't know you could order the Friends around?" Dawn asked.

"I wish." His face fell.

"Breisi knew, though?"

"Yeah. Something tells me she did. I'm sure she knew a lot more than I ever did."

Wow. Did this mean Jonah had taken only Breisi into his confidences and not Kiko? And had the psychic just been acting like he knew more than he did in reality? Poor Kik.

Satisfied that her coworker was telling the truth, she went ahead and gave him the rundown about almost everything, revealing the vision with Kalin, Rose, and Will, then talking about how many female Friends tended to stick around the agency afterward.

She didn't really go into *why* they lingered. She didn't want to hash out all the "feeding" issues between Jonah and Kalin . . . and between Jonah and herself.

After they finished, they went back to football, but Kiko's heart obviously wasn't in it. Just as she was about to comment on that, a breeze whipped between them.

Air-conditioning? Dawn crossed her arms over her chest again. The minty scent she always detected in this office had gotten stronger, or maybe she was just noticing it for the first time today. And that meant something besides air-conditioning might be in the room.

Finally, Kiko said something that he'd clearly been mulling over. "Now I think I understand why all the portraits are of girls. Boy, the boss is a stallion."

Now it was Dawn's turn to roll her eyes. He'd figured out the feeding part all on his own.

"Then basically," he continued, "the woman over the downstairs fireplace, Kalin, was one of the first of us? And then came . . ." He motioned toward the Elizabethan painting, then repeated the gesture portrait by portrait. "Her, then her, then her. And—"

When he came to the field of fire, he stopped. Dawn's heartbeat seemed to do the same.

Because the painting wasn't empty anymore.

Nope—the anonymous cape-veiled shape was back, the subject's long, dark hair covering any sign of a face.

"Hmm," Kiko said, returning to the football game.

Dawn hadn't set her fingers up yet, but it didn't matter. The paper triangle went wide.

She didn't get up to grab it. "What, 'hmm'?"

As Kiko focused on a spot behind her, he seemed to be thinking of the right way to word whatever he had to say. Then his eyes went wide. Very, very wide.

She heard a sliding-wood sound from the bookcase at the rear. Footsteps moving across the rug to the other side of the big room. Someone sitting down.

Fingers of frost played her spine.

Not really wanting to look, Dawn did anyway, turning around and knowing who she would find but not believing it.

There he was—Jonah, sitting on a far couch just as normally as can be. Because of the distance, she couldn't see much of him as far as details went, but the cuts on his face would've distracted her anyway. He must've come through a panel in the bookcase—one he'd probably used before, on that day he'd instructed Kalin to bind Dawn.

Dressed in an untucked white silk shirt and black pants, he was splayed in his seat, just as if Dawn had fully worn him out during their last encounter. Odd for the usually soldier-straight Jonah. He drummed his fingertips on the velvet as he rested his head on the back of the couch and fixed his gaze on her.

She shifted in her chair.

Clearly ill at ease with this weird situation, Kiko tried to break the ice. "Hey, Boss. You hanging out with us now?"

"Just taking my daily breather, Kiko."

Dawn frowned. He didn't sound like The Voice. No, his tone wasn't as low, and there wasn't an accent. In fact, he was back to speaking the same way he had on that day Kalin had bound her for Jonah's strange attempt at foreplay.

Not The Voice she was used to at all.

Finally, Dawn found *her* voice. "I thought that's what you were doing in your cell—taking the breather of all breathers."

She could detect a faint smile from him.

"Boss?" Kiko asked.

Jonah slumped even lower, now tapping his hands on the seat in a bored rhythm, his dark hair clinging to the velvet behind him. "Your third degree makes me think I can't even rest in my own house. You like my seat at the desk, Kiko?"

Jonah had said it with a sense of dry humor, but . . .

"Sorry." Kiko rose out of the chair, more formal than ever. "I didn't realize—"

"Nobody realizes. *Nobody. Realizes.*"

Kiko looked at Dawn, probably to see how she was going to handle this. Hell. Like she knew?

After hefting out a sigh, Jonah latched his gaze on the ceiling. "The conversation you two were just having . . ."

Oh, oh. Was she about to get lambasted for telling Kiko about what'd happened in Kalin's picture? Was she supposed to have kept that a secret? Dawn girded herself for a whooping.

But it never came.

"I'd be frustrated, too," Jonah added.

Dawn's eyes almost popped out.

"In fact," their boss said, sitting up and leaning his elbows on his knees, "I'd be going crazy with not knowing anything about how we operate."

Totally thrown off her game, Dawn stood, prickling with such uncertainty that the thought of not being ready to defend herself was just wrong.

"Don't go anywhere." His gaze was on her again, and there was something plaintive about it.

She stayed. For now. Just to see where this was all going, in spite of her own better judgment.

Jonah sneaked a look at the clock on a Chippendale table next to him, then glanced at her again. She'd automatically focused on his scars, and she lowered her eyes, caught.

"You can't really look at me without wondering what happened," he said.

She wanted to tell him that she'd accepted his face, actually finding his scars intriguing, not ugly. She'd never been much for perfect, anyway; a girl like her—one who'd always suffered by comparison to Eva—didn't aim for pretty boys. Also, she had a couple of wounds on her own face.

But, yeah, he was right. She wondered what the story was behind his injuries. "I assumed you got hurt from one of your showdowns, Jonah."

He touched his face, laughing shortly. "Oh, it was a confrontation of heroic proportions." Then, in the oddest of all that was odd, he flushed, as if shame had settled over him.

At this point, Kiko had taken a spot beside her. His warmth felt reassuring. But when she glanced down at him, she saw that he'd started to sweat.

Before she could call a Friend to help him avert a cold-turkey moment, Jonah had spoken again.

"What if you could see how I got these scars? With help from Kiko, of course."

Holy . . . *What?* Secretive Jonah inviting her to investigate? To get a straight answer? Something was very wrong. . . .

"Don't you want this, Dawn?" he asked.

She nodded way too many times. "Hell, yeah."

"Then come over here."

She actually began to tremble. *Answers.* Taking a step forward, she couldn't resist.

But Kiko grabbed her hand and, in his restraining touch, she guessed what he might be thinking. *This is too good to be true.*

Still, she couldn't pass this up. "Please, Kik."

When he turned his gaze up at her, she saw the caution, blue as a hazy twilight room, in his eyes. He had to be thinking of what had happened with the dagger vision and what could be in store with this one. It wasn't safe.

My God, his loyalty *wasn't* the reason he stuck by Jonah. Not entirely.

"Dawn," their boss said, and his voice held none of the vibrations she was used to getting when he said her name.

But it didn't matter.

Ignoring Kiko's clear feelings, she used all her strength to pull him to her greatest desire—Jonah and answers.

"Hurry," their boss said, checking the clock again.

And she did, grabbing Kiko's sweaty hand. Eyes wild, he tugged back, but she wouldn't let him go. She was stronger, so she forced his touch toward Jonah.

"We really shouldn't. . . ." Kik said.

"Please," she said.

Their boss reached out, seizing the psychic's retracted fingers, forcing them to touch the scars on his face. Dawn's hand rode the back of his.

Too late, she saw that Jonah's eyes weren't topaz, but *blue*—

An explosion came out of nowhere, blasting her into a memory.

She stared from Jonah's eyes at his image in the mirror of a sumptuous marble bathroom, his dark hair disheveled as he anchored his hands on each side of a sink.

His face was clear and beautiful in the light, but his eyes were blue with something like depressed terror.

"You were gone longer than normal," he whispered.

But there was no response from whomever he was talking to.

Out of gloomy desperation, he yelled, "I didn't think you were coming back!"

A breeze ruffled his hair, and Jonah's blue eyes focused on whatever was behind him in the mirror. An unknown companion.

When the guest spoke, the room seemed to quake from a dangerous undertone. An old-world-accented darkness.

"You know I always return, Jonah. I must."

"But I get afraid that you won't."

"Calm down, please. Do not assume—"

Jonah slapped the porcelain. "You're looking for someone else, aren't you? You aren't happy with me anymore."

"Please, Jonah. Let me in and you will not be this upset."

The young man smiled shakily and leaned toward the mirror. "Why? Do you think I might strand you outside? Are *you* afraid of that?"

"Let's not play these games. . . ."

"You think you have all the power, don't you?" Jonah reached for something on the side of the sink. "You think you've got all the control here. Well, what if I . . . ?"

A stab of silver flashed in the mirror as Jonah held up a straight razor.

"No!" yelled The Voice.

Faster than a pulse of light, the young man brought down the blade, yet he hadn't been aiming for his throat. The weapon slashed across his cheek. Pain blinded him, but he slashed again, full of rage, full of vengeful panic.

"Stop trying to get into my head to keep me from doing this," Jonah said. "This is *my* body."

He angled forward, forcefully nudged by the essence from behind, but he kept going, undeterred. Slash. Slash. Slash.

"Jonah . . ." It was The Voice, his tone steeped in sorrow.

"Tell me"—Jonah slashed again, his face a mash of cuts—"you won't leave."

"Oh, Jonah."

"I won't go any lower with this razor if you promise."

The air went icy, and so did The Voice. Everything stilled.

Jonah held up his wrist.

"I will not leave you," The Voice said quickly. Then his tone took on a dreadful, rueful edge. "I promise."

Through the blood, Jonah smiled again, sinking to the floor. . . .

The memory ended gently, the red fading under Dawn's vision as Jonah's real face came back into focus. His beautiful, young, brutally scarred face.

He had removed her and Kiko's hands from his cuts, his blue eyes gauging her reaction.

Dawn's heart was beating so fast it was numb. She heard Kiko's heavy breathing next to her. Drenched with sweat and shivering, he lost his balance and Dawn caught him, getting to her knees so she could cradle his body on the floor.

"Is that an answer for you?" Jonah asked. It was such a young question from a young soul.

Jonah's soul. Not The Voice's.

They were two different entities altogether.

She dragged her gaze back to him, only to find him looking so intent for a response that it almost crushed her heart.

"Please explain what just happened." Her words barely got past the dryness in her mouth.

He parted his lips to answer, but a bolt of cold air cut the space between Jonah and Dawn. His body lifted, slamming back against the couch, while his eyes closed. For a second, all Dawn could hear were Kiko's labored breaths, her own heartbeat in her ears. Fear did a pinching dance on her skin as her gaze traveled to the field of fire painting.

It was empty.

Then, from his prone position, Jonah . . . whoever . . . slowly opened his eyes to reveal the topaz hue she'd come to know so well.

But she hadn't known this. Had never even imagined he could be so different than what she'd expected.

Whoever it was sat up ramrod straight on the couch, once again the warrior.

ELEVEN

THE BREAK

Dawn held the shaking Kiko to her chest as he grabbed on to
her tank.

"Who's in Jonah's body now?" she yelled at the stranger sitting
on the couch so stiffly. *"Who the hell are you?"*

When he answered, he seemed supremely unaffected by what
had just happened. In fact, there was even a streak of cruelty rip-
pling a low, harsh voice that nowhere resembled that of the real
Jonah's tone.

"I am the same man you have known for over a month now,
Dawn, and you should know that even I have my limits. Your med-
dling has finally gone too far."

She ignored that last part, ignored that Jonah had wandered in
here for some random reason and offered himself to her, because
she was stuck on something else he'd said. *"Man?* You call yourself
a man?"

"I have been called myriad things." He forced a horrible smile, his
eyes intensely golden. "And 'man' is what I prefer to most others."

Even through the shakes, Kiko spoke up. "The fire field . . ."

Dawn glanced up at the empty painting, then back to the stranger. She didn't want to keep him out of her sights. "Is that where you rest, just like any other Friend?"

"Yes, but I am not so much like them under it all. Not remotely."

Maybe the pieces should've all fallen together at that point, but she didn't get it. Didn't get any of it.

This lack of control made her feel more helpless than ever, especially when she realized that the room had filled with the scent of jasmine. Friends. A whole jury of them.

One of their voices threaded through the air, feminine and song-like. *"Toss 'er out. . . ."* Dawn thought she heard the spirit say, even though she couldn't be positive.

Kalin?

The stranger in the real Jonah's body hadn't moved a muscle, even when other Friendly voices chimed in to drown out the Fire Woman, to cover whatever poison she was trying to spew.

"I hope you're planning to tell us your real name now," Dawn said to The Voice—because that was all he was to her again. Just a thing. To have him mean any more would remove the last stitch holding her together.

Kiko fought to sit up, but didn't move away from the arm she kept around his shoulders. She was pretty sure he hadn't known about their boss. Hadn't known any of it.

"I can tell you more than just my name," the stranger said.

The Friends' voices rose again, one emerging louder than the others. Kalin's. *"She's trouble . . . too much trouble—"*

Cut off. It sounded like someone—maybe Breisi?—had shut Kalin up. Dawn took advantage of that.

"Stop stalling."

The room seemed to go cold at the commanding tone she'd used.

She thought she saw something sad in the stranger's eyes, but he hid whatever it was by lifting his—*Jonah's*—hand in a careless gesture. "Mr. Limpet is my gracious host."

She knew in her gut that he was referring to more than just living in this house. The Voice's essence—the force that'd been inside her so often—lived in that fire-field portrait, and when he wasn't there, he was in Jonah Limpet's body.

"You've taken him over?" she confirmed. "And he's the one who told Kalin to bind me that day, wasn't he? That wasn't you at all. You . . . you stopped him from going any further. I remember how it sounded like there was a struggle, and then your voice—*this* voice—told me not to turn on the light. . . ."

The stranger assessed her, narrowing his eyes. "Jonah tends to want whatever I have, so during one of his 'breathers,' he sought you out. It was inconvenient."

Good God.

None of the agency's other spirits—the Friends—had usurped a body. Not to Dawn's knowledge. Then again, he'd already said he wasn't like the Friends. So what did that make *him*?

She wanted to know. And she didn't. She really, really didn't.

He must've read the trepidation on her face, because he stopped watching her, as if finally seeing what he'd been expecting in her reaction all along. "Does that satisfy your curiosity, Dawn? Do you have a better idea of what you are dealing with now, and will it finally put a stop to your invasive activities?"

She held on to Kiko, just as he was holding on to her. The sweat from his body was making her arms slippery, dampening her shirt. Or maybe it was her own fear doing that.

This wasn't happening. She hadn't seen into Jonah's head, hadn't made this discovery. Damn it, why couldn't she blank it all out?

"Don't you wish to know more?" the stranger's voice thundered. "Or have you had enough?"

She flinched, but she didn't back off. She just wanted to attack, to take back her mind and put it the way it used to be.

"There's more to tell?" She got to her knees, protectively maneuvering Kiko behind her.

You work for a monster, Eva had told Dawn. Why hadn't she listened, even to her mother?

Jasmine started to press in around her and Kiko, as if flanking them. Dawn's blood began to race, her hearing going fuzzy in panic.

The stranger smiled that unfamiliar, vicious smile again. Where had her boss gone? Had he forgotten how he'd filled her last night? And didn't he understand that Jonah, himself, had given her permission to see inside his head?

"You want to know how I came to take my host over, yes?" the stranger continued. "You and your endless nagging would perhaps cease to drive me mad if you knew my true name, my true self? Do you wish to see the darkest parts of me now? Will that make you happy?"

"What's wrong with you?" Sure, they'd had their moments, but even in his worst hours, he was always respectful.

"Ah, avoidance." The Voice nodded. "Now that it comes down to it, you wish to shut out reality, just as you did with your mom's death. Yet after hearing the truth of that, Dawn, all has not turned out so well, has it?"

Bastard. "Why would you be so willing to blurt out the truth now instead of b—"

Before she could finish, something unseen hit her, bowling her backward until her spine flattened against the rug. Gold—all she saw was the topaz of his irises, and the color, the heat, was sizzling her eyes. His essence had come inside her head, taking advantage of the door she'd always left open for him. He was searching around her brain, violating. . . .

She screamed, pushing against him as he pummeled her memories of being kidnapped by Eva, of going to rescue Breisi, of seeing the woman who'd come to mean so much to her die—

Then, just like that, it was over.

Gagging, she rolled to her side, her shirt clammy, her skin filmy.

"What did you do to her?" Kiko yelled.

She heard his feet pounding the floor. He was charging the boss—the stranger.

Weakly pushing to her elbows, she tried to get up, but she was too late. Just before Kiko jumped at The Voice, the little man was picked up by a whoosh of air, then pinned to an adjacent couch. There, he stayed, punching at nothing.

"Breisi!" he yelled. "Let me go!"

Breisi's essence flew away while other whispers shot toward him, whispers Dawn had heard earlier when the collected Friends had put Kiko, then her, to rest.

Within seconds, he closed his eyes, his head lolling to the side.

Wait—*Dawn* could command the Friends. She'd forgotten because it was such a new power.

She began to order them to leave Kiko alone, but the stranger quashed her hopes.

"My commands take precedence over yours, so do not bother."

She almost preferred being put to sleep over this. Would the Friends be lulling her next? Then why was this stranger bothering to taunt her? *What was happening?*

She got to her hands and knees, unable to stand because of her jelled legs. "What's wrong with you?"

Her guard slipped and, for one moment—just one—she didn't want to fight. She wanted her mentor, her guiding force, back.

She whispered the rest. "What are you doing?"

At that, he seemed to wilt a fraction. But then he went rigid. "I'm being the monster you should have expected. Did your mother not warn you? Were you not paying attention to what she was trying to tell you?"

"Shut up." She almost put her hands over her ears but fought the urge. Blocking out her mother's words from the outside wouldn't do anything when they were already ingrained in her head. They were

burning, scarring a message into her gut that she never should've ignored.

A monster. One of them.

Or maybe even worse?

"What I find interesting," the stranger said, his tone like a slight
retreat, "is that you still don't want to believe what Eva said about
me. I saw that in your mind, as clear as day."

Confused by his change in voice, Dawn hardened herself, avoiding the stranger's eyes now, vowing he wasn't going to get inside
her again. "I'm starting to believe what she told me."

"That's because you will never trust me." He leaned forward.
"No matter how much you learn about me, it will never be enough.
In fact, it will be too much."

It was already too much.

She tried to get to her feet, clawing at the rug in her effort.

The stranger shook his head. "No sense in standing unless you
wish to walk out the door."

She stopped at the return of his razored tone.

"Go on, Dawn. You are free to leave."

Everything seemed to fall down around her. Wasn't the team
supposed to stay locked down? Wasn't it dangerous for her to venture outside?

Or was it more dangerous in here?

"I . . ." she began.

"Invading my host was the last straw. You clearly have no respect for my privacy, though, last night, I thought you might have
cultivated some. But you are unwilling to accept my protection
here in the house without causing distress, and you will need to
leave us."

"But . . . I'm 'key.' "

It'd come off as pathetic. Dawn even cringed, but she recovered
quickly, pissed off that he had the power to make her feel so insignificant.

"Kiko has been wrong before." The Voice leaned back against

the couch, bending a leg so he could rest his ankle on the other knee.

Bullshit. Once The Voice had told her that he had a lot of faith in Kiko's talents. That couldn't have changed so drastically.

She stood her ground. "I don't know what's going on, but I'm not leaving. This is crazy."

"This is necessary," he whispered.

Dawn's toughness slipped a little. A chink in his armor?

"Leave," he said, "before you can never go back. Just leave, Dawn."

Leave? And go where? And do *what*?

"Oh, how merciful," she said, fighting oncoming tears. "Do you actually think I can 'go back' to walking around the streets without knowing what's under them? Do you think I'll ever be the same person again?" Her fingernails dug into her palms, clutching on to something since everything else was out of her grasp. Her nails broke skin but she still kept pressing.

Once, when she'd first come back to L.A., Kiko had told Dawn that she'd never return to her old job as a stunt double. She'd thought he was full of it, but he'd been right.

She'd always been wrong.

Dawn forgot about protecting herself, allowing her gaze to meet the stranger's. What she saw there made her want to cry out in frustration. It was the old Voice, the one who'd taken her under his wing and educated her, even while keeping her at an intimate distance.

Then, as if he'd gotten caught, the stranger's body seemed to steel itself, transforming before her very eyes into the thing she didn't know anymore.

"I cannot afford to care how life will treat you from this point on," he said.

But she'd seen that he still cared, somewhere in that body of his. She knew it, and this was all another one of his games.

She gave it right back to him. "Okay. So when the Underground comes to get me for the part I played in hunting them down, you'll just shrug and chalk it up to life as a Limpet PI. Is that how all your team members end up—deserted if they don't become Friends?"

He was clearly battling himself, like he wanted to argue but wasn't going to.

Unable to tolerate it anymore, she made a dismissive motion. "You *are* a monster—just not one to be that afraid of."

As she began to turn her back on him, her nape tingled. Chills. *What's he doing? What's he thinking . . . ?*

Against her gut instinct, she looked back. He'd come to a slow stand, looming in a rage, his jaw and hands clenched.

"Would you *finally* leave if you knew the true definition of 'monster'?" he asked. "Is that what this will take?"

She didn't like the question, didn't like his nightmare tone. And when he lowered his chin and offered a terrible smile, she regretted ever stepping into the Limpet house.

In his hands, something was gleaming. The dagger—the simple tool etched with a *C* that had shown her the stuff of hell with Kiko's help.

No. No, he wasn't saying what she thought he was saying—

"The mark on this dagger stands for 'Costin,'" he growled. "*That* is my true name."

Dawn's blood hammered in her temples, her vision pulsing until her eyes hurt.

Costin. C. Bloodlust. Monster.

The seer in Kiko's dagger vision.

A wet stream slithered out of one eye, trickling down her cheek. "Stop saying things like that. You're going too far."

He walked toward her, dagger outstretched, as if asking her to take it from him. On a different day, she might've thought he was begging her to remove a burden from his soul.

"I was introduced into this new life through blood," he said. "I know what it is like to thirst for it, to murder for it, to drink it until my every fiber sings with it. As you have seen, I have the potential to be a *monster*, like the vampire Robby Pennybaker who raped your brain." His eyes heated. "Like the mother you claim to hate."

She tasted bile in the back of her throat. The stench of jasmine compounded her nausea. He'd been inside her, with her permission, caressing her, saturating unfilled holes where she hadn't allowed anyone before.

Her legs itched to move, but she couldn't. Damn her, she *did* trust him, because she couldn't believe what he was saying, couldn't truly believe he could be evil, too.

She barely got out her last question. "Are you one of the masters?"

Another awful smile. "I should have been."

The sinister insinuation seeped into her until every last hope she'd been clinging to rotted away. He was just like the Master she hated. Just like a cold killing machine.

"Then goddamn you, whoever you are," she said.

"Too late." Costin stopped short of her, the dagger offered. It lay like a sleeping creature nestled in his hand.

Just like the Master. She wanted to use the weapon on him so badly, but her confusion held her back. None of this made sense. His change in temper, his story, his holding out the dagger right now. He said he had feasted on blood, but why hadn't he taken it lately?

No sense, no sense . . .

Jasmine stifled her, pressing in like the sides of a coffin. She struggled for pure air, but couldn't get it.

A stray thought parted the waves of nausea. Help. Who could help her? One person. One PI vampire hunter who'd told her he could take care of everything.

The dagger winked as Costin shoved it closer. He kept watching her, the scars on his face livid. In his smile, she saw the hint of a Robby Pennybaker, of Eva herself, of a master somewhere Underground who had planned Breisi's death.

Monsters.

Anger and terror exploded inside of her at the same time, and she lunged through the jasmine to grab at the dagger. But with heart-stopping speed, the stranger gracefully removed the weapon from her reach.

"Thank you, Dawn, for making this easier," he said, his lips twisting at her betrayal. "Now get out of my sight."

He'd set her up. The helplessness built in Dawn's soured stomach, pushing up through her chest until it burst out of her head with a force she'd never been able to control.

Until now.

Zoom—she aimed her mind power at him, hitting him and thrusting him backward. He stumbled, then recovered his balance.

For a naked second, she saw something like surprised admiration in his gaze before it went cold again.

"It is going to end this way, then?" he asked, tucking the dagger into the back of his pants. When his hand emerged, it was fisted.

"You don't scare me," she said.

"No?"

He wandered closer, his eyes like magnetic forces. Suddenly, she couldn't move. Hypnosis.

Her mind snowed as he stalked her, circling and maneuvering behind her, then pressing into her back. But she was in such chaos that her body didn't know how to react, not even when she felt the tug of his fingers at her jeans waistband.

"What would it take to scare you off?" he whispered, slipping a finger past the denim so that it brushed the small of her back.

Her body, then her head, split into pieces.

Blood thirst . . . Jonah . . . good guys and bad . . .

Who was who?

It was only when he backed off and came around to the front of her that she could focus again.

Fight him off, her instincts shouted. *Don't let him near you.*

She used her own mind to pound away at the hold he had on her. *Out, get out!*

Shoop—his mind sucked out of hers and she brought her fists up through the perfumed air, bending her knees in a fighting stance. She felt something pulling at her, as if the Friends were keeping her from their leader.

So instead of attacking him physically, Dawn summoned her mind energy again, lashing out.

It was as if he'd been slapped. His head whipped around and, when he faced her again, his hair stuck to his cheek.

He stood strong, ready to take whatever she had to give.

She let loose, pushing, pushing, forcing him back step by step until he was at the couch.

"Save your strength," he ground out. "Stop and leave *now*."

Like she was going to follow that advice, especially from . . . What? Who?

Anger renewed by bewilderment, she struck out again, this time with a mental punch so forceful that he spun to the wall.

As he smacked it, the portraits shuddered, and Dawn's breathing almost stopped.

Slowly, he turned to her again, his mouth red with blood. He licked his lips, as if tasting it. She thought she heard . . .

A slight groan? Or was it the sound of a nearby Friend?

"Last warning," he said quietly. "Go before this continues in a direction no one wishes to see."

There'd been a sting of pain in his words, and that made her even more crazed. Anger took the form of heat, and it flared inside her. This time, when she pushed with her mind, the stranger reacted.

Jonah's body slumped to the ground, as if deserted and, before she knew it, Costin's essence was behind her—smelling of that strange, exotic mint while wrenching her arm up between her shoulder blades until agony consumed her.

"No more," he said, fogging into her mind.

Suddenly, stopping seemed like the best idea ever.

She tried to force the hypnosis out. Damn it, he'd gotten to her again.

But then, as if unable to hold his position or maybe even recon-
sidering it, he retreated from her head. Her arm ached while the
pressure of his essence disappeared from behind her.

The cold wind of him arced away, toward the other side of the
room. Toward the real Jonah. There, the body jerked. Then Costin
aimed a glare at her, secure in his host again.

Revealing an expression so terrifying that she couldn't move.

There really was no going back now. She couldn't be in the same
house as this Costin. Yet there was someplace she *could* go.

Without thinking further, she darted toward the still-sleeping
Kiko, but hit something that felt like a brick wall just in front of the
couch he was lying on. The impact was enough to knock the breath
out of her and throw her to the floor.

She got up again, only to hear a lone voice say, *"Dawn, don't!
Please!"*

Breisi. And she was pleading.

Jarred by that—Breisi never begged—Dawn scrambled in the
other direction. Taking Kiko with her wasn't going to happen. *Matt.*
She needed Matt Lonigan on her side now, because there wasn't
anyone else.

She ran, stumbling down the hall, tripping over the rug, and
aiming herself toward the stairs. She slid down them more than
stepped, then had enough presence of mind to grab her jacket from
the clawlike coat tree near the door in the foyer. Her keys were inside, along with a few small weapons. More of the same would be
in her car.

As she barged outside, triggering the UV lights and shielding her
eyes from the descending sun, she was in such a frenzy that she
didn't stop to spray on any garlic that might act as a repellant to
lower vamps. No, she just fumbled with her keys and prayed her
car would start.

The engine whined, and with every cycle her nerves got closer to
the surface of her skin. Come on, come on, she thought, her eyes
starting to blur with heat, her chest clamping into itself.

Finally, it *vroom*ed, and she skidded into the street, driving into the afternoon sun like a maniac, just trying to get away.

Away from Jonah, Costin, jasmine, monsters—

Dawn flailed to get her phone out of a jeans pocket, then almost dropped the cell.

Blood, thick, red, fangs, Costin.

Cursing herself into steadiness, she dialed Matt's number and then, when he answered, basically yelled that she was on her way and to have the door open when she got there. Maybe he said, "Done," or maybe he didn't—Dawn wasn't sure. All she knew was that by the time she hung up and tossed the phone away, she couldn't see very well, her eyes flooding, hot, leaking. She tried to wipe the tears with an arm, but they still came.

Jonah. Costin. What had just gone on?

She rounded a corner, heading downhill, swiping at her eyes. Costin, Costin, Costin . . .

She didn't know how long she drove, where she was as she floored the gas. She didn't know anything.

But when she turned a corner, nearing Matt's house, she heaved in a breath, pulling back on the wheel and digging for the brakes when she saw something on the road.

A woman dressed in a long flowing dress, standing as if she'd been waiting for Dawn to arrive.

Tires screamed on the pavement, the windshield view going topsy-turvy, showing the quickly approaching woman holding out her arms in supplication. Her blond hair blew in the breeze as she tilted her head.

Eva?

Something broke inside Dawn.

She jammed down on the gas pedal and targeted yet another betrayer.

Her mother.

TWELVE

BROKEN

Sноu⊔d we awaken Kiko?" Costin asked as he stood at the window overlooking the late-afternoon-shrouded street. He had parted the curtains to stare outside, where Dawn had driven in her rush to get away from him.

Gone. She was finally gone.

Next to him, Breisi floated, heavy with sorrow. *"Let's let him sleep. He'll get up soon enough, and he'll have a lot of questions. Put it off for a while."*

"There is always a price, is there not?" Costin pressed his—no, *Jonah's*—head against the windowpanes. Blood from when Dawn had slammed him into the wall still ghosted his mouth. While Jonah admitted to enjoying the taste because of his romantic longing for the adventurous life he thought Costin could provide, Costin himself shunned it.

"You put the modified locator on her?" Breisi asked.

Costin thought of the moment he had gotten close enough to press the tracking device on the back of a denim belt loop. "Yes."

"Then we won't have long to wait."

"If she ever arrives at the Underground."

"Boss, you know that this master would stop at nothing to get her there, and if your suspicions are right, she's unknowingly been in contact with him. And she needed to be driven to him. Otherwise she never would have left this house while you were still in it. And you know Dawn needed to make that choice herself, because if she was hypnotized, she would fight the mind control off eventually. She didn't know who to go to, but she knows now. It was a gamble to depend on scaring her away, but we needed to find the location. Frank is there."

He knew how much that meant to Breisi. It was her only solace these days. "Then it's up to Dawn now."

"Sacrifices," she reminded him. *"You told me from day one that this life would be full of them."*

Costin's shoulders slumped. "I did."

A jasmine weight pressed on his back. Breisi's comforting touch. *"I know it took you a long time to finally get the cojones to carry this off. It took one final feeding for you to have the strength to let her go. Now we have to take care of the rest and worry about the aftermath later."* Breisi paused. *"When Dawn came on board with the team, she said she would do anything to get Frank back, Boss. You're only taking her at her word."*

He forced himself to straighten his posture, to be a soldier. This was a war, and he'd done what was necessary.

"I only hope," Breisi said, *"that Dawn doesn't become the enemy."*

Costin went cold, even though Dawn didn't know enough about his true powers to reveal critical information to an Underground. Let them know he was Costin. Let them wonder.

"God forbid she does," he said softly.

He then allowed the curtain to fall closed before anyone could say they saw a monster framed in the window of this haunted house.

THIRTEEN
The Welcoming

Dawn's car picked up speed in its path toward the woman in the middle of the road. Her foot crushed the gas pedal, gunning it for all it was worth.

Eva got closer, her blond hair blowing, her hands outstretched with her palms up. She wasn't moving an inch, as if she were expecting her daughter to hit the brakes.

Dead, Dawn thought. *I wish you were dead—*

The car's tinny engine roared, unstoppable as the vampire loomed.

At the last second, her mother dropped her hands, stricken, finally understanding that Dawn wasn't going to slow down.

As the car's fender reached Eva's knees, Dawn cried out, impulsively wrenching the steering wheel to the right and closing her eyes at the expected impact.

Screee—

Resistance, as if someone were pushing against the car. It lost speed. . . .

But Dawn was still going fast enough to thunder to a crunching stop.

A flash, a chop to the knees, a yank so sudden that when it was over, she could only sit there, hearing a sound like a hissing, primal breath. She saw a streetlight pole squished against the seething hood.

Got to get Eva, she thought, not feeling anything at all. *Got to try again.*

She attempted to start the engine, but it only offered a droning whine. Again. She kept trying and trying, not grasping that her car was done.

Then she looked down at her knees, which had started to burn. Her jeans had been torn open there, her flesh bloodied. The dashboard . . . Had her knees banged into it? And her seat belt had strained into her chest, hurting it, too. Her Corolla was too old to have air bags and, slowly, it entered her mind that she should've been really injured at the speed she'd been going.

Unless . . .

Dazed, Dawn turned to her window, where Eva waited by the back of a nearby RV blocking the view of a house. Strong, quick . . . Had her mother slowed the car down before it'd crashed?

Dawn didn't like knowing how weak she was against these vamps, didn't like being beaten by Eva yet again.

Always second place, she thought, fumbling with her seat belt and getting her head together enough to grab her cell phone and a couple of weapons from the passenger area's floorboards.

Always left in the dust.

Ignoring her slight wounds, she stuck her cell in her jacket pocket and busted open her door, barging out with a machete in each hand. Then, not even bothering with a hello, she stumbled toward her mother, who was lingering in back of the RV like she was hiding.

Eva made a put-upon face, then darted to the side as Dawn lunged and sliced a machete where her mother had just been.

"You don't want to kill me," the glamour goddess said.

"Wrong." Dawn spun around to find her target again. It took her a second to steady herself.

"You need to sit." Somehow, Eva made hand-to-weapon fighting sound maternal.

Dawn sliced downward with the right-hand machete, just as if she could hack at her emotions. Missing, she immediately raised her left arm for leverage, then swung down with it while reverse chopping the right blade back up at Eva.

The vampire easily dodged, then, quick as you please, exploded into her Danger Form, where she rose in a dazzling mist. Within a millisecond, she had swooped into an almost hidden tree at the side of a house with a For Sale sign in the yard. She wove herself into its leaves, her essence pearled, angelic, and decorated with tendrils waving out and in, like silk ribbons in a wind. Dawn couldn't look away.

She lowered her machetes to her sides because, inside Eva's cloudy form, she saw images of what she'd always wanted: a mother who was reaching out to embrace her.

"I don't know what happened inside the Limpet house to make you drive that way." Eva's voice held all the silverware chime and soulful simmer of dinner being made in a homey kitchen. "But I'm here for you, even if they're not."

Dawn wanted to nod, to go to her mom and imbibe what Eva offered. But a mental twitch kept her from giving in.

When that twitch turned into a nudge, then into full-blown repulsion, Dawn shook her head. Shook Eva right out of it.

"I suppose you were there for me the other night, too," Dawn said, "when you lied about saving Breisi. You were never going to carry through with it."

In the tree, Eva twirled back into solid form. When she was done, she was left sitting in the branches, grabbing an overhead limb, and leaning her temple against an arm in summer-soft repose. "Will you listen to my explanations now, D—?"

Zoom quick, she jerked her gaze away from her daughter to

something behind Dawn's back. When Dawn looked, too, she realized that a family across the street was squinting out the window of their quaint house. She got closer to the tree trunk, using it to shelter herself. They'd heard Dawn's crash, no doubt, and were scoping things out.

So that was why Eva had hidden in this out-of-the-way tree, to remain incognito.

Again, Dawn cleared her head with a good shake, inconspicuously tucking her machetes close to her sides, then taking a better look around. Her vision was a dull sepia that she tried to blink away. But she couldn't. The neighborhood, with its palm trees and white-planked serenity was familiar.

She'd made it to Matt's block, near his cottage.

Dawn peered back up into the tree branches, only to find her mother gone.

Goose bumps lifted her skin, and she backed away. From somewhere, she heard people coming out of their houses.

Taking care to hide her weapons, Dawn crept in the direction of Matt's, minding her balance but dismissing her aches. Maybe she could call a tow truck when she got to him, yet she had no time for going back to the car and taking care of normal-person business now. But, damn it, she didn't want a random, well-meaning stranger going through her weapon stash.

She could care about that later.

When she got to Matt's, with those bird-of-paradise plants blocking his windows, she saw him standing in the open doorway, craning his neck to see what was going on down the street. He spied her, then started asking a question.

She sprinted forward, panic welling in her chest and chills eating her spine.

"Dawn, what's—?"

She stumbled over the threshold, then kicked the door shut. He'd kept it open for her, just as she'd asked. Without a word, she numbly set her machetes on the hardwood floor, took off her jacket, and dropped it.

"I need my car towed," she mumbled.

Now that her adrenaline had clamped off, she felt like she was moving in a vacuum. Colors had drained themselves out of a room that Matt kept so carefully male: the stark entertainment equipment bleeding wires, the blank walls, the bolted closet door with the basketball backboard canting against it. None of it really registered.

"Was that you making a scene out there?" Matt asked. "I was downstairs, finishing up something before you got here. . . ."

His words dissipated when he noticed her knee-gaped jeans, the wounds. He swallowed, nostrils flaring, then grit his jaw.

"Does Limpet have anything to do with this?"

Angry. That had to be why he was reacting this way. Everyone seemed angry these days.

In her cotton-thick shock, Dawn didn't know what to tell him. Where should she start? How far should she go?

"Dawn." He took her hands in his and, faintly, she recognized the scratches she'd given him the other night, baked into the back of his hand in violent reminder.

He guided her toward the couch, and it was all she could do to maneuver her body correctly. But then she took a jittery breath, pulling away from him.

"I've got to . . ." She stumbled back to the front window where, between the thwarted colors of the bird-of-paradises, she could see the street. Eva might still be out there. Dawn needed to get Eva. "Did you see her?" she asked.

"See who?" Matt stood next to her.

"My mother."

He paused. "Isn't your mom . . . ?"

"Dead?" Yes, she was. Dead to Dawn.

She could sense Matt's piqued interest. Once more, he began to lead her away from the window, but she wouldn't let him. She needed to watch for Eva. For any of them. Vampires. Every single one of them was the enemy.

A swipe of Jonah's—*Costin's*—face clawed over her mind's eye, but she shut it out.

"Hey," Matt said softly. "First, let's take care of your knees. Then we'll talk about getting you some . . . medical help."

"No." She hadn't crashed that hard, thanks to Eva.

Matt kept on. "Then we'll get a tow and . . . I guess we'll go from there."

She glanced at him. Even the usual startling blue of his eyes seemed less vibrant to her now.

"For Pete's sake." Taking charge, he lifted her, set her on the long dining table in front of the window. "Happy now?"

She could still scan the street, so she "mmm-hmm"ed. The next thing she knew, Matt had left, then returned with some big bandages, Mecurochrome, liquid soap, and a wet bunch of paper towels. Gently, he tended to her stinging knees, keeping his head down. As he dabbed at the blood with the towels and soap, she thought his hands might've been shaking, but she wasn't sure.

After he cleansed the wounds, he swiped the Mecurochrome over one and she jumped.

"That brought you back a little." He smiled slightly.

"Biting off my tongue usually does that."

Glancing at the bottle, he made a face. "This might be pretty old, but it was the only thing I could find in the medicine cabinet."

"Let's put some of that on one of your open sores, and we'll see how high you can sing."

He laughed, then cut himself short. "I'm being serious."

"So am I."

"I'm not talking about Mecurochrome, Dawn." His gaze was steady. "You know it's not beyond my experience to believe that you saw Eva Claremont outside. What's going on?"

Okay. She could start there. But how much should she tell him? Why not everything?

A red light leeched of its vibrancy beat against her eyes, and she intuitively felt that she should keep Costin to herself. Or maybe not. She had no idea what to do. But Matt deserved to know the basics. He'd earned it with his patience and support.

"Dawn?" he said, tucking back a strand of hair that had escaped from her ponytail. He looked so sincere. "Whatever it is? It's okay to be angry about it."

He grinned, winning her over. Matt understood, even if he had no concept of what she'd gone through today. He was the only one on her side. *At* her side.

"Much to my pleasure," she said, throat raw, "I've discovered that Mommie Dearest is a vampire." A near-hysterical laugh quaked in her chest. "How's that?"

His hands paused as he bandaged one knee. His touch lingered, as if he was memorizing how her skin melded over bone, or how the bruised angles of her were pieced together. Or maybe he was just witnessing her becoming unhinged.

As his finger brushed her flesh, he shuddered.

"No surprise about Eva?" Dawn was positive that she'd never fully confided in him about what her mother had done.

He made an abrupt move away from her knee. "Sure, of course I am." His forehead furrowed. "I suspected it. . . ."

"And you didn't say anything?"

He touched her ankle. "Why worry you? I was just getting started on looking into it."

Okay. She could buy this . . . except for that one fleeting moment when he should've shown more of a reaction. Or maybe she was on such hyperdrive right now that she thought everything should be going *kaboom* around her.

"What do you know about these vamps?" she asked.

"Just a little about Robby Pennybaker." When she widened her eyes, he shrugged. "You weren't the only one following leads, remember?"

She didn't say anything, just tried to figure him out.

"Besides," he added, "I suspect that, next to you, I know nothing." He left that hanging, tending to her other knee.

Dawn allowed herself to relax at his care. At least, she tried. But something vengeful stirred in her as she thought of how Jonah slash Costin would feel if he saw her with Matt now.

See, she thought, *I don't need you, whoever you are.*

"My mother," she said, "decided that long-lasting youth and beauty were way more important than seeing me graduate from grade school or giving me advice on how to wear lipstick. She's part of this . . . network, you could say, of movie-star vampires. They're fooling us all."

Matt had finished bandaging, but he hadn't stood back up. Instead, he was running a hand over her calf. "A community. How do you think they stay hidden?"

She attempted to lose herself in his touch. Failing, succeeding, going back and forth. *Damn you, Costin.*

"They live somewhere underground," she whispered. "That's where they hide."

He didn't say anything, just rubbed her leg. Was he even listening?

"Matt?" she asked.

His eyes were a million miles away, seeming to fog with need for her. But he blinked, ending the illusion.

"Do you want to track down your mother?" he asked. "Is that why you're posting watch out my window?"

Reminded, she fixed her gaze there. An oncoming sunset buttered the street, then burned it into an acrid stain.

"I'm . . ." Dawn leaned forward, fortifying herself. "I'm not sure what I'm going to do."

Matt's hand traveled up her leg, and instead of getting turned on, her veins seized into themselves, hardening her, making her beat with a longing for payback.

Costin.

"Why don't we try to go underground?" Matt said. "You and me."

She forgot how to breathe.

"I know it's a big thing to suggest," he added, "but we can find your mom there and deal with her however you want."

On his knees, he seemed so devout, so worthy. But she'd been screwed over before, oh so very recently. She looked back at the window, and he apparently read her reluctance.

"I'm the best partner you'll ever have." He stood, taking her hands in his. "Or . . . maybe you need persuading. Shoot, if my own mom were here, she'd tell you what a stand-up guy I am."

"And what else would your mom say?"

He grinned. "She'd tell you that if the son she raised to be so justice minded and right seeking ever let you down, he'd never be able to live with himself."

"Now you're sounding like a superhero out of Kansas—not Gotham City."

His pupils expanded and, in them, she could see that he was taken aback by her observation.

"Just giving you a hard time," she said. "Go on. I won't impale you with any more sardonic—"

Something outside caught her jaundiced vision. A flutter of skirts, just like the ones Eva liked to wear. The material had disappeared in the direction of Matt's backyard.

He turned toward the window, too. At the same time, she slid down from the table, her biker boots thumping on the floor.

"It's her," Dawn said.

Matt grabbed her wrist. "She'll just go back to this underground place you were talking about. Are you prepared to follow her?"

"I'd prefer to keep the fight up here." She ripped her wrist away from his grip, striding toward her machetes. Sure, she was still kind of shaky from when her car kissed the streetlight post, but that wasn't nearly enough to stop her.

But Matt was enough. "You're going to end up down there one day."

When she looked at him, he seemed . . . off somehow. She couldn't put her finger on it.

"I mean," he added, "vamps haven't gone public for a reason. They like their privacy. Any heavy business will be conducted underground. Mark my words."

"Okay, then. Marked."

She fetched her weapons, heading for the cottage's rear screen door. Matt dogged her.

As she laid a machete-filled hand on the latch, she asked, "You going to back me up or not?"

He hesitated, then nodded. "I'll get my stuff."

"No." She lifted her other machete. "Eva's mine. If you see me get into trouble, that's when you intervene."

"And what if it's too late by then?"

"She's not out to hurt me. She just wants to destroy Frank's life—and mine, too." Dawn unlatched the door. "I might be a while, so before you call for a car tow, could you get my knickknacks out of it? Thanks."

"Just a second . . ."

But she was already outside. The yard was almost empty, except for an old slab of wood hanging by two ropes from a small oak tree. Maybe it was a toy from a previous tenant, or maybe there was something Matt wasn't telling her about his personal life. At any rate, as it swung in the wind, the rope creaked. The near death of day had left the air warm, but it was cool enough to scrape over Dawn's skin with a chill.

Behind the tree, she caught the wave of a flowy dress peeking out.

"Eva," she said, machetes at the ready.

And just that simply, her mother sidled away from the back of the oak, her dress tickling her thighs.

"Good," her mother said, utterly ignoring Dawn's weapons. "I'm glad you've finally come to your senses."

FOURTEEN

The Family Way

Dawn almost laughed at Eva's ridiculous comment. "You think I'm here to entertain more of your crap?"

Her mother ran a look over the machetes in Dawn's hands. Then, clearly on purpose, she leaned against the tree trunk, as if declaring defeat. The swing's ropes continued to moan.

Dawn's chest seemed to bend inward, deforming whatever had been holding her up. It felt good to wound Eva, to make her lose hope, to one-up the mother who'd always been better even in death. But it also went against every dream Dawn had nourished of *having* a mom.

Perversely, Dawn scraped the machetes together: the lyrics sang about what was right, what was just.

"Eva, what could you possibly tell me that I haven't heard before?"

Her mother didn't react to the machete scrapes. "There's a lot to clear up. Last time you were with me, it wasn't exactly under ideal conditions, and I'm afraid I didn't get my true message across."

"Oh, I think you did. You took me captive and threw me in a hidden room with Frank. And let's not forget the part where you chained me up. That was the biggest true message of all."

"I knew you'd fight before you became rational. You would've chained you up, too, in my place."

"I always fight." The machetes seemed heavier now, almost like Dawn should just drop them and walk away. She could, too. But in which direction would she head?

She thought of what was waiting for her in the Limpet house. It was the same as what was here with Eva. The same as what was waiting for them all everywhere, except few normal people knew it.

"You don't have to fight." Eva had taken hold of the swing with one graceful hand, silencing its groans.

Wrong. That was all Dawn knew. She'd just taken fighting to a new extreme lately.

"What if," her mother added, "the two of us called a truce for now. Even the most ferocious foes would meet on battlefields to attempt an understanding." Eva smiled and ran a hand down the swing's rope. "At least, I think I remember hearing that in some history class I daydreamed my way through."

A school-despising tweak of empathy manipulated Dawn. Like mother, like daughter. But she murdered the emotion.

"I was under the impression that we were talking just fine right now." Dawn could just about feel Matt behind her, watching through a window. Maybe that was why it was so easy to be a smart-ass.

Eva shook her head. "There are ears tuned in to what we're saying. Someplace more private would be better."

"The isolation of a backyard isn't good enough?"

"No."

Dawn barely caught Eva's glance skimming the cottage, and she understood. Matt was a hunter, and Eva might've known it.

Dawn's heart was fisting, squeezed by that little girl within who'd cried in the corners of playgrounds after the other kids had taunted her about having no mother. In a way, Dawn wanted to give in to the fantasy of Eva—the runaway returned, the caretaker resurrected and dedicated to her family. It was all Dawn had ever wanted, especially now, after being turned out by the group she'd considered to be her family.

"*If* I had a sit-down with you," Dawn said, making sure Eva knew how unlikely it was, "where would we go? A coffee shop . . . ?"

"I can't be in public." Eva tucked a blond lock behind an ear, like she was flustered. "You have to understand, with everything that's going on, the community has retreated Underground. In fact, my big comeback movie with Paul Aspen and Will Smith? Is on hold. Some non-Servant producers are up in arms, thinking that Paul and I have run off together because we haven't shown up for work. Our publicists made up a cover story about how Paul got sick and I've checked him in to a private clinic and stayed by his side because I'm so smitten."

Dawn frowned at the name "Paul Aspen." She'd met Eva's costar at a party he'd thrown. There, her mind had been entered and partially wiped. Costin had yelled out in a rage when he'd discovered it.

Sloughing off the memory of his protective response, Dawn said, "It must be killing you since you bought that movie with your soul."

"You're right. It wasn't in my plans to saddle Jacqueline Ashley with a bad work reputation." Her mother wandered away from the swing, close enough to lower her voice. "I know this is asking a lot, but there's a place where we don't have to worry about any interference. Somewhere that's been deserted since I moved Underground for security." She flicked a gaze to Matt's house, her meaning clear. "Come with me?"

More out of curiosity than compliance, Dawn asked, "How do you propose to get anywhere . . . ?"

Her car was wasted, and walking was out of the question. But she had an idea about how Eva, who didn't want to be seen Above, would get her to this private place. It'd probably be the same way the vamp had taken Frank and Dawn to Breisi that night. . . .

Her mother held out a hand. "Just this once, don't resist for the sake of being difficult."

"You need to tell me where we'd hypothetically be going." Dawn hadn't made a move toward Eva's hand.

"My house."

Oh, this was rich. "Really. The place where you stuck me in a dungeon and had a Servant guard me."

"Julia is Below now, and the house is vacant." When she looked into her daughter's eyes, her face went sad. "All this pain I've brought you, Dawn. I'm so sorry."

Thing was, Dawn thought her mother meant it. But maybe it was *acting!* Or maybe it was just what she wanted to see in Eva.

Dawn clutched the machetes. "If you think I'm going to have a slumber party with you, you're on crack. All I see when I look at your face is the traitor who let Breisi die and then made off with my dad for a second time."

Her mother bent her head. Nodded. Guilty?

Eva's obvious regret worked, worming its way through the cracks that the little girl inside was fighting to pull open. Remorse seemed to do that in every good silver-screen story. It could redeem even the worst of villains.

And Eva sensed Dawn's openness.

Quick as a subliminal flicker, the vamp whipped into Danger Form, using her misty tentacle-arms to embrace Dawn and bring her daughter inside her body. Cloudy, warm. Here, Dawn forgot about everything but how Eva felt like pillows under her head, about how there was no sound except for an all-encompassing heartbeat threading through her like a connecting cord.

Time wound into itself, and in an instant—or maybe it was an hour?—she emerged from Eva, the warmth of her mother's body lost as Dawn found herself in the cold reality of a familiar living room. She gathered her wits while sitting on the floor and looking around, discombobulated.

In the corner, she found the small-scale Eiffel Tower that had decorated Jac's house, a place Dawn had visited back when she thought they could be friends. The drawn curtains provided shade, the walls were a muted cream, the furniture a warm wood hue, like notes from a Chet Baker song. Jazz. Something Eva obviously liked, a fact her own daughter had never known.

Her mother was standing behind a couch, respecting Dawn with distance. "Something to drink?" Eva smiled, clearly knowing the answer.

When Dawn didn't say anything, the vamp left anyway, heading for the kitchen.

In the meantime, Dawn realized a few things. First, Matt hadn't even had time to interfere with Eva's taking of Dawn. Second, the back of her neck kind of smarted, maybe from the mini car smashup. She also saw that she was still holding her machetes and, damn it, she hadn't even thought to use them when she'd been inside Eva. Dropping one blade, she rubbed her neck, thinking the ache might hurt a lot more if Eva hadn't lessened the impact of the crashing car, as Dawn suspected.

Then she started to get off the floor, her hand going to the base of her spine at a slight twinge there, too. Once, during a stunt, Dawn had almost broken her back, so she was always hyperaware of any activity there.

But as she gave herself a diagnostic prod, her fingers brushed against something hard on her jeans. Was it a button that she'd never realized was there? She felt a little more. Smooth, metallic . . .

Uninvited, the memory of Costin skimming his fingers against the small of her back intruded.

She tore at the button-object, ripping off part of the weak belt loop it was attached to in the process. Discarding her other machete, she used both hands to wrench at the rest of the denim, hearing the loop pop off of her old jeans. And, there, sucked against the material, was a tiny locator.

Her mind seemed to slant inside her head, like a boat's deck in freak weather. Costin had marked her, then kicked her out of the house. The Limpets had to be tracking her.

Rational thought imploded under the pressure of her temper. Son of a bitch.

Dawn flung the device to the ground, then dug her boot heel into it, crushing the locator into the delicate rug, making it part of the intricately flowered design.

Fuck Costin. Fuck them all.

When Eva came back, water bottle in hand, Dawn quickly picked up the locator's remnants, then shoved the tiny wires and casing into a back pocket.

Dead. They were *all* dead to her. Just as dead as she felt.

Eva gave her daughter the unopened bottle, probably knowing Dawn wouldn't drink from it unless she could be sure there'd been no tampering. The vamp was catching on.

"I left in such a hurry that the fridge is still full." Eva sat on one end of a modern-chic couch, spreading her skirts around her. She wasn't drinking any water. Duh.

"Sit, please," her mother said.

"Nope. I'm comfortable like this." Standing. Waiting.

"Suit yourself."

Dawn opened the water bottle and took a swig. Relief. "How long will this joke of a peace negotiation take?"

"Do you have better things to do?"

"As a matter of fact, yeah. I thought I should probably kill you before all your vamp buddies crawl out of bed and come to your rescue."

Eva froze. "And here I thought you might take advantage of having me at your disposal."

A sidelong glance seemed the proper response. "Come again?"

"I want you to fire away with questions. Go ahead."

Blink, blink. Honesty. Dawn hardly recognized it.

"But . . ." Eva sighed. "Since you're going to kill me . . ."

Dawn bristled, because they both knew damned well that Eva could kick her daughter to the curb if it came down to it. Sure, Dawn would put up a grand fight, but Eva was superior.

"Bummer," her mother said, looking so strangely young, "because we never did have any mom-to-daughter chats. Except when you were *this* big, of course."

She'd cradled her hands and indicated a bundle-sized baby shape. The smile she wore couldn't have been faked. Dawn latched one hand on her opposite arm, half shielding herself.

"During that one month," Eva added, "I talked to you about a lot of things. I told you about when I was a girl. I gave you tips about how to wrap your dad around your teeny finger."

Her mother bit her lip, and even Dawn fell under her maudlin spell a little. Only a little.

"What were you like . . . as a girl?" She really wanted to know. "And no bullshit stories, Eva. It'd be nice to hear nonfiction for once."

"It'd be nice to *live* it, too." She gazed at a curtain-covered window, brown eyes going soft. "I was an only daughter, just like you, but instead of being born in California, I made my grand debut in Milwaukee, crying like a little princess. That's what your grandma said."

Dawn didn't know anyone on Eva's side of the family. Frank had kept her from them, except for one Christmas. Two people who'd wanted her to call them Grandma and Grandpa had joined Frank, Dawn, and her paternal grandparents. The strangers had given a really young Dawn—was she about five?—a tricycle. After they'd left, their eyes teary, Frank had taken the toy away from Dawn and she'd never seen it again. She knew they'd passed away years ago because, once, she'd come across some papers in Frank's house that said as much.

"When did you move out here?" Dawn asked, gripping her arm harder, like part of her wanted to shut herself up.

"When I was eighteen. Remember when I . . . Jacqueline Ashley . . . told you that she won a modeling contest and that it was her golden ticket into Hollywood? Well, that's actually what happened to me." She sent a longing glance to Dawn. "I'm really a lot like Jac."

Dawn pinched her arm. "I thought Jac was human, not a marrow-sucking backstabber. Big difference."

Eva smoothed her dress. It seemed to be a habit when she was gathering herself. "Whatever you think, I really was pretty innocent when everything started out. I never got used to going to parties and being visually prodded like meat at auditions. But when I snuck into a theater that was playing my first movie . . ." Eva held a hand over her heart. "Magic."

The rest was history. Eva's rise had been meteoric. She'd possessed the type of face that defined the fantasies of a generation: an innocence lost, yet still available in the persona of one Eva Claremont, sunny dream girl.

"Still," Eva added, "that moment was nothing compared to when I had you."

As a tear slipped down her mother's face, Dawn shook her head.

"I call bullshit. If you gave so much of a damn, you wouldn't have given me up for your extended career. You wouldn't have given me up for anything."

"I know it'll never make sense."

"You've got *that* right." Dawn's temper goaded her to stalk toward the front of the old-time-movie gingerbread house.

But just as she was about to exit the room, she turned back around, finding Eva on her knees on the couch and holding the back frame, her face a riot of devastation.

Slayed by her mother's quiet show, Dawn stopped in her tracks. Then she gestured toward the living room. "Forgot my machetes."

"Dawn, I never had the opportunity to explain why I gave you up when you were only a month old. I've already told you that I was young and stupid . . . and so impressionable. My handlers were persuasive. It all made such sense when they pitched the idea of going Underground."

Dawn couldn't believe it. Sense? How could being a vampire make sense?

Eva continued. "They said that the faster I went Underground, the easier it'd be to leave you—I wouldn't be so attached after only one month. But they were wrong. So wrong."

"Now's a great time to have a lucid moment."

Eva lowered her voice. "I thought everything would be perfect after my comeback. I thought my time away would make having you accept me easier, not harder."

"How could you possibly believe that?"

"I thought things would turn out differently. I was depending on my comeback to . . ."

"*Redeem* you?"

The vamp lifted a finger. "Listen. Men in Hollywood can deal with age a lot easier, but roles for older women? Good luck. Going out when I was young seemed to guarantee that I could continue succeeding when I made my comeback . . . again and again. It ensured that you'd always be taken care of."

Youth, beauty—both were at a premium in this town. And, clearly, Dawn and Frank had been easy enough to trade in, no matter how many justifications Eva had for doing it.

Neither of them said anything, because it was just too obvious that talking wouldn't make up for what had already happened, every hideous thing.

Out of defensive attitude, Dawn stuck her hands in her back pockets. Her fingers jammed against the guts of the locator.

Nowhere to turn. Nowhere to go now . . .

Eva sank farther down on the couch. "I suppose that does it for the touchy-feely talk."

For a second, her mother looked so real, like a young girl

who'd been disappointed by what affected most girls her age in life. Dawn wondered how much of that disappointment was *really* a part of Eva.

"I have to tell you," Dawn said, leaning her back against a wall, a position that relieved some of the tension, "that what you did with Bre—"

Forcefully, Eva pressed her finger to her lips. Dawn didn't say another word.

While her mother rose from the couch, she gave a meaningful look. What it meant exactly? Dawn wasn't sure.

The vamp went to a table, opened up a slim top drawer, then extracted paper and a pen. After writing something down, she came over and gave the items to Dawn. Then she lingered, seeming to block the paper, as if the two of them were secretly trading "Best Friends Forever" notes and hiding the contents from the rest of the class.

The paper said: *There may be bugs here—they'll know if I disable them, especially after what happened that night. I could be in trouble.*

All right. Why had Eva brought Dawn to her home if there could be eavesdroppers? Had she been instructed by the Underground to initiate some kind of mind game here? Or did her mother want to talk privately, but she couldn't, hence the notes?

Playing along for now, Dawn went to the couch's back, using it as a shield, then sunk to the floor in order to write. She made sure she didn't leave the paper in clear view. While she penned her message, she fake chatted, just as a distraction for anyone who might be tuned in. "I know how special the Underground is to you."

But she wrote this: *They don't know what happened?*

After seeing that, Eva answered out loud. "Right." Then she launched into some more covering chatter while Dawn continued writing.

What you did with Breisi = deal breaker.

While her mother wrote a response, Dawn continued jawing.

Underground bad, not worth abandoning your family for, yada yada yada.

Eva's answer was this: *It would be a deal breaker for me, too.*

Ignore all attempts at sympathy. *Ignore.* Dawn took a deep breath, then let pen loose to paper. Afterward, Eva took the note and Dawn did the talking thing, wondering how Eva would react to what she'd written:

I really did think you were going to help me and Frank rescue Breisi. You almost had me on your side. I might have followed through with that promise you made me take about giving you another chance if you'd just helped us save B. Did you plan to sabotage B's rescue from the get-go, even when I promised that I would give you a chance to be my mom again?

Eva scribbled furiously. *B was coming between us—all of us—* She stopped and exhaled.

She *did* feel something like guilt. Dawn actually believed that.

Something switched on inside her mind, even in the midst of her beaten weariness. The detective in her wouldn't back off.

Dawn took the note and turned it over to a clean side while Eva chatted inanely and went for more paper.

So the Master doesn't know what you did that night? Dawn wrote. *Because you're still with the "community."*

Eva's turn. *Right—he doesn't know. After I brought you and Frank to where B was being held, I left. But then I came back. Too much to lose. I used what you call a "mind screw" to block video transmission into the Underground. So no one saw me interfering with plans to have Cassie kill B.*

Dawn wanted to ask why Eva had bothered. Her master might have been real proud of Eva's decision to let Cassie finally murder Breisi. But Dawn was getting good info here. Why blow it by ticking her mother off?

When the paper was full, Eva went to the kitchen. The sound of running water *ssss*ed, and she returned minutes later. Dawn thought she might have destroyed the messages in her sink by wetting the paper: blurring the words and turning it into an un-readable lump.

"I'm planning to be around my family for years and years," Eva said out loud, transitioning back into the spoken conversation they'd been using as a distraction. "We'll be frozen in the happiest time of our lives. That's all the explanation you need about why I want you Below, Dawn."

"Still doesn't convince me." This was odd. Eva had seamlessly gone from betrayer of the Underground to proponent of it. Did she believe in both views? Was it possible that her mother had only as much use for the Underground as it related to her?

"You're forgetting the part where I get fangs and drink blood," Dawn said. "I'm not so keen on that."

The vamp got an understanding look on her face. "That's all in-cidental. What matters is the way you feel when you become . . . us. Don't deny you're attracted to beauty."

Right—like Dawn hadn't been on an antibeauty crusade her whole life. She'd either worn too little makeup or too much, depend-ing on who she wanted to piss off that day. She'd rebelled against any association with Eva, becoming a stunt double and embracing the habits of a tomboy.

Yet . . . Eva was on to something, wasn't she? As much as Dawn deplored the superficial, she was drawn to it, wondering what it'd be like to be adored. . . .

"Jonah Limpet," Eva said, "wouldn't ever give you the chance to feel this good. In fact, I suspect he makes you feel the opposite."

Every muscle in Dawn's body clenched. "Don't. Ever. Say that name to me. Again."

Her throat felt stripped from the force of her words, and Eva looked just as flayed, too.

"Okay, I understand," her mother said softly.

"No, you don't."

It was a conversation capper and, after an awkward moment, Dawn started for her machetes.

"Looks like it's time to kill me again," Eva said.

"Oh, stop being such a smug pill, would you? If you want me to continue any 'peace talks,' maybe you'll reassure me that Frank is okay so I can at least murder you with that in mind."

"Yes. Frank."

Eva folded her hands, and Dawn couldn't help noticing that her knuckles were white.

"What the hell, Eva?"

"I'm just going to tell you, even though it's not easy—"

"Come on, already!"

"I don't know where Frank is."

Dawn actually did one of those stupid cartoon head shakes. The last time she'd seen her dad, Eva had been enveloping him in her body-mist and carrying him off as he cried out in a rage over Breisi's death.

"Come again?" Dawn said.

Eva carefully exhaled, then returned to the table for more paper. Dawn moaned, and they repeated the process of spelling everything out at the back of the couch while one covered for the other with a conversation about Frank in general now.

Eva wrote, *First, some background for you: I returned Underground after the Breisi/Cassie debacle and gave the Master a—*she hesitated—*certain version of what happened.*

Dawn's turn. *You mean you lied.*

I reimagined. When you deal with the Master, you'll see he exists in a world that's populated by movie stars and fantasy, so revisions are normal. He sees only what he wants, and I've been taking advantage of that.

Hell. Looking at Eva, you saw a harmless, sweet girl blushing in a breezy dress. But, deep down, she had a devious mind. Getting to know it would only help Dawn when she figured out where she'd go after this tête-à-tête.

What are you telling me? Dawn wrote while Eva jawed some more to cover their activities.

Eva again: *Frank escaped under the Master's nose, and I facilitated it. And the Master hasn't asked about the whole story yet.*

Eva went on to write about how she'd, on the spur of the moment, overloaded her husband with her blood and how that had allowed him to sneak out of the Underground undetected.

The blood reference lurched to the shadows of Dawn's mind. But, in all this confusion, she didn't pursue questions about what that meant. She was too caught up in finding out where Frank was.

Why did you let him go? she wrote back. She didn't know what to think about her mother now. Yeah, Dawn knew she still hated her, but Eva's allowing Frank to escape put a different spin on things.

The vamp seemed to think about what she was going to write. *You know the cliché that says, "If you love someone, set them free"? Frank needed that to come back to me. And he will, just as soon as he sees that what's out here doesn't appeal anymore.*

After a second, Eva added more. *I had to crush his delusions about what waited for him Above. He won't like what's there now, and he's not going to be strong enough to deal with daylight. Besides, Servants are on his case. He'll get tired of running, and he won't even be able to approach Limpet.*

More paper. As Eva went to get it, Dawn asked out loud, "Why's that?"

After a warning look, Eva came back to write: *He accepted my bite just before you showed up. You had to know he became a vampire.*

At the blunt comment, everything splattered in Dawn's mind—the blood reference, all her previous suspicions she'd had about Frank when he'd seemed to be able to read Cassie Tomlinson's thoughts in a vampire mind screw. Dawn pulled her knees to her stomach, hugging herself.

"At any rate, I truly don't know where your father is," Eva said out loud while getting up to go to the kitchen again. "He's blocked me out of our Awareness. I was using it Above before I intercepted you, since that ex-boss of yours knows that we exist anyway. If he senses the communication, it won't make much of a difference now."

While Eva ran the water in the kitchen, Dawn wondered if Frank really would be turned away by Costin and Friends. Why would her former boss deny a benevolent vampire when he claimed to be something similar himself?

But Dawn wasn't going back there to find out.

By now, she'd come to a crouch in order to help her stomach calm itself. "It wasn't enough to have Dad with you. You had to make him a vamp."

Eva returned. "It's a beautiful life. Give it a chance."

"No way."

"What would it be like to be forever loved?" Eva whispered. "Have you really thought about that? It's heaven. It's all humans really want."

"You're not going to convince me." She sounded a little *too* emphatic.

"Don't be so quick to refuse. I've told you before that the Master wants you Underground and . . . Well, prepare yourself, because I'm going to be honest with you."

Surprised again by all this truth, Dawn met her mother's intense gaze.

"The Master knows where you are. He's asked me to help ease you into the Underground, thinking I could do it without much turbulence. But . . ." She shrugged.

The rest went unsaid. The Master had no idea what was between Dawn and Eva. He didn't know just how much Dawn hated her mother for what she'd done during the Vampire Killer episode.

"I'm not going to displease the Master, Dawn," she added. "When he sees you, he's going to be very happy."

So happy that he would forget about the other night and the part

Eva might've played in it? It might be just a matter of time before he found out what happened, and Eva probably couldn't afford to make him angry by withholding Dawn.

"That's cool," she said. "You're pimping me out to your big daddy. I knew this mother-daughter thing would be special."

"He can be a perfect gentleman and won't force anything on you. I'll make sure of that."

Agitated, Dawn stood. "And when Limpet comes Underground?"

Eva just laughed. "Don't worry about seeing him again. As the Master's favorites, we won't need to be that involved with fighting. Benedikte hasn't asked me to train with the others."

Benedikte. "That's because you've had alternate duties—like working me over."

"You're right. I have been involved with spy work."

"Hell, I wonder if I should be really impressed. I mean, you're quite the mental soldier, and I had no idea." And here she'd thought starlets were dim.

Eva paused, then got one more piece of paper. Dawn stared at the rug. Then, when her mother was ready, Dawn read the new secret note.

Things will turn out okay if we play our cards right.

It occurred to Dawn that maybe she'd gotten her whole craving for control from DNA—Eva's.

Her mother went to the kitchen again and did her thing. Dawn could hear her voice mixing with the stream of water.

"I know this is probably misguided," Eva said, "but I also want you to be Underground, where Frank can find you. He'll definitely come back if you're . . . there."

"You want to me hang around the vamps until then?"

"I want you to have the time of your life."

The concept should've disgusted Dawn, but there was something small and dark—a pit in the center of her—that grew at the thought of embracing what Eva had promised: beauty, peace.

The opposite of what Costin represented.

Not knowing what else to do, Dawn turned and made for the exit.

"Dawn." Eva's voice stopped her just as she reached the front door.

Needing to get out, to go back to Matt, because this had been such a mistake to come with Eva, she throttled the knob open and . . .

Instead of the welcome hush of dusk settling over a front yard, a rock wall greeted her.

Stunned, Dawn stepped into a hallway, surrounded by stone. She looked up, and a drop of water plunked onto her cheek, let loose from a crag above.

Underground.

Eva hadn't taken her to the gingerbread house Above at all.

"I told you," her mother said from behind her, "the Master knows where you are."

FIFTEEN

BELOW, TAKE THREE

BENEDIKTE stood in front of a full-length mirror in Dawn's new room, shifting into yet another body.

He'd tried on three already, from "Matt"'s pugilistic demeanor, to the form of Thomas Delaney—one of the hottest nonvampire movie stars Above—then to the shape of the surfer-boy weather man from Benedikte's favorite TV station.

But the Master didn't feel right in any of them: the weatherman was too tedious, and Benedikte wasn't understanding Thomas Delaney's "motivation" for being Underground when he hadn't yet been approached about it. And the Master needed this information if he was going to pull off a decent performance.

This brought him to the other rejected body—"Matt." Dawn wouldn't expect her "vampire hunter" to be hanging around in the Underground so casually, either, and Benedikte preferred to save that shape for when he truly needed it with her. After all, even though "Matt" hadn't been able to persuade Dawn to come Underground before Eva had gotten to her, he was the only person Dawn seemed to be at home with right now. This was valuable.

He shifted back into the body he'd worn as a human being—Benedikte. Would Dawn find *him* pleasing?

Checking himself out in the mirror, he decided to bind his hair back in a queue to sport a clean-shaven face. To top off the illusion, he added an oversized white shirt—what they called "poet's style" in today's pretentious catalogs. Leather pants and boots completed the look, and Benedikte was content. Now. To wait for her.

He found himself pacing to the cadence of his nerves. Dawn was Underground, and he couldn't rest. Not when he'd been anticipating her arrival, working toward it for what seemed like forever. He'd taken so many chances appearing Above in "Matt" 's body. He'd put his very safety on the line to make sure he would be with her someday.

And his desires had all started coming true after he'd received Dawn's call for help. Something had happened with Limpet, he knew, and he intended to find out what it was soon after Dawn got comfortable in her new home. Whatever had transpired, it might end up working to Benedikte's advantage.

But, for now, he was thankful Limpet had done something to trigger Dawn's arrival. After her phone call, which had been easy to access because he was always tuned in to "Matt" 's phone, he'd wasted no time in getting Eva Above: she would be Dawn's conduit, transitioning her Underground where Benedikte would finally meet her as the Master. He didn't plan to ever tell her that he'd been masquerading as "Matt," because he knew Dawn's ability to trust was a fragile thing and his deception would shatter any relationship he expected to have with her. No, from now on, the Master would let the real, human Servant Matt Lonigan go about his own business Above, right after Benedikte's version of "Matt" gently broke up with Dawn. In the aftermath of her heartbreak, Benedikte would pick up the pieces and construct her into the shape of his dreams, bettering her.

Luckily Eva had been successful in getting Dawn Below. Then again, he'd known Eva would do her job well, since she wanted to be with her daughter just as much as Benedikte did. He'd just been surprised at the way Eva had accomplished the task.

She'd somehow taken Dawn into her celestial vampire body and transported her daughter. The Master had this power, though he hadn't used it in centuries; certainly he'd never seen an Elite do this before. But he suspected the reason for it. During Eva's last blood infusion, he'd gone overboard, overfeeding her. Was this a result of that impetuous moment when he'd only wanted to express all of his affection?

Aside from that minor surprise, Dawn's move Underground had gone perfectly. With Eva cradling Dawn inside her misty vampire body, Benedikte allowed them inside Matt Lonigan's home. The human Servant had already given all Underground vampires permission to enter, so it hadn't been an issue. Then, Benedikte had led his Elite to the supposed "closet" door—the bolted one with the basketball backboard leaning against it. After opening the barrier, they'd traveled the tunnels to the Underground, and Eva had taken her daughter directly to her chambers, which looked exactly like her home Above.

At that point, Benedikte had bowed to Eva's request to have time alone with her daughter. Dawn would be a tough one to fully transition, Eva had pointed out, and seeing the Master right off the bat would only rile her daughter to the point of rebellion. Knowing this was true, Benedikte had decided to wait in Dawn's room for the big moment, consumed with looking his best for her.

Pacing in earnest now, he couldn't stop the anxiety from overruling everything else.

Benedikte . . . ?

He halted at the sound of Eva's Awareness.

She continued. *We're on our way.*

He felt like he was in one of those romantic comedies that aired on pay movie channels, a film like *There's Something About Mary*.

In particular, the sequence where Ben Stiller, that funny man, was so frazzled when he picked Cameron Diaz up for the prom that he got his privates caught up in his zipper.

But Benedikte wouldn't be that tragically graceless. He'd lived for centuries. He'd mangled men during battles. He was a *vampire*, for the day's sake.

As the door eased open, the Master quickly considered changing back into "Matt." In that body, he knew how to act.

But it wasn't smart. No, he could do this. . . .

Eva preceded Dawn into the room, and the Master caught his breath. His favorite, with her blond hair loose about her shoulders, her skin a becoming pink due to that last, mistake-ridden infusion.

But then Dawn walked in, and the Master almost self-destructed.

It was too much seeing them side by side: one golden and untouchable in her innocent fragility, the other dark and tough as she scowled and looked around at the palatial room he'd designed for her.

Yes, his tough Dawn. But Benedikte knew better, thanks to his time as "Matt." He realized that she had her own brand of vulnerable beauty under all that attitude. It would take some work to reveal it, but the Master was up to the challenge. She would rival her mother in no time, and Benedikte wondered how Eva might react to that—at being so obviously replaced.

The Master waited for Dawn to say something sassy, but it didn't happen. Instead, she just stood there, inspecting the gym set that had been worked into the walls like usable sculpture.

Pity. He'd noticed back at Matt's house that a certain light had been extinguished from her eyes. Again, he wondered what Limpet had done to make her flee and how he could take advantage of it.

He took a step forward, every inch of him wired by excitement. "Welcome, Dawn."

Had she even known he was in the room? When she shot a glare at him, he wasn't sure.

"You're the Master?"

She sounded so unimpressed that Benedikte almost shifted bodies without thinking. Didn't he appeal? How could he—

He stopped and thought about what "Matt" would've done to get her on his side. He would've been mildly amused and, thus, ruggedly charming. Benedikte could do that, too.

"I see you dressed for the occasion," he said, and it came out just as wryly as he'd planned. He motioned to her holey jeans, her dirty sleeveless top that gaped to show a black bra underneath. How they dressed these days.

With "Matt," Dawn might have laughed. She always seemed to enjoy banter, but with Benedikte, she was unresponsive. His chest felt heavy and, as he looked at the holes at the knees of her jeans again, he recalled how he'd tended to her, touched her skin, smelled the blood on it, and battled to contain himself.

By the door, Eva was taking all this in, hugging her arms over her middle.

Dawn gave the Master a negligent look up and down, her eyebrows drawn together. "Do I know you from somewhere?"

The Master masked his surprise. "I'm sure you don't."

She turned to Eva, who lifted her shoulders in a more modest shrug.

"Familiarity bodes well," he said, channeling the smoothness of the vampire he'd always been. There, this was better. She was a human; he was a force of supernature.

Grunting softly, Dawn started walking around the room while running a hand over the rock walls. "This is where I'm supposed to stay? Before Limpet attacks, that is?"

Beautiful—she'd slipped right into where the conversation needed to be.

"The room suits you well."

She walked down to the sunken bed, just below where he was standing in front of the long mirror, his back to it. With an odd look, she touched the delicate veiling that tumbled from the bed

BREAK OF DAWN   163

frame, as if she were almost afraid to come into contact with something that was her opposite.

"To think," she said, "that a couple of nights ago I was sleeping on a couch at a buddy's place."

"The Underground isn't a flophouse." The Master watched the sheer material caress her fingertips.

She seemed to become aware of his devout attention, then dropped the veiling. A hardness cracked over her.

Matt's body, he thought. *I need it—it's the only way Dawn will warm up to me. . . .*

But Benedikte didn't want to be loved as "Matt."

"I don't know what to think," she said, her voice cryptic as she put her hands on her hips. "All you vamps have this baroque thing going on. It's kind of fruity."

He knew her well enough to realize she was getting his goat, as they said.

"Why are you like that?" she concluded.

Now he knew that this was her way of trying to wheedle more-significant-than-it-seems information out of him. They'd gone through that exercise too many times for him to count.

Benedikte paused before answering. Maybe Limpet had staged difficulties with Dawn and had sent her Underground to spy. Well, two could play that game—not that she would ever get the chance to return Above to report to her boss.

Plans formed in his mind: Dawn was a creature who craved endless answers, so Benedikte would give them to her—to a certain extent—if it would win her over.

"Why are we so 'fruity'?" he repeated. "Possibly because we've lived through many gilded ages, and a taste for fine things never dies. We fruity vampires would kill for beauty."

He just thought she needed a reminder.

At the word "kill," she looked down, as if recalling something painful. But she still managed to ask, "How old does that make you?"

Near the door, Eva cleared her throat in a very motherlike way of telling her daughter to be polite.

Benedikte merely laughed. "I was born in the fifteenth century."

"Born. When you say 'born,' do you mean as a vampire?"

He nodded, waiting for more.

"Got it." Dawn peered up, inspecting the mirror poised over the bed. This time she did look impressed.

Was she coming around?

She meandered to the other side of the bed, the veiling partly obscuring her. It set Benedikte's fantasy machine into motion because the seductive sheerness made her look more feminine. More like Eva.

"How do you know Limpet?" she asked.

Oh, how to word *this* response?

Out of the corner of his eye, he saw Eva straighten up by the door.

"I suspect I know him through a brotherhood," he said. "Long ago, we made a vow together. I kept it and, like so many other blood brothers, he did not."

In fact, Benedikte wondered which one of the brotherhood was betraying him this time. It wasn't Andre, who'd perished while trying to take over Benedikte's first Underground. And since they'd all cut off contact from one another—a result of greed and paranoia reaching a peak—the Master had no idea whom he would be facing now.

But he would be ready, along with his small army who would fight to the end for their careers, egos, and home.

Before Dawn could take over this interrogation-cum-conversation, Benedikte spoke. "How much do you know about Jonah Limpet, Dawn?"

Behind the bed veiling, her silhouette froze. The material belled in and out with her breathing.

Would he have to go into her mind to get answers? It was a last resort, a rape of sorts, and it didn't fit into any romantic scenarios the Master had planned. It demeaned him.

She finally answered. "Why would I help by giving you information?"

Near her spot by the entrance, Eva winced under her breath.

"I mean," Dawn continued, "do you really think I want to help *any* of you cretins to stay alive?"

If she'd concocted some sort of fake fight with Limpet just to fool Benedikte, she was acting like a pro. The hatred in her voice sounded too real.

Suddenly, Dawn jerked away from the veiling, almost tearing it from the bed frame. She headed for a shocked Eva.

"Did you want to show me anything else in this place?" Dawn asked her mother. "Or am I confined to this shithole?"

His one—his only—barged out the exit, leaving Eva behind to shake her head in puzzlement at her maker, then follow Dawn into the hall.

Stinging, Benedikte composed himself by straightening the ruffles on his wrists, one at a time.

For a first meeting, it had gone well, he told himself. Yet as he turned around to glance in the mirror again, his body warped back into the only one Dawn would respond to.

"Matt." A subpar form whose appeal he didn't comprehend.

But during their next meeting, he would use it, just one more time: he would indulge her and then . . . then . . .

Despondent, the Master shifted into his blank, ghostly, nebulous nobody form, not knowing any answers beyond that.

SIXTEEN

THE SCREENING

WHAT *a blowhard,* Dawn thought as Eva caught up to her in the rock hallway, their footsteps heavy on the Moorish-patterned tiles. On the walls, electric lights flickered as they passed, casting color that had been leaked of life.

"That was brave of you," Eva said.

"What, I'm supposed to be afraid of a fop?" Okay, she would admit that the Master had been sort of Gary Oldman–as-Dracula intriguing. But, come on, his shirt wasn't exactly a testament to ultimate manhood. He had a quality that she remembered from pictures in high school English-lit textbooks—one of those romantic guys who wrote about Greek vases and shit.

And there'd been something about him. . . . *Had* she seen the Master before?

All the same, Benedikte really hadn't unnerved her. But that didn't mean she was just going to write him off. *Never* trust what you see.

"Dawn," Eva said, gently grasping her arm and stopping her

progress down the chisled hall. In the near distance, there was a sound like wailing, even though there wasn't a breeze. "The Master didn't invite you here so he could pop out of corners and make you shriek. He's not a joke to be taken lightly."

Dawn shirked off Eva's touch, and her mother kept her hand in the air. The sharp keening from down the hall grew louder—it sounded like "home"—and disappeared abruptly.

"At any rate," her mother said, "I appreciate how you didn't put up a fight when it came to seeing Benedikte."

"What choice did I have? I was already Underground, thanks to you. Might as well take the whole tour." Dawn didn't add that her options for being anyplace else were limited to Matt's house and . . . nowhere.

A sense of alienation swallowed her, a mental anesthetic that removed her from everything. She couldn't even feel the soreness of her post-smashup body anymore.

Eva began walking ahead of Dawn, then turned around to see why her daughter wasn't following. "Are you coming then?"

"Coming . . . ?"

"For a tour." Eva smiled. "I don't mean to brag, but this place is going to blow your socks off."

"Sure it will." Living in L.A. had desensitized Dawn to so much that wowing her was unlikely. And with what she'd seen just in the Limpet house alone . . .

Anger ratcheted her body up another notch on the tense scale. She didn't give a crap about the Limpets anymore. Or, at least, she shouldn't. The fact that she still caught herself thinking about Jonah and Costin and all the rest ticked her off.

Dawn went to Eva, careful to leave a chasm between their bodies as they walked.

"Great." Her mother sounded like Jac: chirpy and energized by Dawn's cooperation. "We'll be coming to the emporium first, where everyone hangs out."

"Yay. I get to meet and mingle with your kind."

"You've done it Above. What's the difference?"

Dawn's hackles rose, but she didn't want to give Eva the satisfaction of seeing that the notion freaked her out. She changed subjects. "About Benedikte . . ."

Her mother slowed her gait.

"Do you know your master's history?" Dawn added.

"Not really." Eva wore a guarded look. "Why?"

"Why do you think?"

"Dawn, if you plan to go back Above to inform Limpet of—"

At the name, Dawn's body screamed. Next to them, a lightbulb popped, darkening a circle around their bodies like a deadened halo.

Eva shrank back from the tiny explosion, then gazed wonderingly at her daughter.

"I won't be going back there," Dawn bit out. "Don't ever accuse me of that again."

"All right."

"Now . . ." Dawn casually brushed her hands together, trying to seem in control. "What do you know about Benedikte?"

"I . . . I know that he's old, like he told you. I know that he's a vampire of great power who was born in violence and has murdered his way through the years. He realizes I don't like to see that side of him, though."

"You like to ignore it." To reimagine the Hollywood story.

Her mother sighed, clearly biding her patience.

Once again the persistent detective, Dawn asked, "And how about my old boss? How much do you know about him?"

"Besides that he's evil? We know a monster wants to ruin us, and we've been instructed to exercise our powers to fight him. I've wanted to get you away from . . . your boss . . . ever since you started working there."

Was Eva still playing her? Was she withholding?

"Dawn, forget about all that." Her mother came closer. "Roll with Benedikte, and you'll find out that life can be very easy. It can be everything you've always dreamed of down here. Think of what you'd want the most, and it's yours."

Absently, Dawn ran a gaze over Eva, almost as if her mother were a wishful reflection in a mirror. Then she caught herself, ending the moment with a blanked expression.

"When you're ready to give permission," the actress added, "Benedikte will be there."

The vampire's bite. That was what her mother was talking about. They wouldn't force it on Dawn, though. Supposedly.

Well-worn anger stepped in to ease Dawn's longing for what Eva was dangling. "I'll bet the bite is a real rush."

She was being sarcastic, testing.

Her mother's eyes began to swirl. "It's like nothing you've ever felt before."

"Do you think it's the type of rush," Dawn added, unable to resist one more dig, "that Cassie Tomlinson got when she killed women like Klara Monaghan and Jessica Reese—"

"Lee Tomlinson killed Klara, not Cassie—"

Dawn didn't absorb Eva's continuing effort to be forthcoming. She couldn't even enjoy the answer to one of the questions that'd been dogging her about the Vampire Killer murders.

"Back to the point, Eva," Dawn continued, raising her voice above her mother's. "When Cassie killed women like *Breisi*, did you, as what amounts to an accomplice, feel the rush?"

"No, I felt . . ."

"Nothing, I'll bet, even though you're laden with guilt in the aftermath. I'll bet you thought it all over and realized that remorse was an appropriate emotion to use."

Eva wildly shook her head. "You're wrong."

"Why would I want to go around all empty like a vamp?"

Recovering, her mother pierced her with an astute glance. "Since you do such a good job of acting like nothing matters, I thought you might *like* the blankness, Dawn."

Oh . . . snap.

Jaw clenched, Dawn stiffened before the truth could hit like shot from a gun, spraying more damage than she could endure.

"I'm sorry," Eva said. "I didn't mean—"

Dawn started walking. "Where is this emporium?"

In silence, her mother led her down the hallway, rock encasing them.

Soon they came to a massive door and, with a shy, peace-seeking grin, the vamp made a show of opening it for her daughter. This didn't seem like an act on Eva's part. Her mother was actually excited about sharing what was behind the barrier, just like someone wanting to see a movie they loved for a second time with a virgin viewer.

With a tumble of sight, sound, and scent, everything blazed at Dawn, assaulting her with color in a world that had only been a dull palate. It was like opening the doors to a sensual, archaic Oz.

Stepping inside, she was swallowed by the scent of smoky flowers, the tingle of sparkling laughter over the rustle of silk flying from the ceiling. High above, a golden dome reigned over the rock walls that boasted waterfalls and leviathan screens that flashed music videos. On the marbled floor, tented, diaphanous veils hushed over circular beds, some of which were surrounded by clear pools. And in those pools, naked figures swam, their hair spread out in flowing serenity. On a raised dais, a group of worldly looking vampires sat, languishing in the occasional robe or nothing at all as they applauded the performance of one of their own: she was trotting around with what looked like a sword, acting like Conanita the Barbarian.

"Looks like it's break time from war practice," Eva said.

When Dawn tore her gaze away from the rest of it to look at her mother, she saw that Eva's eyes were gleaming. She loved it here, and the idea that she wanted her daughter to love it, too, did some harm to Dawn's will.

For once, she was too swept away to brace against what Eva wanted. Dawn took in the gaiety, the contentment, the beauty.

But then alienation crept back up on her, reminding her that she didn't belong.

Eva had started for the dais, where the playactress was having her fun with the sword. "Come on," she said, becoming perky Jac all over again.

Dawn hesitated. Should she, could she . . . ?

She followed, keeping her distance.

When she and Eva got closer to the sword performance, Dawn realized the actress was Rea Carvahal, who'd recently become a pop-culture icon because of the antiheroine roles she played in hip, ultraviolent movies. Ironically, Dawn had come this close to getting a stunt gig in one of her flicks.

"Dare to best me, you limp Limpet?" Rea was saying, poking her sword at an invisible foe. Her curly auburn hair, upturned nose, lethal cheekbones, and dimpled chin made her striking in a quirky way. "I am well experienced in your manner of threats."

A smattering of applause met the actress's mocking demonstration of the disemboweling she was going to carry out when Limpet attacked.

Crap, what were these vamps going to do when they recognized Dawn? Were they going to take their movie swords and try to poke at her, too?

Eva leaned over to speak in Dawn's ear, her soft perfume an unwelcome distraction. "Rea—or maybe you know her as Filipa Pratt from her old career—likes to kid around. It relieves tension."

Dawn was still back on the Filipa Pratt part. Damn. Big, bad damn. Ironically, Filipa Pratt used to play sexy vampires in a string of gothic cult monster flicks from the seventies.

"She looks so young," Dawn said.

"She'll always be that way." Eva laughed as the actress leaped in the air and twirled her sword, then pretended to cut off Limpet's ears. "After an Elite is released and our next careers flourish, we sometimes have to use cosmetics to make the public think we're aging gracefully. Then, when that doesn't work anymore, we try for a second comeback by returning Underground and undergoing another surgery and release."

Checking out the vampires surrounding Rea, Dawn recognized a lot of faces from posters in memorabilia shops. Eva had shared with her before, so Dawn had known what the Underground was up to, but seeing them in the flesh . . .

She felt drab, out of place, uglier than she'd ever imagined with her scars marking her skin and the bandages peeking through her torn jeans.

Then a familiar face in the crowd snagged her attention. Paul Aspen, the vampire who'd thrown the party where Dawn had been mind wiped. He was riveted to Rea, his always-a-boy-next-door looks shiny and bright.

"Ahhh!" It was Rea, pointing at Eva with a finger, her sword by her side. "Look, my friends! We are joined by a body from the heavens themselves!"

When the actress's gaze traveled from Eva to Dawn, Rea did a double take. Then, within a heartbeat, she jumped down from the dais, making her ethereal robe flow around her. She came to a graceful landing in front of Dawn, smelling of precious oils that made her skin glitter.

"Why, hello, hunter," Rea said.

The vampires on the dais remained seated. In fact, they were all watching Dawn with wide eyes. Was it because she was Eva's daughter? Because she was wanted by Benedikte? Or had they heard about what she'd done to Robby Pennybaker?

Satisfaction took her over as she stood toe-to-toe with Rea, unfazed by her gorgeous mug. She even looked into her swirling eyes, daring her to try a mind screw, just as Robby had.

"Rea . . ." Eva warned.

The other actress kept facing off with Dawn, as if trying to intimidate her. But Dawn wasn't about to let the vampire know that it might be working, that she felt like a mere speck of dirt in this lovely garden.

Then, without warning, Rea fell to her knees and spread her arms, dropping the sword. "The form of Diana the huntress!" she proclaimed. "The beauty of ages, right before mine eyes!"

Dawn wanted to kick her ass for pointing out to everyone that she was the plain, unspectacular pretender in their midst.

"Drop the act," she said.

When Eva tried to intervene, a grinning Rea held up a hand. "I am only paying homage."

Truly, Miss Carvahal was pretty much every reason Dawn hated the acting masses.

But then Rea fixed her gaze on Dawn again, tilting her head in assessment. In the actress's swirling eyes, Dawn thought she detected an honest admiration.

No. She was seeing things.

"The hunter," Rea repeated. Then she picked up her fake sword, which turned out to be not so fake after all. "Could you best me? I wonder."

"This has gone beyond fun and straight to ridiculous," Eva said, walking away.

But Dawn didn't retreat. Maybe it was because of the challenge. Maybe it was because of the need to hurt something as thoroughly as she'd been hurt today. Or maybe it was because giving as good as she got was just in her nature.

Dawn smiled, and Rea liked what she saw. She swooped back her sword as if to come at her target lightly, not to fight, but to embarrass a real hunter through parody, showing everyone that Limpet's forces weren't anything to fear.

Taking advantage of playtime, Dawn jumped and kicked out, knocking back Rea's sword arm before the vamp could bring it forward. Then, just for good measure, Dawn twirled around in a hurricane kick, bonking Rea gently in the head.

It was the spanking Rea had meant to give *her*.

As the actress put a hand to her skull—probably surprised but not even close to physically injured—the rest of the Elites on the dais tittered. But it sounded like it was out of not knowing how else to react more than anything.

That did it for Rea. As Eva cried out in warning from behind Dawn, the cult actress cocked back her sword, and from the look on her face, Dawn knew it was time to spar for real.

So the bloodsucker wanted to embarrass the visiting hunter? To play with the human yarn ball?

Anger surged, and Dawn blasted with her mind. Rea tumbled backward, feet over head, smacking against the dais steps.

Everything went silent. But after a splintered pause, the Elites began applauding.

When Dawn glanced up at them, she saw more than a pleased audience shouting, "Bravo! Encore!" She saw confusion and even a healthy respect because they weren't sure what else she could do, if maybe she was even strong enough to take *them* on.

Dawn would just make sure they kept wondering.

Blood pounded through her and, out of a dumb, instinctive need to see what her mother thought, Dawn turned to Eva. But the vampire was speed walking out of the emporium.

As Dawn went to catch her, the Elites yelled for her to come back. She just sent them a shrug, then took off.

"What?" she asked, reaching Eva in the hallway.

Her mother kept moving at a rapid clip. "That was classy."

"Hey, you wanted me to be a part of the Underground. Keeping someone from dominating me right away is a start, don't you think? If she's going to try to mark me with her piss, I'm going to deflect it right back at her."

Eva kept zipping along.

"Wait!" When Dawn gripped her mother's arm, swinging the vamp around to face her, she grunted a little, her neck and back reminding her that they were sore. She'd been too hyped up in the emporium to remember that.

Dawn was taken aback by the intensity in Eva's gaze. Was it shame? No, not altogether. Was it . . . envy?

Wow. For once, Dawn had stepped out of Eva's shadow. She'd been her own woman in the emporium, and maybe her mother couldn't stand that.

"It was out of line," Eva said. "Your lack of maturity is astounding sometimes."

"Oh, lovely. *Who's* talking about growing up?"

"No, you're not getting it." Her mother clasped her hands, put them, prayerlike, to her forehead, then calmed down. Music filled the hallway from about twenty feet down, coming from an ajar door that leaked stuttering blue light.

"Dawn, when I was your age, I had already been married with a child. I was *responsible*. I don't know—maybe it's because a lot of other people in our generations take their time growing up, but you've got to think things through around these older vampires. They'll take your inexperience, chew it up, and spit out bone chips."

Crazily enough, Dawn listened to what her mother was saying. Eva was right. At twenty-four, Dawn couldn't even conceive of having a kid and settling down. She really wasn't an adult in emotion.

"Okay," she said, humbled. "Sounds like it's time for me to go back to Matt's."

"No. What I mean is . . . you're welcome here. Obviously."

Sure, obviously.

"You know," Eva continued, "deciding to bring you to the Underground reminded me of those days when I wondered if L.A. was a good place to raise you. So much temptation, so many things to teach you the rights and wrongs of."

"I handled the city just fine." There was a note of unmistakable pride in there.

"Yes," her mother said. "You sure did."

They stood, facing each other, but not meeting gazes. Finally, Eva began strolling toward the music, toward the slit-open door, and Dawn went, too.

"What's this?" she asked.

Her mother made as if to walk on by. "A screening room. The

Master loves to stage retrospectives of all our movies. Let's keep on going."

An extradeep flush had washed over Eva, and Dawn thought she knew why. She recognized the music from one of her mother's films, a weepie in which she'd had a substantial role as the girlfriend of a small-town football player. Eva's character had been the light of his life, his symbolic reason for staying faithful to the purity of the game.

Without a word, Dawn opened the door, then entered, knowing Eva would probably give in and follow.

It was a room of gigantic proportions, a yawn of a cave with a film screen and half-filled, plush seats. Asian trimmings flecked the outside of the screen, adding luster.

As Dawn slumped in the back row, Eva sat upright beside her. They'd walked in on the scene where the hero spots his girlfriend dancing on a bridge that leads out of town, right before one of those hayseed dances you could only find in Americana movies. He was about to leave for the big time, deserting all that was good in his life. But the sight of his girlfriend, so natural, so pure in the twilight, gave him pause.

Watching her mother on-screen, Dawn got lost in Eva's way of moving: effortlessly, achingly unaware of being devoured by an audience. She was so young—younger than Dawn was now—but she had an eternal maturity that came with the mantle of a star.

Unable to help it, Dawn slid a glance to Eva. The expression on the vamp's surgically altered, yet strangely similar, face almost killed her. Her mother had the look of a woman who'd lost a part of herself—more than a child or a husband, but something that had been robbed from the vault of her very being.

At that moment, Dawn realized just how much it meant to her mother to stay young, to always be Eva Claremont.

Instead of being angered by that, Dawn felt a tragic empathy that she couldn't quell.

All of us want to be special, she thought, *don't we? Nobody wants to be set aside and forgotten.*

Biting the inside of her bottom lip, Dawn tried not to lose it. But when she felt Eva's hand resting over the top of her own on the shared arm of the chair, her eyes got wet anyway.

Yet she stared straight ahead until they went dry.

SEVENTEEN
THE WILD ONE

THE following incident could have been avoided if Dawn hadn't allowed Eva to complete the Underground tour. It wouldn't have happened if Dawn had told herself that accepting an invitation to go back to Eva's chambers couldn't do any harm.

But everything that led up to "the incident" played its part, and in Dawn's rootlessness, she found herself giving in to every bit of it.

After seeing more Underground highlights such as the movie-remembrance pavilion and the spa, they'd returned to Eva's quarters. There, she'd prepared some sort of tea and was setting out the porcelain collection on a low table by her living room couches. Dawn didn't intend to drink any of it, but it seemed to make her mother feel good to be serving company.

Since there was no way Dawn was going back to "her room"—that overdecorated brothel where the Master had first met her—she figured puttering around Eva's for a little while longer was a decent option until she could formulate an escape plan. And it would give her time to figure out how she could overcome her mother when the time called for it.

Secretively, Dawn glanced at her machetes, which Eva had bundled into a far corner. Her mother had done the same thing back when Dawn had first uncovered "Jacqueline Ashley"'s masquerade, and keeping the weapons out in the open hadn't mattered a lick. Eva had smacked her around easily anyway.

"What's your favorite part of the Underground?" Eva asked while pouring a stream of brownish red liquid into Dawn's cup.

Um, barf? "Don't have a favorite."

Her mother smiled, then slid the cup and saucer over.

"What's with the happy?" Dawn asked.

"It's you." Eva used delicate tongs to pick up a lump of sugar and offer it. When Dawn declined, her mother put two cubes into her own filled cup. "You act like none of it was the least bit impressive, but you liked it all."

"Well, you vamps did put a lot of effort into things."

Eva stirred her tea like she was Queen Duchess of Fangovia. "Just like *you* put effort into that showdown with Rea Carvahal."

"You going to get after me about that again?" Throughout the tour, Eva had been dropping minor bombs about how to get along with everyone else. How to be *niiiiice*. Frank used to coach Dawn on that, too, not that it'd helped.

"Dawn, they're already keen on you, thanks to the reputation you came with. You don't have to labor for their interest."

"Interest? They can all kiss my ass." And that was why she'd felt so good about the applause after she'd put Rea in her place. Uh-huh.

As Eva lifted her cup and saucer, the steam from her tea wafted over her face, mysterious mist. She still hadn't taken a sip. "Rea's a Shakespearean clown—harmless. She wouldn't have hurt you . . . especially not with me standing right there."

Dawn shifted on the couch to accommodate her slight aches. "You know, Eva, I find it ridiculous that you're lecturing me about schoolyard scuffles. You're the one who mugged Darrin Ryder because the creep gave me a hard time on a movie set."

"Just protecting you, honey."

"No, no 'honey.' I can take care of myself."

The testy comment made Dawn feel like crap, especially after having seen her mother looking so vulnerable during that movie screening.

Carefully, Eva set down her untouched beverage.

Almost against her will, Dawn offered a verbal olive branch. "I didn't know vamps drank stuff like tea."

"I have no taste for it, but I wanted you to feel relaxed."

Ah. Eva had been *acting!*

Dawn realized *she* had no taste for ripping into Eva now. But that didn't mean she wouldn't do what had to be done soon.

"Since we're on the subject of porcine actors like Darrin Rider," Eva said, "I should tell you something else."

Was her mother trying to win Dawn over with a show of honesty again, just as she had with all those confessions earlier in the night?

"Fire away," Dawn said.

"It's about Paul Aspen's party."

"Yeah, the one where my mind got broken into. Good times."

Eva shifted in her chair. "I found out who took advantage of you, and I've been meaning to ask him about it, but, as you know, I've been a bit busy. Believe it or not, I was just as upset about this as you were."

Actually, Dawn did believe her. After all, her mother had smacked that sexually harassing prick Darrin Ryder around for her daughter's sake. Why not get upset about another assault?

"Do tell, Eva." Impulsively, she scooted forward on the couch.

Her mother inched closer, too, and suddenly they were as close as they'd been while writing those notes earlier.

"I can't get into the why of things, but what this 'friend' of mine did to you was out of spoiled greed. We don't mind wipe unless the circumstances are dire, and for him to bite you . . . He disrespected me. Your reputation down here—as my daughter and as a hunter—made you too desirable for him to pass up."

Violated, defiled.

"Who is it?" Anger began to purr in Dawn, a started engine.

Eva seemed to be just as riled. "Paul Aspen, also known as Edward Waters in his former incarnation."

Dawn's head squeezed together, as if trying to recall his attack. But she couldn't, and the clamping sensation traveled to her body.

Paul Aspen, the boyish charmer she'd seen earlier in the emporium. The vampire who'd invaded her.

She stood. "You said you've been meaning to talk to him about it, Eva?"

At first, her mother just sat, posed in something like indecision. But then heat seemed to fill her eyes—maybe because of ire, maybe because she wanted to prove to Dawn that she was truly willing to do anything to make up for Breisi and all the rest of her choices.

Eva rose from her chair, too. "One thing?"

"What?"

"We talk to him my way. I don't want another Rea Carvahal incident."

"Sure, whatever."

And that was how it started, over tea and sympathy. It continued with a knock on Paul's chamber door.

The actor, who would be in his late thirties for a long time to come, answered the summons in a natty Chinese-embroidered robe. Since he was playing hooky from his and Eva's movie production right now, his sandy hair had quickly grown back to a conservative cut without frequent shaving. His hazel eyes glimmered just as jauntily as the earrings he'd gotten for the part of a cinematic buccaneer.

"The party has come to me tonight!" He held open the door, seeing only Eva. "I was just preparing to go out again."

Her mother strolled inside. "We'll be enough entertainment for you, I think."

Dawn felt herself falling into the part of an actress, too. She grinned in greeting as she followed her mother.

At the sight of Dawn, the actor seemed caught in a net, as if he knew that he'd been revealed in taking advantage of his costar's daughter. But when his guests didn't let on that this was why they were here, he stuffed his hands in his robe pockets and playfully bounced up and down on his bare heels.

"It's grand to see you, too, Dawn. We've all been waiting for your anticipated appearance. Eva hasn't been able to talk about anything else for years."

Her mother sent her a sly look, almost as if this were some kind of bonding moment. Unthinkingly, Dawn returned it. Her juices were flowing at the thought of teaching this dick a lesson, just as she'd taught Darrin Ryder what it felt like to have his balls nestled in his chest from a good kick. Power-hungry jerks—male, female, vampire, whatever—were one of Dawn's pet peeves, and since she had nothing to lose now, she didn't mind investing some time and effort in rehabilitating them.

"Care for a beverage?" Paul asked, heading for what seemed to be a fancy cappuccino maker.

"Please," Eva said, going over to his white-on-white living room. Overhead, a massive chandelier tinkled, lending the area a retro-elegant sheen. "But I'm not sure Dawn will join us."

"I understand." Paul went behind the bar and filled two mugs with red liquid. "Rumor has it that you haven't been turned yet, Dawn."

"Rumor's right." Dawn remained standing after she gravitated to the living room, too. "Blood's not my thing."

"Not yet anyway." Paul chuckled and came over with the mugs, handing one to Eva, then sitting on a white leather couch. "Is there something else you'd like instead?"

This guy was either real forgetful or terrifyingly arrogant, Dawn thought. "Last time I got served a drink at your place, it was spiked with some junk that turned me fifty ways up and down. Or . . ."

Dawn put a finger to her lips, tapping them. With every beat, her fury turned up. "Oh, yeah. It wasn't the drink, was it, Eva?"

Paul slowly set his mug down on a glass-topped table.

"You are correct, my dear," Eva said, mocking Paul by setting down her own mug. Now that they were committed, her mother seemed to be having a ball, excited about costarring with her daughter. "Paul, with everything that's been going on, I haven't had a moment to really sit down and chat with you."

Even just watching the actor was bringing Dawn's body to a boil. She felt a pressure at her temples, heating, thrusting.

Paul cleared his throat. "Chat?"

"Hmm, maybe that's the wrong word for it," Eva said.

Pump, pump . . . Dawn's head was about to burst.

"Now, ladies," the vampire actor said in a smooth tone, "let's—"

A flare of heat made Dawn's head feel like it was shattering. She even heard the sound of glass, but when her vision cleared, she saw that it wasn't her mind bursting to pieces at all—it was the chandelier.

A few crystal droplets had zoomed down to pelt Paul, who was raising his arms to cover his precious face. "Wh—"

"You want to see into my mind?" Dawn yelled. "Then take a look!"

Zweek, zweek, zweek—more chandelier shards speared the air, this time embedding themselves into Paul's shielding hands. Blood spurted from his wounds, beading the white couch and carpeting with crimson.

He stood, uncovering his face and revealing a misty grimace Dawn recognized the signs of impending Danger Form.

"Paul!" It was Eva, who was standing, too. "You turn; *I* turn. And, believe me—I'm going to trump you."

The actor shook like an old machine that'd been unexpectedly shut down. Just for good measure, Dawn shot another drop of crystal at his cheek. He startled but didn't do anything because Eva was watching.

But, after a moment, he did turn to Dawn in a visual threat. That was how bullies operated, even if they knew they'd been beaten for the time being. Blood graced his hands and face like grotesque gems.

"Didn't you always want to wear Swarovski?" Dawn asked.

Eva broke in, shooting a shut-up glance to her daughter. "Paul, those wounds are going to heal before daylight comes, so don't get upset."

What her mother didn't say was that the actor's humiliation would last longer. That was what mattered, and that was why he wouldn't tell anyone what had just happened.

As Eva took Dawn by the hand to lead her out of the room, Dawn dug in her heels, still ready to throw down. She wasn't finished, and she had enough fuel in her hatred to go as many rounds as it took with him.

"Stop it," Eva hissed, crushing her daughter's hand in hers until the pain woke Dawn up.

They left the actor standing in the middle of his room, blood splattered and lancing a glare at Dawn.

His former victim.

As soon as Eva closed Paul's door, a rush of adrenaline lifted Dawn so high she could've walked on air.

"Sweet revenge," she said while Eva pulled her along the hallway. "Funny how the tables can be turned like that, huh?"

Her mother stopped, her look hard enough to make Dawn feel like she'd just smacked into a glass door.

"You feel good about what just happened?" Eva asked.

Heartbeat pistoning, Dawn thought about it. But only for a second. "Yeah. Yeah, I feel *great* about it."

Eva resumed towing Dawn. That was when she realized she was holding hands with Mommy. She shook off the connection.

"Where're you headed?" Dawn asked.

"While we were in there, Benedikte summoned me. He'd like to see you in a half hour."

Dawn hadn't noticed Eva getting any Master messages. Then again, would it be obvious? Also, she'd been pretty occupied.

"You're at his beck and call like that?" She laughed and started moving in the opposite direction. She hadn't felt this powerful in . . . ever. "I don't think your master is going to order me around the same way."

"Dawn." Eva's voice required attention. "You do realize Elites like Paul could kill you, don't you? You're not indestructible. Not even close."

A stirring of doubt settled in Dawn's lower stomach. Sure she'd realized it, yet the crystal illusions had overwhelmed her. Still . . . you know what? She'd gotten him, and he could never reverse his punishment.

"And *you* realize," Dawn said, "that I've killed a rogue Elite before."

At the reminder of Robby Pennybaker's fate, Eva stiffened. They'd been costars, friends, just as Breisi had been Dawn's friend.

"I assume killing Robby makes you proud," her mother said.

Not at all, and it made Dawn even bitterer to think that Costin had made her into . . . this. Into something that *had* killed. It made her furious that she'd allowed it, herself, and that she was allowing something even worse to creep up on her now.

Reality cloaked her, then a defensive resentment. Eva seemed to notice.

"You could be so much more, Dawn, if you'd only—"

"If I wanted to be one of you, I'd already have done it, okay? I'm not as desperate about my looks as you are."

Eva reacted as if bitch slapped. Well, she had been, verbally.

Caught up in her black mood, Dawn pressed her advantage. "What are you going to do if the Master gets slain, Eva? Will you finally look your age? I'm not talking about losing your career or providing for me, but becoming just as unspecial as the rest of us."

Eva went stony.

Down the hall, a bunch of vampires emerged from another chamber door and headed toward them in the direction of the emporium. Dawn recognized a bare-chested Jesse Shane along with the silver-eyed Groupies who were flanking him, wearing nothing but delicate chains. His long golden hair made him look like a prince among jewels.

"There she is!" He held his arms out to Dawn. "Eva, where've you been hiding our spectacular newbie?"

As one of his muscle-honed arms slipped around Dawn's shoulders, she got a hot flash. Jesse Shane, action star, had been a buried preteen fantasy of hers, and here he was, in the flesh.

He pulled her to his famous chest and her stomach flip-flopped. Jesse Shane.

You hear that, Costin?

Eva greeted the vamp group while a male Groupie petted her blond hair. She seemed perfectly at home with the attention.

"Dawn and I were just about to—"

"Come to the emporium," Jesse finished, already sweeping Dawn away. "We've finished training for the night, and it's time to . . . er . . . meditate on our future success." He squeezed Dawn to him. "Isn't that right?"

Holy crap, she might faint. Jesse Shane, probably the only star who'd ever risen above her low expectations of the breed. A reluctant crush that she'd kind of forgotten about until now, in his tongue-lolling presence.

She bungled an answer—sounded like a yes to her—and forgot about Eva as Jesse brought her into the domed emporium. The erotic temperature of it soaked into her skin, making it buzz.

Just watch me live, Costin. . . .

Jesse led her to a steaming pool and stepped out of his silk pants. Several female Groupies clung to him, rubbing against his sleek thighs. One even reached out to caress his, well, quite impressive package, if Dawn said so herself. It seemed natural for them to be so carnal, but Dawn wasn't sure what to do with herself. Not here, not now.

Jesse and his perfect, broad-shouldered body slid into the water, and Dawn had to remind herself that she hated actors.

As four Groupies joined him, splashing one another and giggling, he motioned to Dawn.

"You allergic to water?" he asked.

She tried to seem as confident as ever, because, really, this was no biggie. Skinny-dipping and flashing her skin around guys was par for the course. So why was she hesitating?

She looked around for Eva, but didn't find her.

"Dawn Madison . . ." Jesse said playfully. He finger-sprayed some water at her, and the women around him laughed. "If you can't beat us, join us."

He didn't seem to mind her face—the wound from Robby Pennybaker on her check or the stunt-earned scar flicking her eyebrow. He didn't care that she wasn't the second coming of any beauty queen.

In fact, he was looking at her like she transcended a title, like she fit right in with all these beautiful creatures.

Join them. It was the first thing that made sense in a while. What was she holding on to anyway?

And when she saw how the vampires were watching her, with lust and acceptance and even anticipation, she undid her hair, shaking it out and freeing herself.

EIGHTEEN

THE BITING TRUTH

LOOK at me, Costin, Dawn thought as she grabbed the bottom of her shirt and yanked upward. *I can be just like I was before I met you.*

Jesse and the Groupies were egging her on when Dawn felt someone tugging down her shirt from behind, then hoisting her away from the pool.

"Hey—" she started.

But Eva finished. She looked fit to be tied. "Not the time for this, Dawn."

Jesse and his Groupies *oooo*ed in anticipation of a tussle.

Her mother turned on them. "Did you think about what the Master might do if he saw you encouraging her?"

The *oooo*ing stopped. The splashing of the waterfall into the far end of the pool substituted for an answer.

Dawn took up the slack. "Am I not supposed to be having 'the time of my life' down here, Eva? Unless I'm wrong, I think you suggested it."

"I meant with the Master."

"Ah, sublime monogamy." She put on a saccharine smile. "I didn't expect you to be the only prude down here."

As her mother pulled her away from the vampires, Dawn looked at Jesse Shane one last time. He smiled his blockbuster smile, making her want to stay and be a part of what he offered.

But Eva pulled her daughter into the hallway for the second time that night, and Dawn couldn't help feeling like she was being dragged to her room for a good talking-to. *Again.*

"Think," Eva said. "Would the Master be happy that you're cavorting with someone else when you rejected *him* earlier?"

"*I'd* be happy. Seriously—you're protecting my virtue?" She laughed shortly. "How Kiko of you."

Her mother seemed to notice the wistful change in Dawn's tone. Eva stopped, then tilted her head in the way all vamps seemed to do when they were trying to figure you out.

"Kiko," she repeated softly.

It held a note of remorse. While disguised as Jac, Eva had developed some affection for the psychic—at least, she'd acted like it. Dawn chose to believe it was true because, as Kik himself would've said, how could it not be?

The vamp let go of Dawn's hand and moved on, changing the subject. "Besides the Master, I have an ulterior motive for getting you out of the emporium, something that won't take long. We'll see Benedikte right afterward."

"Please elaborate. Because that was Jesse Shane in there. Jesse. Shane."

"I thought you might be more interested in trying to contact Frank."

Ears perked. "What do you mean . . . ?" Dawn caught up to her mother, keeping pace. "How?"

"I've been hoping to make an attempt down here, maybe at an old quarry entrance near the surface to try my Awareness with him. Now that we're prepared for . . . the nameless agency you used to work for . . . it's no danger to use vampire communication Above. It was a concern before because it could be detected. We all had to be careful."

Dawn appreciated that Eva wasn't referring to Costin out loud. It was a small but important sign of simpatico.

"But," her mother continued, "I suppose Jesse *is* waiting."

"We're talking about my dad, Eva." Hell, she hated actors anyway, and it was simple to remember it now that she was out of Jesse Shane's sexual force field.

At her mother's smile, Dawn picked up speed. They had come to a fork in the tunnels, and Eva led her to the right, where electric lights stared and the floor turned to dirt.

A question poked at Dawn, something she'd been wondering for a while now. "Eva, how strong is Frank as a vampire?"

Her mother lost a step, then continued. "I don't have a definitive answer because . . . Well, there's a lot to consider. First, *I'm* strong. During my last blood-taking from the Master, I overindulged, and it boosted me. And"—she lowered her voice, although what she would say out loud probably wouldn't get her in trouble if it were overheard—"I already told you what happened last time I fed Frank. Here's the thing: in our community, blood loses its power with the introduction of every new generation, so that's why we have strong vampires like the Elites and weaker ones, like the Groupies."

"Right . . ."

"What I'm saying is that Frank is no doubt stronger than any of our Groupies. He might be a cross between that and an Elite, so I'm not sure what to expect out of him. Elites aren't interested in making children, really, so Frank's an anomaly."

"And . . . how about this brotherhood I keep hearing about? The one the Master was in." Introducing . . . the detective. It'd appeared in Dawn's mental doorway uninvited, eager to take up the Costin/Jonah case again. "Are all the brothers equal?"

"I have no idea."

They kept walking, the sound of footsteps popping against rock.

As a breeze whistled through the tunnel, Eva slowed down, gravitating toward a wall. She ran her hand over a slightly discolored patch, and a rumble from ahead shivered the air.

While her mother concentrated on her task, Dawn stole a glance at the actress's perfect profile, her forever-young skin.

"What do you think your life would be like if you looked your age?" she whispered.

The vamp's hand flew up, as if wanting to touch her face, then did a slow free fall. "I try not to think about that."

"You'd be . . . what—forty-seven?"

"I don't remember."

"Oh, right." Dawn wanted to hear that her mother really didn't care so much about the youth and beauty part of being a vamp. She wanted to know that the devastation she'd seen on Eva's face in the screening room had been only a reflection from the film, not reality.

"Dawn, I don't want to talk about this."

"Too bad, because I know you've considered every angle of being a vampire. I know you've analyzed what would happen to you if your master died when Limpet visits."

Eva turned, her blond hair blowing from the tunnel's wind. "We don't talk about that, Dawn. You shouldn't, either."

"Would it be so bad if you went human again?"

Her mother got a look that made the skin prickle.

"So it's that bad of a thing to be human," Dawn said.

"No, it's that good of a thing to be long-lived." Bit by bit, Eva collected her poise: first in her posture, then in her expression. "I know you understand what I'm saying. It's in the way you gazed at Jesse. Except, you don't want to desire what we have, so you try to hate us."

The urge to lash out was overwhelming, but Dawn resisted. "You're full of yourself."

"I'm being honest. If you'd think rationally, you'd realize that you could be just like me."

A wave of yearning hit Dawn, so powerful that it felt like her body was winding through itself, traveling paths she didn't want to explore.

Or did she want to? What would it be like to mirror Eva Claremont, to have everything she had?

The possibility knotted Dawn up. She'd tried to tell herself so many times that she liked being her everyday average self, that she didn't want anything to do with her mother. But what if . . . ?

In a last-ditch effort to hold on to her sanity, Dawn struck back, sudden tears edging her words. "It was never about giving your family a better life in the long run. You're down here because of what *you* need, and that's why you'll always serve your master, first and foremost."

Eva reared back and slapped her daughter.

Dawn bashed against the wall, smacking her head and seeing stardust. As a moan escaped her, Eva darted over, holding a hand to her daughter's head. The pain subsided like a wave drawing back from a shore, leaving froth behind.

She nudged her mother away. Eva had done some vamp healing, but Dawn could hardly be grateful for it, seeing as the other woman had caused the damage in the first place.

"I'm sorry," her mother said, one hand fluttering up to her chest. "I'm so—"

Someone cleared his throat.

Both Dawn and Eva straightened up at the sight of a severely handsome vampire. He had straight brown hair that came to just below his wide shoulders and wore all black, including a voluminous coat that undulated in the slight wind.

"More problems, Eva?" he asked in a refined voice. An accent—stronger than Costin's or the Master's—made his tone crisp and officious.

"This doesn't concern you, Sorin," Eva volleyed back.

His mouth formed something like a smile, but it didn't exactly encourage any sparkly thoughts from Dawn.

"I beg to differ," he said, "because the Master has been attempting to contact you, and he sent me to search you out. Your mind is closed to him . . . again."

Even Dawn could interpret this as a bad turn of events, especially after Eva had confided that she'd been keeping the Master in the dark about so many things.

With a defiant glare at Sorin, Eva walked a couple of steps away from Dawn, quiet, clearly getting into that Awareness groove with her master.

This left the male vampire to give Dawn the once-over. She did the same right back. He remained expressionless.

Their standoff was interrupted by Eva saying, "Oh, Benedikte."

When Dawn glanced at her, she found her mother wearing an expression a person might adapt if they disapproved of something a friend was doing but didn't have the power to stop them.

But in the next moment, she was moving in the direction of the Underground. "Let's go," she said to Dawn. "Benedikte says he has something you'll be interested to see."

Even though Dawn was still smarting from Eva's well-deserved slap, she decided to get far away from Sorin, too.

The male vampire's voice rang from behind them. "Eva?"

They both turned to see him running his hand over the control panel. A grumble of rock sliding closed made Sorin's glare even eerier. She'd neglected to shut the entrance.

"Thank you," Eva said coolly. "I suppose I'll have to try to find Frank by connecting with him another time."

"I suppose you will."

This *had* to be the guy whom Eva suspected of bugging her chambers. He was a mean-looking lug.

As they left, Dawn noticed that Eva was walking a little too casually to fool anyone.

When they were well away, her mother whispered, "Sorin is the second-in-command. Don't be intimidated. And Dawn?"

Her daughter continued going right past her, but Eva cut her off at the pass.

"The Master wants you alone this time," her mother whispered, "so if he doesn't behave, just call my name. I mean it."

Whoa. So suddenly Eva didn't think Benedikte would be such a good boy? What was up with this? What had the Master told her during their latest Awareness connection?

As they both headed back, Dawn thrust her mother's strange offer to the back of her mind.

Where she stored all the junk she didn't want to sort through.

After a subdued Eva left her daughter at the door to Dawn's fugly chambers, Dawn knocked, thinking she would just get this meeting over with. Afterward, she could go back to the tunnel exit to see if she could figure out how to open that wall panel herself. Not that she would probably manage to do it without getting caught by Eva or scary Sorin. But how could her mother have shown her an exit without expecting Dawn to take advantage?

Just another thing to mull over. Maybe Eva was being as cocky as she'd been with storing the machetes in the open.

She opened the door by touching the wall where Eva had done the same earlier. Then she walked in.

A trickling from the fountain in the corner hinted at a peace she wasn't feeling while she took a few more steps. The peacock feathers decorating the walls and sticking out of glass vases trembled in a breeze from an overhead fan.

"Hey, Bene?" she yelled.

Something . . . someone stirred from behind the veiling that draped her sunken bed.

And out stepped the last person she expected to see. Her heart seized.

Matt Lonigan, dressed in his new denims and his untucked khaki shirt, kicked at a bedpost with his boot. He shrugged, as if resigned and somewhat amused by his situation.

"Here I am. You get what you ask for, I suppose."

Astonished, she couldn't move. She thought she saw profound

disappointment heft a weight onto his shoulders when she didn't run right into his arms.

He thunked down to the bed, where he came to rest his forearms on his knees. "After Eva took you, I went outside and . . . There they were. I don't remember much after that."

Dawn blew out a breath, coming to her senses. Matt was the only person she could depend on, so his presence should've uplifted her. But it didn't because, now, *he* could be in real danger down here.

Speaking of which, where was the possessive Benedikte? Was he leaving her and Matt alone as a weird peace offering?

Or was he watching to see if she took some kind of unexplained bait?

First things first. She went to Matt's side, her bandaged knees sinking into the silken mattress. "You okay?"

Now he was all aglow. "Yeah, they didn't touch a hair on my head. I have no idea what's going on, though."

Tentatively, she reached out to finger a brown bunch of strands. "If they'd hurt you—"

Without warning, he captured her hand in both of his, pressing it to his forehead and closing his eyes. "Dawn," he whispered.

His intensity stunned her, shooting her through with a slow warmth. Matt—the only person around here who really cared. Her pulse started hammering, pelting away at her veins as if to smooth out all the hard feelings she harbored for the rest of the world.

"How've they been treating you?" His lips brushed against the sensitive underside of her arm.

You getting this, Costin? You see how I can still feel?

"Aside from hanging around with a psychotic mother and being gaped at by her freak master?" Dawn laid her free hand over Matt's arm out of instinct. "I'm fine."

His head had shot up, blue eyes wide and full of . . . anguish? What had she said to cause that?

But just as quickly as the emotion had come, it was gone.

"I've had better nights," she added, still scanning him, "but considering everything . . ." She shook her head. "Okay, aside from meeting Jesse Shane, I can't say it's been great."

"Jesse Shane." His tone seemed forced.

"Yeah, he's one of the undead movie stars, but," she continued, going for some levity, wanting to make him smile again, "don't be jealous. He's only a vamp."

Just as a grace note, Dawn ran a hand over Matt's cheek.

That was when his gaze seemed to get even bluer, deepening and heating.

"Matt?"

His breathing quickened.

A gasp fought its way out of Dawn's chest, but before it could escape, Matt swung her to her back, knocking the air out of her. He pushed her hands over her head, straddling her hips with more aggression than he'd ever shown, his eyes narrowed so that she couldn't really see them.

In her mental chaos, Dawn's body responded, her sex nudging to a hard ache. She wanted this kind of anger, wanted to take it inside and mold the heat into the tight ball that was already burning in the pit of her belly. She didn't care if the Master was watching from behind some hole in the wall, didn't care if anyone was.

See, Costin? Do you see me?

"You're all I can think of," Matt said, tightening his grip on her wrists. "Not being able to be around you . . . You don't know what it's . . ." He choked off.

His bulk made her feel as insignificant as she deserved and, as he hovered over her, she fed off of his feral longing.

"You really missed me?" she asked, breathless.

With a strangled moan, he moved back on his haunches, then leaned back his head. His posture imitated an animal ready to cry out. But when he caught sight of himself in the mirror above the bed, he stiffened, gaze locked to his reflection.

He stared, face wracked with something like devastation caused by what he was witnessing.

"Matt?" she said.

Whatever it was that'd been holding him back seemed to break loose at the sound of her saying his name. He bolted forward, buried a hand in her loose hair, and fisted it until she winced. Then he crushed his mouth to hers in a hard kiss.

That was all Dawn needed.

As they bit at each other, sucking and fighting for dominance, she imagined what they looked like in the mirrors above and surrounding the bed. Two foes fighting, meeting on a primitive field where they would draw blood.

Costin, she thought, *just watch me.*

Spurred on, she reached up to grab Matt's shirt, hauling him down and rolling him to his back. Now she was straddling him on hands and knees, her spine arched while the ends of her loose hair scratched his face.

"You've made me wait for you a long time," she said in a voice that was too raw to be her own. "You'll pay for that."

And for what he'd done when he tried to get her to wear that Eva-like dress.

Still on her knees, she slid down until her pussy skimmed over his arousal. She rubbed, the ridge of him skidding against her, separating her even through her jeans. She pressed harder, needing more.

He gave a small grunt, then reached up to flip her on her back again with a breath-stealing thud. She could tell she'd pushed him beyond endurance—no more gentleman Matt. He was all flesh and blood now, stripped of civility.

As he bent her legs and whisked off her boots and socks one foot at a time, she watched in the overhead mirror, her image a blur, almost unrecognizable.

Are you watching . . . ?

Dawn fumbled with her button snap and zipper, helping Matt to rip her jeans off. When they got to her panties, he hesitated, breathing raggedly.

"Damn it," Dawn said, taking the initiative and removing those, too.

For one odd moment, he averted his gaze from her bare skin, then locked eyes with her. Even in the wildness of his irises, she could see that he wanted all of her, not just an easy lay.

Oh, God, it was the last thing she needed to know. In rebellion, she sat up and began undoing Matt's fly.

"No," he ground out, sliding his hands behind her thighs.

By lifting Dawn, he urged her back to the mattress, bending her legs at the same time. The air caressed her sex, hot, wet. . . . She was ready for him to tear her apart.

When he bent to kiss the inside of her leg by the knee, he seemed so tender that Dawn couldn't watch. Pushing back from him, she flipped to her stomach.

"Do it," she said.

Once again, Matt paused. Then his hands made contact with the backs of her thighs, upward, over her ass.

She imagined a different pair of hands there: invisible, connected to a body that was only lived in part-time. Costin . . . Jonah . . . who . . . ?

She made a low sound of thwarted yearning, opening her legs.

A pair of very solid palms coasted downward, cupping the curves of her cheeks. Then Matt's thumbs slipped between her legs, separating her damp folds and delving in.

Dawn pushed her face into the mattress, biting, tasting the sheets. In her mind, she was in a different room, a different house.

Costin . . .

"Dawn," said Matt's voice.

She opened her eyes as he pressed her clit, massaging it until she gathered the sheets in her fists.

While Matt continued working her with one hand, he slipped his other palm below her hips, raising them. Then she felt him sink down between her thighs, nipping the sensitive inner flesh. His mouth was so warm and wet, so real.

He was quaking now.

She closed her eyes again, not wanting to picture what that meant, what emotion he might be investing while she felt empty.

Almost intuitively, she groaned in response to what he was doing to her. She'd be an actress for him. He couldn't know that she was imagining another man between her thighs, kissing her higher, higher. . . .

She thought she heard a swishing sound. Then more kisses—these cooler, like pinches, flickers of pain—took the place of Matt's mouth.

He traveled over her thigh, her ass, her waist, her back, up to her neck, and she pressed her face into the mattress even harder.

His breath came cool and heavy against her ear, and she remembered how he used to love to play with the blood-moon earring there. Her mind swam as she fought to imagine Matt—this was Matt, not anyone else—making her skin raise with goose bumps.

"Dawn . . ." he breathed, tickling her neck until her jugular pounded in time with her sex.

Then she felt it—a scratch like a razor, like—

She heaved in a gasp, pushing herself up and catching a hint of . . . another man besides Matt? . . . in a mirror next to the head of the bed. Her mind pushed out a bolt of confused shock, and the mirror cracked, fragmenting the image.

Whipping around, she heard the same strange sound, like the one the Elites made when they changed form, and just as it ended, she found Matt. He looked just as shocked as she was, except maybe he was thinking about the shattered mirror . . . or her sudden withdrawal.

Even though her body was one connected, brutal heartbeat, she closed her legs and covered herself. Then something shifted in her memories, creeping to the front of her skull like a thick, viscous flood. Something that'd been bothering her about the night Cassie had killed Breisi.

"You found the Vampire Killer?" Matt had said when she'd come to ask him if he would help her hunt down Eva. *"I saw what was on TV."*

Dawn's forehead throbbed. On the sly, Eva had told her that Cassie's attempted broadcast of Breisi's killing had *not* gone public.

No one could've said that they'd seen the Vampire Killer on TV. No one but an uninformed member of the Underground who didn't know that Eva had told Dawn the truth about the transmission plans.

Oh, God.

Dawn armed herself, forcing a casual smile that almost split her face in half. Meanwhile, she sought her clothing, trying not to fumble as adrenaline screeched at her to run. "I got carried away. We're Underground, maybe being watched. What a time to forget." *Acting!*

But her pulse was screeching.

Matt took a look at the mirror Dawn had mind broken, his breath coming fast and heavy. "I'd think that you, out of anyone, would . . ." He planted his hands on his hips as he remained kneeling.

She got dressed. "I don't want to be vamp entertainment. That's all."

"Okay." Matt knitted his eyebrows. "I can understand. Another time, another place . . . ?"

Her skin was crawling over her bones. "Right. Maybe when things are more settled."

He started to tremble again.

Fear struck a vibrating chord, resonating through her own limbs. "Don't be angry," she said.

"There doesn't seem to be any pleasing you." His voice had changed, warped by embarrassment or rejection or whatever he was feeling.

"Matt . . ."

Out of the blue, his body faded gracefully into another form. It happened so quickly and effortlessly that Dawn's brain didn't catch up to real time until it was too late.

Sitting on his knees before her was the form of Benedikte. *This* was what she'd caught in the mirror—

She gaped, jumped back, away from him, far, far away.

And her horror only grew when she took a better look at him. Only now, with his hair falling free and such a primal expression haunting his features, did she know where she'd seen this being before.

In the seer's dagger vision.

Benedikte was Costin's fierce soldier companion, minus the dirt, facial hair, and leather. He'd been there when Costin was bitten and made a vampire. They'd been friends, these two. They were the same. Very real monsters.

The creature held out his arms to Dawn, as Eva often did when she was pleading. "What do you want? Tell me. I can be whatever you desire."

As Dawn's skin dissolved into shivers, Benedikte's body warped into that of Jesse Shane's.

"This?" he asked.

Dawn choked on air.

"Or," he interjected, "this?"

He changed into Frank.

"Oh, God," she said, nausea coating her throat. "You sick fuck!"

"Show me an image of Jonah Limpet then," Benedikte said, crawling closer as he shifted back into Matt's form. "Give me an idea of what he looks like in a picture where he's not covering his face. I haven't found any, and he's such a recluse. . . ."

She couldn't think of how to get out of this—

If you need any help, just call my name, her mother had said.

"Eva," Dawn whispered.

But then she recalled the sting of her mother's slap.

Damn it, what else was there to do? What were her alternatives—

Picture, Benedikte had said. Jonah.

The option banged through her, knocking at her head. Picture . . . *pictures* . . . Friends . . .

"Breisi?" Dawn blurted out in a whisper. She would help— Breisi, the woman who'd always meant more to Dawn than Eva. "If the locator showed you where I might be, and you're looking for me nearby, I'm here. You can find me Underground here. *Find me.*"

"Matt" was cocking his head at her, as if trying to understand what she was saying and why she wouldn't accept him.

Then terror struck just as soon as she realized what kind of danger she'd put Breisi in by summoning her. Panicking, Dawn started to reverse the selfish request.

But then the door to the room flew open, and Dawn was cocooned in a warm, forgetful mist—Eva? *Eva?*—that clogged her mind, her body, until she found herself spat out into the night air, a minute, an eternity, later, landing on the concrete of a place she didn't recognize.

Until she looked up from her huddled position and found the Limpet house coming into focus above her.

Dawn pushed up from the cold ground, other details phasing into view. An empty swimming pool under moonlight, the pit strewn with leaves. Palm trees swaying in a fading night sky and crying in the wind.

"Eva?" she asked, just now realizing what had happened. Her mother had come to her, just as she'd promised.

But why? Why would she change her mind about leaving Dawn to the Master now . . . ?

Dawn turned to find Eva still in Danger Form, bobbing above the pool like a restless fog, her graceful arms reaching out.

An angel, Dawn thought. A guardian. And she'd dropped her daughter off in the same spot where she'd deposited Breisi after retrieving her dead body for proper burial.

"Remember this," her mother said. "Remember how much I love you."

As she lifted away, Dawn reached out, her throat contracting too much for her to get a word out.

All she wanted to finally say was that she'd always loved Eva, too.

NINETEEN

BELOW, TAKE FOUR

EVA'S vampire body was a part of the howling wind, a part of whatever made the night a fearful thing. She rode the air, telling herself that she could get back Underground before Benedikte realized what had happened.

But she knew she was living on fool's time.

The Master had seen her barge in and then encapsulate her daughter, as if cuddling Dawn back into the womb. He would have no doubts whatsoever this time that Eva had turned on him.

But she'd been aware of the possible consequences when she'd told Dawn to call her if Benedikte crossed any lines. She'd been prepared ever since slapping Dawn when her daughter had pointed out the harsh truth about why Eva had remained faithful to Benedikte.

Youth, beauty . . .

In the near distance, the Hollywood sign burned bright from the husk of a hillside. It shimmered in Eva's heightened vision as she flew closer. But upon a better look, she could tell it was composed of steel, dirtied and lifeless.

She put off going into the Underground, loitering around the sign and looking into the wavering lights of the city. Think, she needed to think. How was she going to explain everything to the Master *this* time?

How could she explain it to herself? One second, she was opening up the Underground for attack by setting Frank free to go back to Limpet, or showing Dawn an old quarry exit and then delivering her Above anyway. The next she was worried that her actions would end up bringing about her master's demise—and her own forgotten humanity. What was she *doing*?

Eva skimmed the edges of the sign, wishing it would cut into her, wishing something would jar her into a more certain reality. Was she the type of brave mother who would give up everything for her family? Or was she really the woman who'd sold her soul to stay beautiful?

She didn't know. She just didn't know, and she was going to pay for the indecision. And, no matter what Dawn said about her mother loving to be in control, Eva knew it was a facade.

But . . . Eva paused on top of the sign. She needed to get back. A show of unity with the Master would help, especially if she could persuade him that she was on his side after all. . . .

Go, she thought. Just *go*.

Before she could hesitate anymore, she shot toward an Underground old quarry entrance, the most remote opening she could think of, though it hadn't been so out of the way earlier when Sorin had caught her there with Dawn. Eva should've expected the second-in-command to be watching her like a gargoyle, but getting caught was nothing next to her need to know that Frank was secure, that he regretted leaving her and wanted to come back.

Had he gone to Limpet? Eva hadn't been lying to Dawn when she'd said that she truly didn't know much about the Underground's foe. She'd really been hoping her husband wouldn't return to the agency, too. Surely he'd have enough sense to just go back to being a vampire version of the Frank she used to be married to and forget about being this new hunter.

Right before the entrance, Eva stopped, building herself up for whatever the Master had in store for her. She would take his punishments; it would be worth her pains because, when the Master had contacted her that second time via Awareness near the quarry entrance, she'd sensed a real desperation in him.

I'll give Dawn what she wants this time, he'd said, nearly giddy with this fresh plan to win her daughter over.

And what's that? Eva had asked, warning bells going off at his tone, even though she couldn't pinpoint the reason yet.

Matt Lonigan. The Master's voice had risen. *She'll fall at his . . .* my *feet now. She'll do anything for me if I'm Matt.*

It was here that Eva had known that if this last-ditch effort to be accepted by Dawn wasn't successful, Benedikte would break. And, seeing as he had some pretty bipolar tendencies, she didn't want her daughter around him when that happened.

She'd seen his monstrous side before.

So she'd impulsively promised Dawn protection. Sure, she knew her daughter could handle a lot—look at what she'd done up until now—but this required more than chutzpah and fighting skills. This required a mother who knew better, a vampire who had retained an echo of humanity, even though it wasn't the real thing at all.

She hovered, her misty shape weaving in and out of itself, as if smoothing down a dress that she would wear in human form.

You're down here because of what you *need,* Dawn had told her, *and that's why you'll always serve your master, first and foremost.*

Her baby was right.

Trembling at the reminder—at the truth—Eva ran an outstretched limb along the wall, undoing the hidden lock.

She would earn the title of "mother." Taking Dawn away from

the Master had been only a start, and she didn't regret it, even though she was probably going to suffer now.

But that was part of being a parent. A real one.

Inside, Eva whirled back into human form, then calmly walked the tunnel while opening her senses to Benedikte so she could go to him.

What I purchased with my soul isn't worth losing Dawn and Frank over, she told herself. And when she arrived at the Master's hidden quarters, she fortified herself with the mantra, arming herself with its abstract, rhythmic comfort.

Even though it was something she would never be able to see in a mirror.

O ПE of the Master's corked soul vials fell from its box on the shelves and hit the rug as he fumbled amongst his collection, searching out a panacca.

But which of his prizes could take the place of Dawn?

Of Eva?

He sobbed, and his form blackened to almost nothing in its nobody-nebulous shape. His outline fizzed with the color of a graying corpse, but inside, he was dark. Closed.

"Master," Sorin said for at least the hundredth time. "You must concentrate on the positives."

Positives?

Ah, yes. An Elite had reported within the last few minutes that they'd caught a curious Limpet spirit Underground and had captivated it in a container much like one of the Master's vials and stowed it in a closet with the others. And, according to Sorin, Eva had played her final hand and exposed herself as a traitor. *Positive* news all around.

"Be rational," Sorin added.

There was fear in his second's voice, but Benedikte took no

interest in that. He continued knocking over vials, partly because he couldn't see well enough to know what he was doing. Instead, his vision was consumed with images of Eva breaking into Dawn's room and stealing his lover away from him. He kept replaying the numbness of watching his one-time favorite zoom Dawn out of the room, out of the Underground, out of his life.

He hadn't even conjured the will to assume his most dangerous form and go after Eva. She had betrayed him and he'd seen it with his own gaze. Nothing else mattered.

No, wait. The disgust on Dawn's face when he'd revealed his identity to her . . . ? *That* mattered.

Losing his strength, the Master grabbed at the boxes that housed the vials, grabbed at the shelving. The structure collapsed on his way down, spilling his collection, the vials rolling over the rug.

As he lay there staring at the ceiling, he felt just like that night in London, decades and decades ago, when he'd lost his first Underground.

Gone, he told himself. There's nothing left.

"Master." It was Sorin again—the one shining light during that first catastrophe. "Please do not sink into your melancholy. You cannot be in this state when Limpet comes."

Limpet. Coming. So what. The Underground had become a means to an end for Benedikte: a way to hold on to Eva. Dawn.

But now it was irrelevant.

"Master," Sorin repeated.

The outline around Benedikte's form fizzled, lacking animation.

His son came to stand over him. "I knew we should have reached into Dawn Madison's mind—rape or not—when she first came down here. Now we have no access to her again."

"I . . ." Benedikte sighed. "I wanted her to give willingly, and she *would* have, if . . ."

"Oh, Master." His son came to his knees beside Benedikte. "Ignoring the truth is not going to aid this situation."

"Don't try to rouse me with anger."

"I would give my soul for that to work. It would mean you have not lost the fire for battle."

He knew Sorin was right, but . . .

Benedikte reached for a vial. Next to him, he sensed his son growing excited, even in spite of his stalwart focus.

"You long for this?" The Master offered it to Sorin.

"No, I—" He cut himself off, rising to his feet and turning his back on his maker.

In the gloom of Benedikte's thoughts, one emerged forcefully. His son was growing into a Soul Taker, just like Benedikte. Could it be that Sorin's new yearning for this sustenance had inflamed the Guards' recent link with humanity, their cries for "hooome"? When Sorin maintained the sentries with his magic, did that transfer a desire for souls . . . *humanity?* . . . to the lower vampires who'd been unwillingly separated from it?

Although Sorin wasn't a parent to the Guards—Groupies were the ones who donated their bite—he kept the troops in line with his powers, and he had a connection with them. . . .

Sorin's voice came out strong now, as if he were fighting off the soul thirst. "I will allow you a moment to wallow in your grief, Master, but then we must face reality."

He would *allow* his maker a moment. Impudence. Benedikte wanted to get angry but couldn't.

"Eva's betrayal could not have been more obvious in the coming," Sorin continued. "Besides all my other suspicions, I found her with her daughter in an old quarry passage. She had opened the entrance, revealing it to Dawn. What if she were planning to gift Limpet with secret access for his attack, Master? Did it ever cross your mind that Dawn and Eva might be siding with the enemy?"

Benedikte dropped the vial. If he could become one with the ground, sinking into it and losing himself there, he would do it. Being a part of the soil sounded so natural right now. . . .

"Eva and that daughter of hers are your downfall," Sorin continued, turning around so that his words could prod at Benedikte's side like a spearhead seeking blood.

But then the Master sensed Eva nearby. She called to him through Awareness.

Master, she said, as if bowing before him in shame.

Normally, he would've melted at her tone, her very presence. But now . . . ? Nothing. There was nothing.

Enter, he thought.

Yet when she did, he couldn't lie to himself any longer. The smell of her hair lured him from the floor to his feet, and when she came to stand before him, his form wavered.

Eva, his love. His heartbreak.

Again, the mental vision of her whisking Dawn away from him stabbed, mutilated all the deep feelings he'd nursed. A spark lit within him, then died. But it left some heat.

She folded her hands in front of her, a knowing martyr. Sorin circled her like an inquisitor of old.

"Are you here to explain," his son said, "or to offer yet another excuse?"

"I'm here to talk to Benedikte and Benedikte only."

Sorin gave the Master a challenging look. *Will you permit this to continue?*

Another spark gasped to life within Benedikte, burning a little longer before extinguishing. *Do not say another word if you wish to remain in one piece, Sorin.*

Then he turned his attention to Eva. Even though he knew that his nobody form didn't show the details of a face, he bet that she could read him just as well. She lifted her chin, as if unwilling to apologize for what she'd done.

A third spark flared, eating Benedikte whole.

Before he knew it, he was inside her head, ripping through everything she'd been hiding from him. Colors of life, bleeding together, images screeching as they crashed together . . .

He saw Eva's duplicity the night Cassie Tomlinson had killed Breisi Montoya. Saw how she'd allowed Frank to escape. Saw how she'd been sharing information with Dawn and exposing the Underground for attack. Every lie. Every betrayal.

With a cutting jolt, he fell out of her thoughts, hitting the floor. It brought him to a quaking, smoldering rage.

"Eva," he cried. "Oh, Eva."

In the aftermath of his invasion, she dropped to her knees, her eyes taking on what they called the Ten-Mile Stare. He'd ravished her . . . the woman he loved. He'd done what he'd promised never to do—taken her against her will, and that destroyed him almost as much as seeing what she'd done.

"It was . . . worth it," she whispered, tears falling down her face. Her lips remained agape, as if she'd been stripped of everything: dignity, privacy, trust.

"Worth it?" the Master repeated.

Then something even more powerful switched on inside of him.

"No!" Sorin yelled, clearly anticipating what would happen next.

But Benedikte's rage had already exploded into a deeper danger: hatred. Hatred for himself, hatred for the world. He felt himself gathering every evil intention that laced the air, felt his form weigh with the nightmares of every child—adult or not—that haunted a night's bloodcurdling attempt to sleep. Expanding, turning, *becoming*, he was the monster under the bed, in the closet, in the cave.

In everyone.

Rising, rising, fangs elongating like curved blades, the abyss took to his very body.

He was terror. He was fear itself.

Benedikte reared back his head, then let out a screech that would shatter heaven if he were anywhere near it.

Then he sped to Eva, stopping just short of blasting against her. She'd gained power during her last infusion, but she would be no match for him. Or maybe she was only accepting what she deserved.

She closed her eyes so she wouldn't have to look into the thing above her and see all her worst thoughts. Then she bowed her head, opening her arms to welcome her reckoning.

Perversely pleased, the Master turned to Sorin, who was already looking away, eyes squeezed tightly shut against all the terrors he was seeing in the form of his father.

Wailing, Benedikte took off, out of control, banging from one side of the room to the other, chipping away rock from the walls, giving the Underground a demented heartbeat. But something on the other side of the room stopped him.

His ghastly, distorted image blurred over the reflection of a dead TV screen, and he screamed in utter horror at what he saw in himself: alienation, a stretched eternity of being alone and unloved.

With a yell of agony that shook the walls, he darted back to Eva, swiped at her with an ethereal claw. She flew in an arc, banging against the rock and crushing the surface of it to dust before slumping to the ground like a pile of discarded, flowered rags. There she remained, unmoving, her hair covering the face he'd so dearly loved.

Was she . . . gone?

A pulse of Awareness told him that she hadn't expired . . . not yet. Heal . . . ? How long would it take her to heal back to the woman he . . . ?

Hating his weakness in not being able to kill her—to kill his pain—the Master shrank back into his original, solid Benedikte body, weeping, stumbling forward until he fell over the top of his desk.

Sorin immediately came to his side. "Thank the day, Master! Finish her—it is the right thing, the only thing! And as for Dawn Madison . . . I see how mother and daughter sway you. They are lethal, and I would kill Dawn myself, truth be t—"

Benedikte punched his hand through Sorin's skull, yanking out his brains in one profane pull before taking his other hand and crush-popping his son's head from his spine.

Sorin's body plopped to the ground.

As blood and gray matter dripped to the tile, the Master stared at what he held.

"Sorin?" he whispered.

On the floor, his son's body bled out, his separated head a mash of unidentifiable red, spangled with shards of white. Then the whole of it disappeared, sucked into nothing.

Even Sorin's brain did the same. But Benedikte's fingers were still coated with blood, and he investigated them, trying to figure out what he'd just done.

"Son?" he asked.

He remembered Sorin's birth night, near the flames of a campfire. A beautiful sorcerer who had enthralled Benedikte with his magic. His blood had tasted of joy, as had his soul.

Then Benedikte remembered the child Tereza had borne him in life, the stiff, blue tragedy of a tiny body that had never even taken a breath.

The Master dropped to his knees, touching the bloodstains from his vampire progeny. Somewhere in this world, there were two vampire women—Sorin's missing preternatural daughters, his only children—who had just turned into wrinkled human old ladies, perhaps even in the midst of a sentence. That was how Benedikte's line worked, and that was how it should have gone with him and Sorin. The father was not meant to outlast the son, not in human life, not in a vampire's, either.

He cupped what was left of his child . . . the best part of him . . . in his palms, cradling his son's blood, looking up as if to ask why.

TWENTY

THE HOMECOMING

In the meantime, seconds after Eva had deposited Dawn by the Limpet house's pool, the back door banged open.

"Get in here—quick!" It was Kiko.

Dawn scrambled, rushing the entry that led to an old kitchen that'd been converted into a stainless-steel haven. It was dreary, curtains blocking the night from looking inside.

The psychic banged the door shut behind Dawn as she got to her knees and hugged him until he pounded at her back.

"Breathe—" he gasped.

Backing away, she still held his arms, taking a good look at him. Last time she'd seen Kiko he'd been passed out on a couch in that office. Now he seemed rested, but there was a hardness to him that went beyond a back brace.

"You okay?" she asked. "Did they—?"

"I'm fine. What's going on?"

Dawn shoved back the hair that had fallen into her face. Wait—before she started talking, there was something. . . .

Breisi. She'd called for Breisi in the Underground.

Hastily, Dawn whispered another command that would hopefully reverse the first, ill-advised summons, praying it wasn't too late. Then she ran out of the kitchen and through the dark halls, coming to the thick door that guarded the lab.

She pulled at it, wanting to go downstairs, to check Breisi's picture, to see if she was down there. "Breisi!"

Kiko caught up, panting. "Don't even try. Most of the Friends have been resting in their portraits, and this door's been locked from the inside, so I have no idea what she's been up to since double dicking me around. But Frank's around here somewhere, safely avoiding me."

Dawn spun around. "Frank?"

"Yeah." Kiko made a weird face. "Your dad? Remember him? He's got this big escape story—"

"I know, I know."

Before she could ask more, Kiko ran a gaze over her disheveled state. "So what the hell, Dawn?"

When she opened her mouth to ask *her* questions, her coworker said, "Na-uh, you tell me first."

She would work at getting the door open while she talked.

Dawn pulled at it some more. "Long story. The thimble version is that Eva took pity on me and got me out of the Underground, which I ended up in after Costin planted his metaphysical foot on my ass." Her head swam, catching up to what had just gone on. She hadn't even recovered from being with the Master yet and here she was trying to get to Breisi. Her perception was still a blindsided mash of surreal fragments, so she rested. Just for a minute. "Eva brought me back here, but I'm not sure I'll stay."

"You're not going back outside. There're Servants watching the house, and we've seen them in midskulk ever since Frank made a run for our door. Don't know if any Groupies or Guards have also been sent up here by now—"

"I think they're all Underground, ready for a fight."

"So what? *You're* staying in here, where none of them has any chance of getting to you. Now, come on, more details."

Dawn shook her head, still not sure if this was the place for her to be. "I appreciate the hospitality, but do you remember what happened? I got kicked out in a major fashion. And . . ." Abruptly, she reached into her back jeans pocket, then brought out the gutted remains of the locator. "I found this on me. Costin set me up to get tracked. He wasn't finding the Underground through meditation or research, so he sent me out there to be his bomb robot."

Kiko took the dead device from her. "Way earlier, after I woke up, Breisi told me about what they did to you. I told her it was wrong, then she got all quiet and went back to the lab. I don't think they care about what they've done, though."

Wiping a hand over her face, Dawn tried to reconcile herself with that. This agency, which had seemed like a savior when she'd first tried to find Frank, had turned out not to be friendly at all.

Speaking of Frank . . . Where was he?

As she went back to door pulling—*Breisi first*—she groaned in discomfort, her body sore from all it'd been through.

"I'm glad you're back," Kiko said.

Aw. "Me, too, Kik. Trouble is, am I in more danger with Costin and the Friends than I am out there?"

"I wish I could tell you, but I'm in your boat. When I woke up, the boss—*Costin*—had locked himself away again, and Breisi got back to work in the lab soon after that. Haven't seen her since and, as I said, I can't get down there. I wanna know what's happening, because from the looks of things, I'm not sure *who* we've been working for. But Breisi still trusts him. . . ." He must've remembered that he hadn't known his other coworker quite as well as he'd thought, either, what with Breisi having been privy to more of the boss's secrets than he'd suspected. "I tell you, I've always been pretty easy about not getting in everyone's business, but I'm thinking those days are gone."

She reached down to squeeze his hand in understanding, but he shrugged away, shoving his hands into the pockets of his cargo pants instead. "I'm just frustrated." His voice was thick. "The crazier things get, the more useless I am. If you were so 'key,' like my vision told me you'd be, why did Costin throw you out? Maybe I was wrong. Maybe my brain has been dying day by day and I'm either getting false vibes or nothing at all." He was talking about what the pain pills had done to his powers—wiped them clean whenever he was stoned.

"Kik—"

"I never even saw it coming—what happened today. Shouldn't the boss's real identity have been important enough for me to catch ahead of time?"

She'd witnessed her coworker go through some major highs and lows lately, but this was rock bottom. Kiko had always taken great pride in his talents. You could even say he was a cocky son of a gun. But to see him brought down like this . . . ?

"The team wouldn't have gotten anywhere without you," she said softly. "You've been indispensable."

"To who?" His eyes got glossy. "To the vamps? To whatever Costin is?"

Dawn shut her mouth, first of all because she had no idea what to say. Second of all because Kiko was inconsolable and there wasn't a thing she could do to change that. She'd never been good at being a friend, and it made her sick that she sucked at it now.

Minding her bruises and aches, she got back to heaving at the door. But Kiko wasn't done.

"Look at your jeans. Look at . . . you. Tell me the rest."

All right, as a friend who was trying real hard here, she'd tell Kik anything he wanted to—

"Dawn?" said a deep voice from behind her in the hallway.

She turned to find her dad framed by the entrance, one arm reaching out to her.

For the longest heartbeat, she got used to him again. His rawhide skin, creased around a mouth that used to love smiling and eyes that had only recently cleared of a reddish drinking haze. His dark hair worn proudly in receding scruffiness. His bodyguard build accessorized with a dark T-shirt and jeans.

Frank didn't look like a vampire—not now anyway.

Wearily, Dawn walked over to him, then rested her cheek against his big chest as he enfolded her. She didn't say anything for a while, just allowed him to be a pillar until she needed to stand on her own again.

So what if there was a slight possibility that he and Eva had cooked something up and he was here only to mess with Limpet? Yeah, she'd considered it. But she didn't want to deal right now. She just wanted to be with Dad.

Finally, Dawn backed away, pushing her hair from her face. "Jonah gave you permission to be in the house, huh?"

Frank jerked, as if a dart had gone astray in a bar and nailed him in the chest. "Go ahead then. Give me hell."

"That's the last thing I want to do."

After assessing her with a cryptic gaze, he sighed. "So why did I let Eva turn me? It's easy. I was so surprised to see her that first night. Day after day, giving in to her seemed real natural, like a reunion. You came right after that, and I realized just what I'd done."

"I suppose if I told you that her death would make you human again, you wouldn't celebrate?"

A harsh glance from her dad answered that. But a perplexed afterglow went right back to confusing everything.

Kiko took to Dawn's side. "I told Frank that if he has anything Underground up his sleeve, the boss is gonna know. We're waiting until Costin comes out again to find out."

"You trust *him*?" Dawn asked.

"Ah." Kiko kicked at the floor. "Who knows?"

Frank swept a concerned gaze over Dawn. "Kiko told me about what happened today. I knew our boss was hiding things, but . . . He's got a lot to answer for."

"Until Costin decides to show himself," Dawn said, "we aren't getting much from him."

"Not true." Kiko gestured toward Frank, obviously intending to launch a few questions on this front. "These vamp powers of yours . . . What are you? An Elite? A Groupie?"

"Can't you touch me and find out, Kik?" Frank asked.

Before Kiko could decide to be pissed, Dawn answered. "He doesn't get vamp readings. Something about you not having a soul anymore." She tried not to acknowledge what that really meant for her dad. God. "Eva told me that you're somewhere in between the two vamp levels. Is that right?"

"I guess." Frank paused. "When I got here, it wasn't hard to out-speed the Servants staking out the house. Same with the lowly vamps who hadn't started snoozing yet when I left the Underground—they didn't even see me go. I couldn't function well in the sunlight, though. It drove me into an abandoned gas station, where I rested in a closet before night came."

"So, all in all, would you call yourself a 'good' vampire?" Dawn asked, recalling how Kiko had mentioned way at the beginning, on that night they'd first gone to Robby Pennybaker's, that some fang-pies could be helpful. That was why the team always had to be careful about attacking a new one.

"I swear on your life," Frank said, his gaze earnest, "that I'm here to help, Dawn."

A crusader, she thought. Costin had once said that this was what Frank had become, and she hadn't believed it until now.

But they would find out if that was true when Costin finally deigned to emerge. Would he even have time for them? Or would he kick Dawn out again, then march off to war?

After spending hours cursing him and growing back some strength, she was ready for whatever happened, especially since she was now armed with the info about "Matt"'s real identity that Costin would want. If she decided he was good for it.

"Strange," she said to Frank, "but Kiko and I tried to get some vibes on you through touch, so we could find where you were being kept." She pointed to the tank she was wearing. "It used to work, but not this time. Not since Eva took you again. I guess we got readings from your shirts when you were human. When you had a soul."

Frank looked ill. "Besides that, when she kidnapped me . . . Breisi was dead—that's what I thought. I wasn't doing much caring anyway."

At the mention of Breisi, Dawn's face went hot, her palms clammy. She had to tell them what she'd done.

"Listen, some shit went down Underground and I . . ." Damn it, she'd been so stupid. "I called Breisi to help me. I didn't think of—"

Frank took a menacing step forward. "You did what?"

"I've already commanded her to get back here. I know—it was selfish and it was idiotic, but I was kind of in shock." Yeah, with the Master—not Matt—kneeling in front of her. Still, it was no excuse.

Frank zoomed to the locked lab door and began pummeling it with his fists. The heavy wood quaked, splinters crunching away from the door. Vamp strength.

"Dad!" Dawn tried to pull him back, but he'd always been as strong as a bull, even as a human.

He was breathing heavily, and when he turned to them, his eyes held a sheen of silver. Both her and Kiko stepped back.

Then Frank let out a bellow. "Cooooosssstiiiin!!!"

His ire shook the air, but there was only silence in the aftermath.

Moaning, Frank turned back to the door, giving it one last epic pound. Dawn went to him, vampire or not, and held his arm.

"I'm sorry," she said. "If I could do anything, I—"

"Don't make promises like that," Kiko said. "You just came from the Underground, and from the looks of it, you *escaped*. Maybe you need to be telling *us* everything."

So she did: she told about almost running Eva over in the car; about going to Matt's house, then being tricked by her mother into coming Underground. Editing out the more personal parts, she re-layed details about how the vamps were training to fight down there, then about finding the locator on her jeans. She was just getting to the hardest part—about "Matt" actually being the Master—when Kiko spoke up.

"Just whose side is Eva on?"

During all this, Frank had slid to the ground, his back against the wall. "She's on her own side, Kiko." His eyes still held a wisp of silver over the green. "Dawn, the Master didn't find out what Eva's been up to?"

"No, not yet." She paused, trying to gauge her father's emotions about his wife. "But Eva did tell me that she let you escape the Underground. She wanted you to leave because she thought you'd decide to come back to her in the end and that would signify your change of attitude and heart toward her."

"Damned woman," Frank said, putting his hands over his face. Exhaustion? Or didn't he want them to see that he still cared?

"Seriously," Dawn said, sinking to the ground next to him. "I can't tell what to make of her, either, most times."

She thought of how her emotions had surged after Eva had dropped her outside by the pool, how Dawn had only wanted to finally tell her mother that she loved her.

"I want," Frank said between his fingers, "to charge Underground and get Eva out of there, even if we don't have a marriage anymore."

Dawn glanced at him hard. From what she'd seen of Frank and Eva, they definitely still had a connection, even if he'd moved on with Breisi more recently. It'd been obvious when Eva had kept them both captive that his feelings for his wife hadn't died, even though *she* had.

But now that Breisi was a ghost . . . ? Man, love was complicated. Dawn hated it.

Frank slid his fingers down his face, leaving pink trails from the pressure. "But," he added, "the other part of me needs to see even more if they're holding Breisi Underground."

None of them commented. The Elites had learned to captivate Friends, and if Breisi had made it Underground, she might very well be a goner.

Frank hit the wall behind him. "Where's Costin?"

A terrible thought slapped Dawn. Wouldn't Breisi have come upstairs to greet Frank no matter what was going on? Then again, Breisi was incredibly focused, and Dawn wouldn't put it past her to keep right on working and put off a reunion. . . .

No. Hell no. Breisi had *died* the other night, and she would be up here with Frank.

Shit. Shit, Dawn had really done it.

"Costin!" Frank yelled. No answer.

Kiko sighed. "He ain't gonna hear you unless he's ready to come out of his voodoo funk."

Driven by fear and anger at herself, Dawn stood, paced. They needed to go. But where? How? What could they initiate?

"Costin!" Frank yelled again.

Dawn followed up. "Costin, get out here!"

Oooh, she wanted to see him. Wanted to—

The host's voice screwed out of the walls. At least that was what it sounded like. There were speakers all over this house.

"Welcome back to you both," Costin said simply.

They all looked at one another, not knowing what to say now that they had the . . . creature . . . on the line. Frank got to his feet.

"Welcome back?" Even Dawn's skin was vibrating now. "That's all you have to say?"

"I assume you found the locator." He sounded so smooth. "We received a partial read on your position before we lost the link, and Breisi followed the lead."

She remembered first discovering the locator in "Eva's house" when she'd actually been Underground. Then she'd destroyed the thing.

"Your plan to use me to find the Underground didn't go as you'd hoped?" she asked, fury straining her tone. "I messed it up pretty good for you, I guess."

"Actually, minutes ago, we found the Underground's location."
Silence again.

Then Kiko wandered away from the splintered door. "How did you manage that?"

The Voice paused. "Breisi was called there, and when she arrived, her escort left her at the entrance and returned here to report the location. Breisi continued inside . . . then went dark."

"Fuck." Dawn clamped her arms over her head, as if she could shield herself. "Fuck me."

Frank merely closed his eyes, probably too wiped out to do anything else.

"We need to get her," Kiko said. "Or is she another casualty of your war, *Costin*?"

"I understand your anger, Kiko. And I have been willing to endure it from you and Dawn since we began. But please believe me when I tell you that Breisi will be taken care of."

"How're you going to guarantee that?" Dawn whispered.

"Just hear me. We are burning the daylight I require—when the lower vampires' powers are at an ebb. I do not need them interfering with my business Underground."

"Costin." The name was a low rumble from Frank, but it threatened to build into so much more.

Then the lab door moaned open.

"I'm ready for you now," Costin said.

TWENTY-ONE

The Confessional

Kiko was the first one down the stairs to the lab, and when Dawn followed him, she thought she caught her coworker putting his hand over his mouth, as if slapping a pill inside.

But maybe her eyes were playing tricks on her again.

She heard Frank in back of her, walking like . . . Well, the undead. *Plod, plod, plod.* The skin on her nape rippled with the hateful, justified gaze he was probably staring into it.

The soulless electric hum from the steel fridge sawed right through to her bones as they entered the lab proper. An acrid smell stifled the atmosphere, something chemical and new. Among the equipment, bedroom furniture, and the nightstand clock with its arms angled just on the cusp of the sunrise hour, Dawn looked to the far wall, as if not believing what Costin had said about Breisi really being gone.

But her portrait was empty, and there wasn't a trace of jasmine anywhere.

I'm going to hell, Dawn thought.

Costin's voice edged out from the darkness adjacent to Breisi's old bed. "Sit, please."

No argument. Dawn, Kiko, and Frank all dragged metal-framed chairs near one another, like they were huddling together without wanting to admit it.

When she peered into the darkness, she thought she saw the flash of Costin's topaz eyes. She'd been anticipating the moment she would see the monster again. And, this time, she was going to beat him.

But, strangely, she couldn't summon much outraged energy. There was only a deep gash of sadness in the pit of her stomach that wouldn't stop bleeding.

"We're sitting," Kiko snapped, obviously still in the pissed stage.

From out of the blackness, the topaz eyes gleamed stronger, as if Costin had ventured closer. "Thank you. For your cooperation, for your loyalty—"

"For our stupidity," Kiko interrupted.

"Wait," Frank said, barely fitting on his little chair. "Let the boss talk. I got to hear why we're just sitting here while Breisi's in the Underground."

"She will be fine, Frank," Costin said with more confidence than all his team probably had, put together. "Until then, I wish to . . . clear the air and make my peace."

Now Dawn understood. His earlier actions, as terrible as they were, hadn't been personal. He was a warrior going into battle, a knight seeking absolution. "Is this your attempt at a confessional? Now . . . after keeping everything from us?"

"You could call it that." His low voice almost sounded too slow, like a man on his last leg of a journey, crawling home.

Fear pricked her. She didn't know if she could take what was about to come. All this time searching for answers, and she was afraid of them.

Kiko let out an exasperated sigh. "Too little, too late. Do you remember what you did to Dawn earlier?"

"Very much so. And before I go, I would like to make amends . . . as much as I can, at least."

"Good luck," Kiko said. Was he slurring a little? No—he hadn't taken a pill that long ago, if that was really what he'd been doing.

"If you wanted me to find the Underground," Dawn said, "you should've trusted me to do it myself. You didn't need to tag me with a locator and . . ."

The memory of his cruelty assaulted her, and she couldn't go on.

"Had you not been turned away from where you felt safe, you might not have embraced the Underground, Dawn," Costin said, clearly having eavesdropped on what she'd already told Kiko and Frank. "It shames me, what was necessary. Yet it was most effective in the end."

"Then you don't regret it."

"I cannot."

Frank stared straight ahead, the former bar bouncer taking it all in. Kiko looked mutinous. Dawn toughened herself up, knowing Costin was never going to fully apologize.

And she wasn't going to arm him with any of the information she'd discovered about the Master. She still had no idea what Costin was about.

Yet . . . *was* that the right thing to do? Weird, but knowing more about the Underground vampires than she did about Costin made it hard to decide who she should be helping here.

In the darkness, Costin's eyes grew even brighter as he came to the edge of the light. "I do not expect you to forgive me for what I have done. Just know that, when I leave this house, I will be fighting for a prize that is much more serious than you can imagine."

"More serious than 'saving the world'?" Dawn asked.

"Not in the big picture." Costin blinked. "But it means everything to *me*."

Dawn narrowed her eyes. "Is your prize this Underground? Are you going to add that to a collection, just like the Friend portraits or your war artifacts?"

It was vicious, but there was no punch behind her bluster.

"No, Dawn," Costin said, stepping into the room, light bathing his scars. "I will be fighting to win back my soul."

And, as he began to tell his story, the phrases wrapped around her like gauze, a thin veiling that covered while letting in a hint of illumination. His words separated her from Frank and Kiko until she wasn't sure they even existed or were hearing the same thing she was.

His sentences took root in her; his voice becoming image; his life becoming hers. . . .

WHENEVER Costin slept, he dreamed of fire.

It consumed him, replacing the soul he had forfeited for the promise of glory, of long-lasting life serving his sovereign. His dreams were lit by hell, tortured by the screams of the forsaken.

But as of late, when he awoke, it was always to darkness.

Eyes blasting open, Costin sucked in the fetid air of the pitch cell, his hands clawing dirt. A shrill cry echoed from somewhere—another prisoner in a far cell?—and he tried to sit up, to sustain himself against the stone wall.

Soon, his heightened vision parted the blackness around him, thanks also to an irregular spot on a wall where the stones had fallen to ruin. It allowed a gush of dull light—enough to make the young vampire cringe out of its path due to practice.

Fury welled within Costin, as natural as the blood he sucked from the rats that dared brave the corners of his cell.

As if summoned, the persistent scratch of little feet on dirt stirred his senses. Costin sniffed, then darted out a hand to grasp his meal. At the scent of blood beneath skin and fur, the change came upon him, his teeth lengthening, his form tingling as he pierced the rat's hide, then drank.

Blood. Not enough to increase his strength to where it had been before, but enough to mock his cravings and keep him alive. If that was how one could describe Costin's state.

The taste of it conjured memory: the crazed yells of a night battle. Cries of death from the foe, cries of joy from Costin and his fellow warriors as they tore out necks with their teeth and grew stronger with each swallow. After taking the blood vow, Costin had indeed followed his sovereign on their journey to eternity, yet . . .

He hurled the rat against the wall, its bones shattering as they hit stone. Horror consumed him as he dwelled upon what he was, what he had become.

Even though there had only been one battle for Costin, he was still accursed. He had been given over to the darkness of a cell, all but forgotten, yet he remained damned.

Just before he had been put here, he had joined his sovereign in defending against the sultan's invasion of their land, killing his first man in the brutal style of a low creature. Amidst the moonlit chaos, the thunder of cannons, many of his companion soldiers had been doing the same, all like starving wolves let out of cages to feast.

Yet Costin's enjoyment of his kill had been short-lived.

It was all so clear: his victim's throat constricting as he attempted to scream. Costin lifting his head from the feeding and seeing how his prey's dark eyes accused him of being the very devil himself.

Beast, he had thought at that moment, backing away from his victim on hands and knees. *I am not . . . human. Not anymore.*

Horror had pushed him away from the battle, that and the still-lingering taste in his mouth. His long teeth had contracted, his will draining from his beast body.

Not human . . .

Time blurred. He found himself wandering in a marsh, sinking to the ground as if being sucked into it by a higher grief. In his ears he still heard the far battle, the screams. In his eyes, he still saw his victim's gaze . . . the beast reflected back at him. . . .

Before the light of day, Costin heard the thud of horse hooves on earth, and he attempted to raise his head. Yet the men—underlings of a noble who sided with the infidels—were upon him before Costin arose. When they stabbed him, he merely laughed. They watched in fascination as he began to heal.

Enthralled, they brought him to their superior's castle, where Costin found himself in this dark cell, where, upon occasion, he heard men outside, attempting to summon the courage to enter and test him again.

He found himself too weak to escape, possibly due to the lack of the good blood his body craved. Or perhaps they had used a curse he was unaware of to keep him here.

Or, perhaps, he was not moved to return to what he was.

Nevertheless, Costin often used his Awareness to call out to Benedikte, but not to his sovereign. Yet it did no good. Perhaps his companion had been instructed not to answer due to Costin's betrayal of the brotherhood. Perhaps Costin was even too weak to send a proper message.

He let out a tormented moan, his body heavy.

"Despair not," came a thready voice from the next cell.

Costin glanced at the lone opening high in the wall. "Sleep more, old man. I will not suffer you this night."

That was not true. The self-proclaimed "raving man" who was kept next to Costin could be quite diverting to a beast who did not wish to think too much.

"First I am tucked away here because I trouble those who have the loudest voices," the old man said. "Yet, now, with you, I am nothing."

The old man, or The Whisper, as Costin had come to call him, claimed to be so ancient that he had forgotten his own name. He also said he had been driven out of a village and held here because no one knew what else to do with him. He refused to tell Costin the particulars of his imprisonment—Why? How? When?—other than to announce that he was on a quest.

If Costin was not a beast, himself, he would fear for The Whisper's health of mind.

"You are hardly 'nothing,' old man," he said. "You are the only reminder that I am not in the true void."

"Oh, my friend, but you are. You very much are."

Through conversation after conversation—For how long? How many nights?—the old man had somehow sensed that Costin was not pure. In fact, The Whisper had attempted religious counsel, which felt to Costin like hot pokers shoved beneath his skin. Perhaps this was the reason Costin dreamed of hell: listening to tales from the old man seemed to conjure fire.

Tonight was no different.

"Once," The Whisper said, "you could tell the void from the light, Costin. Once, you possessed a soul."

"Another attempt to convert me, is this what I must endure?" There was no rancor in his tone. There was actually the hue of a plea.

"You abhor what you have become. Do not deny it."

Costin stood, legs so weak that he stumbled toward the wall with the missing stone and slid until he was sitting. "There is naught to do. This is how I live; this is how I last."

The Whisper came closer, as if he were at the wall, as well, reflecting Costin's position: hand to hand with stone as the only thing separating them.

"What if this raving old man told you," he said, "that he could offer redemption?"

Where the word should have caused agony, now it brought odd comfort. Costin looked to the faint light of the hole. "There is none of that for me. Or have you forgotten?"

"You are a soldier, ripe for the fight." He paused, as if deciding a definite fact. "It is time."

Before Costin could grasp what was happening, a breeze whispered through the hole in the wall, whistling down to circle his head. Terror bolted through him, and he cowered, arms barring his face.

"Harm is not my intent," The Whisper said.

"What do you wish of me?"

"No, Costin, what do *you* wish? The answer is not impossible to guess."

What did he desire? Blood? Costin instinctively choked. No, no. If he could have anything, anything at all, he would take back the moment he had become a beast.

"Yes," said The Whisper. "It is yours."

"My soul?"

The breeze soothed around Costin's head, as if it had become the hands born to cradle him.

"Costin, your fight begins here. Yet, to win your soul, there would be conditions."

He could not believe this. Was he in a fever dream?

The breeze rested on Costin's shoulders. "This brotherhood you are joined with in blood . . . *Every* creature who took part in the ritual must be hunted down and destroyed."

"Every . . . one." His brothers.

"Especially the one who birthed you. The dragon. The wily creature who struck a deal with the devil himself."

Costin's thoughts were still far behind this talk of his maker.

His brothers. Benedikte. They had all become something not of this world, not human. None of them had the soul that Costin might take back if he . . .

He willed himself to wake up. But there was no flash of fire in this dream. This was very real.

"If they all should die by my hand," Costin whispered, testing, "would I be human again?"

"No, it is too late for that. When every last creature is vanquished, you will be granted a true and peaceful death, your soul whole and finally yours. You will not face fire if you succeed. However, there is a boundary to this hunt."

A boundary? Costin's mind was tattered.

The old man continued, as if offering terms such as these every night. "Someday, the dragon will sleep for years and years after he commands your brothers to create societies where they will build in

number and power. Then the dragon will rise to dominate humanity just as he sought to in life. You, Costin, must destroy the dragon
before this later rising."

Yes, this was only a dream, after all. It could not be true in any
shape or form. Yet Costin found himself carried along with the
madness. He had nothing else.

"Who are you?" he asked.

"That is not a question that matters."

What mattered was that Costin was a creature being offered
back his soul, and there was something like a spirit in the room doing the deed.

"How long would I have, old man?"

"Centuries." The Whisper sounded pleased that Costin was not
denying him. "And though that sounds sufficient, it might not be.
Winning back a soul that was willingly cast into darkness is a terrible matter, Costin. This might be all but impossible."

"And if I fail?"

"Your soul will be forfeit to the place you cursed it to. For eternity."

He would dream—*feel*—fire forever.

Images of his teeth slashing through skin, breaking through the
bone that mixed with the blood he wished to consume . . .

"What else?" Costin asked. "What else must I do?"

For the next few hours, The Whisper laid out the rest with the
care of a battle well planned. Costin put aside any thoughts of madness, and he found himself believing. Completely, desperately believing.

Costin would be a "traveler," The Whisper explained. A traveler
just as The Whisper itself was. He must leave his vampiric body behind, because their captors would never unleash a beast like Costin
from its cell, so he would have to discover another way out to begin
this quest—a quiet way.

"This requires," the old man said, "you to be loaned your own
soul so that you might use it in another body since you will never

see this old one again. Yet do not think that this soul is yours just yet."

And there were rules for "traveling," Costin discovered. So many rules. Still . . .

"I accept," he said, out of need, pure and all-consuming.

With the words, his abandoned soul awakened from the flame-ridden prison it had been in. It rushed and joined with his thoughts to cleanse him out of this sin-ridden body, like water through a bloodied valley.

Reborn.

He left that other deadened body behind. Then he flew, flew around the cell unrestrained, in joy, consciousness rejoined with his true spirit. He slipped through the hole in the wall, then arrowed down to the body of the old man who had been deserted by The Whisper traveler and was sitting against the stone with his arms spread open to welcome his new traveler.

With a shattering crash, Costin took refuge, blackness exploding as his soul expanded to fit its new body, pushing the old man's own being down as a fellow companion in this new crusade.

Then Costin opened his eyes to the dark of the old man's cell and held his hands to his withered, tear-stained face—

DAWN came to reality at the same time Kiko and Frank did. They found Costin facing them, arms resting on his thighs as he sat in a chair. He was fixated on Dawn in particular, scars angry, eyes golden.

His intensity didn't do anything to make everything she'd seen co-alesce into rational thought, into a firm opinion of what she should think about him now.

"Years later," he continued, just as if he'd always been narrating in this way to them, "the old man—*I*—was released from our prison. There was no explanation as to why we were being set free, but the castle had changed hands, so I suspect that was a reason. At any rate, the dragon was said to have died, but I knew better. I found my dagger, which had been taken from me, in a pile of rubble. It was a reminder of what I once was—and will *never* be again. A talisman that I have kept in my collection of war relics, a rather random gathering that keeps me grounded. And then I began."

Dawn licked her lips, feeling as if she hadn't spoken for hours. "So you took over that old man's body, just like you did with Jonah Limpet?"

"Dawn," Kiko said, "just listen."

There was definitely some slurring from Kiko.

"Yes, Dawn," Costin answered anyway. "And it was not long before I searched out my next willing body, one that was not as frail as the old man's. Yet one who was just as interested in justice as this volunteer host. When I parted with him and assumed my new form, the old man died shortly thereafter, blessing me in my journey." He stared at the ground. "But I never knew who The Whisper traveler was or how he could possibly have arranged this offer. He would only tell me that there would be answers in the end. So you see, Dawn—you are not alone in wondering because of a Whisper . . . or Voice."

That *really* shut her up.

Costin leaned back in his chair. "In this younger, fight-worthy body, I was naïve. I did not put together a team because I did not have the experience to know I would need one. And I went after the dragon first, even after he was assumed dead."

Frank grudgingly laughed at that—alpha male to alpha male. Costin smiled slightly.

"Ballsy, as they might say today." He tempered his humor. "It was a near-fatal showdown for me. My maker was more amused than anything, I believe, though I was disguised in another body and he could only sense that perhaps one of his own soldiers was trying to assassinate him. After I managed to survive, I guess you could say that I 'went underground' myself for a time, gathering my strength, my wits, recovering from my close call."

"So the dragon was still running around after that?" Kiko asked.

Dawn shot *him* a look now, and it wasn't just because he'd interrupted. If he was on pills . . .

Costin responded. "It took centuries before I tracked my maker down again, only to discover that he had already been buried, for his rising in a hidden location, by an anonymous brother. So every time I face a master, I'm sure to ask them where I must look now. As you can imagine, they have not been so . . . helpful."

They all lapsed into quiet, questions almost palpably dotting the walls.

His soul. How many times had Costin told her how high the stakes of his hunt were? She'd gotten the "saving the world" part, but she'd never realized it was so personal for him.

Wouldn't she do anything it took to get something so vital back? *Hadn't* she?

She made the best choice she could come up with under the circumstances, finally taking a side. She just hoped it was the right one.

"These brothers," she said. "Do you know which one you're dealing with now?"

Her boss shook his head.

"It's the one," she said, "named Benedikte."

Whatever color was in Costin's face drained away.

TWENTY-TWO

THE UNTANGLING

"BENEDIKTE," Costin repeated, destroyed.

Frank and Kiko watched him in sympathetic curiosity, but then turned their attention to Dawn, as if asking what else she hadn't mentioned about the Underground yet.

"You had to know he was going to show up one day," she said to Costin.

"Yet I had hoped I was wrong when I thought it was this day." He bent his head, his hair masking any more emotion.

Just a few hours ago, Dawn would've taken great satisfaction in seeing him so injured. But now . . . ? No. Not after knowing full well what he was fighting for, even if he'd used her to get at it.

But, again, she would've done the same damned thing, and knowing this made it easier to give him the information he would need before going off to fight because, in some deranged way, she realized this was her battle, too. This was everyone's battle. After what The Whisper in Costin's story had said about "the dragon's rising" . . . ?

Jesus. It finally gave "saving the world" a definition. Thanks to

Costin's dagger vision, she'd seen his maker in action, and the bastard wasn't fooling around.

She eased into more of an explanation for him. "Benedikte more or less took off his 'Matt' costume and revealed himself to me when I was Underground, so I recognized him from your dagger vision. He was pretending to be Matt Lonigan this whole time—"

Kiko bolted out of his chair. "What? When you and Matt had lunch at Chez Rose, I shook his hand and there was no sign. . . ."

"Shielding, Kiko." Costin raised his head. "You would not get a reading. As 'Matthew Lonigan,' Benedikte would have been shielding against us all. If done well, shields are hard to detect. Also, the effort would not have allowed him to search into us at the same time."

Throughout this, Costin had exhibited no reaction whatsoever on his haggard face, and that was when Dawn knew.

"You realized the entire time that 'Matt' was the Master?"

"No, Dawn." Voice flat, emotionless, drained. "At first, I only suspected 'Matt' was from the Underground, perhaps just a spy. Soon afterward, I began to entertain the concept of him being a master."

She should've been floored, should've gotten angry at being kept out of the loop once again. But she was impervious to that now, just like someone whose face had been punched so many times it was numb putty.

Frank busted in. "Hold on—I know I'm behind with the headlines, but it sounds like Dawn and this Matt—"

"Not now, Dad—"

"—like the two of them were . . ." He was waving his hands around. "And you let her *see* him?"

"I did," Costin said softly.

When Frank began to get out of his chair, Dawn threw an arm over his chest to stop him.

"I've waited a long time for this," she said. "Save the demolition for later."

With a measuring glance at his daughter, her dad nonetheless got the rest of the way up, moving to the back of their chairs so he could pace in agitation. He was obviously going nuts because of Breisi's captivity. Kiko remained standing, too. Ironically, Dawn seemed like the only one in the room besides Costin who could manage to sit still.

"Now," she said, absently mimicking Costin's posture: forearms on thighs, wilted. "Go on."

He locked stares with her, and an indestructible bubble seemed to fill the space between them, pushing them apart.

"We decided to see what this 'Matt' had in mind in his attempts to know you," he said.

And, by "we," Dawn knew he meant himself and Breisi, maybe even other Friends, too.

"We kept close watch, though," he added, his tone taking a turn for the dark. "Very close."

That familiar scratch of jealousy abraded his words, but Dawn doubted he felt much. Warriors could have only one main passion, one dedicated cause, and she clearly wasn't it.

She shouldn't want to be "it" anyway. She *didn't* want that.

"But even though you eventually suspected 'Matt' could be the Master," she said, "you had no idea that he was your friend Benedikte. Your companion."

"Only now do I know this for certain." In an unguarded moment, the ghost of a smile tilted Costin's lips. "He was always good at ignoring the pain, good at hiding what was truly going on inside of himself. Yet I could always tell. . . ."

Even in the dagger vision, she'd seen that Benedikte had influenced Costin; maybe he had even been more like a true brother rather than a blood one. Maybe.

"I think," Kiko said, "you need to be telling Dawn why else you let her hang out with 'Matt.'" He put his hands on his hips as he glanced at Dawn. "This is something I *do* know."

He'd said it accusingly, and it made Costin blink only once, slowly, in acknowledgment.

Then he began. "Months ago, Kiko had his 'key' vision. You have been privy to that much: the image of you covered in the blood of a vampire, victorious. What I never elaborated on was that we interpreted this to mean you would find this master and symbolically be the key to besting him. Sometimes when Kiko has visions, they might not be literal."

She recalled the prediction Kiko had gotten about "red fingers" and how it had led to finding Frank. Since the fingers had turned out to be the chimneys on Eva's rooftop, she bought what Costin was saying.

"What we didn't reveal to you," he added, "was the second part of the vision."

"A feeling, really," Kiko said, breaking visual contact.

She couldn't blame her friend for not telling her about this before now. Secrecy was how Limpet and Associates thrived. Every step had been a part of strategy, where no one was a person—they were only markers on a map, being moved around by the general in this war.

And she'd wanted to find the Underground just as badly.

"What else?" she said to Costin.

"Kiko felt that this master would be lured out of his Underground because of a fascination with you."

Something Kiko had said to Dawn from his hospital bed after he broke his back got to her. *Bait.* That was what he'd whispered, but she'd thought he meant Frank. Or maybe even all the other times Costin had used her.

But this? She'd been bait for the Master himself? That was why Costin had hired Frank and eventually gotten Dawn to join them due to her father's accidentally fortuitous disappearance?

Costin clasped his hands together. It looked like his fingers were trying to strangle one another.

"I was a decoy," she confirmed. "A worm on a hook."

"More like an irresistible temptation," Costin added, his voice cracking.

Dawn's chest collapsed, but she held herself up before any damage could register.

Then he sighed. "It was a catch-22 situation. You were to flush the Master out, but Kiko also felt that just by being around you, this vampire would regain an interest in life and grow in strength. We debated about what to do: lure him out with a woman who would increase his powers? Or should we go on without you, knowing we would be forgoing a gift and perhaps losing precious time?" He shook his head. "The answer was easy. As you know, I was certain there was a master in the area—I sensed him almost a year ago and immediately began shielding so there would be no chance of him discovering me before I did him—and he must have shielded at the same time. We only hoped you would draw him out before he grew too strong. In any event, I knew he must be destroyed before he held any advantage over me."

Destroyed so Costin could get his soul back. It was all finally making sense, as much as it could.

"At first," he continued, something like self-disgust sharpening his tone, "I was truly reluctant to take you on. My difficulty in sending you out with Kiko and Breisi to the Pennybaker mansion on the night you joined us was not feigned. I knew you were to be bait, but there was no avoiding it."

"At least I had my uses," Dawn said.

"Don't say that." Costin's gaze burned. "You are . . ."

She widened her eyes, and he trailed off. In the resulting quiet, Dawn knew she couldn't compete with regaining his humanity. As if in understanding, her earlobe burned, a phantom throb marking the spot where she used to wear the old Dawn's earring.

Behind her, Frank cleared his throat. She didn't look back at her dad. Couldn't.

"I'm sorry I didn't know all this from the beginning," she whispered to Costin.

Damn it, that sounded pathetic. So, in defensive reaction, she shrugged and acted like she was okay with it all. It felt better that way, even though she and everyone else in this room knew it was a put-on.

Her next words were just as careless. "I mean, I might not have been such a brat if I knew you were in this soul tug-of-war. Then again, if I knew everything, I suppose I wouldn't have been good bait anyway."

"I told you as much as I could."

That chiseled at her. "You didn't tell me squat. But now . . ." She exhaled. There was nothing she could do about anything. Her part was finished. Might as well let it go.

"Dawn . . ."

Her name from his lips. So many times he'd undone her with just that one syllable. She couldn't stand it anymore.

"Why're you telling us everything at this point?" she asked, taking over. "Because you think if you're going to die, you want to do it with a clear conscience? Or because your story would persuade me to tell you what happened Underground?"

He looked bereft at having been robbed of the power to say her name and have it mean something. Then he got back to business, just as she had. It was so much easier that way.

"Untangling a burden is part of this confession," he said. "But, know this—I have not told you enough to endanger myself. Still, none of you is to leave this house after I am gone."

Once again, thoughts of Breisi niggled at Dawn.

"Then I guess with the vision of Jonah earlier," she said, "you just showed us enough to drive me away—so you could find the Underground with the locator on my jeans."

As he nodded, she remembered the night of his last feeding, in the guest bedroom, right before all hell had broken loose and he'd kicked her out.

Whatever happens in the future, he'd said, *know that I am sorry for it.*

Now, Kiko pointed at Costin. "Wait—you always told us that you were keeping us safe by withholding information. What's changed?"

Costin's grip on his own hands tightened, as if shame was devouring him. Dawn squirmed because the gesture made her so reluctantly mortified for him.

"There are actions we can never redeem," he said, "and I knew I would be committing quite a few of them. The less you knew, the better. That is what I believed. I thought that I could postpone the hatred you would inevitably have for me, righteous hatred. That is the reason I would not tell more than what was necessary at the time."

The lining of Dawn's stomach trembled. What was he saying? She knew that he'd been expecting her before she even arrived in L.A., and he'd immediately lied to her. But he couldn't have gotten that strongly attached from just one of Kiko's visions. Or had he become attracted to the idea of the power he kept telling her she possessed?

"You manipulated us," she asked, "because you wanted us to *like* you?"

"I never wished for *you* to hate me, Dawn," Costin whispered. "There is a world of difference."

At this naked admission, Kiko glanced back at Frank, as if asking if they should leave.

"Stay," she said, fighting off what Costin's words were doing to her. "You need to know everything."

"Yes," Costin added, "you need to know why I have been so . . . monstrous." He sent a look to Dawn, as if asking her to validate that, as if hoping she wouldn't.

Something caught in her throat, making it impossible to agree or disagree.

"Often," Costin said, still watching her, "I wonder if my quest has built me into more of a beast than ever. I remind myself of what is really in store for the world if the dragon rises, and that alone seems enough to justify what I have done. I remind myself that when The Whisper cleansed me of that vampire body, I became another type of being. I became something *much* different than a member of the brotherhood."

Even as he said it, Dawn could tell his doubt was growing, that he questioned the choices he'd made with every breath. That, even now, he was attempting to convince himself that he really was more than a damned being whether it came in the form of a vampire or another unnamable creature.

But, as a vampire, he would never have a soul. He probably told himself over and over that he would *never* be one of them; he would distance himself from their evil while hunting them down. Yet he didn't seem sure of that, and it got to Dawn.

As if knowing what she was thinking, he murmured, "Time has bent us all into forms we do not recognize."

She held her breath. Did he know how much she'd been wondering about what she'd become, too?

Kiko had backed away, closer to where Frank was looming by Dawn's shoulder. She could feel them standing behind her.

"Costin, do you know what to expect out of Benedikte?" the psychic asked. It sounded like a way to send their boss off gracefully.

Had Kiko been moved by Costin's unburdening, too?

The mention of the mission at hand seemed to help Costin in sitting up and returning to soldier readiness, his shoulders straight and only slightly pushed down by a personal situation left unresolved. "I can take what we know about these Elite vampires and make an educated guess as to Benedikte's specifics. Yet, as we already know, each blood brother seems to develop different talents based on individual strengths, so I cannot rely on past experience with the other masters to guide me."

"Different talents," Kiko mulled. "Just like the Fantastic Four. The same storm hit them, but one could stretch his body, and one could turn into a fire fiend—"

He cut himself off, realizing this wasn't helping.

"How do *you* work, Costin?" Dawn asked, putting off the inevitable: the moment he would walk out of here. Even with everything he'd done to her, she was getting worried about letting him go

Underground to face overwhelming odds. She'd seen those vampires, seen just a hint of what Benedikte could do with his own body.

"You are no doubt wondering about what you witnessed with Jonah," Costin said, nodding, as if he'd expected to be put on trial for his earlier actions.

"Yeah," Kiko said, "what was with him just wandering into your office? You were always real careful about talking to us through the speakers and never letting us see that Jonah was . . ."

"His own person?" Costin finished. "He is that, even if I am a part of him now. Though Jonah knows he is usually not to contact my team, I asked him to do it, just this one time, in order to goad Dawn to the Underground with the locator."

"That's one question down," Kiko said.

As Costin sat in silence, the ticking of the clock on the nightstand clamored, a banging countdown for the approaching moment when he would leave for the big showdown. With each thud, Dawn's pulse accelerated.

Maybe something will happen so this can all be avoided, she thought. *Maybe he'll change his mind about going and . . .*

Give up his soul in the bargain?

Costin stood, ambling over to Breisi's empty picture, his hands clasped behind his back.

Tick, tick, tick, tick . . .

"When the old man allowed me to enter his body," Costin continued, "I found that I had certain . . . advantages. I could manipulate people with my mind—'hypnosis,' it came to be called. I did have to work to perfect my skills, and I found that I must use them in small doses. Every effort weakens me until I am able to regain strength through rest and occasional sustenance."

Rest, Dawn thought. Like he got when he went into that firefield portrait in his office—a background of the hell Costin had endured in his vampire body. But . . . sustenance?

"Could you use all your powers right away?" Kiko asked. "I mean, the ones you tried to teach me, too?"

"Yes, I came 'fully loaded.' " Costin continued to look at Breisi's empty picture. "Persuading others, creating illusions, reading minds—these are part of my arsenal."

Dawn tried to reconcile what he was saying with what she'd been through with him. That first night she'd met Costin, his voice had seemed so persuasive. It'd even entered her.

Illusions? Mind reading and entering?

"When I met you . . ." she began.

Costin unclasped his hands, his back still to them. "That was me using my powers to test you, Dawn."

"And the time in the boudoir?" she asked, forgetting herself in front of Kiko and her dad.

"Er," Kiko said in back of her, "Dawn, why don't you catch us up on everything later?"

She turned to find the psychic tugging at Frank to come with him.

"Whoa, whoa, whoa—" Frank began.

"No, really," Kiko interrupted. "We can wait for when Dawn comes upstairs."

She realized how uncomfortable Kiko had to be with the subject she'd brought up. How uncomfortable *she'd* be discussing kinky Voice nookie in front of her own dad.

Giving Kik a thankful look, she watched as he urged Frank up the stairs, promising him that he would fill in the other blank spaces while Dawn and Costin sorted their own stuff out.

When they were gone, Dawn turned back to the enigma.

Tick, tick, tick, went the clock.

"Well?" she asked, but the question held none of her usual vinegar. "Do you remember it or not, that time in the boudoir when we . . . well, did it, in front of the mirror?" Back then, her mind had gone fuzzy when he'd first come to her. His Jonah body had been in another place—behind the bookcase—while his voice had seemed to be with *her*.

Now, Costin only allowed Dawn to see Jonah's profile—one

half of his tragically carved face. "At first, I did use hypnosis with you, yes. You wanted to know about me, and that left you open."

And that was how he'd projected his voice and fooled her. "But when I felt you physically, even though you were invisible?"

"My spirit, rented though it is, left Jonah's body to come to you." To feed off of her.

"You felt like flesh and blood," she said.

"I might have persuaded you to think so."

So that was hypnosis, too? Or had it been *him*, a being she'd wanted to feel, to be consumed by?

The question warmed her where she didn't want to be warmed. The heat dragged her down, made her want to cry at truly being so attached to him.

Accordingly, she toughened up. "And when Jonah *himself* came to me in the office and used Kalin to bind me?"

"You already know." Costin fully turned away from her again. "Jonah was taking what he is entitled to take: a breather. It is our understanding that he gets his body back for a short time daily, while I go away."

Into the field of fire picture, she thought.

"And when I found you praying in front of your crucifix in your quarters," she asked, "and . . . Jonah's eyes were blue while he was watching you feed off of me . . . ?"

"I lost control that time, traveling out of body in error, in . . . excitement." He softened his voice. "I could not help myself when you walked in."

Before she could do something silly like fall at his feet, she bucked up. Crazy. This was all nuts. Yet, with each tick of the clock, it was closer to being over. . . .

Oh, God, over. What if Costin lost against Benedikte?

No . . . what if he *won*?

She rushed to ask another question. "This story you just told us, about how you got out of jail? While you were talking, was *that* hypnosis, the way you brought us into the action?"

"Yes, your minds were open and it illustrated nuances that I don't have the luxury of verbally dwelling upon just now."

At her limits, she got out of the chair, but didn't go near him, even though she wanted to. Didn't want to. Did. Didn't—

"Why do you go in and out of Jonah's body?" she asked, fighting to stay away. "Wouldn't it be smarter to—?"

"He is entitled to be himself every so often. It is part of our bargain, although I didn't expect him to begin taking such advantage of his free time, as he did when he persuaded Kalin to bind you. Unfortunately, her temper made her an easy ally against the woman she considers a threat for affection."

Don't give in; don't give in. . . . "Why did Jonah do it?"

"Because Jonah . . ." Costin shook his head and let out a long breath. Even with his back turned, his expression was eloquent. "He covets. Though I do thorough research for each body I desire, I didn't do it well enough with this one."

Dawn looked for signs of Jonah, himself, rebelling to get this body back, but didn't find any. Costin was in control.

"I have made arrangements for another," Costin added.

"Another?"

"I plan on assuming my new host's body after I finish today's work." He put his hands behind his back again and sauntered away from Breisi's picture and to her lab table, aimless. The glass jars and beakers were cloudy with a fresh, silvered residue, as if only recently having been used but not yet cleaned. "Clearly, Jonah is in *this* particular battle with me. And if we survive it, because there is always a slim—"

"You will." It'd come out unchecked, powered by hope.

Costin looked up, the joyful surprise on his face making her backtrack.

"I mean," she said, "the world kind of needs you to win."

"Of course." Not fooled at all, Costin went back to surveying the equipment, a dark smile lingering. "You see, when I first approached Jonah, it was when my former body was on its last legs. We had lived a good life together, vanquishing a master. During my research, I discovered Jonah had lost his parents and was a recluse—a wealthy one. He suited my needs beautifully, and it turned out that he was more than willing to be my next host, even after everything was explained to him. I always find this to be a fortunate thing—my hosts are usually men who lack excitement, all loners disconnected from society in some way, all looking for a cause to justify their existences. All physically strong and vital, yet they crave a new life, and I promise that to them. However, they understand they might die because of my quest." Costin negligently ran a finger over a glass beaker. "In past situations, hosts have been slain, though my essence was able to escape to a new form that I had already secured and I was able to continue my mission. Today, my new body will be standing by, distant enough to remain safe, close enough to be convenient."

"What if you don't get out of a host body before it . . . dies?"

The being before her—she wasn't sure what else to call Costin—loitered over the beaker. "If I am somehow caught in my host's body during his death—if I should need to anchor to the strength and sustenance he gives me because I am too weak to escape, for instance—my quest is over. I will have failed and will perish in damnation since I would not be able to escape the useless host and redeem myself. The effect is that of a collapsed cave; the dead matter would trap me inside and my soul would be forfeit to the fire."

Oh. Dawn didn't know what to say.

In spite of the news, Costin got his arrogant poise back. "I do not anticipate that happening. Jonah is strong."

"But . . ." Dawn narrowed her eyes. "You've picked out your next host already. Who is it?"

"No one you know—a quiet software genius who never makes headlines. I found him a while ago. This did not please Jonah, of course, and I have done my best to appease him." Costin paused in his chemistry set inspection. "Ours is a symbiotic relationship, yet a respectful one. I'm always careful with the bodies because I am in awe of what they are willing to do for the quest."

"Do you ever feel bad for inhabiting them?" Dawn asked.

"Absolutely."

"But the good of the many outweighs—"

"The good of the few. I know it well, Dawn. You have drilled it into my head."

She started to smile but stopped herself.

He must've sensed that he was never going to win her over. She could see it when he stopped messing with the beakers.

"They all have their reasons for wishing to house me," he said, "mainly because of that sense of high justice you love to note. But . . . I came to find out that this was not altogether the case with Jonah, though he is committed. He is a smart man and was able to fool me into believing that he only wanted to aid in cleansing the world."

"What do you mean?"

"I mean he was attracted to my very existence. He thought my offer 'glamorous' and 'romantic.' "

She hesitated, then went for it, not really knowing why she was daring. "And what does this have to do with him using Kalin to bind me?"

Tick, tick, tick . . .

"Is it not obvious?" Costin faced her. "I desire you more than anything, and that means he does, too."

If a body could liquefy, hers would've done it. But a blast of icy reality kept her whole.

He desired her more than anything except for his soul.

Uncomfortable with the obvious intensity of his need for her, Dawn kept talking, hoping it would cancel out the real reason he hadn't left yet, the real reason she was trying to get him to stay. A reason she couldn't admit to.

"Are you saying Jonah's unstable?" she asked. "Would you be looking for a new body even if you didn't need a backup after this battle?" She gestured toward him. "And doesn't Jonah hear you talking about this?"

"He knew back when I first caught on to his real feelings and began to make arrangements. That is why . . ."

Costin motioned to the scars on his face, and Dawn got it.

You're looking for someone else, aren't you? Jonah had said in the cutting vision. *You aren't happy with me anymore.*

"It is only recently," Costin added, "that Jonah's longing for my life has come to a head. I know his thoughts. We share much since my temporary spirit presses down upon his and releases it only when I leave the body. We live in close range, within sharing distance. But now Jonah believes he can *be* me, and my life seems within his reach."

"What's keeping you from going into that backup's body?"

"Jonah has sacrificed much to help me. He is a true believer, in spite of everything else." Costin shook his head. "And I depend upon him just as much as he does me. We are in the thick of the hunt, and he is trained for what must be done. I cannot leave him so easily right now."

Dawn took a couple of steps forward, then reined herself in. "Isn't there a choice? There's always a choice." But she knew she was being idealistic. Yeah, Dawn Madison—Pollyanna.

"Choice does not rate high at the moment," Costin said. "Because you know what is at stake."

She knew. Damn it, she *knew*.

As if she hadn't heard enough, he continued. "And I would suffer a million more centuries of this existence before becoming what I was."

An awareness so heavy draped over her that she couldn't meet his gaze. Not like this. Not until she got back some sense of control.

"So even though Jonah is your cover," she asked, "he can't go outside, either, even during his breathers?"

"That is right. My team does the groundwork while my host and I wait in anticipation of the work I must do in the end. We must hide behind these protected walls from a master's Awareness, which can be developed among the brothers. That is, if a master chooses to risk using it." Costin walked closer to her, yet kept his distance. "Besides, after Jonah scarred himself, he preferred to stay in darkness because he was ashamed of what he had done. So when I finally revealed what I looked like to you . . ."

The night when Breisi had died . . .

"Jonah was angry," he finished. "But I told him that the appearance kept you here, kept your curiosity leveled, and he came to accept my choice. He becomes agitated whenever it seems as if you will leave."

Tick, tick—

The clock banged away, reminding her that *Costin* was about to leave. Almost time, almost time . . .

"I understand now," she said. "You . . . me . . . the feedings . . . You need an attachment."

"Yes. Whether human, whether vampire, there is a commonality. We all have cravings. It is the caliber of them that distinguishes us from the monsters."

Cravings: her addiction to easy sex, her hard feelings toward Eva . . . her yearning to be just like her mother.

They had all flowed from one to the other, keeping her alive, or at least feeling that way.

"Then you live off sex," she asked, "like an . . ."

"Incubus? No. That is not what nourishes me." He clasped his hands. "Humanity. I must take root in it to survive. And the power you have inside of you is enough to fuel me beyond anything else I have felt before."

He came even closer, and Dawn's body reawakened.

"When I am away from Jonah," he added, "I take rest in the field of fire. I dream in fire. I will it to be so, because every lick of flame reminds me of what I have to lose. But I cannot stay away from my host for long—not even with you. Every hour that I am apart from Jonah eats away at my spirit until it is in danger of disappearing."

"What? Why?"

"The Whisper was kind enough to explain that it is a safety

mechanism of sorts—a method to ensure that I keep to my deal and do not attempt an escape from my chosen shelter with my rented soul. I am tied to my duties as an enforcer for the higher powers that have given me this second chance."

"You wouldn't abandon your mission anyway," she said.

"Yet my mysterious benefactors wanted to be certain of my loyalty, and that is understandable. So I never stray far from Jonah. And when I do, it is never for too long or too often."

He risked a few steps nearer to her, increasing the tension between them. Dawn wanted to close the space intersecting their bodies, but . . . After everything he'd put her through?

She broke away, and Costin looked bereft. She tried to take pleasure from that. Tried.

"Kind of like a vamp," she said, emotions flailing until they snagged on the only thing that kept her solid—distance. "What with you needing a willing participant to be your host and allow you inside them. That's just like a vamp."

She'd hit the target. He looked assassinated, stunned, and profoundly disappointed by the attack. The thing was, she saw it only around the lines of his mouth. The rest of him was still a soldier, impenetrable.

Remember, she thought. Remember him using you as bait more times than you can count. Remember that he's lied to you before. Remember that you can't put any faith in him. . . .

Harshly, she motioned toward Breisi's portrait, where the background looked so dead without her Friend in it.

"Come to think of it," she said, "I remember that Dracula had a harem, too. Brides, right?"

His jaw had clenched at the name "Dracula." She'd finally crossed a line. She'd been banking on that.

"They agreed to live on in these pictures." Only a tiny fissure in his tone revealed a crack. "In those portraits, their worlds are intact, and they are happy."

"The worlds they shared with you. How sweet." At this point, she realized she was also working off of a twisted jealousy. "When do their sentences end, Costin?"

Tickticktick—

"When I die peacefully," he answered, a note of longing creeping into the words. "Then they come with me."

His answer echoed like the aftermath of a sonic boom, canceling out everything else.

Death. When he died, he really wouldn't be around anymore. No hocus-pocus, no more miracles. He would get his soul back, all right, but he was telling her that he would be going to a better place than hell. A place he had earned.

And it would have nothing to do with her because she'd resisted joining him.

"That is why I do not allow my Friends to kill while they remain in pure spirit form," he said. "I take on the stain of blood in the state of what should have been their grace. It is part of my penance."

"Aren't you in pretty much the same state? When you kill, doesn't that mean you won't go to heaven?"

Much to her shock, he refused to answer, falling to the floor before her instead, bowing, lowering his head and putting his hand to his heart.

Now it was her chance to apologize for everything, before he left, before he fought and maybe never came back.

"Costin . . ."

He peered up at her, his dark hair falling forward, his eyes burning, his face scored not only from wounds but from the hurt she'd visited on him.

"If there ever was a woman for whom I would give up my soul," he whispered, "you would have been the one."

She choked on her shock, on her grief. Say something, she thought. Do something, stop him—

Ticktickticktick

At her indecision, he arose, then formally nodded to her as if to work around an obvious rejection. She tried to find something to say, anything, but . . .

"Remember," he said, cold and beyond reach now, "you will not come anywhere near the Underground. Breisi is in my hands now."

And Eva? What about her?

God, why was she worried about that?

"Costin—"

"Dawn, our last argument has passed and I have no more time for waiting." His eyes flared to sun gold. "You stay here with Kiko and your father, whose intentions are good, by the way—"

"But *Breisi*—"

The heat of his eyes rushed at her, and she rallied to block the incoming power. But a blast of buzzing color blinded her before she mentally chopped it away.

In the chorusing aftermath, as she stood still, unable to move, all she saw was the gold of his gaze.

The warm, beautiful hues of the daybreak Costin was venturing into for the first time since shutting himself in.

TWENTY-THREE

. . . Action

Dawn did get back her sight, although she didn't know how long it took.

Hell. She'd blocked one of Costin's hypnotic attacks, hadn't she? That was what'd happened? Of course, at the same time, he'd skimmed her mind for everything else she'd seen in the Underground, but she was fine with *that* part.

Partially recovered, she stumbled up the stairs, yelling for Kiko. When he didn't answer, she found out why. He—and reportedly Frank—had been plugging their ears with their fingers while the Friends had vacated the house. They'd done this just in case the spirits tried to lull them to sleep, and the simple solution had worked.

After that explanation, Dawn stated the obvious. "He's gone." She was still blinking away the sunspots. "Costin tried to stall me with his mind, but . . ."

But it *hadn't* worked. Not this time.

Kiko went on to explain how, after the Friends had left, Frank had made a run out the door so he could go and save Breisi. Of course, since it was daylight and Frank wasn't a strong enough vampire to work well in the sun, he'd retreated inside. Dawn found him pacing near the back door, his skin reddened. He was almost in a frenzy to go Underground, no matter what Costin had forbid them to do.

There wasn't even a question about what would happen next.

Dawn went up to her guest room and changed clothes, keeping to the tank top, jeans, and biker boots. She rubbed garlic over her skin out of habit, donned both a locator and a silver crucifix with pointed ends, then gathered weapons, mostly backup: a few throwing blades, a silver-tipped stake, more machetes, a .45 with silver bullets, her whip chain, and a mini-flamethrower. She stuffed most of those into a bag that she slung over her chest. The machetes and revolver had their own holsters.

After binding her hair back into its practical low ponytail, she took out the upper earring in her right lobe, went to her suitcase, and unzipped her jewelry bag to stow the stud. In its place, she donned her blood-moon earring, taking up where she'd left off the night she killed Robby Pennybaker.

Breisi, I'm coming, she thought all the while. *And Eva . . . ?*

They weren't topmost on Costin's agenda, but Dawn had her own mission now.

Yet had he taken any precautions besides the attempted hypnosis to keep them away? They would soon see.

After a stop in the lab to pick up the saw-bow Breisi had given her, Dawn met Kiko and Frank in the connected, darkened garage. There, they bundled her dad under thick blankets in the backseat of a backup, Breisi-modified 4Runner, then blocked the already-tinted windows with tarp.

When they finally blasted out of the garage and into sunlight, they were ready for any Servants who tried to stop them.

But that wasn't necessary.

At the sight of the SUV roaring away, one Servant, a woman

who worked at a private security firm in normal life, sat in her Jeep on the other side of the road and dialed her secure cell phone. On the other end of the line, another Servant, a lawyer named Enrico Harris, picked up.

"They're on their way somewhere," the security woman said. "Don't know if it's the Underground, but you'd better get ready down there."

"Did you see who was in the car?" Enrico said.

"Negative. The windows were blacked out."

The other two Servants lingering outside couldn't have seen inside the 4Runner, either. At least, that was what the security woman thought. And there was something bothering her about an event that had occurred over thirty minutes ago. Before this SUV had blasted away, she thought she'd seen something else—maybe it was nothing at all—come out of the driveway, but her mind had gotten a tad muddled and she wasn't sure it had actually happened. A check with the other Servant watchers revealed that they'd seen—or not seen—the same thing. . . .

Meanwhile, Underground, Enrico Harris had already hung up and was heading for an all-purpose communicator that sat on the surface of an office desk. He was in a reception area, on volunteer watch duty.

He pressed the button on the side of the communicator, and it beeped like an electronic trill. "Master?"

Waiting for his leader to answer, he tapped his foot on the ground. Enrico had expected a quick response, especially under the high-alert circumstances.

"Master?" he said into the speaker again.

Finally, a beaten voice answered. "Yes?"

Enrico paused in surprise, never having heard his master in such a state, but then he rushed on. "We need to prepare. . . ."

On the other end of the line, Benedikte lay on his room's cold floor, one hand on the handheld communicator, the other on Eva's shoulder. He had been trying to help her heal, but something was wrong. Physically, she was recovering, but she wasn't waking up. It was as if she didn't want to.

Through the maze of his mind, he barely heard the Servant on the other end of the communicator, but Benedikte got the gist of it.

It was time.

Slowly, he left Eva slumped against the wall, then shifted into Sorin's body—the one most of the Underground was used to seeing as "the Master." Benedikte made a great effort not to look at evidence of his son's demise on the floor. Phantom bloodstains remained, resembling accusing eyes, burning into what the Master had always thought to be his heart.

Then he numbly made his way out of his room and to the Guard's cells so he could instruct them in Sorin's place before they were let loose.

Once there, all the grotesque centurions stared at him, their eyes red as they crept toward the bars of their cells.

Without much verve—how could he muster it when Sorin was gone and Eva was not much better?—the Master gave them instructions to defend the Underground perimeter and tear apart anyone who tried to get in. He thought he saw a slight bewilderment in their gazes, in their gaped, iron-toothed mouths.

A Groupie spoke into a microphone in the shielded control panel down the cell's hall. "Master, we've noticed that the Guards seem . . . scattered . . . for some reason. They have even less focus than usual."

"Then you Groupies must back them up if anything goes wrong on the perimeter," the Master barked. The lower vampire's comments were reminding him of the way Sorin used to nag.

"Us?" another control Groupie asked. "Master . . . we haven't gone near the Guards lately, not after they've been calling for our blood. Didn't you just say the other day that they might be showing signs of addiction to us in particular?"

And *more* nagging. Not only were they quoting Sorin's notes to him, but they were bringing on fresh pain. An image of Sorin's head exploding with the punch of Benedikte's fist blinded the Master. He held a hand to his temple and closed his eyes.

"Do as you are told," he said, turning to mist—not caring that the Groupies would see the odd change from whom they thought to be Sorin. Then he zoomed back to his room to be with Eva.

He didn't stop to think that, even though he had assumed the shape of Sorin's body, it didn't mean the Guards would obey anyone but their creator. He didn't stop to think at all.

Eager to try healing Eva again, Benedikte reached his room, shifted back into Sorin's body since his son was still on his mind, then prepared to undo the secret lock. But his door opened before he could finish.

In his grief, he merely slipped inside, going straight for Eva, sitting next to her, and taking her limp hand in his. Again, he tried to heal her, placing his fingers against her head, against any inch of skin that might still be wounded.

The scent of jasmine came upon him before he could even identify its qualities. Then a voice sounded from a dark patch on the opposite side of the room.

"Benedikte."

The Master's head jerked up at the familiar tone, and he shrunk back toward Eva. Then realization suffused him like hemlock, bringing a measure of stultifying peace and welcome destiny.

"Costin?" he whispered to the voice he recognized now that it was pure and undisguised. Then he smiled sadly, even though it felt like a scowl. "You're finally here."

TWENTY-FOUR

The Humanity

BECAUSE of some hiking adventures years ago, Dawn knew where the old quarry in Griffith Park was, even though Frank said the Underground entrance was well hidden and apart from the TV and film projects that had previously set up shop in the caves. From under his protective blankets, her dad was helping to guide them to the more out-of-the-way location, which Eva had shared with him.

After encountering a locked gate inside the park, then coaxing it open with the aid of an acid gun Breisi kept stored in one of many added vehicle compartments, Dawn kept her eyes peeled for rangers. Didn't matter if the officials confronted them, though: Dawn and the team were desperate enough to make a run for the Underground and lose any pursuers in the confusion if it came right down to it. Smokey could arrest them afterward.

From there, she pushed pedal to metal and took the SUV on a fire road, cold energy stringing her together as the same things kept repeating through her head: Breisi, Eva . . . Costin.

He kept saying he wouldn't need a team's help—not unless it

were composed of command-ready Friends, obviously—but she wasn't disobeying and going Underground for Costin's sake anyway. Not at all . . .

She drove on, surprised all over again that flying in the face of a creature as powerful as Costin was so easy. Maybe none of them had been susceptible to his hypnotic sway at this desperate point. Maybe *she*, in particular, had gotten too good at blocking, because she had the distinct feeling that his final mind blast at her might've been a method of wiping out most of the information he'd imparted to her before leaving.

But something bugged her about that. Would he do a mind wipe on her when he'd been so upset about it being done by Paul Aspen? Of course. That way Costin could get his confessional *and* trust that Dawn wouldn't be privy to too much information. Kiko and Frank hadn't been there for the nitty-gritty conversation and, with a wipe, Dawn wouldn't be able to tell them about any of what she'd heard.

In any case, on the way over, Dawn had kept Costin's personal information to herself. But the more she stayed silent, the more she realized what they were undertaking. And, too late, she'd started to wonder if a pill-popping Kiko was up to going Underground with her and Frank.

Following her dad's muffled directions to avoid a more well-known quarry entrance and head lower, they ultimately reached a deserted area off a fire road where daylight swallowed the craggy hills, rocks, and dirt. In spite of the rough terrain, she parked under a shaded overhang, near where Frank said there was a fake wall that could be operated by a knowing touch.

She and Kiko got out of the 4Runner, but before they opened the rear door to help her blanket-swaddled dad out, Dawn stopped her coworker. "Maybe you should wait out here."

Hurting his feelings wasn't a primary concern right now, yet when he grimaced, she couldn't help feeling bad. He'd shucked off his back brace and donned a hip holster for his revolver, along with a smaller arsenal bag strapped over his chest, just like Dawn's and Frank's bigger ones.

"I've been fighting these things longer than you have," Kiko said, his words running together—but that could've been out of adrenaline, not necessarily a pill.

She bent and took him by the bag strap. "This isn't about your experience—which barely trumps mine now, by the way. This is about reality. I saw you put something into your mouth back at the house, Kik, and we're going to be hauling ass all over the place. You can't—"

"Come on, it was only for one little flare-up of pain, okay? That's all. Just a quarter of one Vicodin. And treating me like a kid isn't going to keep me out."

She gave him a slight push away. "Don't play that with me. I don't have time for it."

For a moment, Kiko just stood behind her as she went to open the rear door so she could help Frank out. Damn, even a quarter of one of Kiko's pills would set her reeling, yet the psychic didn't seem totally stoned. Had he built up a tolerance for the medication?

Then, his voice showing an effort to talk 100 percent soberly, Kiko said, "I'm gonna go with the rest of the team, Dawn. You know that I won't just stand by while the shit's going down."

She paused, hand on the door latch as she thought, again, of how Costin's previous teams had died. They were probably as stupid, stubborn, and, yeah, loyal as this bunch was. And they probably hadn't believed, either, that their boss could face a whole Underground with just protective Friends as backup.

Was Costin resigned to them dying? Is that why he needed new teams with every Underground?

The shuffle of gravel told her that Kiko had taken a step nearer. "We're *all* going down there, no matter what Costin says. Do you really think he gives a hoot about anyone else now? He's concentrating on that master and, when everything is said and done, he won't care. He just doesn't want to have to keep an eye on us, I'll bet. We're over, as far as he's concerned, and that's why *we've* got to put Breisi first on the priority list. Costin ain't gonna do it. Breisi's an afterthought to him right now, but not for me. Not ever."

From inside the SUV, a *thump* knocked against the door. Frank, waiting for them.

"Let's go get 'em!" he yelled from behind the tarped and tinted window.

"'Em," which would mean "them" in Frank-speak. But was "'em" referring to Breisi *and* Eva?

"Okay." With the heel of her palm, Dawn knocked back against the window. The aggressive reaction helped to tamp down the prefight adrenaline collecting in her like explosives wired to blow. She turned to Kiko, who'd gotten out his revolver and was checking it over for the thousandth time.

"I just wonder," Kiko said as he shoved his silver-bullet-filled weapon into its holster, then took a wide-legged stance as if to steady himself, "if you and Frank are gonna retain any immunity. Maybe Eva negotiated it for her loved ones before she blew it with the Master, but is it still in play like it was when you saw those redeyes with Cassie Tomlinson? *I'm* fair game, but what about you two?"

He seemed fantastically cool in the asking, but Dawn could sense a buzz of anxiety in her friend.

She shrugged, trying to make his important question seem inconsequential. "It all depends if Eva talked her way out of this last game she was playing with the Master. We'll see."

But something told her she needed to fight for her life, to never depend on the Master's whims to keep any of them safe.

What she needed to depend on were things like the lower vamps being weaker during the day, because they would probably act as the infantry once the team got past the entrance.

At the thought of getting on with this, she cowboyed up. She'd fought vamps before; she could do it again. Didn't matter that Breisi *and* Eva's existences were at stake. Didn't matter that Costin could

very well need their help in taking the Master apart limb by
limb . . .

Dawn stiffened. The Master. The creature that had set this all in
motion. Taking him apart was music to her vengeful side. He'd dis-
mantled her life and taken advantage of her for lesser reasons than
redemption—

Struck by her anger, the side-view mirror began to shake. Dawn
calmed herself, saving it for when it would count.

After she pulled open the door, she told Frank to keep the blankets tightly around him, then aided him into the shade, careful to
avoid any hint of sunlight. Once secure, he tested his luck by sticking
a meaty arm out of his coverings. Then, unaffected, he shed his blankets, emerging out of his bulky cocoon with one emphatic shrug.

Immediately, he jogged into one of three dark holes.

Dawn didn't even have time to ready any weapons besides her
loaded saw-bow. Here it went.

From their talk on the way over, Dawn knew Frank intended to
connect with Eva through their Awareness while they all snuck
around the sentry vampires. Right. And if they could manage that
monumental piece of luck, maybe her dad could persuade Eva to lead
them to the captive Friends, and then . . . What?

Wreak Underground destruction? Yell "banzai!" as they fight
for a higher cause than their own lives?

She only hoped Frank didn't have it in him to betray her. She
tried not to think that he could be part of some elaborate plan that
he and Eva had cooked up to ultimately win over their mentally
beaten daughter. Stranger things had happened lately, so it wasn't
out of the realm of possibility, even if Costin had told her Frank
was still decent.

"You get ahold of Eva yet?" Dawn whispered harshly as she followed her dad into the darkness. He was leading through vampire
sight, she knew, but she didn't have time to put on a lighted head-
piece from her goodie bag. Not if she wanted to keep up with Frank
the bloodhound. Besides, there'd be electric hall light soon.

"I can't find her." Her dad was already a decent ways ahead, yet his whisper carried. "But she'll come through. You said she's been waiting for me to get back here, so I'm sure she's open for me. . . ."

Dawn turned around to give Kiko a look, but it was too murky. Still, she heard him breathing behind her.

Good God, what was she doing by letting him come with her and Frank?

She briefly considered tackling Kiko and leaving him knocked out in the SUV, but that would be unforgivable. Injured or not, he knew a thing or two about vamp fighting. Even under the slight influence, he'd studied, trained, and he knew how to use Breisi's gadget weaponry. Besides, he would end up coming inside on his own anyway, the brave fool.

They descended into the ever-increasing cool of surrounding rock, where the sound of their breathing overtook even the bash of Dawn's heartbeat in her ears. When they bumped into Frank, he'd just opened a panel.

The entrance finished grumbling to a gape, shedding minimal light—enough to judge shadows by. All three of them waited, Dawn's saw-bow raised, and Frank aiming what looked to be a compact flamethrower; it had the silhouette of a long, flare-nozzled handheld gun, so she was pretty sure. She guessed Kiko would be using his own flamethrower instead of a revolver so they could enter more quietly.

When nothing moved in front of them, Dawn started to exhale, but she couldn't complete it. Her lungs felt too shallow.

Frank gasped, then whispered, "I think I just got something from Eva. . . ."

He moved ahead, and they did, too, running their free hands over the cave walls for insurance.

Soon we'll come to the hall lights, Dawn thought. Hopefully *very* soon.

Indeed, in the near distance, the breath of yellow beckoned from around a corner. As they got closer to it, time moved by at a fast crawl.

But, when they arrived, a fork in the tunnel caused hesitation. After exchanging glances with her dad, Dawn gestured to the path on the right. They took it, priming their weapons, pulse throbbing in her head.

Once they all were deep into the passage, she allowed herself to breathe again.

Until the lights went out and red-eyes opened to greet them from the top of the tunnel.

A frenzied cry, then two, three, four—*five*—cracked open the blackness. Frank's flamethrower growled, spitting fire up at the descending creatures. Immediately, the ceiling exploded with water, showering down from hidden holes.

Shit, of course vampires would have fire precautions.

"Try the other route!" Frank yelled. His flamethrower lit the dark again, and the lights fluttered back on.

Without hesitating, Kiko and Dawn sprinted away. She looked over her shoulder once to check if her dad was following, but all she saw was Frank lowering into a crouch, then springing in superhuman grace to meet one of the Guards midair.

Damn—Frank. That was her *dad* going vampy in there. . . .

Running for her life, she got it together, knowing panic wouldn't do any good. Amidst screeches from the pursuing Guards, she and Kiko entered the other tunnel. It greeted them with suddenly full-blown electric lighting.

"So much for quiet," Dawn muttered, wondering if now was the time for getting out her whip chain, which would counter those barbed Guard tails. But there wasn't room to maneuver with it in the tunnel, so she stuck with the heavy stuff.

Kiko got out his revolver, his weapon of choice.

A sopping Frank flew at warp speed around the corner to catch up with them, yelling like a happy wrangler, "Here they come! Day hours did make them slower!"

Uh, yeah, and from what she'd seen it hadn't been by much. Maybe they were just slower to freakin' vampire *Frank*.

She aimed her saw-bow as her dad skidded to a stop next to her. Kiko mimicked Dawn with his revolver. Unlike her cofighter, she wouldn't be able to waste blades like bullets, so she forced herself to calm, even if her skin was frying itself away from her muscles.

Take the perfect shot, she told herself. *Nothing less.*

Four nail-on-blackboard cries, all piled one on top of the other, preceded four Guards around the corner. Frank's flames shot out at them, but they were using their long tails to whip upward in stop-start motion, toward the ceiling, out of the stream of fire.

Upon seeing them through the resulting shower of fire-alarm water, Dawn's vision went surreal. Movie monsters, her common sense told her. Nightmares with bald heads, pale skin, iron teeth, clawed hands, and deviled machete-slicing tails. From the first second she'd seen them, fooling herself was the only way to cope.

But a doused Kiko was as collected as a trained sniper. He fired, catching an approaching Guard in its heart.

Whhoo-wiiip. Its body—clothes and all—vacuumed inward until nothing remained.

That left three, one of which went after Kiko by flying through the water toward the gunman. All Dawn heard was a shot from her friend's revolver before she, herself, targeted a Guard on the very left. But when it hesitated, as if not knowing exactly what to do—maybe the Master still didn't want her dead?—she squeezed the saw-bow trigger.

With a sputter of water-shy sparks, the circled blade spun for her prey, catching it in the neck. But, damn it, she'd only cut half its throat. Blood sprayed into the water as the creature gurgled and fell to the ground, grabbing at the wound, its sharpened tail beating into the mud.

From the opposite side of the tunnel, Frank fired his flamethrower. But when it guttered in midgrowl, he dug his other hand into his bag. During this pause, a Guard spit at Frank, and Dawn yelled, "Dad!" because she knew it might burn even in the water-soaked fight. But . . . oh, hell.

Frank didn't need to worry, because he'd zipped out of the line of spit and come to cling to the side of a wet wall, crouched and ready to spring on the offending Guard.

Vamp. Her dad was a crappy v—

Just as Dawn drew a machete from a hip holster and was about to finish off her own half-sawed creature, and just as Kiko's second foe disappeared from a bullet to the heart, Frank's Guard suddenly backed against the opposite wall, as if losing its senses, its purpose. Then it let out a word that almost jolted Dawn out of body.

"Frank . . ." the pitiful thing said, sliding down to the mud.

Her dad's grip slipped on his wall, making him lose his insect-like position. He crouched, hair matted to his head, water streaming down his weathered face. His silver eyes peeked through his drenched strands.

The sitting Guard cocked its head and continued to stare at Frank. "Hooome."

Frank started to shake his head in denial.

"Dad?" Dawn said, leaving her own Guard behind as she lifted her machete and came closer to the sitting sentry.

Why wasn't her dad fighting? Maybe the Guard was seducing him back to their side; he *was* a vamp, she reminded herself, even though she didn't want to.

"Don't!" Frank said, lifting a hand. "Don't do anything—"

The Guard had turned its wet face toward Dawn. "Dawnie?"

The machete almost fell from her grasp.

Then she looked past the red eyes and at its expression. She wouldn't ever have known, otherwise, but there was something about its voice that told her.

"Hugh," Frank said. "It's Hugh Wayne."

Hugh Wayne.

When Dawn had last seen him, she and Kiko had been interviewing the drunk at the Cat's Paw—Frank's favorite bar—about her dad's disappearance. They'd continued to keep tabs on the place, and on her final visit, when she and Breisi had checked in there, Dawn had noticed Hugh was missing. No one knew where he'd gone, but since he had a tendency to land in jail or go on private benders, it hadn't seemed like a big deal. But he had no family, no real friends outside of the bar, so who had been around to care?

Then something about that first night at the Cat's Paw hit her, too. "Matt Lonigan" had been there. "Matt," the Master.

She suspected how Hugh might've disappeared. How each and every one of these buffed-out Guards might've been recruited . . .

"Hooome," murmured the Guard . . . Hugh. "Bloood."

At that word, Dawn gripped her machete, and Kiko, who was just as gobsmacked, raised his revolver. Yeah, they knew this guy, but he was still a vamp. He would kill for their blood, but that wasn't what was spooking her the most.

Her first instinct had been to terminate him without another thought—that was what made her scared.

Frank inched closer to his old friend, cocking his own head as if in understanding. The vamp habit dug into Dawn.

"Hugh?" he asked.

But, just as he got near, something tore out from behind a corner, flying at Frank. Without even deigning to glance at it, her dad easily raised his hand and ripped at the thing's throat.

It was a Groupie skidding over the mud, a scimitar in hand. The woman's silver eyes bulged as she opened her mouth in silent surprise and tested her ripped throat with long, pink-painted fingernails. The chains she wore over her skin got caked with grime, her flowing blond hair growing red where it met her opened neck.

Before anyone could react, Hugh the Guard sprang at the new arrival.

"Blood! Groupie blood, Groupie blood!" He grunted, wrenching back her head to sink his iron fangs into her neck, then drinking deeply.

As the Groupie's eyes rolled back, her mouth formed one beseeching word that looked like "Master???"

From the corner, Dawn's almost-dead Guard began to crawl

through the mud and toward the Groupie, too. "Groupie blood, Groupie blood."

Kiko, Dawn, and Frank all connected gazes, the meaning in each of their eyes clear.

Run.

Frank scooped up Kiko, not even considering the insult of what he was doing to the back-injured psychic, and Dawn hefted her saw-bow to her side. They took off, the mud sucking at her boots until they reached an area where the sprinklers were off. She ran faster when the eerie screeches of "hooome" wavered through the tunnels, as if searching, coming closer and closer. . . .

Thank God none of them had been bleeding. Thank God none of their own wounds had set those Guards off.

As the cries came to a peak, Frank motioned for Dawn and Kiko to halt and wait against a wall. They did, and she pushed her machete back into its holster, then grabbed her .45 to aim it instead. Through a hole in the wall, they could see more Guards screeching past in an adjacent tunnel, coming from other sentry points around the Underground on their way to Hugh and the sacrificial Groupie.

Then Frank lifted his chin, as if listening to the air.

He might've been connecting with Eva now. Dawn hoped so, as she watched a few Groupies dash toward the growing "hooome!" screams.

"I wonder," she whispered to Kiko, "if the Guards can keep those Groupies busy long enough for us to get in and out."

"Don't count on it," Kik said, his breathing labored. He wasn't complaining about being carried around by her muscled dad, so all seemed good.

Frank jerked his head in the "go" signal, and they ran ahead, making their haphazard way toward Eva, then hopefully Breisi, then maybe even . . . ?

How *was* Costin doing?

As Frank ran ahead with Kiko, Dawn cleared her mind, doing her best to stay even with her fast dad.

But when someone's arm sprang out of a crevice in the wall to grab her throat, she couldn't even cry out.

All she could do was watch Frank disappearing down the tunnel with Kiko under his arm while she was dragged into that crevice. Then, as her vision adjusted, she found herself in a small room filled with what looked to be office supplies.

Office supplies? she thought randomly, her throat raw and tender. What the—?

Then her attacker swung her up and pinned her against the wall, holding her high above him with one hand against her chest, making her heave for air as she dropped her weapons.

"Just because the Master likes you," Paul Aspen said, his scars from the chandelier healed to pink reminders, "it doesn't mean we can't settle things between us in a way you won't forget."

He reached up and ripped out her blood-moon earring, laughing as she yelled.

WHiLE Costin's team had made their way Underground—a fact unbeknownst to him—he had stepped out of the shadows to reveal himself in the starkly depressing room known as Benedikte's chambers. Costin had hypnotized his and the Friends' way past Servants, Groupies, Elites, and Guards to get here, mentally persuading the simple beings that they were not seeing him. Ultimately, finding the Master's quarters had been all too easy.

Now, as he stood before Benedikte, he saw that his old comrade was not himself. Literally. He was wearing another being's body: that of a long-haired, brown-tressed male vampire whose face held a barely contained scowl. Yet Costin knew it was his old friend under the surface. He could tell by the window of the eyes.

Casually, he reached into Jonah's oversized coat, grasping the small, tied velvet bags that the Friends would need to guarantee the privacy *he* would need with Benedikte. He'd waited until finding the Master before setting the spirits loose, avoiding any alarms they might trigger on their own.

"Go," he commanded, tossing the bags into the air. The spirits batted them around to push them forward as they left through the open door. Just as carelessly, Costin went to close the barrier, watching Benedikte all the while.

"Shifting shapes," Costin noted as his comrade merely stared with unfocused eyes. "Your powers grew strong. What other talents have you developed?"

As the Master crawled away from the woman he had been cradling—all while never removing his gaze from Costin—memory returned like a night's half-moon.

Benedikte, his fierce yet gentle friend.

He had always fought hard for the dragon, even before the blood vow had been undertaken, yet he had loved a wife beyond all imagining. When she had delivered their stillborn son, it had taken away a vital element in the man; it had perhaps even made it possible for Benedikte to have embraced vampirism with such relish in the end.

Costin watched his companion dart a glance to the breathing vampire woman in the corner, as if to make sure she was safe. Eva Claremont, Dawn's mother. Her eyes were closed, as if in slumber. A look of such longing passed over Benedikte's face that Costin found him to be almost human.

Finally, the Master located his voice. "You entered without incidence. I didn't invite you inside. . . ."

"I don't need such a thing. I am not a vampire like you." Costin shook his head. "Benedikte, I sensed you long ago. You must have wandered aboveground, or perhaps come near an entrance to have shared Awareness with me. You are hard to detect Below."

"You aren't . . . a vampire?" his old friend asked with wonder.

Costin clung to those words. They were all he had besides his rented soul and Jonah's temporary shelter.

At Benedikte's perplexed glance, Costin relented, sweeping a hand over this shape—Jonah's—that must have been so unfamiliar to his old friend.

"I am still Costin," he reminded him.

For a sublime moment, his friend's eyes sparkled, and in that gleam, Costin saw them laughing together over meals, sweating together over the labor of seeing their land remain pure and untouched by foreign conquerors.

As if slipping into a more comfortable suit, Benedikte's body flowed from its present state to one more welcoming. *His* own form. The true Benedikte.

Anxiety invaded Costin. He had bested many masters, but this one . . . ? He was almost a true brother. The bond they had enjoyed remained one of his most treasured human memories.

"My brother," Benedikte said, his tone a testament to better times. But then he cocked his head, his eyes returning to the dull haze that had greeted Costin previously. "You're here to challenge me?"

"Yes, Benedikte."

His old friend smiled tentatively. "Did your Underground fail? Is that why you want mine? I wouldn't turn you out, Costin. You know I wouldn't. Or . . ." He frowned. "No—you were vanquished centuries ago. After the vow, after we crossed the Danube and . . ."

"I did not expire." Costin fought to contain composure. "Not in the conventional way."

Benedikte was clearly frustrated because he did not understand. He had almost regressed to being a child, this man turned poor beast.

Truthfully, Costin did not understand everything, either. But there was one question he needed to ask, one more emotional detail before he would do what he must.

"Did you ever hear me calling to you, Benedikte?" From the prison. From his own hell.

The Master shook his head. "No. Never." For a moment, the

odd light that consumed his gaze clarified. "Had I known you were still among us, I would have answered."

Costin had only wanted to know. "Yes, I believe that." Then he nodded. "But now there is business to attend to."

"Business?" Benedikte pushed the wild hair back from his face and broke into a shaky laugh.

Costin was not certain it was because he found the challenge amusing or if it was because of the many things that must have further scarred his friend during years of pathetic existence.

"When my first Underground was attacked—by Andre, of all vampires," the Master added, "it was a less-civilized moment than this."

Costin knew of the warring between brothers. At times, it made his job easier, if that was how one wished to describe it. Then again, it also caused difficulties when more than one master banded together to strengthen their societies.

"This can be painless, Benedikte," he said gently. He just wanted this to be over. "Can you tell me where our father is buried?"

The blood in Jonah's body began to thrum in anticipation. Though The Whisper had once clarified that the dragon was expected to rise in the late 2000s, Costin knew time was precious.

But Benedikte was not biting—just like the rest of them.

"Why are you here?" he asked instead.

When Costin did not answer, his old friend began laughing—out of control, unhinged while he turned his body toward Eva Claremont again.

"I wouldn't have expected this from you," Benedikte said. "All those rumors about our brothers turning on one another, and I never thought you could ever be one of them, dead *or* alive."

Little did Benedikte know just how far Costin had turned.

But his friend was not done talking. He had rested his back against a wall, his gaze still trained on the woman.

A quiet alarm began to beat in red and blue urgency over the

Master's desk, but the vampire didn't mark it. Costin, however, did. Had someone else breached the Underground?

Dawn. Perhaps she had blocked his final mind blast. He had been depending on its effectiveness, but he should have anticipated her strength.

"I still don't understand," Benedikte said softly, oblivious. "After the world said our father was 'dead,' it should've been so easy. Instead of pursuing his throne from beyond the grave, he decided to quietly enjoy his powers, just like the rest of us. He lay low and allowed his enemies to concentrate on other wars before he formulated the plan of plans to return."

Costin had heard the tale before from other masters, although he had been forced to construct it from piecemeal parts. After his so-called "death," the dragon had enjoyed many gluttonous pursuits. They had never been enough, though, so he had decided to use the element of surprise to regain his properties . . . and then some. Yet just as the maker had been readying those plans, a book had been published in the late 1800s, a work of "fiction" that had brought his legend to light, and it became impossible for him to maneuver undetected.

That was when he had directed his soldiers, his most faithful, to step up their efforts in serving him. The maker was going to rest until his strength increased, and all his sons had to do was create their own societies, their own patriots who would help to populate an entire vampire world—not just a nation—when their father arose like a mighty god. Instead of secret conquering, the dragon was going to use force.

Hence, for a while now, he had lain buried, sleeping in a coffin containing his native soil, gathering power while his soldiers multiplied in number. And when he arose, he would not merely have an army. He would have Armageddon.

Costin repeated the one question that had not yet been answered—the answer to getting his soul back.

"Where is he buried, Benedikte?"

His old friend glanced away from Eva and at Costin, looking startled to discover he was not alone with her.

Costin frowned. And *this* was the vampire who had been lured by a fascination for Dawn . . . ?

Oh. Oh, no. Costin knew how Dawn had endured an Eva complex her entire life, and this was not going to help if she knew that Benedikte might have his own Eva obsession to fulfill with the superstar's own daughter.

The Master came to himself with a start. "I can't tell you where our father is, Costin. Whoever has him never told me. And it's not as if we all keep in contact anymore."

The paranoia, the greed—Costin knew what had separated the brothers and caused them to attack one another.

"Then," Costin said, quelling Jonah's own escalating pulse, "we haven't much else to discuss. I'm not interested in your other vampires." After Benedikte's death, they wouldn't be a factor anyway. Locating the Underground itself was half the challenge. The other was Benedikte, who was the only one here who could match up to Costin.

Benedikte's eyes grew cold, and he became the soldier Costin had once known: proud, strong, a touch mad.

"A soldier's war then." The Master seemed to like the idea of keeping the others out of it. "Just you and me."

Costin bowed to his old friend, out of remembrance, out of a resurrected respect for what they had been to each other. "May the best of us triumph."

As Benedikte's body began to mutate, Costin emerged from Jonah, knowing he did not have much time to fight outside as a free spirit.

TWENTY-FIVE
THE VOID

Dawn's right ear was a wet patch of nerve endings on fire.

Below her, Paul Aspen kept pressing up against her chest to maintain his hold on her against the wall. His other hand held her blood-moon earring.

With a boyish grin, he dropped her to the floor. Blood coated her jaw and neck, and his nostrils flared as he took that in. But instead of begging her for a drink, as Robby Pennybaker had done, Paul jauntily undid one golden hoop out of his own left lobe and replaced it with her earring.

It shimmered in red and silver glee.

The pounding in her ear paced the anger that was gathering. Her head throbbed, as if containing a monster itself.

"Does this make me cool, too?" Paul asked, turning this way and that while taunting her. "I asked the other Elites for permission to get first crack at you, and since I'm one of the oldest ones here, they were fine with it. Well, maybe *they* didn't want to annoy the Master, but I'm past caring with you, sweetheart."

Arrogance—she could always bank on that from a bastard who'd sold his soul for fame.

Her sight became the color of the blood wetting her skin as her head thudded louder.

"You need some lesson learning," he added. "And, sorry to say, but you set off an alarm, so if you think you and your pals are getting anywhere . . ." He flicked the earring, and it danced. "The other Elites will be waiting to take you all to school."

THUD—

Her mind blasted against him, and she just had enough time to enjoy the comical look of shock on his face before he went flying back, knocking over a shelf of paper, sheaves spitting into the air and slowly free-falling. Through the chaos, she caught sight of him splayed against the far wall like a spider whose legs were about to be picked off by a wicked child.

She could tell he'd underestimated her, even though he'd known damned well what she was capable of: it was written all over his drama-king face as his body began to flicker, on the verge of changing into Danger Form.

Dawn whipped out the first weapon she came to in her bag, one that would be accurate at this range.

The small flamethrower.

Elites can walk in sunlight because of drinking the Master's blood, she thought, *but would they truly die by fire?*

She pulled the trigger, flame heaving across the room and catching the last falling paper on fire, just like Paul Aspen's body. He writhed, moaning and screaming in fits while he slid down to the ground, caught in a conflagration. He yawed in a screech, his angelic beauty only an echo in the flames.

Before water could begin raining from the ceiling, Dawn gave him another blast, crisping him to a modern art sculpture—an eternal work that would last through the ages. An Elite would appreciate that.

As moisture from the sprinkler system came down, she dropped the flamethrower, reached for a machete, and cocked it as she jumped at the vampire.

With one swing, his toasted head went flying.

Time seemed to slow into itself, and Dawn took in what she'd done, water sluicing over her face. Paul's separated head was blackened, his mouth gnarled in a whimper. If her earring hadn't been embedded in the freakish charcoal of his flesh, she would've taken it, even though she had no right to the item. Not anymore.

Unlike with Robby's death, she didn't feel any twinge of guilt.

Then, as time sprayed back to normal, Paul's body sucked into nothing.

After cleaning the machete in the water, she went back to collect her dropped weapons and secure them, then reload her saw-bow. The ceiling stopped spraying, and Dawn withdrew out of her bag a capsule of healing unguent that Breisi had once concocted, smearing it on her torn ear. It neutralized the bleeding.

Then she grabbed her revolver, her saw-bow in her other hand, and made her way out of the soaked room. The blood had washed away from her skin but stained into her tank top like a new, pale red emblem.

Detached, she continued in the direction she'd seen Frank and Kiko run, but she didn't get far. She was stopped by Jesse Shane lingering by the door of the emporium, as if on watch.

Eyebrow raised in something like surprise, he smiled that killer smile. "This time when I ask you to play, I'm not going to take no for an answer."

Based on what Paul Aspen had said, Dawn knew Jesse realized that she was now on the Underground shitlist, so she didn't take his invitation to Tiger Beat heart.

This was just part of how Elites fought, both Below and Above: with mind games. With finesse, until their willing victims realized that they hadn't been anything more than a diversion. A toy.

There would be more Elites waiting in the emporium, so she wasn't about to go inside. Besides, she needed to find Kiko and Frank. And where were the Friends since they'd disappeared from the Limpet house along with Costin?

And speaking of Costin . . .

A bruise seemed to swell in her chest at his name. With every pumped heartbeat it hurt more.

Meanwhile, Jesse grinned as he opened the emporium door, looking around behind her at the same time. Had he been expecting Paul to escort her?

The silence from inside the room spoke terrifying volumes.

He jerked his head toward the entrance teasingly, making his summons all the more ominous. His longish golden hair gleamed around his face as he gave a perfunctory glance to her wet appearance, her weapons bag, her saw-bow, and her drawn revolver. Then he lingered over the blood on her shirt and ear, his nostrils flaring only slightly. Maybe the red was too washed out or tamed by Breisi's healing gel, she guessed. It wasn't a fresh temptation anymore.

"Paul Aspen wanted to show me a good time, too," Dawn said. "But I suspect you already know that."

The star raised a bare, muscled arm and leaned it against the wall in a sexy, naughty pose. His eyes began to swirl with the release of his Allure.

But when Dawn blocked it, he raised an eyebrow, startled.

Then he got pissed.

"So what'd you do with Paul anyway?" He was just now acknowledging that Dawn had earned a killing reputation, that she had some mind powers. That she was wandering the halls away from the vampire who was supposed to have taught her a lesson.

"Paul made his last mistake with me," Dawn said, *acting!* for all she was worth. She was Cool Hand Luke right now.

Jesse lost his photo-spread posture, going into a stiff, readied stance instead. Now she wasn't just a toy anymore.

For a loaded second, it was a standoff, neither of them moving.

Don't lose your cool; just draw when you're ready. . . .

He false started, and she brought up her revolver.

But, in a flash, Jesse took her by the waist and tossed her into the emporium. She dropped her saw-bow in midflight: it wasn't a choice if she wanted to land right. Skidding and then balling into a series of rolls, she balanced up to her bandaged knees, aiming her .45 at the first streak of movement to catch her eye.

Yet, before she could fire, a whirlwind cry came from Jesse, and Dawn knew he'd gone into Danger Form.

He swiped at her with a tentacled arm, but she anticipated him, jerking back just in time.

A blow from another one of his arms blasted her off her knees, sending her through the air, and she slammed into . . . something— she couldn't tell what it was at first because everything, including her bones, was ringing.

In the vibrating craziness of her vision, she focused on where she'd landed.

But she couldn't see much. Not unless you counted the Elites circling her, all in misty, flowing, ghost-angel Danger Form. Maybe thirty of them, if she wasn't seeing double.

Out of panic, Dawn pushed out with her mind to swat them away, yet nothing happened.

Angrier, she thought, *you've got to be angrier.* . . .

But, at the sight of their surrounding beauty, she wasn't. No, all she saw around her was the usual reluctant temptation, the in crowd, the startling perfection in every Danger Form.

You can be one of us. She witnessed that in their mist, and she was drawn to it down to the depths of her soul. It was something she couldn't resist, no matter how hard she tried.

Her head tilted as she felt peace hush through her, felt the inebriation of being accepted, even if it was only a fantasy stirred up by discombobulation. . . .

Then she felt her body being picked up by cold tentacles, and an

Elite vampire whipped her around to face its heavenly countenance. As Dawn recognized Rea Carvahal, something told her to grip her revolver. But she'd already dropped it.

Dawn tried not to get lost in the Elite's breathtaking beauty. Instead, she told herself to concentrate on the vampire's prideful ire shining through the mist.

"Tit for tat," the gorgeous vamp said, batting Dawn upside the head with a cloudy limb in imitation of what Dawn had done to Rea earlier.

The cuffing had a gonglike effect. In fact, when Rea tossed her away, Dawn didn't even realize it until she was halfway across the Elites' circle.

Another vampire swatted her in midair—*gong*. Then another. Another.

They laughed at her, laughed and laughed.

With each smack, she flailed in helpless instinct, trying to grasp on to something but catching only air. With each progressively harsher punch, she groaned, her ribs sore, her body pummeled with more than just physical violence—with mortification, too.

They laughed harder. And harder.

Finally, one vampire missed, and Dawn hit the floor, barely avoiding dinging her face on the marble. There, they allowed her to gasp for breath. She felt pulverized, shamed.

"What about Eva?" she heard one of them say in the fuzz of her hearing. The voice was ethereal—angelic and demonic at the same time.

More laughter. Then someone answered in that same preternaturally tinged tone—male, female, Dawn couldn't think what gender it was.

"Screw Eva," that vamp said.

Hilarity ensued, and Dawn's throat tightened at the cruelty. She was back to being twelve, teased by the other Hollywood kids for being a tomboy and not having a mother to go home to.

Between the strands of their laughter, Dawn thought she heard something distant, out in the hall. A yell . . . maybe a cry.

The Groupies, the Guards . . . Was it them? Were they coming now, too?

As a pressure built from her chest to her throat, making her perspire with damp panic, she tried to push away from the floor. But a tentacle snapped out to slap her down. The side of her face met the marble, making it spike with pain.

A different Elite spoke up. "We heard you've been a bad, bad girl, Dawn. The Master's supposed to be mad at you—that's the rumor. And thinking you could walk around with weapons to use on us . . . ? Who do you think you are?"

Weapons—she needed them, just one of them. . . . Face smashed against the floor, Dawn snuck her hand under her belly, toward her bag.

"Do you think the Master would like to be in on this?" another asked.

Dawn touched something hard near the top of her bag. A silver-tipped stake—a close-range tool. She tried to dig deeper.

"He can tell us later, when he gives us an update about what's exactly happening now," yet another vamp said, extending the lazy discussion that had gone from surreal to rude, now that Dawn's head had stopped buzzing.

"Update?" Was that Jesse Shane's altered voice? "We kick ass on anyone who enters with a bag of weapons; that's what the Master would want. That's *my* update."

They all laughed again, like they were at a cocktail party listening to the action hero talk big. It gave Dawn the opportunity to squirm her hand way down into her bag.

But when one of the Elites spanked her with a tentacle, Dawn froze, mouth opening in a stifled cry.

Don't you let them see your shame. Don't, *Dawn.*

"Bad girl," the random vampire said. Actually, it sounded like

Rea Carvahal. "I'll get you again if you don't tell us if Limpet came in with you."

"The Master would let us know if *he* knew," yet another vamp said, leading to even more comments.

"Maybe the Guards have already taken care of the rest of them?"

"Or maybe the Groupies did."

"It'd be nice to have that update. . . ."

Another smack on the butt made Dawn flinch. The burn in her throat made her choke back threatening tears.

Her head began to tighten.

"Tell us, you little bitch!" Another spank from what had to be Rea. Then another.

Outside the emporium, there was a shriek, this one closer. Dawn didn't know if it was in her own head or for real.

Another spank. With every one, her poise took a hit. But her helpless outrage flared.

Something barged into the other end of the emporium, making most of the Elites gasp and stir, but Dawn could only feel a tentacle sneaking beneath her body to undo her jeans for a bare-assed whack.

A furious sob came from Dawn, and her mind exploded.

Vision blurred, she levered to her hands and knees, directing her fury at Rea. Meanwhile, the rest of them were whirling around the room, frenzied by whatever had come into the emporium.

At Dawn's mind punch, Rea's mist and tentacles had spun away like an unraveling ball of silk threads. The vampiric mass crashed into a pillar, then banged to the ground.

Quickly, Dawn groped over the floor, toward her dropped revolver, aiming at Rea and plugging it in the heart.

As she squeezed off a shot at another vamp that was fleeing toward the door with the rest of the herd, the room went to an even higher level of chaos. Something had clearly won their attention away from Dawn.

Her silver bullet pierced her target's heart and, just then, Dawn realized which Elite she'd gotten. Charity Flynn screamed and clutched her chest. Then, like a career gone into free fall, her celestial beauty sucked into where the bullet had struck, a star collapsed into nothing.

Wobbling to her feet, Dawn began to stumble toward a pillar for cover. But one Elite wasn't letting her go anywhere.

Jesse Shane.

She aimed at him. *Bam*—her bullet caught the silver fringe of his Danger Form, and he jerked back but didn't implode.

Damn—silver anywhere but in the heart poisoned but didn't immediately kill.

Shaking his head, Jesse got into a compacted attack position, then charged her. Dawn rolled away, shooting again, missing altogether this time.

He whizzed above her, intimidating her by hovering, then zoomed down to attack, his mouth opening in a silvery, fanged grimace.

"Costin," she said under her breath as she raised her revolver. Probably her last word, and she'd spoken *his* name.

It all came rushing back—an avalanche of emotion that destroyed all the containers where she'd been keeping her real feelings: a flash flood of heat, remorse, bewildered anger.

Crasssshhh!

At her mind punch, Jesse spun backward, as if hitting a shield.

Steeped in everything she'd always tried to white out of her, Dawn now opened herself to the anguish Eva had initiated, the self-hatred Dawn herself had nursed all these years. She used every burst of it to pound back at the ever-weakening Jesse, wielding the fear of not knowing how long she could keep this up to feed her even more.

But each mental smash was losing power. . . .

Costin, bait, using each other—?

Now her repulsing grew in strength and, soon, Jesse dropped to the floor, swishing back to his more human form while he held his waist where her bullet had nicked him, poisoning him.

She sprang up and came to stand over his body, leveling her revolver.

"Mercy?" He was still playful, grinning at her as if his charm could win the day. But he was nervous, too.

Aw.

Dawn planted a bullet in his heart and his smile disappeared in an inward rush of full-body oblivion.

Then she ran—no, *tripped*—to the other end of the emporium, where shrill cries strained her ears. What she found surprised the tar out of her: the smell of jasmine—*Friends!*—plus the sight of all but two Elites frozen statue still in their more human forms: she recognized Tamsin Greene among them before she realized that two remaining vampires had flown up to the golden dome, plastering their Danger Forms against it like filmy webs.

What the hell? They were *afraid* of the Friends, even though the vampires knew how to captivate them . . . ?

Then the truth hit. Duh—these Elites didn't want to be statued like the others. But how were they getting statued?

At the reprieve, Dawn got out her flamethrower to see if it was working well enough to cover the range. Then she heard Kiko's voice; it hardly registered.

He'd run to her, now that the Friends were in control. "Those last two Elites are peeing their pants so hard that they're not even thinking of captivating our girls. The others"—he gestured toward the statued Elites—"never knew what hit them."

Slowly, Dawn turned to the psychic, finding his gaze on the dome. Frank walked up to them, too, towering over them both as he scowled at the mini Elite gathering.

Then Breisi's voice whispered into Dawn's right ear. *"I shouldn't have expected you to follow the boss's orders and stay home."*

All the heaviness, the anger, left Dawn in a shaky moan. "Breisi."

An indistinguishable nattering from a second Friend shook Dawn's other ear. There, the jasmine was overpowering.

"Aw, Kalin," Kiko said. "Shut up and do your thing."

He tossed a hand-sized velvet bag into the air and, just like that, all the jasmine swept up and away, toward the dome, the bag juggled aloft, as if an invisible force or ten were batting it around.

Even Breisi got in on the action. *"Here we go."*

But first her jasmine trailed toward Frank. He smiled, reached out a hand as if to touch the scent, then lowered his arm as he watched the spirit-woman he loved go to work.

Kiko indicated Dawn's washed-out, bloodied shirt and her ripped ear. "I see you've been busy." He nodded toward the traveling Friends. "After you disappeared, one group of Friends caught us in the halls before we could even find Eva. On the way, they neutralized some Elites with—jeez, wait 'til you see what they have in those bags—and then shuttled us to a little closet room where vials were being kept. That's when we all let Breisi and the other captivated Friends out of those containers. Then, just like nothing happened, they all went to work on the rest of the Underground. They were protected by the last of a hypnotic spell that Costin used to let them sneak around undetected, so none were captivated this time out."

Costin . . .

She let go of the name and instead took in how, for the first moment in ages, Kiko seemed confident, redeemed by finally getting to play the stud again. True, he was slurring slightly, but what could they do about that now?

"Only thing is," Kiko continued, keeping his eye on the spirits as they swarmed near the two leftover Elites, "the Friends wanted to get back to a room of souls—the ones the Master was collecting from his Elites. I don't know what we're gonna do with what's in that room, but the Friends won't be quiet about seeing to them."

Dawn imagined that Costin probably had plans for those Elite souls: releasing them so they could return to their humanized owners after the Master was vanquished? Or would that happen automatically?

She glanced around for her saw-bow, then picked it up and came back to watch what the Friends were up to with the remaining Elites.

"They had everything in check before we even got here," Kiko said. "Kick-ass former vamp hunters, huh? They haven't lost it. You know how the Friends were all secretive in the lab? That's 'cause Breisi was helping Costin make this . . . stuff."

"Stuff?" Dawn secured her bow on the floor, then reloaded her revolver while keeping her eyes raised above.

Near the dome, out of seemingly nowhere, something sprayed out of the bags at the Elites, as if forcefully spread by the Friends.

Silver sprinkles?

The Elites seemed to inadvertently inhale the matter, moaning as they struggled to breathe.

"You'll see," Frank said. "The Friends made some silver-based dust that should put every vamp but the Master out of commission while Costin does his own work. Once that silver concoction's in the Elite's system? Loss of body control—poison. Friends say they already took care of all the Elites who weren't hanging out in this room."

"Except for Eva," Kiko added. "They said she's with the Master and she's not moving around anyway."

Dawn's stomach flopped, and she turned to her dad. When he didn't react, she wondered if he still wanted to go after his wife, even though he didn't need her help to find Breisi anymore.

At that moment, there was a wailing from above, and it consumed her attention. Silver dust showered down, blocking Dawn's view of the action at first. But then she saw something wondrous: the two Elites changing from Danger Form to their solid bodies. Their silk clothing fluttered as Friends guided the vampires down, down, like comets streaking from the sky.

By the time the bodies were laid on the floor, they'd become flesh-and-blood statues.

Dawn got closer to inspect them, gritting her teeth at the aches in her joints and bruises on her skin.

"It's just temporary until the boss can take care of the Master," Frank said, sounding proud at Breisi's genius in creating vamp weapons. "The Friends don't have to kill to be efficient yet ruthless."

Speaking of ruthless. Dawn thought about Eva again. What if the Master had punished her mother and that was why she wasn't moving? What if she needed their help?

Dawn had to get more information before deciding how to go about phase two of her own personal Underground mission. "And the Groupies and Guards? Are they out of the way?"

"We got other Friends seeing to the lower vamps," Frank said, "but from what we heard, the Groupies and Guards pretty much took care of one another. Groupies got snacked on hard."

"Any Servants?"

"Friends said they've all gone Above. They're nothing anyways."

"And the surviving Guards?"

With one last look at the Friends tending to the motionless Elites, Frank hefted his flamethrower and started for the door. "We're going to try more dust on them. Breisi said that Costin was going to take care of euthanizing Guards after he finished his job, but I volunteered to do it first, since we're down here anyway. I figure I might as well stay on his good side."

"Let's go then," Kiko said, untroubled by the possibility of getting busted. He was still flying high in hero mode and, really, it was good to see.

Still, Dawn's first instinct was to stop them from putting the not-running-on-all-cylinders Kiko at risk again, but she decided she would go with them instead. She would talk to Frank about Eva on the way. If he wanted to help, great. If not, oh well.

"So," she said carelessly—*acting!*—"it sounds like Costin's no doubt doing okay in his part of the Underground. He had everything planned, all right, but—"

"Don't even," Kiko grumbled as they headed for the door. "I don't have to read your mind to know what you're thinkin'."

Even though her body felt pulled to another side of the Underground, where Costin was probably even now fighting with Benedikte, Dawn forced herself to follow her group.

They entered the hallway, where more Elites lay frozen on the tile, no longer a factor. Then a stream of jasmine joined them while the team readied their weapons for any unexpected Guards, Groupies, or even Servants.

The lights in the hallway flickered with malicious warning while they patrolled, up and down, all the rock walls looking the same. But the Friends kept them on course by zipping ahead and reporting back. Plus Frank was familiar with the surroundings, thanks to Eva.

When they heard a massive scream that shook the walls, they all looked at one another, knowing exactly what it was. The Master, or maybe Eva . . .

Or it could've even been Costin.

Dawn sprinted toward it, knowing nothing could keep her from where she really wanted to be.

WHILE Dawn was facing the Elites and the Friends were dusting the house, Costin and Benedikte were meeting head-on.

Perhaps the Master was withstanding the attack so deftly because he knew Costin's limits in battle: the hesitation he had shown before taking the vow, the loyalty that had linked him to the sovereign for only as long as Costin could endure, the humanity both Benedikte and Costin had shared in their bond as friends.

But now, in Benedikte's frenzied state—one that Costin chalked up to a disease of the mind, cultivated through the madness of living too many years without a soul—he was all but unstoppable.

In Costin's rented spirit form, he had advantages a monster like Benedikte did not: Costin could dart here and there, disappearing in collapsed pockets of air and popping up somewhere else to attack. Yet Benedikte had the strength of insanity on his side, flashing from human form one moment to a hell-beast mass of smoky matter another.

Now, as they circled each other in the Master's room, Benedikte wore this *last* terrible shape. Costin could see hints of nightmares inside his brother's abysmal form, yet the images did not affect him. He had lived with these nightmares every day, and they had only served to drive him in this quest to rid the world of the dragon and his ilk.

In a spurt of quickness, Costin jammed Benedikte against the wall, then popped from left to right, emerging and disappearing as if he were a sparring boxer, putting off the foe until weakened. Soon he would have to retreat back to Jonah, who was still recovering on the floor from the sensation of Costin being out of body. But first Costin needed to get the Master into a more helpless state that would leave him open for the final attack—

As Benedikte took a swipe at him with a meaty, translucent-yet-solid claw that rent the air, Costin popped into a pocket of atmosphere, then reconstituted on the other side of the room.

"This is not worth the effort you are expending, Benedikte." He was using what Dawn had always called The Voice, his ultimate weapon. Out of Jonah's body, the undiluted power of it was always a master's undoing. In body, it was not enough weapon to fight any brother who had taken the blood vow. At least thus far. Unfortunately, Benedikte was taking longer than most masters since he seemed to have more than just an Underground on his mind: was Benedikte also fighting for Eva? To get her back somehow? Or was he thinking of Dawn, too . . . ?

At the repeated thoughts of Dawn, Costin faltered, then forced himself to concentrate. "Does the thought of happiness, eternal and bright, not appeal to you?"

He had sensed this longing in his brother's mind before Benedikte had shut him out. And, just as Costin had hoped, the Master's dark form finally withered, as if touched by the possibility.

He stilled, then drifted, stormlike, over to the unconscious Eva

Claremont. Her mind was blank to Costin, and he had not the strength to concentrate on both vampires.

Suddenly, Benedikte's black form shuddered, and even Costin reacted, his essence ruffling in discomfort.

"Happiness does not exist," the Master said, warped voice shaking. "It is a lie."

Encouraged that a little hypnosis might end up going a long way with a master in such a torn state, Costin continued. "It was not a lie with your wife. Remember?"

Costin detected a smudge of recollection wipe through Benedikte's sheer form, an image of Tereza, who would have died centuries ago as a human. She had the same innocent smile that had made Eva Claremont a superstar.

Now was the moment to end this.

Summoning every ounce of energy—energy he could only conjure out of body—Costin cast a solid-looking image of Tereza, blond and tiny and pale. This was more than the usual hypnotic vision—this would be life itself to Benedikte. This would be the Trojan horse carrying his destruction.

Costin's essence shook with the effort of aiming Tereza on the other side of Eva Claremont, manipulating the vision into holding out her arms to Benedikte in a plea for him to return to her.

"Come to me," he made her say to Benedikte, juxtaposing the fantasy next to the movie-star vampire who had betrayed her master. Anything to get Benedikte to lower his defenses.

The labor in completing the fantasy, coupled with being away from Jonah's body, was sapping him moment by moment. While Costin hovered near Jonah's slumped form, his soul jerked in anticipation of returning.

As for Jonah himself, the boy knew what to do now: he fumbled with a small flamethrower beneath his coat. Fire always seemed to work on masters—it was far more concentrated than the mere sunlight most could withstand. Costin prayed it would be the same with a weakening Benedikte. . . .

Across the room, the Master's form had started to shift again, flickering back and forth between the deadly smoke and the body Costin knew as Benedikte—a form most open to decimation just as soon as the vampire committed fully to it. His bound hair had fallen loose from its band, slumping over a brow as he reached for the Tereza vision.

Yes, Costin thought. *Forget everything but her! Become yourself again, Benedikte.*

When he felt a tug of need consume his body, urging it to get back to Jonah soon, he ignored it. He was almost there, almost done with this master, and he could not maintain this caliber of image unless he was out of Jonah's body, unblocked by human matter.

"Happiness," Costin whispered in his Voice. "She wants you to join her, Benedikte. Join her as *yourself.*"

Still flickering between smoke and Benedikte form, the Master began to weep as he got closer to the wife he had so loved. The wife who had indeed brought him such joy during their life, even through their trials.

Then Benedikte remained in humanlike shape for a longer time, flickered to smoke again, and finally went back to being himself. . . .

A mighty yank drew Costin nearer to his host, a costly distraction.

At the same time, a whole-bodied Benedikte leaped forward to embrace Tereza—a vision that his arms cut right through.

Costin recovered. "Jonah—now!"

Even with his slumping lack of energy, Jonah brought up the flamethrower while the Master screamed, blowing the door clean away from his room. It burst to dust across the hall.

"Another lie . . . !"

Then, with another cry, Benedikte exploded back to that smoky nightmare cloud and rounded on Costin.

"Jonah!" Costin yelled, thinking this should have been over by now.

But it was just beginning again. The Master had seen the

flamethrower and bolted forward to knock it out of a terrified Jonah's hands as the boy closed his eyes. But he'd also made forceful contact with the human, too, and the boy hurtled through the air, smacking into the wall.

Costin heard bones crunch.

Blood leaked from Jonah's head as he struggled to crawl away from the wall, reaching into his coat in spite of his clearly debilitating injuries.

Before Benedikte could hurt Jonah any more, Costin swooped over, barging against the Master's form—solid invisibility against solid invisibility—and slammed him away.

At the same time, he fought to stay out of his host's body, but he could feel a click of neediness signaling that his time was counting down.

The brothers went at each other like dogs, tearing and maiming, devouring with a passion for survival. With every swipe, every maneuver, Costin became less and less.

Body . . . my home . . .

Unable to cope anymore, he flew toward Jonah, entering, booming inside the body and expanding to fit once again. Both Jonah and Costin heaved in a high-pitched breath, and the boy's agony rooted to Costin. Their vision was near dark as they fought off the pain together, as Jonah had been trained to do, their shared body going numb.

Nonetheless, Jonah had already grabbed another weapon with his good arm, a silver stake, the nearest thing at hand in his coat. Now, with Costin's reentrance and added power—what was left of it—Jonah clutched the weapon.

The pain . . . Costin clung to Jonah's injured humanity and battered psyche, feeling just how serious his host's wounds were.

He'd waited too long to stay out. He'd allowed Jonah to get hurt. . . .

A voice was yelling from where the door used to be—it had consumed the Master's attention and changed him into humanlike form.

"Stop, Benedikte!"

It was Dawn, wet and bedraggled, aiming a saw-bow. Pink, washed-out bloodstains streaked her shirt.

The Master darted over and swiped in one lightning-quick flash, knocking her into his desk, where she merely crashed into the wood and sat stunned, her saw-bow dropped.

He could have done worse, so much worse. Had he been holding back?

Then a ruckus in the hall drew the Master's attention. Kiko and Frank. The Friends would be with them, as well—

Benedikte yelled, and chairs went flying into Kiko and Frank, bashing them outside. Then the Master cried out again, and the opening squeezed together, sealing the entrance so tightly not even a Friend would be able to slip through.

He had blocked out everyone but Dawn.

Costin began to pray, his mental whispers ever weakening.

The Master turned on her. "Why do you return!" But then his scream fell to a whisper. *"Why?"*

Even as he questioned, Costin and Jonah's vision went gray, lifeblood gagging Jonah.

Did Costin have enough strength to leave this dying body? He had to get out, flee before this personal cave crashed down on him and trapped him—

He pushed upward, but he couldn't leave. Instinctively, he needed to cling, to root, a parasite without choice.

He couldn't . . .

Helplessly, he watched as Dawn flicked a glance at her mother, then checked Jonah, as well.

Costin forced Jonah to blink as a message—*I'm alive; I'm still in here*—and her face became a masterwork of relief and released affection.

Then the room got darker, and it didn't hide her terror-ridden realization at what was really happening to him.

As his host's body closed in around Costin, he mused, *She came.*

Jonah was thinking the same, and their thoughts merged in an avalanche of oncoming death.

Even when commanded to stay away, she was too powerful to obey.

Thank the Lord she came. . . .

TWENTY-SIX

The Inhumanity

When Dawn saw the lights go out of a severely bloodied Jonah's—*Costin's*—eyes, she began to scream. Too late, she thought. I'm too . . .

Unable to look anymore, she dragged her gaze to Eva. Her vampire mother was bloody, too, but the red was dry on her skin and she didn't seem as bad off as Jonah and Costin. She was either alive or peacefully dead, though it didn't look like she'd been killed like a vamp should be.

Was she in the process of healing, bolstered by her stronger preternatural powers?

Then Benedikte's voice speared into her thoughts. But it wasn't the Master's voice anymore. It was Matt Lonigan's.

"Why did you come back?" he asked again.

Dawn looked at the man who'd earned some of her affection once. At least she'd thought so.

Matt's—the Master's—pugilistic features seemed more wounded than ever.

Oh, Matt. She wanted to ask "why," too. Wanted to know why she'd been taken in by him so easily. Why she'd betrayed Costin by gravitating toward his rival.

"Why what?" Dawn asked, containing a quavering sense of loss as she kept thinking of Costin in Jonah's battered body. She was doing another acting job now, pretending to be calm; it was becoming natural. "Why am I down here?"

"Yes, Dawn. You left me with Eva's help, and I thought you wanted it that way. Are you . . . ?" "Matt" looked so hopeful, but then his face crumbled into a frown.

Dawn hurried before he lost it. "Matt," she said, using this name in the hopes that he would think they were still on nice, delusional terms. *Please believe me, please.* "Did you know that your Guards freaked out and ate the Groupies? The Underground is defenseless right now."

Benedikte just stared at her, his frown melting. Then he began to laugh. It was scalloped with a tinge of crazy.

"Sorin," he whispered, more to himself than anything. "Without him, the Guards wouldn't obey." Then "Matt" locked onto her again. "Why would *you* care about my Underground?"

She just smiled at him, hoping that it would pass as an answer. She couldn't think anyway because her mind was still on Costin. Was he dead? She still couldn't grasp that, wouldn't let herself believe it— an unfeeling blankness didn't allow her to even consider it. And everyone else was blocked out of the room, including the Friends, thanks to Benedikte's spaz attack. But she thought she heard some movement on the other side of the wall, as if everyone were banging away at the stone.

It was up to her, wasn't it? She was key. She was going to be the one to bring down this master after all.

The sense of importance, control, fulfilled her when it shouldn't have. She should be doing this for a higher purpose, not ego. Still, no matter what her motivation, it was going to get done. She just needed to keep the Master calm, then ratchet up her anger and use her mind on him . . . or better yet, use a silver stake to the heart or even a bullet.

"You had me fooled for a while," she said to "Matt," standing slowly from the wreckage of the desk. Damn it, her right arm hurt where she'd been wounded by Robby Pennybaker once. It was a little numb, and her lobe was beating where Paul Aspen had ripped out her earring. But the realization of what he'd done hurt more than the actual wound, which was healing under Breisi's unguent.

"I had you fooled?" The Master didn't seem to know what she was talking about until he glanced down at "Matt"'s body. "Oh, this."

Oh, this?

"You wanted me," he said, "just as I wanted you. That's straightforward enough."

"I guess it is." They *wanted* each other. "That night you met me at the Cat's Paw, I was"—she swallowed—"attracted to you. It's true."

She sounded collected, even if she was grossed out.

"Seeing you in real life and not merely in pictures was a different experience." The Master got a dreamy gleam in his eyes, telling Dawn that this walk down memory lane was keeping him at bay for the time being. "I recognized another lost soul in you. And you reminded me of Eva, but she just wanted Frank. Yet we—you and I, not me and her—were compatible. I wasn't meant for Eva at all."

Dawn got attacked by the heebie-jeebies . . . and the same garbage that'd been dogging her ever since she was old enough to know who Eva was. A pulse throbbed in her temple.

The Master closed his eyes and leaned back his head. "I only came Above to find answers about some vamp hunters who were causing trouble. But I found you at the same time. I lied to myself, thinking that I was only going to win you over so I could extract information from you, but then you . . . came onto me." He looked uncomfortable with that term. "You were interested in this body, Matt's body, and . . ."

He didn't have to continue.

She watched a comatose Eva out of the corner of her eye. Not moving—not moving at all. Watched Costin and wished him back to life, if he'd really gone and died.

Died. A sob choked her as she listened to the clanking noises outside where help was coming.

Cry later. You're key. You're the only *one who can take care of this now.*

Slowly, her shattered will reconstructed, even though a lone echo inside kept asking, "Costin?"

"So you were moonlighting as one of the Underground's spies," she said.

"I took a big chance." "Matt" was looking more hopeful the longer she kept him talking. "I opened myself to another master's Awareness by going Above, but I was always careful to shield, except for one night at Matt's home. I had to try to get information from you, had to see if it would work."

She knew exactly what he was talking about. That night, she'd felt a twinge of invasion, and this was the reason. But unlike other vamps, he hadn't needed to look at her to mind screw. He was more powerful, pure-blooded.

"Sorin never agreed with what I was doing." The Master seemed agitated again. "He thought it was too risky having me Above. But I was effective, wasn't I? I brought up the subject of vampires with you because I knew Limpet was already on to us, so why not misdirect you with Matt's stories about other vampires who dwell Above? Non-Underground vampires."

"It worked for a while, Matt."

"I tried so hard to earn your trust so you would tell me everything without my having to enter your mind. I wanted you to permit me one day. I wanted you to be willing, Eva."

At that, both of them stared at each other. Then the Master glanced at the movie star still propped against the wall. Dawn didn't bother. She didn't yearn for Benedikte, but everyone yearned for Eva. Always had, always would.

"Dawn." The Master was shaking his head in apology. "You made me feel alive again when your mother couldn't."

What he's saying doesn't matter; don't let it matter. . . .

"You're good," she said, awkwardly moving her uninjured hand closer to her revolver bit by bit, so as not to provoke him. "You're a hell of an actor. Was that blade you wore at your back a prop?"

He seemed pleased that she'd noted this. "Method acting."

What was this guy about? Then she thought of his society: movie stars, screenings. Benedikte was the ultimate groupie.

"I even thought," she added, "you tried to kill Robby Pennybaker with that machete."

"No, I'd never kill my son."

Benedikte crumbled, sinking to his knees and uttering something like, "Sorin," under his breath.

Dawn had to work quick, had to carry on with Costin's quest.

She contained herself at that. *Later . . . cry later. . . .*

What had Costin said? That he always asked where the maker was buried before dispatching a master. She needed to do that, too. But how was she going to get around to the subject without Benedikte wigging out?

Keep working at it, she thought. *Use what you've learned.*

"You seemed very human," she began, following her own advice.

The Master halted his dramatics. She'd never seen anyone turn on and off this fast. . . . Wait. Yes, she had. On a movie set during a break, an actor had gone from slaphappy to suicidal within two seconds and they'd escorted him to his trailer, then taken him to his doctor.

This wasn't out of the ordinary for someone who lived close to the skin. And actors did. They banked on emotion, or the semblance of it.

"Yes, I passed for a human very well," Benedikte said, smiling, even with his eyes bleary. "I took the shape of a Servant, studied his ways, emulated him. If you'd met the real Matt, you wouldn't be able to tell the difference."

"Well-done." *Get to the dragon.*

"I had to cover my bases. I wasn't sure if Limpet was actually investigating the Underground or not, and I couldn't assume his interest in Robby's case meant he was on to us."

"And you definitely got my sympathy." As thoughts of Costin crept into her again, her legs started to shake. She hurt. And, damn it, her saw-bow was across the room.

She kept inching her left hand toward her firearm, hoping to use it after wheedling the dragon's location out of Benedikte. "Adapting the Batman story was smart. Murdered parents, who drove you to hunting vampires . . ."

"A flight of fancy that almost cost me since I deviated from the real Matt's story." The Master sat on the ground. "And you almost caught on until I had a Servant plant Internet database stories and paperwork about the other name I gave to throw you off my trail: Matt Destry. The name I told you I'd shed after my parents' deaths." It sounded like he was giving her some credit for keeping him on his acting toes. "To think, after all these years of gaining immunity to things like garlic, sunlight, religious items . . . I can't overcome a woman as easily."

Stay on course. "Your powers are impressive." She gestured to his body, indicating his ability to shift. "But your acting . . . I mean, how did you talk on the phone with Costin and avoid detection? You had actual voice contact with him. He no doubt altered his own, but how did you fool him?"

"Shielding." Now he was trying to impress her. "But it voided my ability to reach out and sense what he was in return. I had to rely on good old-fashioned detective work. I hoped that Limpet . . . Costin . . ." He paused, then started up again with a confused slant to his face. "I hoped he would reach out and try to sense me, giving himself away, but he was shielding, too."

Yet Costin had me to draw you out, Dawn thought.

"You, though," he added, "*you* were reason enough to risk everything. When I didn't see you for that entire month between Robby's death and the Vampire Killer murders, it tested me. All I wanted was to be Above with you, but Robby's demise forced me to take stock down here. My children needed me. We all locked down together until security was partially reestablished."

Dragon—how could she get to the dragon from this without giving herself away? If she pulled a weapon, then asked, he would kick her ass mano a mano.

"Dawn," he whispered, and she knew that she'd come to the end of this Sherlock-paved road.

He cocked his head at her. "I've been waiting for you to come to me. I thought there was no chance after Eva took you." He went livid. "I get it. You came back because it was her fault, wasn't it? She *did* take you away from me. Jealous. She was only jealous." He stopped, laughing.

Out of Dawn's peripheral vision, she thought she saw Eva stir.

Mirth subsiding, Benedikte held out a hand to her. "I wanted you to come, master to loved one. 'Matt' would get you down here, and I knew you'd ultimately stay because I could give you anything you ever wanted."

She tried to block against his reasoning, but he was right. She could've been one of them, but on her own terms. She really could've been her mother's daughter.

Her gaze came to rest on Costin in Jonah's still body. If he had stayed intact, maybe her longing to be like Eva wouldn't have mattered eventually. Costin had always wanted Dawn for what *she* offered—

As if sensing her grief, Jonah's eyes came open to a slit. Dawn didn't move a muscle, not believing what she saw. But when he closed his eyes, her body resurrected, heart pounding.

Alive? She could still help him. What had Costin said? Oh, God . . .

*If I am somehow caught in my host's body during his death—if
I should need to anchor to the strength and sustenance he gives me
because I am too weak to escape, for instance—my quest is over. I
will have failed and will perish in damnation since I would not be
able to escape the useless host and redeem myself. . . .*

If Jonah died, Costin would lose his soul. It wasn't fair. This
couldn't happen. . . .

Then, with a crash of conscience, she knew what she had to do.
So simple. So obvious. So *right*. Costin might kill her, but it was the
only way.

After all, the good of the many outweighed the good of the few.
Costin would agree with that.

Blind and deaf to everything but the bigger picture—and to
Costin—she went forward, no matter the sacrifice. She really *was*
key. She was Costin's only chance.

Clink, clink, clink went the team outside as they tried to find a
way in. But they weren't here yet.

She swallowed back the nausea of what justice was demanding
she carry out.

"You'd give me anything?" Dawn whispered to Benedikte, sinking to her knees, slipping off her weapons bag in a show of trust.
"Even after all the hard feelings between us?"

"Matt" shifted into his Benedikte body, his eyes lighting up
with hope. Hell, why couldn't he have stayed in "Matt"'s body? It
would've been so much easier.

"I would give you the world," he said, excitement lacing his tone.
Make him believe; make him believe. . . .

"I want to be like Eva more than anything else," she said, the
words enticing her when they shouldn't have. "Please."

A small sound emitted from the other side of the room, where
Costin lay.

His inability to go out of Jonah's body emphasized just how bad
off he was. She would bet he was in there, trying to get out and he
couldn't.

But she was going to take care of that.

As she offered her neck to the Master, Dawn turned her face toward Eva. And just as Benedikte reared back and dove for Dawn's throat, she saw that her mother was indeed awake, woozily pushing away from the wall.

"No, Dawn—!" she whispered weakly.

The Master's fangs entered her, and Dawn held back a shocked groan, clenching his arms as she instinctively arched. Stabbed, invaded . . .

Memory exploded, and she saw stars, just as she had when someone else—Paul Aspen—had bitten her.

A tear of agony slipped from her eye as Benedikte sucked at her, draining, pulling at her jugular. In Dawn's blurry vision, she saw Eva crawling toward her, but she mouthed, "No!" and opened her jaw in incomprehensible reaction to the Master's stimulated drinking.

The only way, she thought, *the only way to help Costin . . .*

With a joyous breath, Benedikte stopped nursing at her, then tore open his shirt and slit his breastbone with a nail. Blood seeped from his flesh, and he took the back of her head and led her to it.

At first taste, she took to the liquid, clinging to Benedikte. Good. Perfect. More. More. More—

Everything flowed into her: power, glory, love, knowledge. A drugged rush of completion. She heard the roar of crowds showering devotion at her feet, felt the caress of ticker tape falling over her as she paraded by the masses while they hung over barricades just for the chance to see her, maybe even to touch her.

The silver crucifix against her young vampire chest began to warm up, but she didn't care. She was strong, all-powerful, almost immortal.

She thought she heard weeping from Eva, silence from Costin. Still, she drank and drank, Allure drowning her in its fantasy.

"There, there, my darling," Benedikte whispered in her ear. "You're me. You're my everything."

She pulled away, looking into his glowing eyes and panting, wanting more. She felt as light as ether, and just as potent.

Shot through with ecstasy, Dawn pressed against the Master, feeling the vampirism taking painful root, feeling her limbs grow strong and healed. Every minute was torture as the new blood thudded into the place of the old, stretching her veins, heating them, making her into someone more exponentially wonderful than anything she could've dreamed.

Finally, after forever seemed to have passed, Dawn lifted her head to look at Benedikte. In her emerging heightened vision, she saw how his skin glowed, how the blood traveled beneath it in neon patterns.

More time passed as her body heaved and adapted. Eva continued crying, but she didn't do anything to stop Dawn.

Her daughter had more than enough time to wonder why.

Then, as she opened her eyes again to take in a room that had grown in color—so vivid it almost made her cringe—she held the Master away from her.

"I'm almost as strong as you?" she asked.

"You're my pure child, and have taken more blood than any Elite. You're my best work."

With true gratefulness, she whispered, "Thank you, Benedikte," and tore off her crucifix, cocking back her hand, then spearing the sharpened silver into his neck with superstrength. He opened his mouth in surprise.

"Stop. . . ." It was Eva.

Her plea ripped at Dawn, but she forged on, diving away from the Master and toward her bag. With more power than she could almost handle, she whipped out a silver-tipped stake, just as he was curiously touching the crucifix sticking out of his throat. He was clearly shell-shocked at this last betrayal, unable to react at having what he'd wanted taken away from him so quickly.

She flew at him, plunging the stake into just above the Master's heart, keeping him alive but weakening him. In a burst of unexpected speed, she dove toward the silver stake in Jonah's hand, too, then returned to pin the Master's other side.

She felt nothing, only the urgency of needing to keep the Master alive. He *had* to stay alive, to keep her a vampire.

"Dawn?" he winced, merely staring up at her.

After firing a few silver bullets into his gut, she left the chemistry to do its job. *Damn it, please do your job. . . .*

Then she barged over to Costin. Jonah's mouth was open, the achingly beautiful red of his blood seeping out and onto the ground as he tried to say something. But then his eyes rolled back at her, as if in accusation. She was one of *them* now, but she'd done it for him.

"You can't leave Jonah's body, can you?" she said to Costin, stroking his hair back. Jonah was so breathtaking with Costin's topaz eyes. "You're too weak and you need to be anchored to his humanity, but he's dying, Costin, and I won't let that happen."

"Dawn . . ." It was the Master. His tone had lost gusto. Silver was infecting him. Like the vampire children he'd borne, he could die of slow poisoning, too, but she couldn't let that happen yet.

She carried through with what she'd started, doing it because it was the only way she could think of to keep the quest for Costin's soul going, and he would hate her for it. . . .

She reared her head back, fangs springing from her lateral incisors. Then, with a moan that sounded like a homecoming, she pierced Jonah's jugular.

Imbibing like a thirsting animal, she got drunk on him, not wanting to stop because this was ecstasy—this was what she'd been looking for every time she'd gone to bed with a man. This was beauty, sublime and everlasting, this was what she should have grown up to be—a woman everyone would've thought worthy of being Eva's, a mirror reflection of her wonderful mother.

A monster—

She forced herself to stop, wrenching her mouth away with a wince. Her heart felt sunken, as if it had tried to bury itself away from what she was feeling, doing.

Go on. . . . She cut her own wrist, imitating what Benedikte had done so she could feed Jonah, initiate the exchange that would turn him, heal him, and free Costin from the body.

She hoped. This had to work.

As her blood dripped to his lips, his eyes widened, and she thought she saw the color go blue—Jonah's blue, as if the host had briefly taken over in his craving for a life that might be even more exciting than the one he already had.

Just when his gaze went back to topaz, his body seized, and she knew the change had come on him. Jonah's soul was deserting the body. More importantly, he'd begin healing and, hopefully that would allow Costin to depart Jonah's working body and resettle in his waiting backup.

Hopefully.

With one last stroke over his temple, she rose, fetching her saw-bow, stepping past Eva, who was still weeping against the wall.

She shut out her mother's agony, mainly because she was focusing—but she also wondered if Eva was mourning what was about to happen, too.

Dawn stood in front of the Master, who was trying valiantly to change into his own Danger Form, though she shuddered to guess at what that might look like. Almost sadly, she touched her face, feeling the lack of scars on her skin. She hesitated, reveling in the last moments of finally becoming everything she'd always longed for.

No more looking inside from a window. No more enduring the measuring glances that would find her lacking.

Perfection—she had it now.

Behind her Costin was groaning. The sound of grumbling stone from where the door used to be indicated that Frank, Kiko, and the Friends were almost inside.

She imagined how Kiko would react to what she'd done—how Frank would, too. She couldn't endure their disgust—not along with the censure she expected from Costin for turning him into what he most despised, even if it might only be temporary.

Facing the Master, she cocked her head, taking in the devasta-tion on his face as he continued his pathetic attempts to change. Her new, incredible vision took in his pulsating form, every move-ment fascinating.

"Where is the dragon, Benedikte?" she asked.

He sputtered. "I . . . don't know. . . . Dawn, believe me, please. I am poisoned. *You* . . . poisoned me."

She lifted her saw-bow, using this just in case the Master needed more than silver to the heart. She sighted it on the vampire who had taken Eva away from her.

"Blood . . ." Benedikte opened his hands but couldn't move oth-erwise. Blood would chase the poison from his body.

Targeting, she gave him one last chance. "Give me the location, and I'll give you my blood."

He groped for an answer, and she knew he didn't know.

"Please, Dawn," he begged. "Your blood can cleanse me."

But this is going to cleanse me, she thought.

She fired the saw-bow, a twist of sparks blocking the moment the blade sliced off his head.

A body-eating pain gnashed at her, flooring her, but out of sheer determination, she overcame it and withdrew her silver-bullet re-volver from its holster.

From her hands and knees, she shot Benedikte in the heart, his body indeed heaving into itself, disappearing like any of his chil-dren. Just like one of them, after all . . .

Doubling with anguish, she hugged her knees to her chest, wracked by seizures. Her blood churned, a strange alchemy that twisted and tied her body into bent shapes.

Soon, but not nearly soon enough, it was done.

She came to, finding herself feeling heavy and human again, even though there was something different—something that weighed like grime on the inside.

Nevertheless, she breathed in the musty air of Benedikte's cham-bers, the atmosphere spiked with the stench of blood. When she rolled over, she found Eva stretched out alongside her, as if her mother had crawled over, devoid of much strength.

Then Dawn looked into the face of the human woman who'd given birth to her.

Crow's feet graced Eva's tired eyes, and she had the look of fresh skin that had lost its dew. She was still beautiful in her cosmetically altered appearance—would always be—but she wasn't the age of indestructible grace anymore.

They stared at each other, as if meeting for the first time. And when Eva began to weep, Dawn held her hand.

"It's okay, Mom," she said. "We're going to be fine."

But when she heard Costin give a cry of strangled rage, she knew she was wrong.

TWENTY-SEVEN

ĴUST BEFORE DAWN

Three Months Later

In a buried cove of pines in the San Bernardino Mountains, Dawn cut the engine on the Limpet Agency's backup 4Runner. A secluded chalet waited at the rear of the graveled driveway, its windows shuttered against the light day would soon bring.

Mist speckled the windshield as she waited behind the wheel, her breathing shallow.

Costin had finally contacted her via phone last night. He hadn't said a word, but she'd known it was him. And since he'd opened his mind to her, she could also sense where to track him now, similar to the traditional Awareness the Underground vampires had possessed.

She and Costin had a link—one she couldn't research because there wasn't any lore about how a vampire-turned-back-to-human master related to her vampire child.

They hadn't spoken since the vanquishing of the Underground, but she'd known he would come around some day, and she'd given him the time, given him the space, aching for him every minute of the wait.

Aching to make up for the choice she'd made.

Not long after Frank, Kiko, and the Friends had broken into the Master's room and everyone had checked up on one another, Costin had disappeared in the confusion. When he hadn't reappeared, they had taken it upon themselves to wait for him, cleaning up in the meantime. They discovered that all the vials in the Master's sick collection were already blasted open, the Elite souls easily led back to their human shelters, just as Eva's had been. And the souls that didn't have an Elite body to return to? Dawn hated to guess where they'd ended up.

All the same, the silver statue dust had soon worn off of the other surviving Elites, and they had awakened in their restored human states. Unsurprisingly, many of the glamour vamps had reacted badly to their Master's death and the resulting wrinkles. Some ran off not to be heard from as of yet. One group had undertaken a suicide pact, and the Limpet team hadn't realized what was going on in time to stop them from carrying it out.

There'd been no trace of Groupies or even Servants—not unless you counted the gore in the halls. And the Guards who were left to giddily wander around with blood ringing their mouths and a gleam in their eyes as they smiled and murmured, "Hooome?" had been taken care of by Frank, who'd made good on his promise to euthanize them. He'd taken special care with Hugh Wayne, his old friend from human days.

For weeks afterward, Dawn had hoped hard for Costin's return. She'd occupied herself by helping Frank, Kiko, and the Friends to close up Underground loose ends, then seal the entrances like they were locking a case in a vault.

When Costin still hadn't returned, she'd tried to get back to normal life. It was impossible. Her stunt career was pretty much dead—she accepted that now—and it didn't seem like she could go back to it anyway. She'd been through the real thing, no special effects, no choreography, so how could she sell the fake when it paled in comparison?

Now, sitting in the 4Runner, Dawn took a steadying breath, trying to get the courage to go inside the chalet where Costin was waiting. She reached for her duffel bag, which she'd packed last night while Kiko had sat on the bed after their boss's phone call.

"What I still don't get," he'd said, "is how you didn't look anything like my 'key' vision when we finally got into the Master's room that day."

They'd been debating this for weeks and weeks, and Dawn had come up with the same answers every time. "I recall Costin saying that your visions aren't always literal. So I wasn't bathed in the Master's blood? Things turned out anyway."

"I don't know about that."

His pupils seemed extrabig, and she was keeping her attention on them. He'd been on pills again because he'd overextended himself in the Underground attack and was even now hurting. She'd done everything but camp out in the doctor's office with Kik, but maybe it was time to force him into rehab—an option he'd been fighting tooth and nail.

Yet . . . he seemed happy, mainly because his "key" vision had otherwise come true in a lot of ways. He'd been validated and was already talking about the "next master hunt" after Costin decided to come out of his seclusion. What an optimist.

Dawn didn't remind him that, one, Costin might not make a habit of using the same team twice, even if they survived. And, two, she wasn't positive that the quest's rules still applied to his new vampire self, though she'd risked so much to bet on that. But she tried to believe that Costin could carry on, mainly because it was obviously Jonah's body that had lost its soul in the vampiric transition, yet Costin remained because he was unable to get out since Jonah was animated although technically dead.

She wanted to feel bad about what she'd done to Jonah, too, and she would if she didn't suspect that he might be pleased with this exciting turn of events.

"Something occurred to me a little earlier," Kiko had said as

Dawn hauled the duffel from the bed on her way downstairs. "I think *you're* gonna get the dragon, not Costin. That's what my 'key' vision really meant."

She almost tripped while entering the darkened hallway. "Bite your tongue, Kik."

"That's why Costin is getting in touch with you again, because you're still 'key.' " Kiko stayed at her side as they descended the stairs. "I'll bet he wants to get the band back together."

As they entered the foyer, Dawn dropped her bag at her feet, her gaze skimming the portrait where Kalin was resting, just as most of the other Friends, save Breisi, had been doing in Costin's absence. In spite of Kiko's read on the situation, Dawn had been hoping their boss had summoned her for very different reasons than resuming business. Disappointment made the edges of her heart furl back like burnt paper.

"Kik, you remember that Costin and I didn't part on the best of terms. Killing the Master brought back *my* humanity since I was his child, but it didn't do that for Costin, who is *my* child and wouldn't be directly affected by the termination." That sounded weird. But it also drove home her responsibilities—the crusade she'd undertaken since that day.

"What're you gonna do to cheer him up then?" Kiko chuffed. "Get killed so Jonah's body goes human again? *That* would probably release Costin and make everything hunky-dory."

It was supposed to be a joke, but neither of them ended up laughing. It only emphasized that Dawn had to find a way to save Costin from being the monster he'd detested for centuries, the enemy he'd fought to vanquish.

Worse yet, in trying to save him, she might've locked him into Jonah—the host he'd been planning to replace with a new one who had obviously been put on the back burner.

But she would take care of everything, whether Costin had to wait decades for her to die off or if that happened while she pursued another master—and the dragon—for him.

Yet she would need his help to do this because she wasn't equipped with the powers he had possessed. She only hoped *Costin* was still equipped with them, but shouldn't he be? All that had changed was that Jonah was a vampire now. His body was still in good working order for Costin's needs.

And maybe *that* meant Costin could continue the quest since being in a vamp body wasn't exactly like being trapped in a dead-dead body. Jonah was *un*dead. Would Costin's operating base really matter that much as long as it could walk and breathe and fight?

She thought of how, long ago, The Whisper had forced Costin from his original vampire body, but that had only been out of a need to smuggle Costin out of the jail, right? Could Costin even undertake a holy mission in a cursed body? Was that allowed by the powers that had given him this quest?

And she wasn't even going to dwell on how she'd put him in the position of ultimately escaping Jonah's vampiric shell. Damn it, she'd really created a problem out of her good intentions.

Kiko tugged on the long-sleeved Henley she was wearing, getting her attention. "You're still worried that you've already screwed up his deal with The Whisper. You're worried that anything you do won't matter."

"Yeah, I'm worried." But since Costin himself hadn't forfeited the deal with The Whisper, there was still a chance that he would get his soul back if he stopped the dragon from rising. She kept believing that.

"So he'll just have to undertake the rest of the quest as a vampire," Kiko said, shrugging. "There'll be advantages."

"Why don't you just break into an Orphan Annie song?" Dawn bent down, hugging him. "You take care of yourself until I see you again."

"I will."

She broke away before she could mist up. "No, I mean it. You freakin' take *care* of yourself. Frank's going to be here to watch."

Speaking of whom . . .

With a warning look that made Kiko roll his eyes, Dawn stood, then made her way to the kitchen. The aroma of herb-encrusted pork wafted out of the stainless-steel room, where Frank sat at a table, leaning on his forearms and smiling at the air. His hair moved, and Dawn knew that Breisi the Friend was touching him.

Eva was at the counter, tossing a salad. She had her back to the room, looking like any other mom cooking dinner for her and Kiko. But Dawn could detect the forced line of her body.

She'd explained that she'd been too weak to help fight the Master during the attack, and regretted that she couldn't join in, though she said she would have if the Master had gone into his ultimate form. Luckily, he hadn't managed, thanks to Dawn and the silver.

That was well and good, but, sometimes, Dawn wondered if Eva's story was altogether true. She didn't doubt Eva had been healing during the battle—that wasn't it at all. There were just times when she caught her mom staring off into space with a glance so sorrowful that Dawn didn't know what to do. Did Eva miss everything she'd had as a vamp? And had her mom resisted killing the Master because of what it would destroy?

Her beauty and youth.

Or maybe she kept looking so down because Frank had chosen Breisi over her.

Whatever it was, Eva had taken to maternal life like it was a new mission—and why not? Jacqueline Ashley's burgeoning acting career had already guttered. Like many of the other Elites, the "starlet" had quietly disappeared from the public eye, just like so many other Hollywood careers often did. But, as for the Elites who'd become superstars again? No explanations. To the world, their disappearances were a disturbing mystery played over and over on the tabloid shows.

Thus, Eva now stayed indoors here at the Limpet house exclusively, even though Kiko was working on securing a new identity for her. She doted on Dawn, doing things like cooking dinner, tak-

ing care of her daughter's laundry, and serving tea in the late afternoon. But her perfect family plans weren't quite complete with
Breisi in the picture.

And there was another thing that weighed: what was going to
happen to Eva's restored soul after human death? She'd told Dawn
that it felt "dirtied" now that it'd come back from its limbo.

Dawn knew the feeling, because her own soul had returned the
same way. But that was secondary to Costin's issues since it'd been
her choice that had put them in this position.

She said good-bye to her parents, whispering to Frank that he
needed to watch over Kiko. He agreed and followed Dawn to the
door, Breisi's jasmine by their side, too. Kiko took up Dawn's other
side. Eva trailed behind them all.

Then Dawn took off in the SUV, tuning in to the open sensory
path Costin was leading her on. Fairly soon, she found the cabin in
the woods. The hideaway.

Ultimately, she decided not to take her bag just yet—too pre-
sumptuous. Instead, she emerged from the 4Runner into the lifting
darkness.

The door was unlocked, so she entered, pulse choking her.

"Costin?" She didn't know why she even bothered to ask for
him, because her body was pulling toward a room on its own, as if
hooked.

She found him waiting in a chair behind a desk, shadows from
an electric crystal lamp playing with his face. His scars had disappeared, thanks to vampire healing. It left him brooding and beautiful, with only sadness as a more obvious wound.

As she stood in the doorway, shivering because of the unheated
house and something even deeper, he spoke.

"I have sensed another."

Overwhelming emotion, unidentifiable in its mixture, rushed
upward to consume her. He sensed another master—that meant his
quest was on. That also meant . . . What?

He got out of the chair, coming to stand in a slant of shadow, topaz eyes burning bright. This was it—the condemnation she deserved.

As he paused, his body jarred for no reason, and he reached for the wall, as if balancing himself. It made Dawn wonder if Jonah's vampire body might have some control over Costin's soul now.

Even though guilt took her over, she said, "I can't regret what I did." The words were like exposed cuts. "Not if it's going to save you in the end."

"Not even if I am cursed to carry through in this body?" He clutched at the wall. "Not even if it has made you *my* master now?"

She shielded against the comment because, truthfully, she would've loved this turnaround three months ago. All the control she'd craved—it was hers. The user was at the mercy of the used.

"You don't really have a choice but to tolerate me," she said. "Kiko thinks that maybe I'll have something to do with getting the dragon, so you need me."

And I need to redeem myself to you *at the same time you're redeeming yourself.*

She took a breath to continue, but he abruptly held out his arms, interrupting her as if he'd finished with holding back.

"Come here, Dawn," he said, the name soaked in desire, his eyes filled with it, too, taking on a hint of silver.

Heart bursting, she went to him, not holding back, either. When he embraced her, she lost herself in a scent that seemed more appropriate for another lifetime than this one. Spices, exotic memory, vampire.

She had become many things: hunter, slayer, even an actress. But right now, she was finally herself, finally with the only person who could truly understand the changes, the becoming, the horrific acceptance.

"Dawn . . . ?" he breathed before longingly stroking her throat.

Had he been waiting for this—to feed on her again?

Without hesitation, she opened herself to his pleasure, her eyes opened wide to focus on the dim light of the lamp as she bent to offer her neck out of mutual yearning. Out of taking responsibility for him, too.

A sunburst, she thought as the lamp's colors sparkled and illuminated. A beginning.

Above her, Costin reared back his head, and she grabbed him, forcing him down to her, wanting with her entire heart to embrace everything about him—about *them.*

As his fangs pierced her jugular, she pulled him tighter, feeding him, keeping him alive, and guarding his very soul. The sunrise colors expanded, exploding, shedding warm light.

Shining the serenity of a new day over every open space inside of her.

Dear Reader,

Thank you so much for coming on this ride with me. This series has been a lot of fun with all its twists and turns, but I'm happy to tell you all that the ride is going to carry on even after Book Three ends!

A Drop of Red will continue the Vampire Babylon series in March 2009. In fact, it's the start of a new VB trilogy. You've come to realize that this series isn't structured like most: it's told in trilogy arcs that concentrate on one basic story. While each individual novel focuses on a central mystery, which is solved by the end, the three books together build character and mythology arcs/mysteries until everything culminates in the third book. In the second VB trilogy, you're going to discover a new Underground as well as further adventures of Dawn and the team, so I hope you're as excited as I am to explore it.

Until then, happy hunting, and thank you once again!

Chris Marie Green